SHATTERED VOWS

Courtenay Shelburne's world was cruelly shaken when his beautiful bride of two months ran off to Italy with his closest friend. Enraged, the hot-tempered Earl of Warbeck swore he would someday have his revenge on the traitorous wench—all the while tormented by the knowledge that he desired her still.

PROMISE ME

Now, five years later, Philippa has returned to England—no longer the shy young miss Warbeck once married, but a sensuous woman of proud bearing, falsely damned by lies and vile, secret stratagems. And though vengeance is finally within his grasp, the embittered earl cannot extinguish the passionate fire Philippa's presence ignites . . . nor can he still the voice within that begs him to welcome love back into his heart.

KATHLEEN HARRINGTON

PROMISE ME

An Avon Romantic Treasure

AVON BOOKS ◆ NEW YORK

PROMISE ME is an original publication of Avon Books. This work has never before appeared in book form. This work is a novel. Any similarity to actual persons or events is purely coincidental.

AVON BOOKS
A division of
The Hearst Corporation
1350 Avenue of the Americas
New York, New York 10019

Copyright © 1995 by Kathleen Harrington
Published by arrangement with the author
Library of Congress Catalog Card Number: 94-96570
ISBN: 0-380-77833-5

First Avon Books Printing: May 1995

AVON TRADEMARK REG. U.S. PAT. OFF. AND IN OTHER COUNTRIES, MARCA REGISTRADA, HECHO EN U.S.A.

Printed in the U.S.A

RA   10   9   8   7   6   5   4   3   2   1

With love and thanks to
Dorothy Northrup Persinger,
my sister-in-law
and
Rick's other Mom

Your warmhearted generosity
will never be forgotten

Let me not to the marriage of true minds
Admit impediments. Love is not love
Which alters when it alteration finds,
Or bends with the remover to remove:
O, no! it is an ever-fixed mark
That looks on tempests and is never shaken;
It is the star to every wandering bark,
Whose worth's unknown, although his height be taken.
Love's not Time's fool, though rosy lips and cheeks
Within his bending sickle's compass come;
Love alters not with his brief hours and weeks,
But bears it out even to the edge of doom.
    If this be error and upon me proved,
    I never writ, nor no man ever loved.

—SHAKESPEARE
116th Sonnet

Prologue

Bussaco, Portugal
The Peninsular War
September 1810

"**M**ajor Shelburne is over there, sir." The sergeant sprang from his place near the campfire to snap a quick salute. The burly hussar pointed toward a solitary figure barely discernible in the gathering dusk, then stroked his huge mustachios and eyed Lieutenant Colonel Tobias Howard, Viscount Rockingham, warily. "The major doesn't like to be disturbed unless it's mighty important," he warned.

In the glow of the flames, the other dragoons watched the newcomer with open curiosity. They knew from his uniform that he was one of Wellington's staff officers and quite probably carried orders that would determine in large measure whether they lived or died on the following day. The fear of death stalked the encampment. Only the muffled sounds of harnesses being repaired, rifled muskets cleaned, and sabers sharpened broke the silence. On the night before a great battle, few men had the cool nerve it took to chatter sociably with their fellow soldiers.

"The major prefers his own company," the sergeant clarified, then added reluctantly, "but I'll take you to him if you wish, sir."

"No, that w-won't be necessary, S-sergeant," Tobias

said. "Major Shelburne and I are old friends." He re-mounted and rode out along the ridge. As he drew near his childhood companion, Tobias studied the dejected slump of Court's massive shoulders. He stood beside his horse, looking out across the dark-ening landscape as though he carried the weight of the world upon his broad back. What in blue blazes was that maggot-witted fool doing out here past the sentinels? Tobias wondered. Trying to tempt some sniper to put a bullet through his broken heart and put him out of his misery?

At the sound of Tobias's approach, Major Court-enay Shelburne, the earl of Warbeck, turned with an irritated scowl. The instant he recognized his visitor, his face lit up in a welcoming grin, and he straight-ened to his full, forbidding height. "Rockingham!" he bellowed happily. "What the hell are you doing here?"

Tobias slid off his saddle, and the two men clasped each other in a fierce bear hug. "I just delivered d-dispatches to Craufurd," he explained, gasping for air. Court had arms like steel bands. "Old Hookey has s-some last minute instructions for the b-battle tomorrow. The general t-told me the Light Division was encamped on this r-rise, so I came looking for you. C-come daybreak, all hell's going to break loose."

Together, they turned and gazed across the rolling meadow, thick with heather, to the fir-clad hills be-yond, where sixty thousand Frenchmen waited for the morning light. "My regiment has been ordered to delay the advance of Masséna's first line of attack," Court said quietly. "I wanted to review the lay of the land one last time."

"Aye, I know," Tobias answered with a solemn nod, fully aware that the ensuing carnage would be appalling. Napoleon's heavy cavalry, big men on big horses, and frequently armored, had the duty of smashing British formations and riding down broken regiments with their long, deadly lances. "I can't stay b-but a few moments," he said apologetically. "I'm w-waiting for Craufurd to write his reply and I'll be off."

"Then quickly, tell me all the news from home," Court said. He patted his restive horse, running his hand down its long, sleek neck in a soothing motion. "It takes so blasted long for the mail pouches to reach us. I haven't received a letter from Lady Augusta in months. I suspect we get only a small part of what's actually been sent."

"Y-your grandmother is d-doing f-fine," Tobias replied, the stutter he'd fought to control since childhood worsening dramatically. "I was b-back in L-london s-six months ago to c-carry dispatches to the Horse Guards. Lady Augusta l-looked in the b-best of health." He tried to ignore the knot of foreboding that tightened in his chest. Devil take it, this was going to be every bit as hard as he'd expected. Court would know something was wrong before he could even prepare him.

"And Belle? Any chance she's carrying the next Viscount Rockingham?" Court asked with a teasing grin.

Tobias shook his head. "N-no luck there," he admitted with a flush of embarrassment. "But w-we'll k-keep trying."

Court clapped him soundly on the shoulder. "Good man." His smile faded as he peered into Tobias's guarded eyes. "Something's wrong, though. What is it?"

Tobias pushed his wire-rimmed eyeglasses farther up the bridge of his nose and gulped. He took a deep breath, and both air and words came out in a rush. "Belle got a letter from Philippa."

Court's head jerked up, a lock of his blue-black hair falling over his forehead. Tobias watched the emotions that flickered across the earl's handsome face as he fought the demons that rose up inside him at the mere mention of his former wife's name. "She's safe somewhere, I take it?" he asked tersely, a muscle working in his neck. His hooded gray eyes were shards of ice.

"They're in Venice. Alive and well."

Court shrugged to indicate that he didn't give a bloody damn, but his next words were laced with a bitter cynicism. "I suppose it would have been too much to hope that their ship had sunk to the bottom of the sea. Philippa and her lover seem to lead charmed lives."

Tobias swallowed nervously. Philippa's lover was their lifelong friend, Arthur Bentinck, marquess of Sandhurst. The three men had been bosom chums since boyhood. Their Kent estates bordered each other's. They'd attended Eton and Oxford together. Then one horrible day, Court had discovered his wife in Sandhurst's arms. The two adulterers had fled England before Court had the satisfaction of shooting the marquess in a duel.

"There's m-more, Court," Tobias said, determined to get it over with. He shrank from his self-appointed task, hating what he was about to say. But Court had to be told the truth. And Tobias knew he should be the one to tell him. "Sandy and Pippa were m-married as s-soon as they learned that the divorce b-bill was passed in P-parliament. They had a child s-sometime last year. A little b-boy."

Stunned, Court closed his eyes as though to block out the painful images the announcement had conjured up. In the fading light, his hawkish features appeared drawn and haggard, making him seem far older than his thirty-two years. He turned with a stumbling lurch and clenched the saddle's pommel with one hand. Head bowed, he leaned against his mount for support. "Damn them," he cursed softly. "Damn them both to hell."

"I'm s-sorry," Tobias croaked, his voice hoarse with regret. Burn it all, why did he have to bring such wretched tidings? And why here and now? But this was not the time for evasions or half-truths. There was a good chance they might never see each other again.

"Colonel Howard," someone called from behind the picket line. "The general's ready with his reply to Wellington."

"I'll be r-right there," Tobias answered. Heartsick, he stepped closer to his grieving companion. "I have to g-go n-now. I'm sorry."

Court turned at once to offer his hand, and Tobias caught the glitter of tears in the tortured gray eyes. "Good-bye, old friend."

The look of utter despair on the earl's face sent a jolt of alarm through Tobias. "You're n-not thinking of d-doing anything f-foolish?" he demanded. "Time heals, Court. Things will look b-better when this blasted w-war is over and we're h-home in Kent once again."

"It's been two years since she ran away," Court countered with a sardonic grin. "The pain hasn't lessened, but, hell, neither has the anger. I'll have my revenge someday."

Grasping his hand, Tobias searched Court's haunted features. "Good-bye and good luck."

"I won't need luck tomorrow," he replied with an arrogant lift of his chin. "Just a strong horse and a good carbine. Give my best to Belle when next you see her."

Tobias rode slowly past the guards and through the row of cannons and howitzers positioned along the high ridge, certain he would never see his friend again. He glanced back over his shoulder to where Court stood staring across the heather to the wooded hills beyond. The isolation and loneliness of that brooding silhouette wrenched Tobias's soul. He saw, once again, the quiet desperation on Court's face when he'd turned to bid him farewell. Sweet Jesus, London's most notorious rakehell, a man who'd fought countless duels without a hint of compunction, had wept over the birth of a baby boy. From the blank look in Court's eyes, Tobias knew the earl of Warbeck believed he had nothing to live for.

Damn that scoundrel Arthur Bentinck! Why couldn't he have found a wife of his own?

Chapter 1

London
June 1814

"**T**he dowager marchioness of Sandhurst requests the honor of paying a morning call, Your Grace."

Court looked up from the stack of papers on his desk and stared at his butler in astonishment. If Nash had announced the arrival of the Archangel Gabriel with a flourish of trumpets, Court couldn't have been more astounded.

"Lady Harriet is here? At this moment?"

Nash threw back his shoulders, drew himself up to his full five-foot height, and replied with a flustered scowl, "Her ladyship is waiting in the blue salon. Shall I inform her that you're out, sir?"

Court shook his head. "No, I'll see her."

He glanced at Neil Tolander, who stood in front of the wide mahogany desk. His young secretary's usually placid features revealed his shock. There wasn't a person in the duke of Warbeck's employ, from the house steward to the lowliest scullery maid, who wouldn't instantly recognize the potential for disaster in the coming interview. For years, not a single soul on his entire staff had dared to mention the hated name of Sandhurst.

"Bring Lady Harriet to the study, Nash," Court added as an afterthought. He could hardly refuse his

7

godmother admittance to his home. But if she had the effrontery to pay an unexpected visit after nearly six years, he wasn't going to make it any easier for her by offering tea and biscuits. He couldn't imagine what momentous occasion had brought her to Warbeck House.

"I'll work on these accounts in the library, Your Grace," Tolander said as he scooped a sheaf of papers from the desktop. "Please ring for me when your visit is over." He headed for the door with long, hurried strides, anxious, no doubt, to avoid being caught in the middle of the impending storm.

Less than two minutes later, Lady Harriet Bentinck marched into the room. She was dressed for a formal morning call in shades of purple. The Empire silhouette currently fashionable did nothing to flatter the older woman's robust shape. The printed muslin gown's high waist made her ample bosom appear even larger, while the straight fall of the narrow skirt emphasized the sturdiness of her big-boned frame. Undeterred by the unflattering vagaries of fashion, she met her godson's eyes with a look of fierce determination. "Courtenay," she boomed in her deep contralto, "thank you for seeing me."

He reached for his cane, rose from the desk chair, and moved to the center of the rug, his limp wretchedly noticeable. They'd seen each other on rare occasions when some social function had brought them together briefly under the same roof. But other than a cursory nod or a quick salutation, neither had spoken. He supposed she was well aware of the extent of the war injury that had nearly cost him his leg, since his grandmother had continued her friendship with Lady Harriet, their Kent neighbor, despite his scathing objections.

"Lady Harriet," he said in a belated attempt at good manners, "how kind of you to visit."

"Fustian," she barked. "I haven't come to make a social call, and well you know it." In spite of her sharp words, she offered her lavender-gloved hand. When he took it, she squeezed his fingers in a stout-hearted manner. Harriet Bentinck was as tall as most men and nearly as strong.

He gestured to a green settee, and she sank down with an ungainly plop, her knees sticking up gracelessly beneath the flimsy dress.

Court rested his hands on the sculpted dragon's head handle of his cane. "Why *did* you come?" he asked coolly.

"Not to be insulted by a blockheaded knave, I can tell you that, sir."

He smiled at last. His godmother's abrupt ways were only a rough outer shell. He knew the tender heart that beat inside her capacious bosom. During his childhood years, she'd been like a second mother to Court, showing him the maternal affection his own flighty, self-centered mother had been unable to give. As an adolescent, he'd spent more time at Sandhurst Hall than he had in his own home.

He noted for the first time the sprinkling of gray that now dulled the red-brown curls peeking out from under her bonnet. Who, more than he, could fully understood the tragic sorrow she'd suffered? Court sensed that, in spite of the terrible chasm that had opened up between them, she loved him still. Loved him more than his parents ever had.

Every day, Court was deluged with invitations to soirees, parties, and balls from members of the ton, who yearned to impress their friends and acquaintances with the social coup of having a duke in attendance. Whenever he made an appearance in public, he was surrounded by sycophants and toadeaters, all hoping to curry his favor. But he could number on one hand the people who truly cared about him. This time he spoke with sincere affection. "Shall I ring for tea, Godmother?"

She grinned back at him and shook her head, making the lavender plumes on her bonnet sway. "I won't be troubling you that long, my boy. I came to tell you that I've just returned from Italy."

Court stood frozen in the middle of the room as the full portent of her words struck him. "Oh, have you?" he said at last in a hoarse whisper, furious that even now, after all this time, such an oblique allusion to Philippa could leave him momentarily breathless.

Lady Harriet pretended not to notice his strong reaction. "Yes, I have. I sailed to Venice the minute I learned that peace had been declared, and it was safe to travel abroad." Her pale green eyes regarded him with keen circumspection. "I take it you didn't know that I'd been away these past two months?"

He tried to keep the bitterness from his voice. "I knew nothing of your trip. My grandmother failed to mention it, although I'm certain she was aware of your departure and your ultimate destination."

They stared at each other in taut silence, neither voicing aloud the obvious reason his grandmother had kept such a startling piece of information from him.

Lady Harriet was the first to speak. "Since you're too stubborn to ask, Courtenay, I'll tell you what you're probably burning to know. I went to Venice to see my daughter-in-law and grandson. And to bring home my son's remains."

Court turned and walked back to his desk. Propping his backside against its edge, he rested his black hickory wood cane on his thigh in a pose of nonchalance. A muscle twitched in his jaw, ruining his attempt to appear bored. "Am I supposed to inquire politely if they're well?" he sneered.

"Hardly. I didn't come to watch you play the hypocrite." She rose from the sofa and moved to stand beside him. A thoughtful frown puckered her forehead before she met his daunting gaze. "I've brought my son's remains back home to be buried alongside his father's," she told him. "While I'm sure that's neither here nor there to you, I came to tell you that I've also brought Lady Philippa and her son back to England, where they belong."

Court straightened, all intention of remaining aloof forgotten. "My God, you can't be serious."

"Indeed, never more so. They're staying with me right now in Cavendish Square. I'm asking you, as your godmother, not to cut Philippa publicly, should you happen to meet her. If you have any tender feelings for me at all, Courtenay, I'm begging you to heed my wishes in this matter. Put the past behind you, my boy. Don't do anything to drag up the scandal of your divorce. If not for me, then for the child's sake."

"What makes you think I give a damn what happens to Sandhurst's little bastard?"

Lady Harriet snorted in disgust. "Kit is my son's legitimate heir and the new marquess of Sandhurst. And whatever else you may think, Warbeck, you certainly must agree that a five-year-old boy is innocent of his parents' sins. I'm expecting you to treat the child with some measure of compassion."

Court snarled through clenched teeth. "I'll treat the brat and his wayward mother exactly as I see fit."

The dowager marchioness snatched up her reticule and eyed him with disdain. "I was told by more than one person that these past five and a half years had turned you into an unfeeling monster."

Court grinned with what he hoped was diabolical glee. "Five years and ten months, to be exact."

"I've also heard that you're called Warlock by half the people in London. Until now, I refused to credit such a rumor."

"Until now, I thought I knew the full extent of the Bentinck family's unprecedented gall."

Lady Harriet met his belligerent gaze, a blaze of wrath and disappointment in her eyes. Then, without another word, she left the room, slamming the door behind her.

In the aftermath of her departure, the only sound

was the ticking of the tall pendulum clock in the far corner of the study. Court walked slowly to the fireplace and leaned one hand against the carved oak mantel. His head fell forward. His heart thumped erratically as a tumult of emotions churned inside him.

Perhaps there was a God, after all.

Philippa was back. He would have his revenge at last.

Court's grandmother smiled in welcome as he entered the gold-and-white drawing room later that day. "There you are," Lady Augusta called from her place on the sofa in front of the tea table. "I was beginning to think you were going to forget me, and I particularly wanted to talk to you this afternoon." She lifted a china pot decorated with pink roses and poured tea into two delicate cups.

"How could I forget you?" he teased. "Our teatime together is my favorite part of the day." Court leaned on his cane, bent over her upturned face, and pressed a kiss on her brow.

"Save your preposterous flattery for your fiancée," she advised with her usual acerbity. "I read about your exploits too often in the gossip columns for you to play the simple country squire with me."

But Court's pleasure in his grandmother's company was sincere, and she knew it. Whenever Lady Augusta came to stay at his town house in London, he always shared a few minutes with her in the afternoon.

His busy schedule left him little time. After a brisk ride in Hyde Park, he spent his mornings in lengthy discussions with his bankers, business partners, and political allies. Neil Tolander frequently ate the midday meal with Court in his study as they reviewed the status of his many and varied investments. Court would then issue directives at lightning speed for the enormous daily correspondence to the land stewards of his far-flung estates. Late afternoons found the

duke of Warbeck at one of his clubs in St. James's
Street, for besides White's, he belonged to both Boo-
dle's and Brook's. He generally had at least two or
three invitations every evening, begging his attendance at the countless social gatherings given by the
ton's ambitious hostesses. And the early morning
hours found him in whatever love nest he was currently providing for the latest bit of muslin who'd
managed to catch his fickle attention.

Pulling up a side chair, Court sat down next to the
tea table. Lady Augusta handed him the cup and
saucer. The familiar fragrance of the steaming Bohea
tea wafted about them, evoking memories of times
past, when they'd shared their vastly differing opinions on politics and religion, and their mutual enjoyment of the foibles and follies of the human race.

"What's so important that you were worried I
wouldn't join you this afternoon?" he queried. "We'll
see each other at Belle's party tonight. We can visit
all we want across the dining room table."

His grandmother sat perched on the edge of the
gold satin sofa with the straight-backed posture of
their sixteenth century ancestors. Now in her mid-
seventies, she was as elegant as ever in a wine-
colored silk gown trimmed with a darker burgundy
velvet. Beneath her black lace cap, her hair was a
cloud of white.

"Then you are still planning to go to the Rockinghams' dinner party?" she asked. Her intelligent gray
eyes studied him with unwavering attention.

"Lady Gabrielle would have my head if I didn't
show up for her birthday celebration this evening."
He arched an eyebrow in curiosity. "Why? Have you
changed your mind and decided to ride in the town
carriage with Clare and me?"

She waved her blue-veined hand impatiently. "No,
no. The count and countess de Rambouillet are stop-
ping here on the way to their daughter's home. I'll
go with them." A corner of her mouth curled up in

a sardonic smile as she shook her finger at him. "I wouldn't want to interfere with your chance to seduce such an alluring fiancée."

Court looked up from stirring his tea. There was more than a hint of sarcasm in his grandmother's voice. Lady Augusta had received the news of his engagement six weeks ago with unveiled skepticism. "Let's not squabble over Clare this afternoon," he said gruffly.

She lifted her eyebrows in exaggerated denial. "When have I ever argued with you over your pending nuptials? I merely pointed out that you'd have to go to bed with your clothes on, if you didn't want to freeze to death between the sheets. How you'll manage to sire an heir fully dressed is certainly not my problem."

He shook his head in grudging amusement. "I'll admit, Clare is not this season's most vivacious debutante."

"Debutante!" Lady Augusta exclaimed. "Clare Brownlow has had enough seasons to ensnare ten prospective husbands. It's no secret that she's known as the Snow Queen of Almack's." His grandmother took a sip of tea, then frowned as she met his gaze over the fluted rim of her cup. "But that wasn't what I wanted to talk to you about."

The dowager duchess of Warbeck was a tall, thin, imperious woman who usually treated the slight annoyances of life as too inconsequential to notice. From the concerned expression on her features, Court knew she was disturbed about something.

"I visited your godmother in Cavendish Square yesterday," she announced a little too loudly. "Lady Harriet told me she was going to call on you this morning." His grandmother met his frigid gaze for two quick seconds, then busied herself rearranging the scones on the rose-patterned plate in front of her. It was the first time in his life he'd seen his autocratic grandparent betray the slightest hint of nervousness.

"Lady Harriet came to see me earlier today," he informed her in a tone of warning that even an imbecile would recognize. He sipped his tea and waited for her to retreat.

Ignoring the ominous atmosphere that suddenly blanketed the drawing room, his grandmother forged ahead. "She asked me to speak to you on behalf of her daughter-in-law and grandson."

"If you mean Philippa Bentinck, say it!" he snapped. "Do you think I'm going to start raving like a lunatic at the mere mention of her name?"

"You had better not!" Lady Augusta snapped back. "Everyone in London will be waiting with bated breath to see if you'll make an ass of yourself again. Our world is too small for you to avoid her completely. Sooner or later the two of you are bound to meet. I'm advising you not to do anything that would precipitate another furor now that your former wife is back in England. Leave her in peace, to make whatever life she can. God knows, it will be difficult enough for her without a public pillorying by her previous spouse."

"Why should you give a damn what happens to that deceitful witch?" Court slammed his cup and saucer down. The tea sloshed onto the gleaming cherry tabletop, and Lady Augusta reached across the porcelain tea service to wipe up the warm liquid with her serviette.

Furious at his grandmother's duplicity, he gripped his cane and moved to his feet. "You didn't even have the decency to tell me that Arthur Bentinck's mother had gone to Italy to bring back his grieving widow. Where the hell is your loyalty to me?"

"My loyalty, first and foremost, is to the House of Warbeck. If you have the least shred of doubt about that, you've not half the intelligence I've credited you with." Lady Augusta crushed the soaked linen into a ball and tossed it beside the sugar pot. She looked up and met his gaze with narrowed eyes. "Heed my advice on this, Court. There's a blameless child to be considered."

"Bugger the child!"

Lady Augusta rose and glared at him. "You'll keep a civil tongue in your mouth, sir, or I'll find another place to stay when I'm in London. You may be a duke now, and a celebrated war hero, but none of that gives you the license to talk like riffraff to your only living relative."

Court glowered at his grandmother. Her stiff-necked intransigence on the matter of his divorce had always been a bone of contention between them. "The woman ran off and married my friend!" he thundered. "How in the hell am I supposed to act?"

"If you hadn't divorced Philippa, she could never have legally married Sandhurst." Lady Augusta stepped around the tea table, continuing her lecture in spite of his mounting anger. "If you'd only listened to me and not insisted upon pushing a bill of divorcement through Parliament, she'd still be your wife today."

"What good is a wife who runs off with other men?"

The dowager duchess smirked derisively. "A husband is supposed to make the marriage so pleasant that his bride wants to stay at home."

"I never mistreated Philippa," he uttered quietly. "She had no cause to run away."

"Hah! What did you think the girl would do when you threatened to kill her lover?"

Infuriated by such an idiotic justification of Philippa's betrayal, he took one step toward the door, then paused. "If I hadn't obtained that divorce," he said through clenched teeth, "I would have tracked them down and killed them. And unless she keeps out of my way, I'm not certain but what I might not still do just that."

"Sandhurst is already dead," Lady Augusta

pointed out. "And Philippa has a child to raise alone. Why not consider the score settled?"

"I'll see her in hell first." Court slammed the door behind him.

Chapter 2

"**Y**ou're coming to my dinner party tonight," Belle insisted. "I won't take no for an answer." She plopped down on the edge of Philippa's bed and folded her arms across her chest.

"We're not starry-eyed schoolgirls anymore," countered Philippa with a coaxing smile. She knew how persistent her friend could be when she set her mind on something. "We can't expect the rest of the world to cater to our foolish dreams."

Belle picked up a ruffled bed pillow and placed it on her lap. She drummed on the satin with plump fingers. "I don't think I was ever starry-eyed," she said. "I certainly never dreamed I'd be a viscountess and you'd be a marchioness. And neither did the other girls at the Lillybridge Seminary."

Philippa sat down beside her. "Nor did our teachers," she conceded with an impish grin. "At least, not when it came to a little orphan named Pippa Moore. You, on the other hand, Lady Gabrielle Jacqueline Mercier Howard, were ordained by birth to marry a title. The misfortunes of fate may have conspired to deprive you of your true destiny, but your innate goodness overcame evil in the end."

Behind her round spectacles, Belle's dark brown eyes grew somber as she recalled the story they both knew so well. "I was only two when we crossed the Channel in a fishing boat, disguised as *sans-culottes*.

Yet even to this day, *ma mère* has nightmares of Madame la Guillotine."

The two of them sat side by side in companionable silence. Twenty-two years before, the count and countess de Rambouillet had barely escaped the Terror with their lives. Except for the countess's jewelry, all their possessions had been left behind. In their reduced circumstances, the once-wealthy French émigrés had been forced to enroll their daughter in a boarding school in Chelsea.

"*Eh bien*, something good came from all the suffering," Belle said with a sigh. "I met you."

"And took me into your home as well as your heart." Philippa clasped Belle's hand and squeezed it gratefully. "How I loved staying with your family during the holidays. You'll never know how much it meant for me to share your loved ones with you. I often pretended that André and Étienne were my brothers, too. Especially when they pulled my braids and called me a silly little cabbage." She smiled wistfully at the memory of those bygone days.

With a puzzled frown, Belle tipped her head to one side and gazed at Philippa. "Why did you stop accepting our invitations, *chérie?* You refused to make any explanation at the time, except to say that you had to make use of every moment to study."

"It wasn't because I didn't want to come," Philippa avowed. "By the time I was fifteen, I realized I didn't have the proper clothes or the rank to fit into your world. I didn't belong there. I knew it would only cause you embarrassment if I continued to come to your family gatherings dressed in my serviceable school frocks. What is considered charming at twelve is gauche at sixteen."

"*Vraiment*, you were wrong, Pippa. You have nothing to be ashamed of." Belle waved an impatient hand. "Look at you! Dressed in the latest *à la mode anglaise*, surrounded by beautiful things, you're the

picture of elegance. Why, you outshine any duchess
I've ever met!"

Philippa glanced down at the stylish day dress of
sheer pink muslin with its flattering classical lines,
then gazed about her at the sumptuous room. Lady
Harriet had ordered it completely refurbished before
she'd departed for Italy. Clearly, her mother-in-law
had done everything in her power to make the prod-
igal child feel welcomed. Profound gratitude for the
unexpected kindnesses that had been bestowed upon
her since her return welled up within Philippa.

"Oh, Belle, it's so good to be home again." Tears
swam in Philippa's eyes as she put her arms around
her friend and hugged her tight. "Your letters meant
the world to me. Only someone with a heart as pure
as yours would have remained loyal to a notorious
woman all these years."

Lady Gabrielle returned the hug. Then she pulled
back and met Philippa's gaze. "*Imbécile!* I've known
you since we were ten years old. Not once have I
ever doubted your integrity." A wry smile curved
her lips. "Your common sense, perhaps, but never
your character, never your soul."

"If I had any common sense, I would have stayed
in Venice. Which reminds me, I have a gift for you."
Philippa sprang off the bed and hurried to the low
chest at its foot. She raised the lid and lifted out a
miniature gondola, complete with singing gondolier.
Kneeling in front of Belle, she balanced the porcelain
figurine atop the pillow on her friend's lap. The
shallow-hulled craft seemed to be sailing on a sea of
purplish blue satin.

"Oh, Pippa," cried Belle, "it's exquisite!" She bent
her head to examine the delicately painted replica
more closely, her smooth brown ringlets framing her
pretty face.

The ebony canal boat was edged in gold. The boatman, his head thrown back, his mouth in the shape
of an O, was garbed in a blue-and-white-striped shirt

and black trousers. Everything was accurate, down to the tiniest detail.

"Shh, listen," Philippa urged. She turned a small metal key and the notes of a romantic Italian ballad tinkled charmingly.

"It's a music box!" Belle cried.

"You should see the gondolas as they glide along the canals," Philippa told her. "They look like sleek, black swans. The Venetian ladies, in their finest gowns, step into the swaying boats from marble landings directly in front of their homes."

"Is Venice truly as romantic as it sounds?"

Philippa nodded. "Our palazzo overlooked the Grand Canal. From the upper portico, I could see the golden domes of St. Mark's Basilica and the loggia of the Doge's Palace. In the long summer afternoons, the sunshine would sparkle off the water and bounce off the pink-and-white marble buildings with their lacy frescoes, till my eyes were dazzled by the beauty of it all." She traced the line of the boat's graceful bow with one fingertip, nearly overcome with nostalgia. "In the early evenings, just before twilight, Sandy would sit on the loggia with Kit perched on his lap. Together, we'd watch the gondolas glide up and down the canal and listen to the haunting strains of the gondoliers' love songs."

"Were you very lonely?"

Philippa met Belle's sympathetic gaze. "No," she said. More truthfully, she added, "Yes, sometimes. For the loved ones I'd left behind. But we made many new friends and were accepted by everyone." At the look of surprise on Belle's face, she laughed. "The aristocrats there were not so squeamish about my divorce and remarriage. After all, we were merely heretic Protestants. We couldn't be expected to behave any better. At first Sandy and I were simply amusing oddities. Then as he grew more and more ill, many compassionate people rallied around us."

"One was the duke you wrote about?"

"Yes, particularly the duke. From the very first, Domenico had his own surgeon attend Sandy. His Grace paved our way through the political and social quagmire that is Venetian society."

"He's wealthy, I take it?"

"Enormously. But more than that. Even though Venice is officially under Austrian rule, he holds tremendous power. After Sandy died, I would have been lost without his guidance and protection."

Philippa didn't add that Domenico Flabianico, duke of Padua, Vicenza, and Verona, had fallen in love with her. The day before she left for England, he'd begged her to remain in Italy as his wife. She knew she could always return to Venice and the duke's protection, where she would be shielded from hurtful slander. But if she went back, it would be at the cost of her son's education in England, for she'd never leave Kit behind in someone else's care—not even his doting grandmother's. Philippa was willing to face any snubs, any cuts, any cruelty in order to ensure her son's legal inheritance.

"Now you have us to guide and protect you," Belle said softly. "All my family will be there tonight. André and his wife, Sarah, Étienne with Dora, his shy new bride of two weeks, and my mother and father. They're all anxious to see you again. We love you, Pippa. That includes my own dear Tobias. He'd issue a challenge to any man who dared to insult you. No one's going to let you be hurt."

"Don't talk nonsense," scolded Philippa. "You know very well I can't go to your dinner party tonight." She jumped up from her spot in front of Belle. Scooping up a straw bonnet that had been tossed carelessly on a chaise longue beside the fireplace, she smoothed its wrinkled green satin ribbons and fluffed the crushed silk flowers that encircled its flat crown. Then she steadfastly met her friend's disappointed gaze. "Be reasonable, Belle," she pleaded.

"I'm still a divorcée from my first marriage, even though I'm a widow from my second. In case it hasn't occurred to you, I remain a fallen woman."

Holding the fragile gondola in both hands, Belle rose to her feet. She wore a morning gown of embroidered lawn, and the contrast of her dark curls against the fine white linen enhanced her dusky coloring. She was Philippa's opposite in appearance. Philippa was tall for a female, while her friend barely reached her shoulder. And Lady Gabrielle had the dimpled fullness that was so admired by all the members of the opposite sex.

Through the lenses of her spectacles, Belle's lovely eyes glinted with disapproval as she scowled at Philippa. "So what do you plan to do, *mon amie?* Hide in this bedroom for the rest of your life? You can't avoid the world forever."

"I realize that sooner or later I'll have to brave society and its hypocritical ways," admitted Philippa. She sighed with resignation. "I have no choice. I must reestablish myself in England in order to give Kit the home and station in life to which he's entitled. Believe me, Belle, if it weren't for my son, I would never have agreed to come back at all. When I left Venice with Lady Harriet, my intention was to return to my homeland with as little fuss as possible. The last thing I want to do is stir up memories of the scandal that set London spinning. I've only been here three days. I'm definitely not ready to go out among other people yet."

"I beg your pardon!" Belle cried indignantly. "Since when are your loved ones 'other people'?" She placed the porcelain boat carefully on the dressing table, then turned to face Philippa once again. "Only my family and my closest friends have been invited tonight. It will be an intimate little dinner party. And everyone who's coming knows that you'll be there." She stopped suddenly, as though she'd just recalled something rather unpleasant.

"Except for whom?" Philippa demanded.

Belle's serious eyes clouded with misgiving. She clasped her hands in front of her. "When I sent out the invitations for this evening, I had no idea you'd be in London on my birthday, *chérie*. Lady Augusta had said you weren't expected for at least another week."

Philippa clutched the broad straw brim with tense fingers. "We enjoyed excellent weather. Who else is coming?"

Belle reached out and pried the bonnet from Philippa's grasp. Opening the tall armoire, she stretched up and placed the hat on the top shelf. Then she closed the heavy door with its elaborate carvings, turned, and leaned back against the Chinese fretwork, as though to support herself. Her voice was hushed with suppressed excitement. "Court."

"Are you insane?" Philippa flung her arms wide in disbelief. "Do you actually think the high and mighty duke of Warbeck would stay in the same room with his former wife? The moment he lays eyes on me, he'll cut me dead. After which, His Grace will stick his arrogant nose in the air and leave. All the other guests will immediately follow his lead, and your wonderful party will be turned into an unmitigated disaster."

Belle took a step closer and spoke with earnest conviction. "No, Warbeck won't make a scene. Toby is going to talk to him this afternoon. Either Courtenay Shelburne comes to our home accepting the fact that you're going to be there as my dearest friend, or he's not coming at all."

A hysterical giggle bubbled up in Philippa's throat. She pressed her fingers to her chest to stifle the sound of her panic. "You're both daft if you think you can dictate to a man like Warbeck. If he knows I'll be there, he won't come. I'd stake my entire dowager settlement on it."

"Then there's nothing to worry about, is there?"
Belle replied, beaming with satisfaction. "If you're
certain Court won't be at the dinner party, you can
feel completely safe in attending."

Irrationally, Philippa fought the urge both to laugh
and cry. "There's more to it than that, you
puddinghead. If you publicly befriend a divorced
woman, you'll be leaving yourself open to vile innu-
endo."

"*Mon Dieu*, did you think I was planning on being
your friend in secret?" Belle stomped across the rug
and stood directly in front of Philippa. Her dark
brows met in an irate scowl, but she spoke in a more
reasoning tone. "You're putting too much emphasis
on the past, Pippa. During the divorce proceedings,
the press was far more critical of Court's well-known
reputation as a rakehell than of your inexplicable behavior. You were an eighteen-year-old bride who'd
been married only two months. Except for the elopement itself, no evidence was ever brought forward to
prove you were an errant wife."

"I was *never* an errant wife. When Sandy and I set
sail from England, we were both innocent of adultery."

"I've always been certain of your innocence. I've
known you too long and too well to believe otherwise. Now I'm asking you to be as brave as you are
blameless. Please, Pippa! Come to my celebration tonight."

Philippa pressed a hand to her forehead. How
could she refuse the request of her beloved friend?
Belle had risked her own reputation by correspond-
ing with her, a shameless exile. And now she was all
too willing to face a barrage of scurrilous gossip in
order to stand beside her. Philippa's shoulders
slumped in defeat. Heaven help her, who on this
earth could say nay to that kind of loyalty?

"Very well. Since I'm certain that Warbeck will
never agree to come once he learns that I'll be there,

I'll attend your party." She looked up, still dubious. "You're positive that Tobias will tell him this afternoon?"

"*Absolument!*" Belle grinned in triumph. Going back over to the wardrobe, she swung open its tall carved door. "Now let's see. What will you wear?" She started pulling out evening gowns and flinging them onto the bed.

"Mama!" a child's voice called from the doorway. Kit barreled into the room, well ahead of his nurse. "I fed the ducks in the park! They came right up to me and took the bread out of my hand."

Philippa bent down and hugged her son. "Hello, darling. Were you a good boy for Miss O'Dwyer? You didn't go near the water without her, did you?" She kissed his smooth cheek, then drew him over to the chaise longue, where they sat down side by side.

"I was good," Kit assured her. His gray eyes were enormous with the ingenuous sincerity of a five-year-old.

"Oh, my lady," the nursemaid said with a gasp as she entered the room. "The young master was as good as can be!" Her freckled face shone with pride and satisfaction at the success of their first outing together.

Philippa had hired the seventeen-year-old redhead only the day before. She wanted a cheerful, outgoing person for her son's nurse, someone who wouldn't purse up her lips in rebuke when she learned the story of the child's scandalous mother. Oonah O'Dwyer had listened to Philippa's brief explanation of the circumstances surrounding the family in Cavendish Square without once blinking her big green eyes. Then, without a single comment on the shocking tale she'd just heard, Oonah had assured Philippa that she'd helped her mother care for her ten younger brothers and sisters, and one small boy wouldn't be a lick of trouble. Philippa had hired her on the spot.

"That will be all for now, O'Dwyer," she told her with an encouraging smile. "Come back in about an hour, and you can read to Kit while I get dressed for the evening."

"Did you see the gondola your mother gave me?" Belle asked the boy as the nursemaid left the room. She pointed toward the magnificent porcelain.

"Yes, *Signóra Bella.*" Kit flashed her a happy smile. He popped up from the chaise longue and raced to the dressing table. "Mama showed it to me before we left home. I've been in one just like this," he added grandly. His face shining with pride, he touched the black cap on the gondolier's head with the tip of his finger. "When I grow up, I'm going to be a boatman."

Belle sat down on the edge of the bed. "Your mother was just telling me about your home in Venice. We're so happy you've come to visit us, Kit. I'm going to show you my home in the country. It's right next to yours, you know."

"Do you have a pony, *signóra?*"

Belle nodded and smiled encouragingly.

"Can I ride it?"

She laughed as she looked at Philippa. "That's up to your mama, *mon enfant.*"

Kit returned to stand at his mother's side. "Can I, Mama?"

Placing an arm around her son, Philippa drew him close and kissed his temple. "We'll see, sweetheart. Now, tell me everything that happened at the park this afternoon."

A polite tap interrupted Kit's tale of his adventure. The butler stood in the open doorway, and Philippa gestured for him to enter. She took a note from the silver tray Corbyn extended and then nodded a dismissal. Philippa broke the seal, opened the engraved card, and stared in surprise at its message.

"What is it?" Belle asked.

Philippa met Belle's worried gaze. Wordlessly, she

held the card out to her. Belle snatched the note from Philippa's hand, certain it was some horrible insult penned by an interfering, razor-tongued busybody. With a gasp of shock, Belle read the name inscribed on the top of the folded card: Lady Augusta, Dowager Duchess of Warbeck. Opening the missive, Belle read the single word written in exquisite copperplate.

Courage

Court lounged back in the leather wing chair, lifted a glass of port to his lips, and stared out absently at the busy throng on St. James's Street. Late afternoon shoppers strolled past the thoroughfare's large store windows displaying the costly goods of bootmakers, jewelers, goldsmiths, wine merchants, and greengrocers. Barouches, tilburies, and high-perch phaetons as tall as a first floor window clogged the street, their liveried drivers calling out boldly for the right of way, while street venders, hawking everything from strawberries to sand in their melodic, rhythmical chants, weaved agile paths among London's most noble and propertied citizens. Beneath Court's disinterested gaze, the *beau monde* patronized the street's celebrated shops, ogled the fairer members of the opposite sex, and gossiped as though their very way of life depended upon it. Perhaps it did.

He sat in the wide bow window of White's, apart from his many colleagues in the exclusive club's gaming rooms who were engrossed in the play of whist, faro, and macao. He knew no fellow member would approach him without a friendly smile of encouragement on his part. This particular spot by the window was reserved for the regent and the chosen few he considered his personal cronies. Court wasn't especially fond of the Prince of Wales, but for some reason Prinny had offered his friendship and admiration despite the fact that Court was a leading Whig. No doubt, the entree into the regent's magic circle

had been paved by the heralded tales of the duke of
Warbeck's deep coffers.

Despite his outward show of calm, Court seethed
with anger. He was furious, not just at Philippa for
coming back to stir up the old, tormented feelings inside him, but also at himself. Something deep within
him had leaped for joy at the mere thought of seeing
her again. He was determined ruthlessly to squelch
any wavering in his intention to seek revenge.

Court wondered how long it would take for the
news of his former wife's return to spread through
London. At the moment, no one even glanced his
way. But it wouldn't be long before every head
would turn as he entered this club or any other.

Hell, he'd survive. He'd done it before, when the vicious cartoons caricaturing him as an evil wizard
about to disrobe a sobbing bride of her wedding dress
with his curving talons had graced the newspapers on
a daily basis. No gentleman had dared to smirk in his
face or utter one salacious comment. Nor had there
been a single wager entered in White's infamous
betting-book on the amount of monetary compensa-
tion the aggrieved husband would finally be awarded
in the court of common law. Not even a speculative
hazard on the ultimate destination of the eloping couple had been written down for curious eyes. But he
could imagine all the snide remarks and high stake
gambling that had been carried on behind his back.

Of course, the city's hoi polloi had never been so
inhibited. Ribald taunts had been shouted from the
crowds that lined Parliament Street as he'd entered
the House of Lords each day of the divorce proceedings. To London's lower element, his personal tragedy had been better than a circus at Astley's
Amphitheater or a bearbaiting at Bartholomew Fair.
In those days of public humiliation, he'd discovered
a real sympathy for the tormented bear. Lady Augusta was getting dotty in her old age if she thought
the score between him and Philippa should be con-

sidered settled merely because the marquess of Sandhurst had died in exile.

They had been such close friends as youngsters—Court, Sandy, and Toby—that the populace of Chippinghelm had named them the Three Hussars. Through their childhood, they'd played with their wooden soldiers, learned to ride their first ponies, and triumphed in rugby and cricket over the local village lads. Later at Eton and Oxford, where the competition had been fiercer, they always played on the same team and usually won.

More than once, the other two boys had saved Court from a thrashing by his strict father, for Court had always been quick with his fists and frequently landed himself in trouble. One day he'd pounded Jem Hutton right into the dirt after the ruffian had dared to make a jeering remark about Court's mother. The bully had been a big, strapping fellow, and Court had suffered a bloody nose and a split lip.

"Mama! Mama!" Sandy had hollered as the nine-year-olds raced into Sandhurst Hall after the fray. "Mama, come quick! Court's bleeding!"

"What?" Lady Harriet cried, hurrying into the back parlor. "Let me see." She lifted Court's chin with one finger and carefully inspected the damage. "This time you really got yourself in trouble, young man," she chided. "Who did you fight with now?" Before he could answer, she pressed her snowy handkerchief firmly against his nose and squeezed the nostrils shut, cutting off the flow of blood.

"H-he fought J-jem H-hutton," Toby explained excitedly. "C-court knocked h-his front t-tooth out."

"The blacksmith's son?" Lady Harriet peered at Court in surprise. "Why he's five years older than you, Courtenay, and outweighs you by a good forty pounds." She shook her head and tsk-tsked her disapproval. "What's your father going to say?"

"Court can't tell Lord Warbeck," Sandy confided in a rush. He moved closer to his friend as though to offer protection. "That's why I brought him here, Mom. You've got to help us."

She looked from one to the other suspiciously. "And just why can't he tell his father?"

Sandy and Toby exchanged guilty looks, while Court tensed and glared a warning. He squared his shoulders and clenched his fists, daring his pals to repeat the vicious slur Jem had made against Lady Warbeck.

"W-we can't t-tell you, ma'am," Toby said with a gulp. Behind his spectacles, his serious brown eyes were enormous. "B-but it w-wasn't Court's f-fault. The other b-boy started it."

Lady Harriet's stern features softened. "I see." She favored Court with a bracing smile. "Well, let's take you into the kitchen and get you cleaned up. We can talk about who started the fight later."

"Yes, ma'am," he said in gratitude. The marchioness of Sandhurst might look tall and plain to others, but to Court she was a beautiful guardian angel with red hair and an oversized mouth.

"Thanks, Mom," Sandy said, a relieved grin lighting up his attractive features. "We thought maybe you would send a servant over to the Castle with a note asking if Court could stay here tonight."

"Humph," she snorted. Still pinching Court's nose, she led the errant threesome into the Hall's enormous kitchen. "It's going to take more than one night for Courtenay's swollen lip to heal. But I suppose it will give you young jackanapeses enough time to perfect the story you're going to concoct for Lord Warbeck. I'll send one of the grooms over to the Castle as soon as we get our pugilist bandaged up."

"You're the most wonderful mother in the whole world," Sandy avowed. He rolled his green eyes and sniffed appreciatively. "Gosh, I think Cook's just baked scones. I love to get home right when they're coming out of the oven. Maybe we could each have one after you fix Court's lip."

"Maybe you could," she said with a wry smile. "Maybe then you'll stay out of trouble for the rest of the afternoon."

Lady Harriet ministered to the battered warrior, then sat them all down at the kitchen table and fed them warm scones topped with whipped cream and fresh raspberries. The boys smiled at one another, glorying in their success. Once again, Sandy's magic way with words had saved the day.

After they'd finished eating, the trio headed out to the stables. They clambered up to the top of a haystack and sank down in its sweet-smelling warmth, hidden from view.

"What w-will you t-tell your father?" Toby asked Court with a worried frown.

Court shrugged. "I'll think of something."

Sandy flopped back on the soft hay and folded his hands beneath his head contentedly. "Tell him you were climbing up a tree to rescue a frightened kitty and the branch broke and you fell and cut your mouth."

"That's a g-good story!" Toby exclaimed in admiration.

"I've never told that one before," Court admitted thoughtfully. "So he'll probably believe it. And he won't be angry because helping a stranded kitten is a kind thing to do."

Sandy sat up and held out his hand, palm down. "All right. That's the story we'll stick to, no matter what."

Court and Toby stacked their hands on top of his. "Three against the world," they chanted. "If one betrays another, our bones will turn to mush and our blood to treacle."

In the midst of his reverie, Court felt the presence of someone nearby and glanced over his shoulder. Tobias Howard, Viscount Rockingham, stood just behind his chair, solemnly watching him. From the ex-

pression on Toby's sharp features, Court realized that
his friend was well aware of the tidings that would
soon entertain a shocked and fascinated ton. Christ,
he should have known that Philippa would contact
Toby's wife, Lady Gabrielle, the moment she set foot
on English soil.

He lifted his glass to his companion in salute.
"Here's to the newly arrived émigrés," he toasted,
and then drained the port in one quick swallow as
Rockingham settled his lanky frame into the soft
chair across from him.

"G-gad, I was afraid you wouldn't b-be here."
Toby expelled a deep whoosh of relief. "I st-stopped
by Grosvenor Square, but your s-secretary didn't
seem to know where you'd gone. S-said you'd
stomped out of the house hours ago."

Court tried to ignore the vein pulsing in his temple.
"Where the hell did you think I'd gone? To some miserable public alehouse to hide like an accursed dog?"

"N-no," Tobias responded cautiously. He surveyed
Court from behind the thick lenses of his spectacles.
"I just didn't know which of y-your clubs you'd
g-gone to this afternoon."

The two were silent as a waiter set down a tray
with two glasses of wine, which Tobias had apparently requested. "What's so important it couldn't
wait until I saw you this evening?" Court demanded
the moment the servant had left, though he had a
fairly good idea what had brought Rockingham to
White's. "If you've come to tell me Philippa's returned to England, you're late. Two people have already had the pleasure of trumpeting the unwelcome
news. Along with their unwanted advice for the
former husband."

"I-I know." Tobias fidgeted with an enameled
snuffbox in his graceful, scholar's hand, flicking the
lid open and shut with his thumbnail. As usual, his
stock was a travesty, his wrinkled coat appeared too
large for his bony frame, and one lace cuff was ink-

stained. He'd probably just leaped up from the laboratory table in his attic, where he'd spent all day over his chemistry experiments without even pausing to eat, suddenly realizing that he was too late to find Court still at home and would have to chase him down at one of their private clubs.

Idly, Court lifted his goblet and watched the dark red wine swirl against the cut crystal. When Toby merely sat there without uttering another word, his thin shoulders hunched forward in nervous expectation, Court glanced over the rim of his glass. "Well?"

Rockingham cleared his throat. He met Court's stare with unflinching brown eyes. "I-I came to tell you that Belle has invited Lady S-sandhurst to tonight's festivities."

"That wasn't necessary. I was already aware that the dowager marchioness planned to attend. It won't be the first time my irascible godmother and I are under the same roof."

Dropping the snuffbox back in his coat pocket, Toby ran one finger under his limp cravat and frowned unhappily. "I w-wasn't referring t-to Lady Harriet, though of course, she'll be there as well. The dowager will be escorting her d-daughter-in-law."

Jesus, why couldn't any of them just say Philippa?

As the full import of Rockingham's disclosure hit him, Court tipped his head back and rested it against the chair's cool leather upholstery. The rational part of him admired his own calm, collected front, while a bitter, aching disappointment at his friend's betrayal sliced through the spot where his soul would have been—if he'd still had one. But trust and fidelity were for those demented fools who still believed that mankind had been created in the image of a loving and merciful Father.

"You'll forgive me," he drawled with icy detachment, "when I confess that I'll not be able to attend this evening's fete, after all. A matter of gravest importance has arisen which cannot be put off to another

time. Please express my deepest regrets to Lady Rockingham and extend my felicitations on her birthday."

"D-damn it, Court!" Tobias exploded. "Don't take
that snotty, stiff-necked attitude with me! I'm your cl-
closest friend."

"*Were* my closest friend," Court corrected. He refused to acknowledge, even to himself, the aching,
empty feeling inside him. He set the wineglass down
on the side table, reached for his cane, and rose. A
sharp twinge of pain lanced through his thigh.

Tobias followed him to his feet. "You have so
m-many friends, then, that you can afford to throw
one away?"

Court grinned in sardonic self-mockery. "It would
seem I have a chronic inability to retain another's affection."

He started toward the door, and Tobias stepped in
front of him. Toby lowered his voice and grated in a
hoarse whisper, "It's Belle's s-sincere hope that you'll
attend as you promised and b-behave yourself like a
ci-civilized gentleman."

Court spoke through clenched teeth. "I can't possibly come to your home this evening, Rockingham,
since my former spouse will be there. Lady Gabrielle
made the choice between us when she invited the
strumpet. Your mistake was in acceding to your
wife's foolish wishes. Though no one knows better
than I the effect a pair of beautiful eyes can have on
a man's good judgment, I simply can't overlook your
disloyalty to me."

As Court kept walking, Tobias stayed right at his
side. "Blast your eyes, man! Belle can invite anyone
t-to her home that she sees fit. And I'll stand
b-behind her. No one can t-tell me or my wife whom
w-we can and cannot befriend."

Ignoring the heads craning to discover the reason
for the commotion, Court took his hat and gloves
from the steward. He strove to keep his voice low
and controlled as he leaned toward the viscount. "Far

be it from me, Rockingham, to try to tell you anything. But the next time I lay eyes on Philippa Bentinck, I'll snub her so thoroughly that no one in this bloody, sniggering town will have any doubt as to my feelings about her. And I'll make damn sure she won't be received in society by anyone higher than a scullery maid."

Shocked by the vicious intensity of the threat, Tobias paused at the top of the stone steps and watched Court descend, then charged down after him. He grabbed his arm and pulled him to a standstill on the busy thoroughfare. "I d-don't know what awful p-punishment you have pl-planned for Philippa, but I have s-some advice for you, Warbeck, whether you w-want to hear it or not. If you p-purposely hurt her, you'll lose the sympathy of every p-person who still cares about you. You'd b-better get a rein on that temper of yours and think before you strike out at a helpless female. And for God's sake, d-don't do anything until you've s-seen the child."

Before Court could wish the boy and his confounded mother to perdition, Viscount Rockingham whirled and stalked off down the street.

Philippa quietly opened the door to Kit's bedroom and tiptoed across the rug. From her chair in the corner, Oonah O'Dwyer rose and came forward. "Can I be helpin' you, me lady?" the red-haired nursemaid asked softly in her thick Irish brogue.

Philippa placed a finger to her lips. "I just wanted to be sure Kit was tucked in. He's a restless sleeper. He often kicks the bedclothes aside during the night."

"Oh, he'll be perfectly fine," Oonah said with a reassuring smile. "You have a wonderful time at Lady Rockingham's dinner party, and don't be worryin' none about the little lad. I'll be lookin' after him for you."

"Go on to bed, then," said Philippa. "I'm going to

sit here beside him for a few minutes before I leave for the evening."

The buxom girl dropped a quick curtsy. "Goodnight, me lady. And by the by, you look perfectly smashin' in that lovely gown. All the fine young gentlemen will have eyes for no one but you."

Philippa glanced down at the dress she wore. It was fashioned in the current classical style, but instead of the usual pale color, it was the deep lavender-blue of hyacinths. "Thank you," she said, a wry smile twisting her lips. She didn't bother to explain that the only fine young gentlemen there tonight would be Lady Gabrielle's two married brothers.

After O'Dwyer left, Philippa went to stand beside the canopied bed. In the lamp's golden glow, Kit's dark hair stood out starkly against the white linen pillow slip. Just as she'd expected, he'd already started to push off the comforter. She lifted the cover up over his shoulders and tucked it around him gently, touched by the adorable picture he made. His thick black lashes lay against his cheeks, his pink lips were parted in a slumber so tranquil he looked like a cherub resting on a cloud. Bending over, she pressed a kiss to his forehead. Then she sat down on the edge of the feather mattress and smoothed back his tousled locks.

"My little angel," she whispered. "How precious you are." She lifted his small hand and placed it in her palm. His fingers curled reflexively around her thumb, bringing a tender smile to her lips. Love for her child filled her completely. On the day he was born, she'd made a vow that he would never suffer the terrifying feelings of abandonment that she'd known as a little girl. She would guard and protect Kit with her life. She would stand beside him till he was a strong young man ready to go off to the university.

Her conversation with Belle that afternoon had brought back images of her own childhood. Philippa had been six, only a year older than Kit was now,

when she'd been orphaned. Her earliest memory was
of her uncle taking her to the boarding school where
she had lived until she married at eighteen.

She stared absently across the dimly lit chamber,
seeing herself and Belle at twelve, lying in their narrow beds on the top floor of the Lillybridge Seminary. They shared a tiny room by themselves, a
privilege generally awarded only to the older girls.
But Philippa's unique status as a full-time resident
had prompted the Misses Blanche and Beatrice to
give her and her best friend their own cozy little
nest. During the holidays and summers, Philippa had
the room to herself. Not that she liked the weeks she
spent alone. She lived for the day when the fall term
would begin and all the other young ladies would return, filled with wondrous tales of their adventures.
To Philippa, their homes in Sussex and Devonshire
and Surrey seemed as far away and exotic as the jeweled palaces of Cathay or the nomadic tents of Araby.

"Try harder, Pippa," Belle had whispered on that
long-ago winter night. "Try harder. You *have* to be
able to remember your mama. She didn't die till you
were six. I can remember when I was four and Papa
and Mama gave me a beautiful doll for Christmas."

Lying flat on her back, Philippa screwed her eyes
tight and tried to concentrate once again. What had
her mother looked like? Had she been tall and thin?
Short and plump? Philippa was certain her mama
had been beautiful, with a wonderful smile and a
sweet, gentle voice. But she couldn't picture her. She
couldn't hear her. Always, it seemed the image remained just beyond her reach. No matter how hard
she struggled to regain the lost memories, her life before she'd arrived at the school remained a void. "I
can't remember," she said with a frustrated groan.
"Truly, Belle, I've tried and I've tried, and I can't remember what she looked like."

"Then how about your papa?" Belle encouraged.
"Try to remember him. Maybe he was fair like you. He

was probably a wonderful rider, and took you up before him on a prancing horse. Think about a tall, handsome man riding with you across a grassy meadow."

Once again, Philippa shut her eyes, searching in her mind for an image—any image of a man, tall and handsome or short and homely. "It's no use," she said dispiritedly. "I've tried so many times to picture him. Why can't I remember?"

"Do you remember the fire?"

"No."

"Sometimes you dream about one."

"But I never recall the dream when I wake."

It had always been a source of wonder to those around Philippa that the only emotional scar from the tragedy that killed her parents was a deep and abiding fear of fire. Once, a curtain had accidentally brushed across a candle flame in their room. Philippa had stood by, frozen in terror, while Belle calmly quenched the blaze with a pitcher of water. That night, when Philippa had awakened screaming from a nightmare about the fire, she'd sobbed over and over, frightened by the image of a "bad man with a torch." But in the morning, she was her usual happy self with no recollection of the incident.

They lay there in the still, darkened room, their breathing regular and even. From outside came the faint sounds of a handcart being pushed over the frozen cobblestones. The iron wheels crunched and squeaked across the thin layer of snow.

"Belle," Philippa said at last, "do you think my parents loved me?"

"*Bon Dieu*, of course they loved you!" Belle's whisper was hoarse with exasperation. "All parents love their children. Why, your mama and papa are in heaven, looking down on you right now. And they love you very, very much. I'm certain of it."

Philippa rolled to her side and stared at where her friend lay in the darkness, barely able to make out the lump of her shape beneath the pale quilt. "Then why can't I feel their love?" she asked. "I pray to them every night. I beg them to let me know they're thinking of me. But I never hear anything. I never *feel* anything."

"I don't know why," Belle answered truthfully. "Perhaps it's because they know that Miss Blanche and Miss Beatrice are looking after you now."

Philippa smiled at the comforting thought. "Maybe you're right. I have two adopted mothers who love me very much. So I shouldn't feel alone, should I? It's just that when the other girls ask about my parents, I have nothing to tell them."

"I didn't know that bothered you." Belle's voice revealed her surprise and concern. "You always seem so happy. No one would guess their questions upset you. They don't mean any harm, you know. They're merely curious."

"I don't mind their curiosity. I just don't want anyone feeling sorry for me," said Philippa stubbornly.

"Well, they don't, *imbécile!* Everyone thinks you're so much fun to be with. You're the cheeriest girl in the school."

Philippa knew what Belle said was true. All of the other students at Lillybridge believed she was happy-go-lucky in spite of the fact that she was an orphan.

Early on, Philippa had learned to hide her sense of isolation behind a bright smile. When Philippa was only seven, Miss Blanche had sat the tearful child on her lap and told her that it did no good for a person to feel sorry about what she didn't have. All the crying and fretting in the world wouldn't change a thing. But a sunny disposition made everything seem brighter, and pretty soon you started to feel happier, too. "Act the way you *want* to feel," Miss Blanche had told her. "Before long you'll find that it's the way you *do* feel." Philippa had taken the advice to heart.

"Anyway," Belle said, "you're coming home with me in three more days. You'll be able to meet Mama and Papa and Étienne and André. We'll have a wonderful Christmas together."

"Oh, Belle, I can hardly wait!" Philippa's words rang with excitement. She could scarcely believe her good fortune. "Are you sure they want me to come?"

Belle's throaty giggle was contagious. "Want you? Why they'd be so disappointed if you didn't come, I'd have to stay here at school during the holidays, myself."

Giggling, Philippa plumped up her pillow. "We'd better get to sleep," she warned, "or we'll never pass our arithmetic examination tomorrow."

"Okay, good night." Belle yawned loudly. "And don't worry about meeting my family. They're going to love you."

Philippa snuggled beneath the warm comforter, thinking about the coming holiday. Belle had told her all about the Merciers. They sounded loving and kind, just like Belle. But the thought of meeting her friend's older brothers was most unnerving. Males were mysterious creatures as far as Philippa was concerned. She was simply never around one. When it came to conversing with fashionable young gentlemen, Philippa knew she'd be at a complete loss.

Once, she'd asked Miss Beatrice what men were like, and her surrogate mother had explained that there was just no understanding them. "I'm no expert, mind you," the peppery female admitted, "but it seems to me that men don't think the way we do. When something of great import is involved, they appear to make their decisions by cold logic based on the facts alone, not even attempting to see into the heart and soul of the matter." As Philippa had grown older, she'd found that the spinster had been very wise, indeed.

Breaking away from her reverie, Philippa looked down at the child sleeping so peacefully. She lifted his hand to her lips and kissed it gently, then eased it under the warm bedclothes. "Sleep tight, *carissimo*," she whispered. "Mama loves you."

Philippa loved her son with all her heart. Kit was the reason she'd fled England. Once she'd realized that she'd lost her husband's love, completely and irrevocably, she knew that she had to protect the unborn babe. She was convinced that Court, rejecting her as he had with such venom, would also reject her child. Had he known of her pregnancy, his pride would have demanded that he take the baby from her at the time of birth. But he wouldn't have loved it. If the infant had been a girl, she would have lived her days, like Philippa, locked away in a boarding school. If the baby was a son and heir, his father would have kept him at Castle Warbeck. But every time he'd have looked at the male child, he would have seen his loathsome mother and hated him.

Philippa rose and blew out the candle on the night table, making certain it was completely extinguished. With ingrained habit, she glanced at the cold hearth. The evening was balmy, with no need for a fire. Yet she never left Kit's room without checking twice to be certain there was no chance of a flying spark landing on the rug and igniting while he slept.

With one last, fond glance at her son, she started for the door. This evening, for Kit's sake, she would reenter society among those kindhearted Merciers she'd come to love so dearly. She would make the first, tentative step toward building a normal life for herself and her son.

The terror she felt inside left her quaking in her satin evening sandals. She fought back the urge to return to the safety of her bedroom, where she could remove her fancy dress and climb under the covers to hide. Instead, she squared her shoulders and pinned a smile on her face. The advice she'd received years ago had always stood her in good stead. She would act the way she wanted to feel, for crying and fretting never changed a thing. But a bright, sunny smile cheered everyone around her, including herself.

Chapter 3

⟨◦◦⟩

"**H**ow nice," Lady Clare Brownlow murmured as they crossed the threshold and entered the hallway. She held out her arms to allow Court to remove the fringed Paisley shawl draped across her elbows, striking the unconscious pose of a female used to being constantly waited upon and taking it completely for granted.

As he lifted the wrap from her shoulders, Court glanced around at the familiar setting. "Yes, isn't it?" he agreed, hiding his amusement at her faint praise.

Nice would have been an understatement at the worst of times. But tonight the spacious entrance hall of Rockingham House fairly dazzled the eye. Candlelight thrown from the polished brass sconces along the walls bounced off the genuine Roman columns that decorated the oval antechamber. A blazing chandelier hung from the vaulted ceiling, casting its light on the gilded statues mounted on top of the black marble pillars that had been rescued from the bed of the Tiber in the middle of the last century.

The perfume of spring flowers filled the room. Drifts of yellow and white daisies, velvety purple irises with magnificent fleur-de-lis blooms, great yellow and red tulips on the slenderest of stems, and delicate lavender and pink larkspurs, all potted in priceless Tang dynasty vases, crisscrossed the black-and-white marble floor and paraded up the curving double staircase at the far end, leading to the cham-

43

bers above. In the center of this opulent entryway, the Viscount and Viscountess Rockingham greeted the members of Belle's family and directed them toward the grand salon, where the faint sound of earlier arrivals chatting with one another could be heard.

The duke of Warbeck surrendered his hat and gloves, along with his fiancée's shawl, to the waiting butler and guided Clare through the lavish floral display to meet their host and hostess. Court and Clare were apparently the last to arrive, for Tobias and Belle were already rewarding each other with smiles of mutual satisfaction.

The viscount had retained his unfashionable spectacles, but in honor of the special occasion, his wife had put hers aside for a pair of scissors glasses, their ornate handle held in one white-gloved hand.

"Court!" Lady Gabrielle said breathlessly when they approached. "How good of you to come to my party." She extended her hand, and he brought it to his lips. Keeping hold of his fingers, she squeezed them gratefully before turning to the striking woman beside him. "And Lady Clare," she continued in a rush, "how pleasant to see you again." The bright stain on Belle's cheeks betrayed her surprise at their presence. Her husband had evidently told her of Court's callous refusal to attend earlier that afternoon.

As the two women exchanged pleasantries, Court turned to Tobias. The childhood friends stared solemnly into each other's eyes without saying a word. Above his white cravat, Rockingham's prominent Adam's apple bobbed as he swallowed uncomfortably.

"I see Lady Gabrielle insisted on dressing you this evening," Court gibed with a wry grin. "You look like you're aspiring to be the queen's new majordomo."

Tobias cracked a slow smile, relief flooding his

worried features. "D-dash it all, m-my wife thinks I'm d-destined to knock you off the top of the sartorial ladder. Hope you won't hold it against me."

"You'll have to displace Beau Brummell first. And I believe he's still two rungs below me." Court reached out, and they shook hands with a quick, firm grasp. "You were correct about one thing, Rockingham," he added quietly. "I can't afford to throw any of my friends away. Least of all, one I've known since I was in leading strings."

"Thank you for c-coming," Tobias said.

"Don't thank me. I came against my better judgment, knowing I could never purposely hurt your lovely wife. I guess when it comes to Belle's pretty brown eyes, I'm just as big a fool as you are."

On the carriage ride to Portman Place, he'd asked himself over and over again why he was doing such a bloody stupid thing. He hadn't come up with a clear answer yet. Partly, it was just as he'd intimated. He refused to extinguish willingly the two pure lights that shone like twin beacons in his embittered, cynical world. Tobias and Belle had remained loyal to him during the period of uncensored drinking, gambling, and wenching that had immediately followed his divorce. He wouldn't easily surrender their friendship or their love. Especially not to someone so unworthy of their affection.

And partly, it was the decision to control the time and place of his first meeting with Philippa Bentinck that had made him come. Rather than happen upon her at some unexpected moment, he preferred the luxury of having himself well in control. His year with the Spanish guerrillas in the Peninsular War had taught him the danger of being waylaid. Forewarned was forearmed.

He shouldn't have brought Clare, however. He glanced at her now as she chatted with her hostess, pleased with the picture of elegant sophistication she made. The ice blue satin of her narrow gown was a perfect complement to her flaxen hair and light blue eyes. She was tall and thin, with a haughty bearing and a practiced air of ennui which, he surmised, was about to be transformed into righteous indignation. She would be shocked when she realized the identity of a certain guest. Some perverted wish to flaunt his exquisite fiancée under Philippa's nose had kept him silent, for Clare would most certainly have refused outright to attend the gathering had she known that his former wife was going to be there. Who could blame her? Genteel ladies did not readily countenance the presence of a divorced woman in their midst.

The only child of a prominent and wealthy Whig statesman, Clare was a gentlewoman of unquestionable reputation; her charitable works for the less fortunate were well-known throughout the city. It had been a major coup for a divorced rakehell, reformed or otherwise, to secure the promise of her hand in marriage.

For some quirky reason he'd refused to examine, he wanted Philippa to realize that he had attracted an heiress of unsullied repute to become the next duchess of Warbeck, the title she'd so wantonly abandoned. The fact that the title itself was probably the strongest enticement for Lady Clare irritated him not at all. A twenty-nine-year-old spinster could hardly be expected to contract a lifetime alliance on the basis of an emotional attachment. Clare's cool demeanor suited him just fine. He could buy passion in his mistress's bed for the price of a diamond trinket. Impeccable social standing was harder to come by. Court offered his arm to Clare with a small smile of victory.

From her position above them on the wide stairway, Philippa looked down in horror at the dark-haired man who'd just shaken hands with Viscount Rockingham.

It couldn't be!

Warbeck had come after all!

What a fool she'd been to think he wouldn't snatch at his first opportunity for revenge. Sheer panic, disorienting and immobilizing, battered her senses. She should never have come. She reached out blindly and clutched the balustrade with trembling fingers. Taking a deep breath, she fought the feeling of suffocation that threatened to smother her.

Dear God above, why, why did he have to look so magnificent?

And so frightening?

Several inches over six feet, the duke of Warbeck was dressed in severe black evening clothes subtly tailored to reveal his superb physique. In the jutting angle of his strong jaw, in the sharp, patrician features, in the taut, proud stance, there was about him a formidable, even sinister, tension. It was no wonder she'd always been a little afraid of Court Shelburne. An aura of invincible power hovered around him.

Then he turned to take his companion's arm, and Philippa saw the gold-headed cane, the stiff posture, the impaired stride. Her heart ached at the sight of the man who'd once been the embodiment of masculine grace. She lifted a hand to her chest to stifle an unexpected gasp of compassion. No one had told her that he'd been severely injured.

Her attention moved to the woman at his side. The svelte blonde looked up at him with the tranquil complacency of a spoiled house cat. Warbeck bent his head and said something in her ear that earned him a brief smile. But the humor never quite reached the pale eyes that exactly matched the washed-out blue of her gown. Astonished, Philippa wondered what a man with Warbeck's passionate nature was doing with such a cold fish. Then he turned and looked up at her, and Philippa's heart leaped with fright at the undiluted loathing in his silvery gaze.

Gowned in diaphanous silk the rich color of hyacinths, Lady Philippa Moore Shelburne Bentinck,

marchioness of Sandhurst, stood poised halfway
down the stairs, watching Court with those deep,
dark violet eyes he remembered so well. The startled
look on her face told him she hadn't expected to encounter her former husband tonight. Good. She
needed to realize that he wasn't turning his dearest
friends over to her without a struggle. A struggle he
intended to win. When he was through with her, she
wouldn't have a friend in the world.

She released her hold on the curved mahogany
railing and retreated upward one slow, cautious step.
She was frightened, all right. For a second, he
thought she was going to whirl and dash pell-mell
up the rest of the stairs to hide in the nearest bedroom until he left. But he wasn't to be so fortunate.
Never once breaking their locked gazes, she raised
her stubborn chin and descended the carpeted staircase with all the inborn arrogance of a princess, till
she came to a halt on the bottom step.

Court was vaguely aware that Lady Harriet, in a
dress of scarlet-and-black stripes that rustled omi-
nously as she moved, marched right behind her
daughter-in-law like a colonel in His Majesty's Life
Guards. An enormous black ostrich plume curved
over the top of her head, bobbing up and down with
each redoubtable step she took. But he didn't meet
his godmother's warning glare. He couldn't take his
gaze off Philippa.

He hadn't laid eyes on the wench since the day
he'd caught her wrapped in her lover's arms.
Wretched disappointment knotted in the pit of his
stomach at the sight of her. Bloody hell. She was
even more beautiful at twenty-four than she'd been
at eighteen. In spite of her tattered reputation and
her sin-stained soul, she had somehow retained an
air of untouched wholesomeness. Her wide-set eyes
sparkled just as much as before, her complexion
glowed as smooth and creamy. Her golden hair was
piled high on top of her dainty head in thick, un-

tamed curls. Nothing, absolutely nothing about her revealed the fact that she was a lying doxy—a heartless jade who'd run off with her paramour, leaving her stunned, bewildered bridegroom to curse and rail and throw furniture across his forsaken bedroom like a raving maniac.

He hated her for that.

He hated her for the pain of a wound that had never healed. More than anything, he hated her for looking as innocent and untouched as a schoolgirl in the first, fresh bloom of youth. She ought to be haggard and corroded by her sins. Her deceitful face should be seamed with wrinkles—one for every time she'd taken Sandhurst in her arms, one for every goddamn time she'd lain down in bed with him.

But Court was acutely aware that it was he who'd aged before his time. He was a wreck of his former self. Lord knows, he felt far older than his thirty-six years. The silver in his black hair had appeared over five years ago, etched by the bitterness in his heart. He walked with a humiliating limp, a souvenir brought back from Wellington's campaign against the *Grande Armée* on the Peninsula. Christ, if she could see the mangled flesh of his thigh, she'd draw back in horror.

Rather than pull away, Philippa stepped off the staircase to stand directly in front of him and sank into a deep, graceful curtsy. "Your Grace," she murmured.

That was all.

No blushing, shamefaced stammer. No contritely lowered lids.

How many times during these past years had he pictured their first meeting? Her, penitent, humble, with hands clasped in supplication and tears of sorrow falling down her withered cheeks. He, aloof, righteous, with not a whit of forgiveness in his cold heart.

She rose and stood before him with her head held

high, as though she had a perfect right to be there. There wasn't a hint of regret for the dishonor and suffering she'd caused him. Not a shadow of mortification clouded her impudent gaze. He'd be damned to hell and back if he'd stand there and suffer her puffed-up airs.

Without a word of acknowledgment, Court gripped his cane tightly and pivoted. He caught Clare's elbow and started toward the front entrance. From the corner of his vision, he could see Belle take her husband's hand and lean against him for support, her dark eyes enormous in her pale face. But this time the price of their friendship was more than he could pay.

"W-warbeck," Tobias called, clearly confused at the reason for his sudden departure. The viscount held out his hand as though to beg him not to leave.

Court didn't glance his way. Blind fury engulfed him. He wanted only one thing. To get away as quickly as possible.

Philippa's spirit sank in resignation as she watched Warbeck stalk toward the front door with his exquisite companion in tow. He must have come for just this purpose. To coldly and methodically deliver an ultimatum to the few people who cared about her: anyone who befriended his former spouse would be cut out of his life. She knew this was only the beginning of his quest for retribution. His ultimate goal would be to ensure that no one in polite society would remain in the same room with her for fear of drawing censure upon themselves. She could read his intentions in the unbending posture, the wide shoulders stiff with rage.

All hopes for quietly resuming the way of life she had led before she ever met him were dashed beyond repair. He was too strong, too aggressive, too dangerous to defeat. But this time she wouldn't turn and run. No, this time she'd stand and meet whatever thunderbolts he'd hurl her way. And she'd survive. For Kit's sake, somehow she would survive.

At that moment, Lady Augusta hurried out of the drawing room, took in the scene at a glance, and moved to block her grandson's exit. "Ah, Court, you're here at last," she said. She placed a gloved hand on his sleeve, taking no notice of the fact that he was taut with anger. She eyed him briefly up and down with a critical air, then touched the knot of his perfectly tied stock with one fingertip. "How smart you look this evening, my dear. Dawkes has outdone himself." Before Warbeck could respond, she took both the younger woman's hands in her gnarled ones and beamed at her with overweening appreciation. "Don't you look splendid, Lady Clare. That color certainly becomes you."

The willowy blonde dipped in the slightest of curtsies. "As does yours," she replied abstractedly, scarcely glancing at the gown Lady Augusta wore.

The feathers on his grandmother's turban brushed Warbeck's shoulder as she dropped a swift peck on his companion's cheek. "Now aren't you a sweet child to say so to an old ruin like me? But I've been waiting to talk to you for an age. Come into the salon with me, girl. There are people anxious to meet my grandson's new fiancée."

Philippa refused to acknowledge her start of surprise at the words. Blast it, she didn't care if Warbeck was planning his nuptials. His future was no concern of hers.

Clare looked to Court for guidance, and he could see the confusion in her eyes. "Well," she hedged, "I'm not sure we're going to be here much longer, Lady Augusta."

Court was surrounded by the people he loved most in life, and they were all traitors. "We're not staying," he told his grandmother in a forbidding tone.

"Nonsense. Of course you are!" she contradicted.

She tugged at the black cashmere shawl draped across her slight shoulders and drew it tighter. Meeting his belligerent glower with uplifted brows, she slipped her arm under Clare's elbow as though to lead her into the drawing room. "The count and countess de Rambouillet have never met your fiancée, my dear. Nor have their sons and daughters-in-law. Whatever would they think if you left before they could become acquainted with her?"

Court met his grandmother's appraising look and recalled her admonition not to create another scandal. When he turned his head to his host and hostess, intending to bid them good-bye, he found Belle gazing at him with imploring eyes, while Tobias stood gravely silent, refusing to plead again.

The words of his best friend echoed in Court's mind: *Don't do anything until you've seen the child.* What in the devil had Rockingham meant by that confounded warning?

Lady Augusta, Lady Harriet, and Tobias Howard had all appeared convinced, when they'd called on him earlier that day, that he should place the boy's welfare above his own wishes, even if it meant forgiving the wayward mother. For some incomprehensible reason, they seemed to think they could appeal to his compassion for a snively little bastard who'd sprung from the loins of a traitor.

Unease ruffled Court's determination. Perhaps the child was misshapen or crippled in some way. His heart lurched painfully at the thought. Until he found out why the trio had formed a common front for the defense of Sandhurst's brat, he would forgo the pleasure of snubbing Philippa. He wasn't canceling her punishment, merely awarding a brief reprieve.

Offering his arm to Clare, he nodded his acquiescence to the dowager duchess of Warbeck. "Come, Grandmother. Let's introduce my betrothed to Lady Gabrielle's parents."

His cane tapped softly with each step on the black-and-white marble floor as he accompanied Clare and Lady Augusta into the Rockinghams' formal drawing room.

From her position at the staircase, Philippa wondered whether she should laugh or cry. Had Warbeck stayed as a sign that he wouldn't interfere with her attempt to reenter society? Or was he waiting till he had everyone's attention before he struck his next blow?

"What do you think, Court? Will the Little Corporal stay put on Elba where he belongs?" The countess de Rambouillet shot a piercing glance at him from directly across the table. Catherine Mercier had the same dark eyes as her daughter, alert, intelligent, serious. The storm of revolution that had ravaged her native land and wrought such personal havoc in her life had left the middle-aged woman with a keen interest in political affairs. Seeing the concern on her kindly face, he had to be honest.

"Though I'd like to be more optimistic," he answered thoughtfully as he set down his glass of Madeira, "I'm not so certain we've seen the last of Napoleon yet."

From her place beside the countess, Lady Augusta nodded in emphatic agreement. Her gray eyes snapped with ire. "They should have taken the scoundrel out and shot him. Then we'd be certain he'd never disrupt our lives again."

The Honorable Étienne Mercier looked up from his plate heaped with venison and gravy. "They say the crowds in Paris met Louis Bourbon with cheers as he entered the city. The people of France have had enough of that madman Bonaparte!"

"Truly, they must have," his wife agreed passionately. Dora Mercier wound the pearls at her throat through agitated fingers, and stared across the fragile crystal and china at Court with stricken eyes. "How many brave men died because of that fiend! Or were gravely wounded, as you were, Your Grace."

From down the length of the table, Philippa turned her head to gaze at Warbeck, certain now that he'd received his injury in battle and hoping he would make some mention of what had happened. The duke was seated at their host's right, his fiancée next to him. Lady Clare had scarcely spoken a word the entire meal, though the subjects had ranged widely, from the policies of the present Tory cabinet to Tobias's latest experiments in chemistry.

Belle had ignored social precedence and placed Philippa on her right and her brothers and their wives in the middle of the table, thereby putting the greatest distance possible between the two adversaries. For added protection, Lady Harriet and the count de Rambouillet had been seated close to Philippa. Thankfully, during the free-flowing chatter no one had made a point of the fact that Philippa had been absent from England for some time and knew little of current government policies.

The beat of Philippa's pounding heart had gradually slowed to the point where she was able to contribute a few words now and then. She found that, if she kept her attention fastened upon the comments of the people around her, the presence of her former husband didn't seem quite so threatening. But each time she met his silvery gaze, however briefly, she felt a shock of cold fear as though she were being battered by a storm-tossed sea.

Warbeck smiled kindly at Dora, who was now blushing in embarrassment at her emotional outburst. Philippa had learned from Belle's letters that Étienne's wife had lost an older brother, whom she'd idolized, at Trafalgar. The new bride shyly lowered her lids, till her young husband reached out and took her hand, his brown eyes soft with tenderness.

"Next you'll be asking the duke to show us his medals," Étienne gently teased. He shook his head at her, coaxing a smile. "You know a gentleman can't boast of his exploits on the battlefield. Not even if he owns a good half dozen ribbons for valor."

"N-not even if he w-was given a dukedom for his br-bravery," Tobias announced proudly. From behind his eyeglasses, he darted a quick glance at Warbeck and added with a knowing grin, "Which just h-happens to be the case."

"Leave off," Court complained good-naturedly, though when he next had Toby alone he planned to throttle him. "At least till the ladies have left the table, and I can properly defend myself." He turned to Clare with an encouraging smile, hoping to bring her into the discourse. Throughout the meal, he'd had the chilly sensation of being seated next to a snowbank. "I don't intend to bore you with war stories, my dear," he reassured her. "Not until after we're safely married."

The corners of her lips turned up in a hint of a smile, but she made no response. Somehow, she must have deduced the former identity of the golden-haired woman who'd been introduced simply as Lady Philippa Bentinck and whom the others treated with such affectionate familiarity. Clare may have remembered Philippa from the past, but he doubted the two women had ever said more than a few words to each other, if, indeed, they'd ever met.

"André never worries about boring me with his feats of heroism," Lady Sarah complained with a mischievous smile. "I've heard the tale of every horse race he's ridden to glory in and every card game he's won." The attractive brunette rolled her sloe eyes dramatically. Her face glowed with love for the husband she'd just maligned. "Naturally the losses have never been reported," she added, laughing. Enormous with child, the young woman was radiant with good health and the look of complete serenity that often comes with pregnancy.

"In about two more months, you'll long for the

days when you were bored," André scolded his wife with a wag of his finger. But his smile belied his reproachful words.

"What, has André grown into a settled old man?" Philippa teased. "I can't wait to see him playing the role of the proud papa. Then we'll all be falling asleep in our soup as he drones on and on about the clever little darling!"

With a sheepish grin, the expectant father wadded up his serviette and threw it at her.

Philippa caught the white linen neatly in one hand, while her fellow diners laughed at their high jinks.

"*Petite chou*," André taunted, "you always were too saucy for your own good."

"Oh, no," protested Philippa. "I'm merely pointing out that any offspring of yours will unquestionably be a genius."

Beside Court, Clare stiffened and sat even straighter, though her spine hadn't touched the back of her chair since she'd first sat down. Her look of disapproval made it clear she thought the entire gathering was far too informal for a person of her strict upbringing. She inclined her head to the count de Rambouillet as though waiting for him to reprimand his grown son for such unruly behavior.

"There was never a dull moment when my children were young," Lucien Mercier explained to Clare once the merriment had died down. Chuckling, he turned to his daughter and took her hand. "And I'm not certain they're grown up, even now. You two young ladies," he chided indulgently, "brought the state of giggling to a high art by the age of thirteen. Now, on the occasion of my daughter's twenty-fourth birthday, I can only say that I've earned every one of these gray hairs that cover my poor head."

"Why, Papa," Belle said, dimpling, "we were only trying to entertain you, so *you* wouldn't feel bored."

"That's right," Étienne asserted with a plucky grin. "Few parents have been the object of such devoted attention."

"Attention to nonsense and tomfoolery," his father retorted, barely able to repress a smile. "Now that you're all too big to spank, I'm at a loss to maintain the proper respect for my authority." He folded his hands as though in prayer and looked up at the ceiling. "And, by Jupiter, how I'd love to know the sweet solace of boredom."

The entire family burst into laughter once again.

From his spot at the end of the table, Court strove to keep his eyes off his former wife and pay proper attention to his fiancée. It wasn't easy. He was aware that while he'd surreptitiously watched Philippa, he'd been the object of covert scrutiny up and down the table. He clenched his jaw, determined to maintain his cool facade. Hell, he'd be damned if he'd let them think her presence bothered him.

Madame Mercier's more serious tone interrupted Court's wandering thoughts. "Now that peace is here once again," she said, "I hope to see England blessed with prosperity. And perhaps my homeland as well." Left unspoken was the dream that she might one day return to her abandoned château on the Loire.

"It won't happen while the Tories remain in power," Court cautioned gravely. "Not one member of the cabinet has any experience in guiding this country, other than in wartime."

Lady Harriet set her knife down with a clink, betraying her concern. "Surely Castlereagh and his fellow ministers have made some plans to ease our transfer to a peacetime footing?"

"Not that I've heard." He met his godmother's shrewd eyes with solemn consideration. "We're going to see vast numbers of soldiers demobilized and unemployed. Manufacturers who've been filling the demands for military supplies will be left with invested capital that must be transferred to other fields. If the continental market doesn't open up as everyone's expecting, we'll see the worst depression of the public funds England has ever known."

"D-do you really think it will be as b-bad as all that?" Tobias asked. He pushed his spectacles farther up the narrow bridge of his nose in a worried gesture. "Many merchants are l-looking forward to s-selling their huge stocks of wares to Europe now that the bl-blockade has been withdrawn."

"Yes, but will the people on the Continent have any money with which to buy them?" Court calmly sipped his wine as everyone at the table stared at him in consternation. The Mercier family had a vital interest in commerce. Since their emigration from France, they'd struggled mightily to overcome the enormous losses caused by the revolution. It was no accident that both sons had married the heiresses of prosperous businessmen, though it was also clear that the two young men held their wives in great affection.

"In my opinion," Court continued, "the resumption of peace will result in the complete dislocation of a national economy that has been based upon war for the last twenty years. The transfer from wartime to peacetime government will be extremely painful."

"What do you propose, then?" André asked with a shrug. "Should we look for another war?"

Court met his troubled gaze. "Though we may not have seen the last of the fighting yet, peace will come eventually. When it does, those who've invested in the goods and services of the future will benefit the most."

"Such as?" Étienne prodded.

"St-steam engines!" Tobias announced with glee. He lifted his glass in a toast.

"Steam engines?" Philippa couldn't keep the astonishment from her voice. "But, Toby, I thought you were working on a table of the atomic weights of the elements."

"I am. It's Court who's interested in them. He's b-bought the patent on a steam carriage that can carry eight p-passengers along an iron tramway."

Fascinated, she swung her gaze to Warbeck. "You invented such a machine?"

"Hardly," he answered crushingly. It was the first time he'd spoken directly to her, and his icy gaze impaled her. "I'm merely financing it. A man named Trevithick is the genius responsible. He's already built a steam locomotive that carries a load of ten tons from the Pendarren ironworks to the Glamorganshire canal. Someday people will ride in cars pulled by great steam-driven locomotives."

"Pish!" snorted Lady Augusta. "What person in his right mind would actually ride in such a dangerous contraption? Why, the wheels would slide off the track and kill every fool on board, if the engine didn't explode and blow them to smithereens first. Steam carriages, indeed!"

"I'd be willing to ride on one," André declared.

Dora flapped her hand in front of her face as though the very thought of it would make her swoon. "Oh, my goodness, not me!"

"I would," said Philippa, carried away by the marvel of it all. "Surely the thrill of riding such a new-fangled machine would be worth the risk."

"Somehow, it doesn't surprise me to hear you say that," Warbeck replied with acid irony.

Philippa kept her clenched hands well hidden beneath the tablecloth. She felt a flush suffuse her cheeks as she sat mortified and speechless. But she refused to look away. She met Warbeck's lethal stare and lifted her chin proudly.

An awkward silence descended upon the dining room. Everyone, including Lady Clare Brownlow, had understood the true meaning behind his words. For the first time since she'd arrived, the skinny blonde beside him was smiling in genuine amusement.

"I think it's time the ladies withdrew," Belle said cheerfully. "We'll leave you gentlemen to your port and your war stories. But don't be too long. We have some parlor games for everyone's entertainment."

Chapter 4

Court was in no mood to be entertained. When the men joined the ladies in the informal salon that also served as a music room, he found Clare engrossed in a game of cribbage with Madame Mercier. Philippa was nowhere in sight. The count went to sit next to Belle on one of the matching Empire sofas in front of the fireplace, where she was visiting with the two dowagers. Tobias ambled over to their little gathering, as well, and perched casually on the upholstered satin arm beside his wife.

Near the open French doors that led to the terrace, Dora and Sarah were seated side by side in front of a magnificent pianoforte. They called to their young husbands to come and help them choose compositions to play for everyone's enjoyment. André and Étienne looked at each other with laughing eyes and groaned lightheartedly. They moved to stand behind their wives and offer their advice, which seemed destined to be disregarded, since the ladies were clearly dissatisfied with the gentlemen's suggestions of marching songs and battle hymns.

Rather than inform Clare immediately, as he'd planned, that it was time to leave, Court stood behind her chair and watched the card play over her shoulder with a barely hidden abstraction. It didn't surprise him that Philippa was absent. No doubt, she was staying overnight with the Rockinghams and had wisely retired early.

When Court had decided to come that night, he'd had no idea just how disturbing he'd find Philippa's presence. Hell, the elopement was ancient history. Restless, he left Clare counting the points of her crib and wandered through the open double doors into the June night.

Moonlight bathed the terrace garden in a shimmering glow, casting deep shadows in the corners and beneath the cultivated shrubbery. The scent of night-blooming woodbine floated on the warm breeze. Court inhaled a deep draft of its sweet perfume and willed himself to relax. This nerve-racking evening was nearly over. As soon as the cribbage game was finished, he'd collect his fiancée and leave, never to speak to Philippa again.

From her spot on a stone bench beneath a blooming rhododendron tree, Philippa watched Warbeck draw nearer, certain he was, as yet, unaware of her close proximity. The moment she had dreaded all evening had arrived, and her pulse raced. She was well and truly terrified of him. She would never have come had she believed he'd attend the dinner party. There was only one explanation for his inexplicable behavior. Retribution.

Philippa studied him in silence. The gold-headed walking stick was no affectation. He leaned on it heavily. But although he walked with a noticeable limp, the rest of his well-muscled physique appeared to be in excellent condition. There was a glint of silver at his temples that hadn't been there before. And she'd nearly forgotten how tall he was. Or how his sharp features and swarthy coloring gave him a dangerous, predatory air. But she would never forget the way those thick, black lashes and brows framed his startling gray eyes. Tonight, in his severe evening clothes, Warbeck looked extremely handsome. Handsome, arrogant, and very, very angry.

Phosphorescent moonbeams fell across the deep violet of her gown, turning it the same lavender-pink as the giant blossoms above her head. Warbeck was almost upon her before he noticed her hidden within the natural camouflage. He pulled up short, and Philippa heard the sudden intake of breath the moment he realized she sat quietly watching his approach.

"Are you enjoying the party, Your Grace?" she asked. She fluttered the white lacy fan she'd brought back from Venice, praying her voice hadn't revealed how jittery his nearness made her. Seated deep in the shadows, she knew all that was visible to his steely gaze were the moon-dappled folds of her skirt spread across the garden seat and the pointed toes of her satin shoes peeking from beneath a wealth of gossamer petticoats.

His brows snapped together in a ferocious scowl. "Could I be expected to enjoy this farce?" he snarled through clenched teeth.

"You weren't expected to come," she pointed out calmly. But her stomach twisted into a knot of trepidation. He was the one responsible for their scandalous divorce, yet he made her feel like the guilty party.

He took a menacing step toward her, one hand clenched at his side. "Nor were you expected to ever return to England."

Suddenly breathless, Philippa snapped her fan shut and gripped it tightly on her lap to still her trembling fingers. From behind him came the haunting refrain of an old ballad that told of unrequited love. Two sopranos, a tenor, and a baritone sang the tragic words with a purity of pitch and a dramatic tenderness that touched the soul. Philippa blinked back the tears that sprang to her eyes. What in God's name was wrong with her? Their impassioned love had quickly burned itself out, like a wildfire that takes everything in its path and leaves only charred, dead ruins behind. It was past and gone. And she was glad of it.

His irate voice cut across her daze of self-pity, the words curt, clipped, and insultingly precise. "How dare you show your face in London again?"

Alarmed, Philippa sprang from the bench. Warbeck had a terrible temper when he was roused. Not that he'd ever turned it on her until that horrible day when he'd found her in Sandy's embrace. But she knew he was capable of ripping a person to shreds with his tongue. His brilliant mind was razor-keen, and she was no match for him now. Not to-night. Fighting a mounting fear, she tried to move around him to the open doorway.

He shifted his black walking stick and, with one insolent move, effectively blocked her escape. "You're not leaving until I get an answer."

"All I want is to live quietly at Sandhurst Hall," she told him in a tone that was far more defensive than she'd intended. The knowledge that he was completely justified in being so angry brought a guilty flush to her cheeks. Six years ago, she'd fled without giving him a hint of her intentions, too panic-stricken to leave so much as a note of remorse for her cowardly behavior.

"You've more nerve than wit, Lady Bentinck, if you think you can come back to England and play the part of the poor, bereaved widow. You should have stayed in Venice with the rotting bones of your dead paramour." He laughed harshly, the unnerving sound low and filled with scorn. "But I understand my meddlesome godmother has brought those holy relics back with her."

His callous insult of the beloved friend who'd died such an agonizing death stung Philippa more sharply than anything he could have said about her. She longed to slap his contemptuous face, but immediately bit back the scathing retort on the tip of her tongue, not daring to antagonize him further. Since her return to England, she'd learned from several sources that the duke of Warbeck had become one of

the wealthiest and most powerful peers in the realm.
She desperately needed his tolerance, if not his good-
will, for Kit's sake. Anger and fear warred within
her. It took every ounce of her self-control to appear
composed and unruffled.

"Pray excuse me, Your Grace," she said with consummate politeness. "I'd like to rejoin the others."

At the aloof expression on her lovely features, the
blood in Court's veins pounded in his ears. His hand
tightened around the dragon head cane as he
watched her perfect brows arch in disdain. Philippa
looked at him as though he were some loathsome
creature that had just slithered into her fairy garden.
In the iridescent moonlight, the golden, flyaway curls
framed her face like a halo. Her deep violet eyes
seemed almost black.

But she was breathing in quick, rapid pants. Above
the low neckline of her gown her perfect bosom rose
and fell in a tantalizing rhythm. He knew frigging
well her breasts were perfection. He'd memorized
each smooth globe with his tongue. Bloody hell, he'd
kissed every silken inch of her slender, nubile body.

A tumult of emotions raged through him as he
stood so near to the woman he'd once adored. What
was it about him she'd found so repulsive? He'd
never come close to Sandy's good looks, but, damn
it, few males had. The marquess of Sandhurst had
been the quintessential English gentleman, fair-
haired and bonny, with fine-boned features, emerald
eyes, and a charming smile. Had the dashing buck
simply been too beautiful for her to resist?

Only inches away, Philippa was standing as
straight and stiff as the ramming rod of a jaeger rifle.
Court could see the frantic beat of her pulse throbbing at the base of her throat. She was scared to
death of him, and he intended to keep it that way. He
longed to wrap his fingers around that graceful neck
and choke the truth out of her. Why had she left
him? Was it, as people inferred, because he'd intimi-

dated her with his forceful, aggressive ways? Lord knows, he'd tried to be gentle, to stay always in control during their lovemaking. But in the heat of passion, he may have frightened her with his unbridled ardor. Damn it to hell, all he'd ever wanted was to surround her with love. Was it his own lustful nature that had driven her away? Or was it Sandhurst's mincing, priggish, mealy-mouthed enticements? For his own sanity, Court had to resolve the unanswered questions that had haunted him for far too long.

Philippa swallowed convulsively as she watched Warbeck lean heavily on his walking stick and bend closer. His arrogant face had hardened into a mask of rage. Beneath the straight black brows, the pale eyes glittered like chips of ice in the moonlight. He seemed to be fighting an impulse to strangle the life out of her. Mercifully, his better judgment won out. He flung one hand up in a wordless, mocking flourish, stepped aside, and allowed her escape.

Philippa fled past the open French doors that led to the music room, and hurried, instead, into Rockingham's empty library, where she sank down on a deep leather sofa. Warbeck's scalding bitterness had shocked her. He'd always been volatile and quick to anger. But never cruel. Never malicious. What part had she played in the terrible vindictiveness she'd just witnessed?

Staring blindly at the gold-embossed volumes that lined the shelves on the opposite wall, she fought back tears. Dash it all, she couldn't return to the party with red, swollen eyes. She'd never cause Belle unnecessary concern on her special day. And she'd never, ever give that caustic bully the satisfaction of knowing he'd succeeded in making her cry.

The hallway door opened, and Philippa heard the unmistakable rustle of taffeta as someone entered the room. Seated with her back to the door, she lowered her head and furtively wiped the corners of her eyes with her fingertips.

"There you are, child. I wondered where in the world you'd disappeared to. I was certain you'd bid me good-night if you intended to retire for the evening." Lady Augusta closed the door firmly behind her and moved to stand near Philippa. If the dowager duchess noticed the tears, she was too polite to mention them.

"Yes, I . . . I wanted to have a little quiet time," Philippa explained with a tiny sniff. "Since I arrived in London, I've scarcely had a minute to myself. I hope I didn't offend anyone."

The elderly lady dropped down beside her on the wide cushion with a skeptical cluck. "The question is, my dear, has someone offended *you?*"

Philippa fidgeted with her fan, opening and closing it several times before she answered untruthfully. "Of course not." But for all her stubborn determination, a single, telltale tear slowly made its way down her cheek. Warbeck's remarks had cut her to the quick.

Lady Augusta withdrew a lacy handkerchief from inside the cuff of her long sleeve and dropped it on Philippa's lap. "Humph," she snorted. "My grandson, no doubt, has behaved in his usual combative style. His acid tongue could singe the whiskers off a bishop. Why Courtenay has to turn everything into a battle for supremacy is beyond me. His manners, which were never scrupulous to begin with, have become shockingly ragtag in the past few years. You mustn't let that fire-eater throw you off your stride."

"No, ma'am, I shall be fine," Philippa murmured as she handed her back the handkerchief.

"You used to call me grandmother," Lady Augusta protested mildly. "I wish you would indulge an old lady's whims and call me that now."

Philippa blinked away the last trace of a tear and managed a weak smile. "Very well, Grandmother."

Lady Augusta peered at her thoughtfully. "You were brave to come tonight, my dear. In the next few months, you're going to need all the courage you possess. But you've got enough spunk to stare down the inevitable gossipmongers and, one day, you'll laugh in their teeth."

Philippa shook her head doubtfully. "I don't think so. Not if it's going to be as painful as it's been tonight. When I left Italy, I'd hoped to resume my life in England with as little notice as possible. I planned to live peacefully at Sandhurst Hall."

"An excellent idea," Lady Augusta agreed. "Go to Kent. It will be much easier in the country, where your neighbors remember you with such warm affection. The Rockinghams will help you resume your place in local society. And so shall I."

"I've no wish to reenter society."

"Balderdash! Of course, you do."

The look of sincere compassion on the proud old dowager's face touched Philippa deeply. Yet she was astonished at the offer of help. How could Lady Augusta want to aid the woman who'd deserted her grandson? Philippa was racked with guilt over her own part in the scandal and ensuing divorce. The loving kindness of friends, who'd rallied around her since she'd returned, filled her with unworthiness.

"I'm a social outcast," Philippa said without rancor, "and nothing in heaven or on earth will ever change that. I'll never be invited to a royal drawing room or allowed to enter the hallowed halls of Almack's. Nor will I be received at balls or soirees given by the Quality. But I'll not waste my life pining for things I can't have. Until I married Warbeck, I'd never been part of your world. I have no desire to be part of it now."

"Tut, tut," the elderly lady scolded, "don't talk nonsense." She rapped Philippa's forearm gently with her jeweled quizzing-glass. "You're a marchioness, my dear. And an exceedingly wealthy one at that. You *are* the Quality. Hold your head high and pay no attention to my grandson's pyrotechnics. Had you stayed around long enough, you'd have learned that the boy's bark is much worse than his bite. Even as a youngster, he always did throw a marvelous temper tantrum."

Philippa had no answer for such an amazing pronouncement. One of those marvelous tantrums had irrevocably ruined her life.

"Let all of us help you," Lady Augusta counseled. Her snowy eyebrows pulled together in deliberation. "We can smooth the way for you, child. After all, you did marry the man you eloped with, and you are now an honest widow. Both facts combined will make a strong case for respectability. The Rockinghams will do everything possible to support your cause, and that includes Lady Gabrielle's entire family. Lady Harriet and I have a great deal of influence with the people who count, many of whom owe us favors. Put yourself under our mutual protection. You'll find that not everyone in the countryside will bar you from their door."

Philippa smiled ruefully. "Honestly, I appreciate your kindness, Grandmother, but I don't need to be accepted by the ton in order to live a happy life. My years in Venice taught me that there's a very large and interesting world out there. A world that extends much farther than England's top ten thousand. An exciting world, filled with people who've never even heard of the duke of Warbeck. I've no desire to be accepted as a member of the aristocracy."

"You intend to spurn your title?" The dowager was aghast. Her voice creaked in horror at the very thought. "What kind of revolutionary talk is this?"

Philippa couldn't help but laugh at the astonishment in her companion's alert gray eyes. "To the contrary, Grandmother. I have no intention of renouncing the Sandhurst lands or titles. Indeed, my only goal is to see that my son enjoys the rank and station to which he is heir."

The dowager duchess beamed her approval. Taking Philippa's hand, she squeezed it encouragingly, a bright smile lighting up her wrinkled face. "That, child," she stated without equivocation, "is my only goal as well."

Court woke in the middle of the night, some slight noise having disturbed his restless slumber. Rising up on one elbow, he glanced at the Wedgwood clock on the stand nearby. Its ebony hands were visible in the beam of moonlight that drifted in through the parted drapes a careless lackey had failed to shut completely.

Four in the morning.

Bloody hell.

It felt as though sometime during the night, an intruder had buried an ax in his skull. His head was splitting. He groaned as he recalled the events of the past evening. After the confrontation with Philippa, he'd made a hasty departure from Belle's birthday fete, barely attempting to offer his excuses to his disappointed host and hostess. Then, without any apology to Clare for his surly behavior, he'd left that unhappy female on the steps of her parents' town house and spent the rest of the night at White's, drinking and gambling to a disgusting, and quite satisfying, excess.

He put a hand to his aching forehead and grimaced at the self-inflicted pain. He couldn't remember going to sleep, but apparently he'd done so. He was home alone in his own bed. He closed his eyes and willed sleep to come. . . .

Light, hurried steps, accompanied by a faint swish of silk, caught his attention. He was instantly alert, ready to reach for the loaded pistol that lay in the drawer close by. Turning his head on the pillow, he peered with a scowl at the doorway. What Court saw in the gloom of his spacious bedroom sent his heart smashing against his ribs with the force of a cannonade. He sat up with a start, unable to believe the vision that appeared before his eyes.

Philippa was standing in front of the closed door, still dressed in the filmy violet gown she'd worn earlier that evening. Wordlessly, she stared at him across the darkened room. In the dreamy light that encircled her, her eyes were enormous in her pale face. She was leaning against the door for support, one hand behind her, as though still holding the latch.

"Get out," he warned, his voice low and filled with venom. "Get out, before I throw you out."

She released the doorknob and moved toward him. "Please," she implored in a hoarse whisper. "At least allow me to speak before you send me away."

"Whatever you're trying to accomplish by this vulgar comedy, you're wasting your time. And mine." Furious at her audacity, Court tossed off the covers and swung his legs over the edge of the bed. He slept mother-naked. If it embarrassed Philippa, it was her own fault. Hell, if nothing else, she should have remembered that much about him.

Before he could reach for his cane and move to his feet, she floated across the room and stopped directly in front of him. Bathed in moonlight, she appeared to be surrounded by an otherworldly glow. He blinked, trying to bring her into sharper focus.

"I came to plead with you, Court, to beseech your forgiveness," she said, her words plaintive and urgent. "To tell you how sorry I am that I wronged you so shamelessly."

"What the devil . . ."

Astounded by her temerity, he watched as she fell to her knees at his bare feet, the draped folds of her dress pooling around her, her fair head lowered in supplication, her graceful hands clasped as though in prayer. His breathing constricted high in his chest at the sight of her. She resembled a frightened angel who'd fallen to earth with a broken wing.

Philippa lifted her face to meet his gaze, her beautiful eyes swimming with tears. Catching his hand in both of hers, she brought it to her trembling lips. Tears splashed on his fingers, and a feeling akin to awe swept through him.

"I'm begging you to forgive me," she said, weeping as she kissed his hand over and over. "Please, take me back."

Cautiously, he laid his free hand on her bent head as if bestowing absolution. She didn't shrink from his touch, only continued to move her soft mouth in light, featherlike kisses across his knuckles. The feel of her silken curls beneath his palm sent a shaft of desire spiraling through his groin. One by one, he removed the pins from her thick hair, allowing the golden locks to fall across her slim shoulders. In spite of all past resolutions, her weeping melted his frigid heart, the anguished tears washing away the empty years of bitterness and hate.

"Don't cry, darling," he soothed, "don't cry. All you ever needed to do was ask for my forgiveness."

She looked up at him, her lower lip quivering. Her voice broke when she tried to speak, and she gulped back a sob to begin anew. "Oh, Court, I've been . . . I've been so miserable. I was such a fool to leave you. I swear, I didn't want to go away. Sandhurst tricked me into thinking you didn't love me anymore. It was all his doing, not mine."

Gently, he placed a finger on her lips. "Shh, little girl. It's all right." Cupping her chin in his hand, he bent to kiss her. "No explanations now," he whispered against her mouth. "We'll have time to talk later."

For nearly six long years, he'd craved the taste and touch and sight of her. He covered her tremulous mouth with his open lips, penetrating hers with his tongue, sweeping the warm moistness that awaited him. The hauntingly familiar scent of spring flowers filled his nostrils, arousing him with its glorious

memories. God above, she'd worn that same intoxicating perfume on their wedding night. Deep inside
the frozen recesses of Court's being, his embittered
soul began to awake. His worst suspicions had been
correct. Sandhurst had tricked them both. But it
didn't matter anymore.

She was home in his arms at last.

With a sigh, she raised her graceful hands and slid
them around his neck. The feel of her cool skin on his
fevered body inflamed him. He lifted her onto the
bed, his heart beating madly as he laid her down on
the soft mattress beside him and kissed away the
salty tears that glistened on her cheeks. At his gentle
ministrations, she clutched his upper arms, her fingers pressing against the muscles that bunched and
tightened beneath her touch. Sweet, delicious memories of those dainty hands moving over his naked
body battered his senses.

Tenderly, he eased her to her side and slowly, lingeringly released the tiny buttons that followed the
delicate curve of her back. This time, he wouldn't
frighten her with his wild, unbridled passion. Tonight, he would keep a tight rein on his rampaging
sexual ardor. He would stay in complete control as
he brought her the drugging pleasure he yearned to
give.

Whispering hushed endearments, he eased the
gown's short puffed sleeves over her shoulders and
pushed the bodice down to her slender waist. His
breath caught in his throat at the sight of the firm,
rounded, pink-tipped breasts. He lowered his head
and brushed one cheek and then the other against
the twin mounds, breathing in the heavenly smell of
her. He laved the pliant nipples till they were hard
buds against his tongue. His heart thundering, he
slipped his hand beneath her gauzy petticoats, tracing a path of seductive persuasion up her shapely
calf to the garter that rode high on her silken thigh.
At the touch of his fingertips on her bare skin, she

whimpered softly. It was the ragged, breathy sound of female surrender.

"My sweet, sweet love," he murmured huskily, "it's been so long."

The fever in his veins raced like a fire storm. His pulse grew frantic. Stockings, shoes, and undergarments were off in a matter of seconds. The skirt of her gown was pushed up around her naked hips, revealing a puff of golden brown curls at the apex of her thighs. He slipped his hands beneath her, fondling her smooth buttocks.

He was burning, raging with desire, his loins aching, his staff rigid and heavy. Just as every other time he'd taken Philippa in his arms, he was nearly crazed with a hunger that only she could satisfy. For countless nights, he'd dreamed of loving her in every way possible, his mouth tasting everywhere, his tongue exploring everywhere, his fingers caressing everywhere, his body, heavy and taut, covering her slender form as she writhed in ecstasy beneath him.

Court knew he had to slow down, to subdue the fierce, savage, primal beast within, whose instinctive drive was to conquer and claim, to take at will, whenever, however he chose, in a mating ritual as ancient and elemental as survival itself. He wouldn't shock Philippa's refined, schoolmistress sensibilities with his blatant male eroticism. He would teach her the art of love slowly, with infinite care. And little by little, he would wipe out all memory of Sandhurst.

"Tell me you want me," he demanded hoarsely.

She met his gaze, her thick-lashed eyes dreamy with a sweet, sensual languor. "Yes, oh, yes, Court, I want you. Only you. No one but you."

Easing between her thighs, he rose up on his hands, ready to sink deep into her welcoming warmth. The need ... the need for her was beyond anything he'd ever known. Would ever know. No other woman but Philippa could satisfy this deep, soul-searing hunger.

With one powerful surge, he buried himself in her beautiful body . . .

And woke from the dream.

The same damn bloody dream that had tortured him for the last six years.

Dream? God, no! It was a recurring nightmare.

Soaked with sweat, he threw off the bedclothes, letting the night air cool his heated body. It had been eight months since he'd suffered the hellish thing—not since he'd decided to marry and get himself an heir. When Clare Brownlow had accepted his proposal, he'd thought he was free of Philippa at last. Christ, he was a fool! In every dream, he'd forgiven her. Every bloody, damn one. Only to wake and find it'd been a mirage.

Court grabbed his cane and left the bed. He moved to the tall window in the pitch-black room. His heart still pounded in the aftermath of that voluptuous carnal illusion. Pulling aside the heavy velvet drape, he stared down at the street below. It was raining. Thunder shook the house. Streaks of lightning lit up the sky. An early summer storm washed the pavement of Grosvenor Square clean and new again.

Looking out at the pelting rain, he recalled the day he'd first met Philippa Hyacinthe Moore. It had been at Rockingham's wedding. Court had been a groomsman, with the rank of earl at the time—before he'd been named a duke for his near-suicidal exploits in Portugal. She was one of Lady Gabrielle's gaggle of chattering bridesmaids. He looked across the nave of St. Paul's Cathedral to behold a heavenly vision and been struck by a thunderbolt.

She stood bathed in a pool of rosy light thrown from the stained glass window above her. Wearing a blue satin dress and a crown of white blossoms in her golden curls, she looked as though she'd just floated down from the host of cherubim painted on the ceiling.

At the reception held later in the Merciers' town house, he followed her into the garden when she slipped away from the press of the crowd. He found her standing beneath a weeping willow, drifts of daisies, narcissus, and daffodils outlining the curve of the brick pathway at her feet.

"Miss Moore," he said with a reassuring smile as he approached. "may I introduce myself once again? I'm Court Shelburne, one of Viscount Rockingham's groomsmen. We met immediately after the ceremony."

"How do you do, sir?" Returning his smile, she curtsied prettily. Her lavender-blue eyes sparkled with a contagious joy that tugged at his jaded heart. It was as though a warm light was shining directly into his cold, dark soul, dispelling all the shadows of the past. He yearned to discover the source of such unalloyed happiness.

"Toby said that you're a close friend of Lady Gabrielle's," he continued, drawing nearer. "I can't believe we've never met. Where have you been until today?" he teased.

A blush heightened her naturally vivid coloring at his flirtatious tone. "Why, nowhere that I shouldn't be," she pertly replied. Her eyes danced with puckish mischief. "Are you familiar with *all* of Belle's friends? She has quite a few, you know. At least half a dozen."

Court grinned at her impudence. "I only met Lady Gabrielle a month ago at her betrothal party," he admitted, "but I know for a fact that you weren't there. Nor have I seen you at Almack's or any of the balls this spring—or we wouldn't just now be getting acquainted."

A giggle bubbled up spontaneously, as though he'd made a marvelous jest. "Oh, I don't attend balls," she told him. "And I've never been to Almack's."

"So you've just arrived from the country," he concluded aloud. "That explains why I've never seen you until this morning."

She bent and plucked a daffodil. An engaging smile played about the corners of her delectable mouth as she examined its bright yellow petals. "Do I resemble a milkmaid who's just come from the country?" she inquired with the slightest hint of a pout. "I didn't realize I looked so provincial." She peeked up at him from beneath her long, curly lashes, a spark of deviltry in her impish gaze.

Court's heartbeat accelerated at her unabashed playfulness. He wanted to run his tongue across her sulky lower lip and taste the sweet, fresh nectar of her mouth. That thought sent a spiraling heat through his lower body, and he realized he was hardening with desire. Ordinarily, his female companions were sultry temptresses, chosen for their wanton expertise in bed. He'd never met any woman who looked so breathtakingly pure and untouched. Nor had he ever reacted to one with such immediate urgency. He fought to keep the rasp of sexual need from his voice; the last thing he wanted to do was frighten the young lady away.

"At the moment, Miss Moore, you resemble a woodland nymph tarrying among the flowers of springtime. Did you know a magical glow surrounds you?" Her lips parted in surprise at his provocative question. He quickly followed with another just as outrageous. "Does the halo accompany you everywhere or only shine when you're standing knee-deep in blossoms?"

Her startled laughter rang out, and his heart leaped as though wanting to follow the bell-like tones up to the clouds. The brilliance of her luminous eyes staggered him. "You're very fanciful for a sophisticated London gentleman," she observed wryly.

His hands fairly itched to pull her to him. She had an aura of unblemished innocence and youthful grace, making him want to know everything about her. "Where is your family's estate, Miss Moore? Not in Kent, I'll vow."

She lifted her eyebrows and studied him with dubious regard. "Why? Are you interested in genealogy or geography?"

"Neither, unless it has to do with you." He moved even closer, and she stepped back, only to find herself trapped against the thick trunk of the willow.

Her reply was a trifle breathless. "My family's not from Kent, as you so astutely surmised."

He ventured a wild guess. "Shropshire?"

Philippa shook her head, her violet eyes alight with merriment. It was clear that, in spite of her wary response to his nearness, she enjoyed his teasing and had no intention of telling him the truth without a battle of wits. He wondered what she'd do if he tried to steal a kiss.

The urge to touch her was nearly irresistible. He longed to run his fingers across the curve of her smooth cheek and trace the outline of her beguiling lips. Instead, he placed one hand on the rough bark behind her. "Must I name every county in England or will you take pity on a poor mortal and tell him where you're from?"

"You're giving up so soon?" She pursed her lips disparagingly at his lack of adventure.

He rose to the bait and continued the interrogation. "I don't recall ever meeting anyone named Moore. Certainly not at Eton or Oxford. Do you have any brothers?"

"None at Eton or Oxford," she answered saucily. "What about you, sir? Do you have any sisters?"

"No." He decided to try a different tack. "How long have you known Lady Gabrielle?"

"Since we were ten. Belle and I were schoolgirls together."

Court vaguely remembered Tobias saying that his new bride had attended a female seminary somewhere near London. "In Chelsea?" he hazarded.

Philippa's reward for his brilliant deduction was a bewitching smile. "Clever man," she said in approval.

"And where do you reside while you're in London?"

She wrinkled her nose at his clumsy tactics. "I can't give away all my secrets."

"How can I pay you a call," he pointed out with decisive male logic, "if you won't tell me where you live?"

"For such a quick-witted fellow, you show very little aptitude for solving mysteries," she taunted.

Her high-spirited vivacity was mesmerizing, and a feverish excitement flooded his veins. "Are you mysterious?" he asked huskily. "A young lady with a hidden past, perhaps?"

"Perhaps."

"Or are you a princess who's been sleeping for the last hundred years and awaits the kiss that will awaken her?" Court lifted a springy curl entangled in the cluster of orange blossoms above her ear. The silken strand twined around his finger as if it had a life of its own.

Philippa chuckled. "First a wood nymph, then a milkmaid, now a princess." She clucked her tongue in deprecation. "You're not very good at riddles are you, my lord?"

"Call me Court," he insisted. "The close friend of my closest friend's wife shouldn't have to stand on ceremony."

"Oh, my, yes," she instantly agreed. "With such *close* ties, we're practically related. Perhaps I should address you as uncle."

He scowled at the insinuation that he was far older than she. "Do I look so ancient?"

"A veritable graybeard," she avowed, her eyes bright with laughter. "Indeed, if you wish, you may lean on my arm, and I'll help you return to the house so you can lie down for a rest."

Knowing she intended to do no such thing, he immediately took advantage of her goading. He placed his hands on her slim shoulders and drew her nearer. "Only if you'll lie down with me," he murmured.

The smile froze on her lips. She surveyed him through narrowed eyes. "I think not," she retorted in a clipped, cold tone. She moved as though to leave, but he held her in place with ridiculous ease.

"I've shocked you, little sprite," he said contritely. "How can I make amends?"

Her lavender irises darkened to a stormy midnight blue. "You can start by releasing me," she suggested. "After which an apology would be in order."

He placed both hands on the tree behind her, freeing her at the same time he effectively imprisoned her with his arms. He gazed at her tantalizing lips, then dragged his eyes up to meet her frosty glare. "What good would it do me to write a poetic apology?" he cajoled. "I wouldn't know where to send it."

"Are you a poet?" asked Philippa, clearly intrigued.

"I've never written a line of verse in my life," he confessed. "But if it would coax a smile back to your lips, I'd recite a sonnet from Shakespeare."

"Which one?" she demanded.

"Which Shakespeare?" he quizzed, stalling for time while he tried to recall something suitable.

"Which sonnet would you recite?"

Court racked his brain for a single rhyme. He'd never been one to read the damn stuff, let alone commit it to memory. Then inspiration struck. From somewhere in the back of his head came a verse he'd learned in his university days. He leaned forward and spoke softly in her ear. *"Had we but world enough, and time, This coyness, Lady, were no crime."*

She tipped her head to one side and frowned. "That's not Shakespeare," she corrected. "It's Marvell's poem entitled 'To His Coy Mistress.' "

Court cursed himself for a fool, certain she'd assume that he'd purposely chosen the scandalous verse to titillate and entice. "I meant no disrespect," he assured her hastily.

Philippa's brows arched in surprise. "I don't think Shakespeare would be offended. Andrew Marvell was a very respected poet." The corners of her mouth twitched with winsome amusement. "Besides, I promise not to tell William." The guilelessness in her clear eyes told Court that the idea that he'd intended a sly inference hadn't even occurred to her.

"Do you know that you're absolutely enchanting?" he asked huskily. "I think you really are a wood sprite come to enthrall me and then leave me bereft. Say I may call on you tomorrow, if only to prove me wrong."

She looked down at the daffodil in her hand, suddenly serious. "I cannot, Lord Warbeck. I'm going to be quite busy all day tomorrow."

"The next day, then," he pressed.

"No, but I thank you kindly."

"You're not being kind at all, and I refuse to accept that answer."

She met Court's gaze, her eyes clouded with sincere regret. "You haven't any choice," she said soberly.

All at once, a likely reason for her stubborn resistance occurred to him. "How old are you, Miss Moore?" he asked with mounting suspicion. "Don't tell me you haven't made your debut yet?"

Philippa tossed her head and issued a jaunty rejoinder. "I'm the same age as Belle."

Court breathed a sigh of relief. Eighteen. Old enough. Then a horrible thought struck him. Some families promised their daughters in marriage long before celebrating their coming out. His words were hoarse with apprehension. "Surely, you're not already betrothed?" At her stunned silence, he hastily continued. "Even if you are, it'll make no difference. A lady is allowed to change her mind."

"And what would make me change my mind if I were already betrothed?" she queried.

"This." He bent his head and brushed her lips with his. It was a chaste, fleeting kiss that wouldn't frighten the most inexperienced virgin.

Philippa stiffened and pushed against his shoulders. Her magnificent eyes blazed with wrath. "You forget yourself, Lord Warbeck," she said, her lips quivering with indignation. "But since you are Belle and Toby's friend, I shall strive to forget this ever happened." With a quick movement, she ducked beneath his arm, picked up her skirt and petticoat, and raced down the path to the house.

Court stood beneath the weeping willow and watched her flee. As he inhaled the sweet perfume of spring flowers, he grinned in delight. He intended to make damn sure she would never forget that kiss. For that first kiss was only the beginning.

But when he'd asked Belle where Miss Moore resided so he could pay her a formal call, the new Viscountess Rockingham had refused to tell him. Though he'd only met Gabrielle Mercier Howard a few short weeks before the ceremony, it seemed his reputation had preceded him. Belle insisted that her dearest Pippa was not the right woman for the earl of Warbeck. Lady Gabrielle was far too polite to mention aloud the words *notorious rakehell*, but he could read the true explanation in her compassionate, nearsighted eyes. Court appealed to Tobias, and the bridegroom admitted ruefully that the only thing he knew about Philippa Moore was that she'd attended school with his lovely bride.

The Rockinghams departed on their wedding trip, leaving a frustrated Court knowing no more than Philippa's name. During the three weeks Belle and Tobias were gone, he'd haunted every ball, soiree, garden party, and musicale given by the London ton. He searched for Philippa in countless crowded rooms, his heart racing each time he caught sight of a dainty golden head, only to be cast down when the lady turned to reveal a pair of eyes any color but that marvelous, magical lavender-blue. Hell, he'd even ventured into Almack's, much to the pleased surprise of its patronesses, and listened to the stodgy matrons drone on about that Season's flock of insipid debutantes, till he thought his eyes would cross from sheer boredom. But no one he questioned had ever heard of Miss Philippa Moore. It was as though she'd vanished like the woodland nymph he'd called her.

At last the bridal couple returned. In no uncertain terms, Court declared that he would bivouac on their doorstep until Belle revealed the whereabouts of her beautiful friend. Lady Gabrielle took pity when she realized the intensity of Court's feelings. She told him of the orphan's tragic childhood. . . .

A rumbling crash of thunder shook the night sky, and Court's reverie was broken. He looked around in dazed contemplation. Christ, he should have listened when Lady Gabrielle insisted her dearest friend was not the woman for him. Belle had been right. He never should have married Philippa.

His greatest regret was that he'd ever laid eyes on the beguiling witch. She'd destroyed every vestige of pride within him. She'd broken her marriage vows two months after taking them. She'd dragged his already tarnished name through the stinking morass of a public scandal. Yet even after she'd left him for another man, he still dreamed of her coming back to him. And what was infinitely worse, he still forgave her.

In his mounting rage, Court swore a blistering oath. He reached up, jerked the drapery from the wall, and flung it aside with a roar of fury. The bell pull, entangled in the curtain, snapped, and in the servants' quarters the jangling noise must have wakened half the staff. The brass rod crashed against the far wall with a resounding boom. In minutes, the bedroom door opened cautiously, and Dawkes peeked in.

"Is everything all right, Your Grace?"

"Get the hell out of here, you idiot!" Court shouted. He picked up the clock from the night table and hurled it at his valet. It smashed against the hastily closed door, and the olive green jasperware shattered into a hundred pieces.

Behind the door, he could hear the blasted fool call to the other servants, who'd come running down the hallway at the first sound of the disturbance.

"Don't go in there," Dawkes wisely advised. *"The master is at it again."*

Chapter 5

Philippa's uncle, Erasmus Crowther, sat at his small dining table reading the *Morning Post* over a breakfast of sirloin and ale. The paper was only five days old, having arrived at the sleepy village of Hamble Green yesterday on the Portsmouth mail coach and then been brought to the manor by his stable boy. Erasmus enjoyed reading the news of London's high and mighty. It brought him a chuckle, now and then, to learn that someone, who'd once been pointed out to him as a top-lofty gentleman, had squandered an entire fortune at the gaming tables or been reduced to debtor's prison through a foolishly exorbitant life-style.

He took another swig of ale and scanned the last page of the *Post*, his gaze falling on a small article in the bottom corner. The mouthful of ale exploded across the paper as he choked and hacked in surprise. Befuddled, he wiped his sleeve across his wet lips and then across the smeared print, staring in disbelief.

MARCHIONESS RETURNS

The widow of a late Marquess and former wife of a Duke has returned to England from a long exile in Italy. The reader may remember that the Fair Lady was the center of a notorious divorce scandal recounted in this paper over

85

five years ago. It is reported that she will live in semiseclusion in Kent with her son, the present Marquess.

Hell and damnation! She'd come back! Who'd have dreamed Philippa would have enough nerve to set foot on English soil again?

Erasmus lurched to his feet. "Swithun!" he bellowed. At his summons, the housekeeper hurried into the room. "Tell Whiggs to get the traveling coach ready. Then pack my bags. I'm leaving on a journey this afternoon."

Erasmus knew why a look of astonishment contorted her thin features. During the four years she'd worked for him, he'd never left Moore Manor, or what remained of it after the fire eighteen years ago, except to go into the village once a month to see his banker. For that short trip, he always drove the two-wheeled dogcart. The large berlin that had once belonged to Philip and Hyacinthe Moore sat in the far corner of the stable, covered with straw and dust.

Oh, there was plenty of money. Stacks of it, just waiting for him in the bank at Hamble Green. Enough to rebuild the manor in all its former glory and support Erasmus in the comfortable style of a wealthy squire. But as long as Philippa remained alive, he couldn't reveal those hidden funds. Questions would be asked that Erasmus Crowther couldn't afford to have answered.

Eighteen years ago, he had been married to Philippa's Aunt Anne, a pale, quiet woman. They lived at Moore Manor, dependent on the generosity of Anne's family, for Erasmus had no income of his own. But from the first day he saw Anne's sister Hyacinthe Moore, he'd had eyes for no one but her. Day and night, he dreamed of seducing her, of burying his hot flesh in her soft, silken body. When Hyacinthe swore to divulge his thwarted attempts to ravish her, he'd decided to remove both her husband

and sister from his path. To Erasmus's horror, his carefully laid plans had gone afoul. He'd lost the very person he'd coveted to the point of madness. There were times, after Hyacinthe's death, when he'd wondered if he *had* gone mad.

Mrs. Swithun tipped her head to one side and stared at him, her eyes bright with curiosity. "How long will you be gone?"

"Pack enough clothes for a week," he snapped, irritated at her prying ways. "And put in my best garments, if you please. Now go on and get busy."

Erasmus picked up the newspaper and reread the startling paragraph with a thoughtful frown. He didn't like traveling. Hated it, in fact. Hated staying at inns where they gouged you of every shilling they could get their hands on. But he didn't have a choice. He had to go to Sandhurst Hall to offer his condolences to his poor, bereaved niece.

Since the fire, he'd lived in the only remaining tower of the destroyed manor house, first as Philippa's guardian, and then as a dependent upon her spouse's generosity. Her first husband had spoken of rebuilding the mansion, but the earl of Warbeck had been married to her such a short time that construction was never begun. And during Sandhurst and Philippa's exile in Venice, the marquess didn't seem to take much interest in things back in England. Both men, however, had paid Erasmus a generous salary to act as caretaker of the ruined estate, which he'd quickly squirreled away with the other funds. He didn't want anyone in Hamble Green to think he spent money too freely. Some envious busybody might get suspicious.

Erasmus feared the rebuilding of Moore Manor nearly as much as he hated to see his niece return to England. For seeing the country house in its previous magnificent state might trigger something in the deep recesses of her mind. He lived in dread of the day Philippa would recover from the loss of memory she'd suffered at the age of six. Something told him that, now she was back, it was only a matter of time until that happened.

The morning after Belle's dinner party, Philippa sat in her mother-in-law's town carriage and peered out through the downpour at the solid edifice on King's Road in Chelsea. Her lips curved as she read the inscription carved on the stone lintel above the tall green door: The Lillybridge Seminary for Females.

The four-story building looked exactly the same. The redbrick walls were covered with ivy. The black iron railing that guarded each dormer window glistened with a fresh coat of paint. And the cupola atop the tiled mansard roof was still a bright, exotic blue.

How well she remembered the day Erasmus Crowther had brought her to the boarding school. Her large, forbidding uncle had stood beside her in the wide entry hall, where they were met by the two headmistresses.

"So this is the child you wrote us about, Mr. Crowther," Miss Blanche Lillybridge had said with a cheerful smile. She bent and gazed at Philippa with bright black eyes, reminding the girl of a little sparrow. "How old are you, my dear?"

"She's six," Uncle Erasmus boomed from his towering height.

Philippa stared at Miss Blanche gravely, then turned to study the woman beside her. The two ladies looked exactly alike. They weren't very tall for grown-ups, but still much taller than she. There was something warm and welcoming about them, and Philippa's heart responded with a hopeful bound.

"Can you speak to us, Philippa?" Miss Beatrice Lillybridge asked with a coaxing smile.

Frightened, Philippa gazed at the second woman blankly, struggling to remember some words, any words, that would please them.

"The little chit used to chatter like a magpie," Uncle Erasmus announced in his deep, gruff voice. "But she's been mute since the night of the fire, three weeks ago. The doctor who examined her thinks it's likely she'll never utter another word. *Shock*, he called it. But there's a chance she may regain her speech eventually."

"Oh, my!" Miss Beatrice exclaimed with heartfelt sympathy. "She might never talk again?" The twin sisters exchanged glances, their expressions guarded and thoughtful.

"Well, as to that, who's to say?" Erasmus assured them with a broad smile, clearly worried that they'd refuse to take the little girl off his hands. "You could at least give her a chance for a month or two."

"We don't ordinarily accept such a young child, Mr. Crowther," Miss Blanche explained. "Our girls are ten years old when they're first enrolled."

Miss Beatrice added with a doubtful shake of her head, "Yes, and one that doesn't speak ... I don't know. Perhaps she should remain in more familiar surroundings."

"Her familiar surroundings don't exist any longer," Erasmus reminded them with a glum scowl.

Tears burned Philippa's eyes. She edged slowly away from the burly, pockmarked man, the ache in her chest growing more painful by the minute. She didn't like Uncle Erasmus. He was big and loud and always crabby, shouting at her for no reason. Once, he'd shaken her till her teeth rattled in a futile attempt to make her talk. Two large teardrops rolled down her cheeks and plopped on the front of her dress. If only she could beg the two sweet-faced ladies to keep her with them.

Miss Blanche met Philippa's blurred gaze and her features softened compassionately. "Come here, child." Philippa inched two small steps toward her. "If we let you stay, will you try very hard to be a good girl?"

"She'll be good," Erasmus stated with an intimidating glower at his niece.

Philippa looked up at Miss Blanche in despair. More than anything she wanted to remain with these two kindhearted ladies with their sparkling eyes and friendly smiles. But not a syllable crossed her lips. She couldn't remember how to tell them she'd be good. Something overwhelmingly black and ugly had happened, leaving a wordless emptiness inside her. Silently, hesitantly, she reached out and touched Miss Blanche's arm in a pleading gesture.

"She's a pathetic dummy," Uncle Erasmus growled in disgust, "but I can promise you both she'll give you no trouble. She can help with the kitchen work if she can't perform in the schoolroom. She's a lot stronger than she looks."

"We'll keep her," Miss Blanche said crisply. "And when she begins to speak, we'll enroll her in our academic program." She took Philippa's hand and clasped it tightly. Philippa could feel the gentle woman quivering with indignation.

"Wave good-bye to your uncle," Miss Beatrice instructed. When Philippa only gaped at him in befuddlement, Miss Blanche lifted her small hand and helped her wave farewell.

"One more thing," Uncle Erasmus had added before he turned to go. "She's deathly afraid of fire. Can't be around so much as a candle flame without going into hysterics."

"Considering the circumstances, Mr. Crowther," Miss Blanche had replied sharply, "one can hardly blame her."

Philippa's contemplation of the past was interrupted when her liveried footman opened the coach door and quickly ushered her up the walk under the protection of his great black umbrella. Before she could ring the bell, the door was thrown wide.

"Pippa! Oh, Pippa!" Blanche drew her into the entryway and hugged her tightly, then relinquished her to Beatrice, who did the same.

"My dear, my dear," Beatrice said with tears of joy in her eyes. "Look at you! Why, you're simply ravishing."

Philippa put her arms around them both at once and pulled them close. She bent her head to buss each one on the cheek in turn. Less than five feet in height, the Misses Lillybridge charged through life with the exuberance of an entire squadron of His Majesty's dragoons. "It's wonderful to see you again," she said, swallowing the lump in her throat.

"But you didn't bring your son," Beatrice said in disappointment when she realized that Philippa was alone. "After your delightful letters, we were so looking forward to meeting him."

"I couldn't bring him today," she told them kindly. She understood their disappointment. The spinsters considered her only child their grandson. "Lady Harriet had already asked if she could spend the afternoon with him," she explained. "I'll bring Kit to meet you next time."

With her arms still around their slight shoulders, Philippa looked about at the familiar setting. The formal salon, where she had performed at countless music recitals, was on the right. To the left was the enormous dining room with five long trestle tables and ten perfect rows of high-backed chairs. The kitchen and servants' quarters were in the basement. Just off the large foyer, a wide, curving staircase led up to the second floor, where the schoolrooms were located. Above that was one floor of dormitories for the younger girls and another of tiny, spartan bedchambers for the older ones.

From the landing above them came the sound of chatter and girlish laughter, punctuated by several playful, high-pitched squeaks.

"Let's go into the study," Blanche suggested, after she'd taken Philippa's damp cape and hung it on a coat rack. "We won't be disturbed by the children there."

"I don't mind if they disturb us," Philippa replied with sincerity. "It's been a long time since I've heard a classroom full of little girls reciting their lessons." Sending a last, fond glance upward at the polished oak banister, she followed them down the narrow hallway to the rear of the boarding school.

The sisters' living quarters were in the back of the building. Identical twins, Blanche and Beatrice Lillybridge owned and ran the academy. Although the institution was not popular with the snobbish aristocracy, whose offspring were taught by private tutors and governesses, the seminary provided the most progressive education in England to daughters of high-ranking army, navy, and diplomatic families. Its reputation for excellence had spread as young ladies who graduated from Lillybridge took their places in society.

A china tea service sat waiting for them on the tea table in the room that doubled as both a back parlor and an office. The lamps had been lit to augment the weak light coming in through the windows on that cool, rainy morning. On one side of the room, two matching desks sat facing each other, their tops covered with neat stacks of papers. On the other side, by the fireplace, stood a sofa and two comfortable chairs, each with a colorful quilt thrown across its tufted back. Bookshelves, filled with vintage encyclopedias, dog-eared art and music books, and well-worn volumes on history and literature, lined the walls.

With a feeling of absolute delight, Philippa inhaled the aroma of dried rose leaves, steaming Hyson tea, and musty old books. She twirled around, her arms crossed in front of her, hugging the burgeoning nostalgia close to her heart. "Oh, it's so marvelous to be truly home again."

She grinned in exultation at the sight of her diminutive mothers. They were dressed exactly alike, in dove gray gowns with long sleeves and high necks, as befitted their dignified positions. Sparkling white lace at throat and wrist matched the proper caps on their steel gray heads. Neatness, precision, and order were the qualities their costumes conveyed to the inquiring, finicky parent. Few, besides Philippa, knew that beneath those conservative gray bodices beat two hearts filled with a love of romantic novels and mythic tales.

Returning Philippa's lighthearted grin, Blanche sat down on the sofa and patted the cushion beside her. "Come, sit here between us, Pippa, and tell us all about Italy. We want to know everything. What museums you visited. What churches you saw. Don't leave out a thing."

"But we must converse entirely in Italian," Beatrice added in a rush as she plopped down on the other end of the settee. "That's the only way to describe Venice. Did you make it to Rome, love? Tell us everything." She poured the tea into three fragile cups.

"I will," promised Philippa. "Every detail. But first, tell me how things are here at the academy. How many girls do you have now?"

"Sixty," Blanche said proudly. "From ten to sixteen years old."

Beatrice beamed at Philippa, her black eyes alight with love. "You were the only child we ever enrolled at the tender age of six, dearest."

"I know," she answered with an affectionate smile for both. "And no child was ever more fortunate to have been given shelter in this loving place. I thank God each day that you didn't refuse to take me in."

"Oh, my dear, we couldn't have said no," Blanche exclaimed, startled at the thought. "Mercy, me! When you stared at us with those big, sad eyes, our hearts were captured."

Beatrice took Philippa's hand. Her ebony brows were drawn together in distant reflection. "You stood out there in that great entryway, so somber, so serious, looking up at us as though you'd never smiled in your life. Why, we had to take you in, just to see if we could teach you how to laugh again."

"And ended up calling you Pippa Pixie for your impish ways!" Blanche added with a gurgle of laughter.

Philippa's heart constricted at the pet name. Warbeck had heard that silly appellation once and immediately adopted it as his own. He'd said she must be a sprite, because there was something magical and contagious about her sunny disposition. He claimed he'd caught her happiness like consumption and would surely infect the rest of the world with the malady, if he didn't die of it first. Giggling, she'd assured him that no one had ever died of happiness.

Philippa shoved aside the poignant memories, knowing that to dwell on them would only bring her pain. Biting her lower lip, she took the cup of tea Blanche offered and guided the conversation in a different direction. "Are the two teachers who replaced me doing well?"

"Not two, three!" Beatrice replied with a pleased expression. "Your late husband's generous endowment has provided for three positions. One young lady teaches French, one history, and the other mathematics."

"The late marquess was exceedingly generous," said her sister. "In addition, we've had the extra funds to buy new books, new maps and globes, even new furniture for the formal drawing room. Your husband must have been a very kind man."

Holding the saucer in one hand, Philippa ran the tip of her finger around the edge of the bone china cup. "Sandy was open-hearted and magnanimous to a degree unequaled in most men."

There was a pause, as each woman recalled the tragic circumstances surrounding Philippa's hasty departure from London.

"The marchioness of Sandhurst came to see us the day after you'd left with her son," Blanche said quietly. "She told us that it had all been a terrible tragedy which could never be righted. It was clear that Lady Harriet held you in the highest esteem. We knew, of course, that you were incapable of doing anything dishonorable."

Beatrice touched Philippa's elbow, her words soft with compassion. "The innuendos in the public prints were quite vicious toward the earl. Did Warbeck beat you, child?"

"No!" Philippa answered sharply, squirming with guilt at their naive assumption of her complete innocence. Her voice rose in agitation. "He never laid a hand on me, except with love. This is the first I've heard of such vile accusations."

"Well, it's all over now, dearest," Blanche said. She rubbed Philippa's shoulder and back with maternal sympathy. "We love you as much as ever, Pippa. Put the past behind you and look to the days ahead."

Philippa frowned thoughtfully as she sipped her tea. She'd departed before a single word of the scandal had been printed in the society columns. In their letters, not one of her loved ones had given a hint of the scurrilous gossip that must have entertained the ton for months. A chill went through her. Evidently, the papers had claimed that he beat her. No wonder Warbeck had looked at her last evening with such contempt. Sick at heart, she realized that one day she would have to tell the truth behind her flight. She couldn't allow the world to think that he'd been a cruel, abusive husband, when nothing could have been farther from the truth.

"Tell me about yourselves," Philippa said, trying to push the matter out of her mind for the present. "What have you been doing now that there are three other teachers to lighten the load?"

Blanche couldn't keep the pride from her voice. "I continue to instruct the young ladies in etiquette and dancing. At fifty-one, I can still do the Scottish Reel. I even teach the waltz, though with insistence on strict adherence to the proprieties, of course."

"And you still teach music and Italian?" Philippa asked Beatrice, who nodded happily.

"As well as this," the older woman replied, tapping a book that lay beside the Spode teapot on the cherry wood table in front of them. Curiously, Philippa picked up the volume, then lifted her brows in surprise. It was a copy of Mary Wollstonecraft's *Rights of Women*.

Blanche smiled mischievously, her jet eyes twinkling. "Naturally, we don't tell our patrons that we espouse the women's cause. We just spoon a little of it to the girls at the supper table, in between lectures on proper decorum and readings from the Bible."

Philippa laughed in elation, pleased to learn they were still filled with irrepressible energy and scholarly excitement. The two unmarried ladies who'd raised her were as eccentric and freethinking as ever. She shook her head in mock admonition, brought their hands to her lips, and lovingly kissed their fingers.

Then, as Beatrice had requested, they spent the next hour conversing entirely in Italian.

Philippa refused the invitation to have a light luncheon with Blanche and Beatrice in their study. She insisted that they join their charges as usual, saying she'd disrupted their routine for too long already.

While the schoolgirls were eating the midday meal in the dining room with their instructors, Philippa visited the empty classrooms where she'd learned and later taught. She entered a long, narrow room filled with small desks cluttered with copybooks, pens, and inkwells. In front of a scarred bench, where she had once sat as a young student, a brand-new map of the world had been fastened to the wall. She sat down at the teacher's desk, recalling the day, as an eighteen-year-old schoolmistress, when she'd been summoned from her classroom to Blanche and Beatrice's study.

"Come in, Pippa," Miss Blanche had called with a cheery smile. She stood beside her twin sister in front of their matching desks.

Miss Beatrice nodded her agreement. "Yes, sit down, dear, we have something important to tell you."

Philippa entered, wondering if there was a problem with an unhappy parent, for her schedule during the school day was rarely disturbed. "Is something wrong?" she asked in mystification.

"No, quite the contrary, dear," Blanche said, a look of excitement on her kindly features. "We have some lovely news for you."

As she walked across the rug, Philippa suddenly realized that a gentleman sat in one of the high-backed wing chairs facing the desks. So that was it, she thought in relief. A new student being enrolled at Lillybridge was about to be entrusted to her care. The tall, black-haired man rose as she approached and turned to greet her. Philippa's welcoming smile froze on her lips. The earl of Warbeck met her astonished gaze, a look of fond amusement on his sharply chiseled features. Merciful heavens, the man was even more handsome than she remembered.

Philippa flushed with mortification. A month had passed since she'd met the engaging peer at Belle's wedding. In the intervening weeks, she'd gone over every word they'd spoken to each other in the Merciers' flower garden. She'd been forced to admit to herself that she'd flirted with him outrageously. Why else would he have assumed she was willing to kiss a man she'd only just met? Yet no matter how often she told herself that she'd never see the captivating nobleman again, she hadn't been able to get him out of her mind. And now he stood here before her, like a magnificent Adonis stepping out of her dreams.

"You know our visitor," Blanche said to Philippa, her jet eyes glowing with motherly pride.

Philippa dropped a quick curtsy. "How . . . how do you do, Lord Warbeck," she stammered, wishing she could sink through the floor. He must have come to enroll his child at Lillybridge. Good God, she'd dallied amongst the daffodils with a married man! Of all the schools near London, why did he have to choose this one? She realized in a daze that Belle must have recommended their alma mater to him.

"Please sit down, Pippa," Beatrice urged. Philippa dropped into the nearby chair just before her knees buckled under her.

Miss Blanche's face glowed with happiness. "Do you know why Lord Warbeck is here this afternoon?" she asked lovingly.

"I . . . I suppose he wants to enroll his daughter," Philippa responded in confusion.

The sisters laughed gaily as they exchanged knowing glances. "No, Pippa Pixie," Beatrice corrected. "The earl of Warbeck has asked our permission to pay his formal respects to you. In fact, his lordship has just returned from Surrey, where he received your uncle's consent to call upon you here at the academy."

Philippa gasped in astonishment. She swung her eyes to Warbeck, meeting his amused and affectionate gaze. "I . . . I don't know what to say."

"Say I may call upon you," Warbeck replied with a tantalizing smile. "Your guardian has already approved. And Miss Blanche and Miss Beatrice have agreed, as well."

"Sir, I'm flattered," she began with firm resolve, only to flounder awkwardly as she gazed into his warm gray eyes, "but I . . . I don't think . . . that is . . ." Philippa looked from one smiling face to another, her heart spinning on end. It would be impossible for her to explain to the earl that a courtship was out of the question, without Blanche and Beatrice immediately demanding to know why. Besides, she wanted with all her heart to see the devastatingly attractive man again, if just for one more time.

Miss Beatrice's eyes sparkled in delight. "Lord Warbeck will pay you a call next Sunday afternoon following church services."

"And he has our permission to attend Mass with you the Sunday after that," Blanche added.

There was nothing Philippa could say. She couldn't blurt out the fact that she had no intention of ever marrying because she owed her twin mothers far too much ever to leave them. Lord, she hadn't meant to flirt so shamelessly with the earl. But while she'd been in his presence, all her high-minded resolutions had vanished like fairy dust.

The next Sunday, Warbeck appeared with violets for Miss Blanche and Miss Beatrice and a huge sack of peppermints for Philippa's young charges. The front salon was already filled to overflowing with the enormous bouquets that had arrived daily for the courted young lady herself. Philippa perched self-consciously on the sofa beside the earl, while the two chaperones took up their positions across the room, where they sat reading contentedly.

"Thank you for the flowers, Lord Warbeck," Philippa said, drowning in embarrassment. "We've all been enjoying the beautiful arrangements." She dragged her gaze from a vase of yellow roses to meet his eyes, conscious of the undiluted male power he radiated. He was dressed impeccably for a social call, his long, well-shaped legs shown off magnificently by a pair of skintight buff breeches, his broad shoulders encased in a coat of dark blue superfine.

"I'm glad you liked them," he answered very properly, a smile lurking at the corners of his seductive lips. "Since I don't know your favorite flowers yet, I sent a variety in the hopes of including the ones that would please you most." He didn't seem the least bit uncomfortable about the fact that the two spinsters were listening to their every word. Maybe he'd done this before with other young ladies in other drawing rooms. But surely, even the worldly and polished earl had never gone courting in an academy for females before!

The sound of smothered laughter floated down from the landing above them. Philippa and Warbeck turned to see a row of schoolgirls gawking curiously at them over the railing of the wide, curving staircase.

"There are some children who would like to meet you," she told him with a laugh. She rose and beckoned to the youngsters. "Come down, young ladies, and meet his lordship," she called.

A dozen girls, ranging from ten to twelve, scampered down the stairs and lined up before the tall gentleman. The students were all her special charges, and Philippa knew how interested they were in the daring London blade who'd come to woo their teacher.

Warbeck extended his hand to each child as Philippa introduced her. He didn't seem the least perturbed by their awkward shyness, but had a special, teasing remark for every one.

"Now, young ladies," Blanche said, looking up from her novel, "go back upstairs and leave Miss Moore to visit with her caller in peace."

"Let them stay for a while," Warbeck urged. "I don't often get the chance to visit with so many pretty damsels all at once."

Covering their mouths with their hands, the girls tried to conceal their ecstatic giggles, while four of the most outgoing, Evelyn, Druscilla, Lilith, and Mary Ann, crowded to the fore.

"They may stay for a few minutes only," Beatrice conceded.

"Did you come to pay a call on Miss Moore because she's so pretty?" Lilith asked, her dimples flashing adorably.

"Yes, I did," Warbeck boldly admitted. Philippa's startled gaze swung to meet his, and he had the audacity to wink at her in front of the entire assemblage.

"We think Miss Moore's the prettiest teacher in the whole, wide world," Evelyn informed him earnestly. With huge brown eyes, she stared up at the dashingly handsome man, obviously expecting his immediate and full agreement.

"So do I," he agreed, not one to disappoint an impatient eleven-year-old.

"Miss Moore told me not to worry about my freckles," the redheaded Druscilla confided. She put her small hand trustingly on his sleeve, leaned closer, and spoke in a sweet, soprano voice. "She had spots just like me when she was little."

"You don't say!" Seemingly incredulous, Warbeck turned to study Philippa's nose, and the young ladies broke into gales of laughter once again.

"Girls," Philippa interjected, ignoring his exaggerated mock scrutiny, "why don't you tell Lord Warbeck what you're studying this month."

"Miss Moore's teaching us all about ancient Rome," Mary Ann explained. She pushed her spectacles up the bridge of her pug nose and gazed at him with lofty regard. "Can you name all the emperors starting with Julius Caesar?" she queried.

Warbeck turned to Philippa with a wicked grin. "Isn't it time the little dears went back to their rooms and conjugated Latin verbs for the next three hours?"

Philippa burst into laughter. "Don't quiz Lord Warbeck so," she chided her brightest student. "It's probably been years since he's studied history."

"The next time I come," he promised Mary Ann, "I'll recite the Roman emperors by heart or I'll owe everyone here a trip to Piccadilly."

"Hurrah!" the girls cried, seemingly certain of their reward.

Mary Ann cast a sideways glance at her teacher. "I didn't think he'd know them," she whispered *sotto voce*.

With the two chaperones and the twelve little girls in attendance, Philippa had found it impossible to speak privately to Warbeck as she'd planned. So the next day she wrote him a letter, explaining that, while she was both honored and flattered by his attentions, it would be wrong for her to encourage him. She intended to devote her life to teaching, and she respectfully asked that he not call at Lillybridge Seminary again. Philippa had been very careful not to let her copious tears fall on the paper and give away her true feelings.

The following morning, just as she was readying her young charges for lunchtime, she caught sight of Warbeck from the corner of her eye. He was standing in the schoolroom doorway, dressed in the height of fashion, with a tall beaver hat in one hand and a gold-headed walking stick in the other. He watched her in stony silence as she sent the girls downstairs and then returned to the classroom. He followed her inside, closed the door firmly behind him, and laid his hat and cane on a nearby desk.

"Who is he?" Warbeck asked, his gray eyes cold as winter frost.

"Who?" she countered nervously.

"The man who's won your affections." A muscle twitched in his jaw, revealing the raw emotions he was trying so hard to conceal.

She gaped at him in stupefaction. "What are you talking about?"

"This!" He reached into his pocket and pulled out her crumpled letter. "I received it less than an hour ago."

"I said nothing about another man in my letter," she disclaimed. "You're jumping to conclusions."

He searched her eyes, and what he saw there must have convinced him she was telling the truth. Gradually, his harsh expression softened, and the wrinkled paper drifted to the floor, unheeded. "I apologize," he said quietly, the pain in his voice unmistakable. "I'm such a damn prideful fellow, I immediately assumed that if you didn't want me, you must be enamored with someone else. I failed to consider my own, all too obvious, shortcomings."

Scarcely able to breathe, Philippa whirled and moved to stand in front of her desk. She put out her hand to steady herself, her head bowed in misery. Dear God, she hadn't meant to hurt him. The agonizing truth of it was, she was falling in love with Warbeck. "I never said I didn't want you," she whispered hoarsely, her throat constricting with tears. "And I never meant to imply that you were being rejected for your faults. Indeed, if you have any shortcomings, I'm certainly not aware of them. I've never met a more witty, charming, *wonderful* gentleman in my life."

In less than a second, he stood directly behind her. "Then why?" he asked thickly.

Philippa closed her eyes and drew a deep breath, knowing she would have to tell him the truth. Reluctantly, she turned to meet his troubled gaze. "The problem lies not with you, Lord Warbeck," she said in an aching voice, "but with me. I simply can never marry."

Warbeck framed her face with his hands, his thumbs tracing her cheekbones. "Because you want to be a schoolteacher?" he asked with a gentle smile. "Marry me, Pippa, and I'll give you your own academy."

Her eyes misted with tears at the impossible proposal. "Please listen," she said as she covered his hands with her own. "There's something I need to explain."

He released her and propped his backside against

the large teacher's desk. Folding his arms, he nodded for her to begin, but the uncompromising expression on his hawkish features warned her that nothing she could say would sway him from his course. He wanted her. And he intended to have her.

Philippa clasped her hands together and began. "As you must have learned when you traveled to Surrey to meet my uncle, I was orphaned by a fire. I was enrolled at Lillybridge when I was six and have never left." The profound compassion in his gaze was nearly her undoing, but she forced herself to go on. "My life here was happy, filled with friends and studies and caring teachers." Smiling briefly at the memories her words conjured up, she released a pent-up breath. "Then at fifteen, something happened that changed the direction of my life.

"One summer afternoon, while I was browsing through Miss Blanche and Miss Beatrice's large collection of books, I accidentally knocked a volume down from the top shelf. A letter fell out. It had been written by Erasmus Crowther, my legal guardian, when I was only ten years old. My uncle told the Lillybridge sisters that he was impoverished. Since there were no other living relatives, the only suggestion he could offer was that they place me in a factory, where I could earn my own livelihood."

"Damn his useless hide!" Warbeck exploded. He lurched to his feet, his jaw clenched in fury. "That bastard should have lied, cheated, and stolen before he let you face such an infamous fate. My God, Philippa, you would never have survived!"

"I realized that when I read the letter," she said, blinking back the tears that stung her eyes at his overwhelming concern. "I was stunned, horrified at the thought of what might have happened to me had Blanche and Beatrice listened to my uncle's advice. But they never showed me that letter nor once mentioned the unpaid tuition. Instead, they reared me like their own daughter." She smiled tremulously.

"Teaching in their school is the only way I can ever repay their loving generosity. That's why I can never marry. I owe my twin mothers far too much to ever leave them. For if it were not for Blanche and Beatrice Lillybridge, I wouldn't be alive today."

With a muffled groan, Warbeck pulled Philippa to him and enfolded her protectively in his sheltering arms. He brushed his lips across the top of her curls, then lifted her chin with the tip of his finger and gazed into her tear-drenched eyes. His deep voice was choked with an aching tenderness. "Miss Pippa Pixie, this country is filled with any number of schoolmistresses who can teach at the Lillybridge Seminary, but there is only one woman in this whole, wide world whom I will ever want to be my wife." He bent his head and gently, lovingly kissed her. . . .

A church bell sounded in the distance, pulling Philippa back from her absorption in the past. She looked around her at the empty schoolroom and sighed pensively. She'd never told her suitor what Erasmus Crowther had written about her parents' deaths in that same letter. Shame and a deep sense of unworthiness had kept her silent. Had the proud earl learned the truth about her family's tragedy, he would certainly have pulled back in disgust. So she'd kept the ignominious secret locked in her heart, unwilling to admit to anyone—least of all, the man she adored—that neither her mother nor father had ever loved their little girl.

Warbeck had refused to accept her decision never to marry—with characteristic stubbornness, as she was later to learn. Unaware of the hidden past that tormented her, he had promptly declared that he'd finance the salaries of not one, but two teachers, to replace her, if she would consent to marry him. Hesitantly, knowing that she'd been less than completely honest with him, Philippa at last agreed that Warbeck could commence his courtship.

But when the spinsters finally agreed to allow

Philippa to attend outings, with the Rockinghams acting as chaperones, Warbeck had been fiercely jealous of any man who dared to flirt with her. He seemed to fear that her head would be turned by all the flattering attention showered on her by his very fashionable friends and acquaintances. The fact that richer, handsomer men surrounded her at balls and at the theater was a constant source of annoyance to him. She tried to reassure Warbeck of her loyalty and devotion, but there was always a part of him that didn't believe her. She sometimes suspected that he thought she'd agreed to marry him only because she never dreamed that anyone so wealthy and titled would come along. The latter part was true. But the fact was, to her eventual sorrow, she'd fallen madly and irrevocably in love with Courtenay Shelburne.

Leaving the classroom and its bittersweet memories behind, Philippa returned to Blanche and Beatrice's study. She pulled down a volume of poetry from the top shelf and flipped through the pages. There was the letter, still tucked, forgotten, in the verses of Chaucer. With trembling fingers, she unfolded it.

19 March, 1800

To the Headmistresses of the Lillybridge Seminary for Females

Dear Misses Lillybridge,
  It is my unfortunate duty to inform you that I will no longer be able to pay the tuition for my niece, Philippa Moore. Alas, I am now destitute and will, no doubt, find myself in the county poorhouse before the year is through. So I must sadly advise you to place Philippa in a factory that employs children of her age.
  While I grieve that you must take such a step,

I cannot condemn myself. The full blame must lie upon her parents. Had those two selfish, wicked creatures shown more interest in their little girl than they did in their carnal affairs, the child would not now be abandoned to such a fate. For the fire that took their lives was caused by their own libidinous follies. Hyacinthe Moore threw a burning candelabrum at her husband, Philip, when he dared to confront her about her scandalous affairs, thereby setting off the conflagration that took their lives, along with many other innocent people.

'Twas my deceased and childless wife, Anne, who, alone, loved and cared for their little girl. Such are the frailties of human nature that the cold-hearted mother who bore her and the callow father who sired her had no tender feelings for my poor, unfortunate niece. I trust you will keep these harrowing disclosures confidential.

I remain yr. very humble and obedient servant,

Erasmus Crowther

Philippa folded the letter, replaced it in the *Canterbury Tales*, and returned the book to its shelf. She'd been devastated beyond belief when at fifteen, she'd first read those ghastly words penned five years before. Even now, after all this time, she felt heartsick and filled with shame. She asked herself once again the question she'd asked over and over. Why hadn't her parents loved her?

Four days after the Rockinghams' dinner party, Court was on his way to Kent. Improbable as it seemed, he was going to Chippinghelm to attend the memorial services of the late Arthur Bentinck. He drove his high-perch phaeton at a wild pace, his freckled-faced tiger, Slaney, up on back, holding on for dear life and wishing, no doubt, that he were lucky enough to be traveling with Dawkes and Tolander in the barouche that followed behind at a saner speed.

Chippinghelm lay in a valley partly surrounded by the remains of an ancient forest. As Court pulled around a fast-moving coupé on the narrow road that sloped down to the drowsing hamlet, Slaney tooted a blast on his yard of tin in a warning to let them pass. But the other driver had no intention of being bested, and the back wheels of the two vehicles touched for the slightest of seconds. Inside, the passengers howled as though they'd just been attacked by highwaymen. Court smiled mirthlessly at their indignant curses.

The burly coachman driving the closed carriage drew back his arm, threatening to turn his long black horsewhip on the phaeton's driver. Court brought his own whip back, ready to retaliate in kind. He'd never used the lash on his superb team of matched chestnuts, who were stretching their necks in a reckless gallop to outdistance the showy bays next to them. But by God, he'd flay the coachman alive if the idiot tried to use that scourge on him, his tiger, or his cattle. For a few brief minutes, the two vehicles raced side by side. Then the sleek phaeton shot past, leaving its rival in the dust. Behind Court, the coupé slowed, then pulled to a halt, allowing the squawking passengers to descend and reassure themselves that they and their fancy carriage were unharmed.

Slaney shouted in admiration. "Yer left 'em chewin' the dirt, Y'r Grace."

Court made no reply to his ebullient red-haired tiger. Without another backward glance, he turned his attention once again to the road and the picturesque church of St. Aldhelm at the far end of the village.

Court was in an evil temper. The day after Rockingham's dinner party, Lady Augusta had announced that she was leaving for Castle Warbeck. He'd been astounded when she'd asked him to accompany her to Chippinghelm and attend the interment of the late marquess of Sandhurst's remains in the village churchyard. Furious at his grandmother's disloyalty, he'd refused in vitriolic terms. He hadn't even said good-bye to her the morning she left. After instructing his secretary to see that everything had been prepared for the duchess's protection and comfort during the short journey, Court retreated to his study. The silent condemnation in Neil Tolander's eyes when he came in to say that Lady Augusta was safely on her way had only made Court more distant and remote.

In the end, the stillness of the near-empty house, after the dowager and her large retinue of servants left, had eaten away at Court's cold self-justification. He spent the first night at his club, where, in the hopes of forcing a duel on some hapless fellow, he glared at anyone foolish enough to glance his way. Not a soul so much as spoke to him. And no one mentioned the word *marchioness*, let alone *Sandhurst*, within his hearing. The second evening, he sprawled on the sofa in his study and drank his way toward oblivion. But the fumes of alcohol hadn't erased the memory of Philippa as she'd looked in that damn lavender dress or Rockingham's succinct advice that Court do nothing until he saw the child.

As he broached his third bottle of Bordeaux, Court reached a decision and saluted himself in the mirror over the mantelpiece. His stubbled face twisted in an ironic smile. If everyone thought Sandhurst's bastard was so blasted important, he'd just go have a look at the curst little brat for himself.

The next morning, Court had left for Chippinghelm. It wasn't until three hours into the journey that he remembered he'd promised to escort Clare to the theater that evening. He should have sent a note of regret, at the very least, telling her that he was leaving for his country seat. He scowled without any real concern. He'd apologize later with a ruby necklace. Early in the courtship, he'd learned that nothing lit up his fiancée's pale blue eyes like a piece of expensive jewelry.

The village of Chippinghelm, which dated back to medieval times, when it was the marketing center for the surrounding countryside, lay at the northern edge of the Warbeck lands. A small bridge straddled the brook that curved through the town, its banks lushly willowed. The gentle village green and the welcoming inn with its old courtyards, stone archways, and heavy oak doors were sights familiar from his childhood. Court eased the chestnuts into a smooth trot as he tooled along High Street, past the half-timbered shops and houses with their tall gables and steep tiled roofs to the church he knew so well.

St. Aldhelm's had been built in the fourteenth century by Cistercians, who'd had ambitious dreams for their abbey. At the time of the dissolution, it had become a parish church. Its square Norman tower rose up above the hamlet that time and commerce had passed by, visible over the spreading oaks that lined the narrow cobblestone streets.

Barouches, gigs, curricles, and cabriolets were scattered across the church grounds. All about the thick, green lawn, liveried coachmen, footmen, and postilions gathered in clusters to gossip and smoke while their masters prayed inside. The thought that so many of Court's friends and neighbors had come to pay their last respects to Arthur Bentinck rankled. Court cursed under his breath as he reined the team to a halt. Slaney jumped down and raced to the horses' heads before the phaeton had completely stopped. Steadying himself with his cane, Court descended from the high seat, walked up the brick pathway, and entered the vestibule.

His mouth hardened into a grim line. It was the

first time in nearly six years that he'd set foot in this church or any other.

St. Aldhelm's had remained untouched by the passing of the ages. The interior was dark and cool and slightly musty. Along the thick walls, stone effigies of the Shelburne family lay in tiered shelves, reclining rakishly on their elbows. Succeeding generations of Court's ancestors had contributed to the soaring edifice. There wasn't a stained glass window or shiny walnut pew that hadn't been donated by either the Shelburnes or the Howards. Those latecomers, the Bentincks, hadn't built their original Hall until the time of the Stuarts.

A band of ice squeezed around Court's chest as he gripped the dragon head cane and slowly started up the long, vaulted nave to the altar. He'd been married in St. Aldhelm's. The congregation had watched his gorgeous bride, blushing and smiling with happiness, walk up the same aisle, just as they were watching him now. But this time, they weren't beaming in admiration.

Little by little, an unnatural hush fell over the church, till the only sound was Court's measured tread on the hard floor and the rap-tap-tap of his cane. Heads turned, then craned in disbelief. Here and there, someone let out an incredulous gasp.

Court refused to acknowledge any of them. They were worse than fools. They were dupes to the Bentinck family's misplaced pride. They'd come to honor a cheat and a coward and to offer their condolences to a guileful widow.

With his back straight and his jaw clenched, he moved to the front pew and joined the dowager duchess of Warbeck. Lady Augusta reached over and touched his sleeve the moment he slipped in beside her. Lifting her snowy brows, she pursed her lips and shot him a compelling glance, then tapped one finger on his forearm, whether in silent exhortation or grandmotherly compassion, he wasn't sure. Attired in a muted plum dress and black plumes, she was her most severe, autocratic self. He came by his arrogance honestly.

In the bench directly across from him, Tobias and Belle turned their heads to view the newcomer. Behind their twin spectacles, their dark brown eyes widened in amazement. Then Toby awarded his friend a slow, welcoming grin.

The Reverend Zacariah Trotter, from his position high on the elevated pulpit, waited for Court to be seated before continuing his eulogy. With a nearly imperceptible nod of greeting to the late arrival, the vicar launched once again into an emotional recollection of the man whose remains they were burying that morning. Court listened to the asinine tripe with half an ear. Even Sandy would have laughed at the absurdity of it all.

The Bentinck family pew was directly behind the Howards. As the clergyman continued his touching oration, Court shot a glance across the center aisle. Philippa sat at the end of the bench, dressed in ebony satin. A wide-brimmed poke bonnet with a gauze veil hid her features. Next to her was Lady Harriet, similarly clad in deep mourning in honor of the solemn occasion. Both women stared straight ahead, seemingly oblivious to his presence. Court was about to turn his attention back to the Reverend Mr. Trotter when a slight movement caught his eye. A child, wedged between the two black-garbed women, peeked out at him. Leaning forward, the boy propped one elbow on his mother's knee and smiled shyly at Court, as though unsure if the man who stared at him so ferociously was friend or foe.

For one breathless second, Court's heart stopped. He felt as though he'd been struck in the chest by a ball from a sharpshooter's rifle. The sight before his eyes rocked him as no sight had ever done, not even on the grisly, blood-soaked battlefields of the Peninsula. For Philippa's child didn't have her soft features and golden curls, nor the wavy, coppery hair and green eyes of the Bentinck clan. Here was a boy with silver-gray eyes, straight black hair, and the undeniable, hawkish profile of the Shelburnes. The youngster gazing up at Court with open curiosity was a miniature replica of himself!

With a jolt of comprehension, Court realized that he was looking into the eyes of his own son. A son he never knew existed until that moment. A son whose destiny was to become the second duke of Warbeck.

He tore his gaze from the child to study Philippa once again. Her deceitful face was concealed behind the wide brim of her black satin bonnet. She was looking up at the vicar, listening intently as he extolled the virtues of the miserable, lying knave whose closed casket stood before them. The boy—what was his name? Kit! Lady Harriet had called him *Kit*. Kit leaned up toward his mother, cupped one hand to his mouth, and whispered something in her ear. Philippa immediately turned her head and, through the film of black netting, met Court's accusing glare. In that fleeting instant, he could read the stark terror in her suddenly rigid posture.

She knew that he knew the truth.

Then she quickly looked down at her prayer book, as though hoping to find forgiveness there for her perfidious, abominable lies.

Aghast, Philippa turned her head slightly and peeked from the corner of her eye as Warbeck rose slowly to his feet. Dear God above, he'd actually come to Sandy's memorial Mass! *Here* at St. Aldhelm's, where there were such bittersweet memories that she'd felt nearly suffocated the moment she'd stepped through the door. Never, *never* would she have believed it possible. Warbeck's appearance at Belle's dinner party had surprised her, but his attendance today was beyond comprehension. Had the thought of such a possibility once entered her mind, she'd have left Kit safely at home with his nurse-maid. But it was too late! Too late!

Warbeck knew.

She was certain of it.

Unable to move, unable to think, she watched in dazed horror as he stepped into the center aisle, his face hard and inscrutable. The vicar nodded his bald pate to the choir, and its members began singing the *De profundis*. For one panic-filled moment, she thought Warbeck was going to come over to her and demand in a thundering voice, before God and the other parishioners, the return of his only child. The child she'd stolen from him. To her relief, he moved past her, leaning heavily on his gold-headed walking stick. From the chancel floated the hauntingly beautiful prayer for the dead, mercifully drowning out the soft thud of his cane and the faint echoes of his halting steps. The entire congregation glared in censure as he walked slowly to the arched portal in the western transept and left the church.

Philippa drew a shallow breath at last. Looking down at her lap, she realized that she was clutching Kit's small hand far too tightly, as though she were afraid it would be wrested from her grasp at any moment. Kit peered up at her in puzzlement, aware that she was very upset. His gray eyes, matching exactly the short jacket and trousers she'd chosen for him, were enormous with fear. Kit's alarm wasn't surprising. Anything that could frighten his mother would shake his little world.

"Who was that man, Mama?" he asked in a whisper.

"Shh, not now," she whispered back, putting a finger to her lips. "I'll tell you later, darling." She slipped her arm around his shoulders and pulled him close. No matter what Warbeck might threaten to do, she'd never let Kit go. And no matter how wealthy and powerful he might be, all the irate duke *could* do was threaten her. Her deceased husband had seen to that.

As the service continued, Philippa tried to concentrate on the liturgy, but found it impossible to collect her scattered thoughts. She was tormented with guilt for what she and Sandy had done.

"Merciful Father," she silently prayed, "You know that none of this was my idea. I didn't play any part in the devious scheme, not from its initial planning to its final execution. I didn't even know about the deception until it was an accomplished fact."

But she expected no answer to her plea for understanding. For when she *had* learned of the subterfuge, she'd gone along with it. And she fully intended to keep up the ruse for as long as possible. No matter how great the sin, she was willing to pay the price in eternity. To admit the truth to Warbeck now would be to lose her son forever.

Outside, Court wandered through the peaceful graveyard beside the church, a prisoner to his own turbulent thoughts. Carved stone crosses, some dating back to the Wars of the Roses, leaned at crazy angles, while guardian angels watched over their fallen charges, their once-white marble robes stained with age. Wild clover dotted the rye grass that grew up about the tombstones. In the still June heat, honeybees droned incessantly as they sipped the sweet nectar of the small white blossoms. Four-leafed clovers were a symbol of good luck. Since ancient times, it had been said they endowed the finder with the power to detect witches and to understand the language of birds. The power to detect witches . . . what a fortunate gift.

From the branches of a nearby beech tree, a thrush poured out its heart in a flutelike melody. Scarcely aware of the beautiful song, Court trod over the resting places of the silent dead. An open grave yawned gruesomely, the thick black clods of earth piled to one side on the soft green carpet. Court moved to its edge. An engraved tablet already stood at the head, placed in the Bentinck plot four years before, when word of Sandhurst's death had reached his heartbroken mother.

REQUIESCAT IN PACE
1778 - 1810
ARTHUR ROBERT BENTINCK
FIFTH MARQUESS OF SANDHURST
BELOVED SON, HUSBAND, AND FATHER

Father!

What a filthy, despicable lie!

Court tilted his head back and glared up at the sky as though searching for the dead man's face in the canopy of blue above him. The fiend! The diabolical fiend! Sandhurst hadn't just run off with Court's lovely young bride. The wretch had stolen his son as well.

"Damn you, Sandhurst!" he called to his treacherous friend. "Damn you to hell for what you've done!" Court raised one fist and shook it at heaven. "I swear to God," he cried, "I swear by everything that's holy, come what may, I will reclaim my son."

Chapter 6

⚬⚬⚬⚬⚬

Court stood beneath a spreading horse chestnut a
short distance from the others and watched as
Sandhurst's coffin was carried out of St. Aldhelm
and lowered into the waiting grave. He forced himself to remain outwardly calm, while a maniacal
beast raged within. He had been royally tricked!
Duped in the cruelest of ways. But it'd do him no
good to behave like a madman in front of his friends
and neighbors. Nor would it benefit the child. He
couldn't tear the boy from his mother's arms and
flee, though that was brutally close to what Philippa
had done.

After the Reverend Mr. Trotter said a few short
prayers, the mourners gathered briefly around the
family to offer their condolences. Then the solemn assembly began to disperse to the waiting carriages.

Court made his way through the crowd, which
parted silently to let him pass. He was drawn to his
son by a force so powerful, he couldn't have resisted
had he tried. In a small group lingering beside a barouche adorned with black satin ribbons, Lady Augusta stood talking to Philippa, Lady Harriet, and the
Rockinghams. Kit waited at his mother's side, watching Court's approach with somber interest.

Court could scarcely take his eyes off his son. As
he passed by a cluster of smartly dressed gentry, all
of whom he'd known since childhood, several cast
furtive glances from him to the boy and then leaned

closer to whisper among themselves. He ignored the gossips with icy disdain, not surprised that he wasn't the only person to detect the uncanny resemblance between himself and the young marquess of Sandhurst.

When he joined the party beside the open carriage, Lady Augusta turned and smiled benignly, drawing him into their circle. Her fond look told him she'd already pardoned his boorish behavior on the morning of her departure. "The guests are going to the Hall," she said in her regal manner. "There'll be a luncheon set out, so those who've come a long distance won't have to start their homeward journey on an empty stomach. I'm going to help Lady Harriet and her daughter-in-law receive their visitors. Why don't you come with me?"

Court stared at his grandmother in astonishment. Surely, the last person the Bentincks would welcome into their home was the duke of Warbeck.

"Yes, do come, Courtenay," his godmother interjected, her deep contralto carrying to the farthest knot of onlookers. "Come up to the Hall with Lady Augusta."

Attired in matching dark brown outfits, Tobias and Belle appeared as surprised by the suggestion as Court felt. They glanced swiftly at each other, then smiled their tentative encouragement. "G-good idea," Tobias said. But his worried eyes told Court just the opposite might be true. "B-been wanting to speak to you about s-some horseflesh I've been l-looking at."

"If it's that pair of flashy bays you've been talking about, I passed them on the way into the village. All show and no stamina," he answered, barely glancing at the friend who'd had the audacity to be one of Sandy's pallbearers.

Court swung his gaze back to Philippa, a scornful refusal on his lips. She was staring at him in mute consternation. She'd lifted the netting up over the wide brim of her black bonnet, and he could see the delicate features clearly now. Her smooth brow was puckered in dismay, her deep violet eyes clouded with misgiving. She made no attempt to second the invitation to Sandhurst Hall.

He touched the brim of his beaver hat in greeting. "Lady Philippa."

Her face white and stricken with fear, she nodded curtly in reply. Holding her son's hand, she began to edge away from her companions toward the nearby carriage. "Let's go, dear," she urged Kit softly, tugging him along beside her. Mesmerized, the boy stared gravely up at Court as though afraid the dark-haired stranger looming over him was some evil sorcerer come to cast a spell.

Court fought the impulse to grab Philippa's elbow and hold her anchored to the spot while he drank in the sight of his young son. The lad was tall for his age and perfectly formed, with a robust frame and strong, sturdy legs. His eyes were a familiar, silvery gray, alert, intelligent, and sensitive. It would have been arrogant to say Kit was strikingly handsome. But damn it to hell, he *was* a fine-looking youngster. The thought that he'd never had an inkling of his own child's existence set the beast inside Court howling in impotent rage.

Trying his best to appear impassive, he purposely loosened the death grip he had on his cane and slackened his rigid stance. He was certain that if he attempted to smile, he'd fail to deceive anyone, including the child.

"Perhaps I should come with Lady Augusta," he said to no one in particular, his gaze still riveted on the boy, who was watching him with eyes as round and serious as an owl's. "We need to start getting acquainted again. We are, after all, neighbors."

Philippa started at the soft-spoken words and edged a bit nearer to the coach behind her.

"Excellent," affirmed Lady Harriet. "We'll see you

at the Hall." She tipped her bonneted head in farewell and turned to join her daughter-in-law.

Before Philippa could make good her escape, Lady Augusta stepped closer and caught her gloved hand. "I'll be there shortly, my dear. I'm looking forward to visiting with you in the days ahead. And you, too, young man." She patted Kit's thick black hair and beamed at him lovingly. "I want to see that picture of a gondola you were telling me about."

"Yes, ma'am," Kit answered brightly, a contagious grin dispelling his pensive air. "I'll draw another one, and you can keep them both."

Bending over the youngster, the elderly lady stroked his cheek in a light caress. "I'd like that. But I want you to call me Nana. Will you do that?"

Kit nodded.

A footman, attired in the Sandhurst livery of green and white, assisted mother and child up into the carriage. Lady Harriet climbed in, settled her mannish figure on the seat opposite, and the door was shut. From her place in the open barouche, the dowager marchioness met Court's gaze with the calm, direct frankness of bygone days. Her pale green eyes mirrored the acceptance of her son's loss, and all that might have been, with her customary, down-to-earth practicality.

"Come to the Hall, Courtenay," she repeated as she popped open her black parasol and lifted it above her tall beehive bonnet. "It's been far too long." Their coach pulled slowly away, followed by a long cortege of vehicles draped in mourning.

"Well, then, we'll see you both shortly," Belle said to Court and his grandmother. The young woman's rosy cheeks dimpled in a smile, but behind the glint of her spectacles, her soft brown eyes grew doubtful. She looked directly at him. "I hope that you'll be . . ." She paused, too uncomfortable to finish what she'd started to say.

"Don't fret, Lady Gabrielle," the duchess interjected. "I'm certain my grandson will be on his best behavior."

"C-course he will," Tobias admonished. "N-never knew C-court to d-disrupt a f-funeral!" But the look on the viscount's thin face was anything but confident.

Court gave them a tight smile and made no promises. "I'll see you at the Hall."

As the Rockinghams walked away, Court motioned to his groom, who came running. "Take the phaeton on to the Castle," he instructed. "I'll be going to Sandhurst Hall with the duchess." His tiger started off with a delighted grin.

Taking Lady Augusta's elbow, Court escorted her across the trampled lawn to her closed landau. She tipped her head to one side and studied him as they walked. "I take it you've forgiven me for attending Arthur's final rites."

"Don't be too certain," he snapped. His jaw ached from the tension of trying to hide his feelings for the past hour. At least with his grandmother, he could speak his mind. His words were low, clipped, and precise. "I don't understand how you can be a part of this travesty. Damn it, you saw the boy this morning. You've still got eyes in your head, even if your wits have gone begging."

She shrugged. "Lud, I saw the child long before this. I met him in London the day after they arrived."

Court came to a halt and leaned closer, making sure she wouldn't miss his glare of disapproval. "Then why in the hell are you going to Sandhurst Hall as though nothing of consequence stands between the Shelburnes and the Bentincks?"

A glimmer of amusement flickered over the dowager's patrician features. "Because, my addlepated fire-eater, I have no intention of alienating myself from the mother of my only great-grandchild." As she stepped up into the carriage, she added over her shoulder with an admonitory sniff, "Particularly, since he's likely to be the only one I will ever have."

For the next three hours, Philippa responded mechanically to the consolations of her deceased husband's friends and neighbors. The Bentinck family was widely respected throughout the Kent countryside. With her unflappable aplomb, Lady Harriet had ruled over the local gentry since she'd come to Sandhurst Hall as a new bride. She was second only to the dowager duchess of Warbeck in social prestige. In deference to both peeresses, the landed gentry had obviously decided to overlook the fact that Philippa was a divorcée and recognize, instead, her legitimate status as a widow—at least for the day of the memorial services. Many of them she'd already met during her brief two-month marriage to Warbeck. Not surprisingly, they all remembered her. A notorious woman was seldom forgotten. But it was difficult for Philippa to recall the names and faces of people she'd hardly known and who approached her now with a cool, reserved civility.

The two dowagers had seen to the ordering of the large staff, taking that responsibility off Philippa's shoulders. Extra chairs had been set out, bouquets of Madonna lilies graced the tables, and tall windows stood open to let the early summer breeze circulate in all the rooms. In their pristine black-and-white uniforms, servants hovered nearby to offer refreshments to the many small groups engaged in subdued conversations. Everything was flowing smoothly.

Yet beneath her outward calm, Philippa was suffering frazzled nerves. While she chatted with her guests, she tried to ignore the fact that Warbeck was prowling about Sandhurst Hall as though he owned it. She told herself it was only natural for him to be completely familiar with his childhood friend's home and equally at ease with the throng of strangers she found so intimidating. But she was reminded of a great, wild cat she'd once seen at Astley's Amphitheater, pacing restlessly back and forth in its cage. A stab of fear lanced through her each time she caught a glimpse of his dark head above the rest of the crowd.

The moment she'd arrived back at the Hall, she'd sent Kit upstairs with Belle, who carried orders for his nursemaid to put him down for a rest. Kit had protested, saying he wasn't the least bit tired. Inwardly, Philippa agreed that he was getting too old for naps, but it was the only way she could ensure that Warbeck wouldn't find the child and make a scene in front of a dozen captivated spectators.

Court waited for the moment when he could catch Philippa alone. She remained in the center of the formal blue drawing room, shaking people's hands and conversing quietly. Lady Augusta and Lady Harriet stayed close to her side, guiding her through the introductions and standing guard, he surmised.

Time seemed to stretch on interminably. Restless and volatile, Court roamed through the first floor salons, then joined Toby in the gold-and-white dining room, where a generous buffet had been set out.

"H-how long w-will you b-be staying at the C-castle?" Toby asked. He ran one finger beneath his wrinkled cravat, and his prominent Adam's apple bobbed up and down above his starched white collar.

"I'll stay as long as I have to," replied Court acidly. He waited for Toby to ask his meaning.

But Toby didn't inquire any further. With a mumbled excuse to Court, he accepted a plate laden with food from a lackey and headed for the only empty seat, along the wall next to Squire Bingham and his plump family, who sat watching Court in fascination, seven pairs of beady eyes glittering with morbid curiosity.

Court ignored the feast laid out across the white lace tablecloth and continued to pace through the spacious home. He mingled with people he'd known

since infancy. The wealthy landowners from the surrounding countryside, the prosperous shopkeepers
from the village, the vicar and his gentle wife, all
came to make polite conversation, thrilled, no doubt,
to be able to tell their friends that they'd actually
seen His Grace at Sandhurst Hall. That juicy tidbit
would be in the London papers before the week was
out.

He wondered if the amazing similarity between
the young marquess of Sandhurst and the duke of
Warbeck would be reported as well. Hell, he didn't
care if the whole world knew that he'd been cheated
of his son for the past five years. Let them snicker.
When he took the boy from his weeping, broken-
hearted mother, his revenge would be that much
sweeter.

After the guests departed, Philippa sought the
quiet solace of the library. She wanted to regain control of her feelings before she went upstairs to talk to
Kit. He would be full of questions, especially about
the dark-haired stranger who'd stared at him so in-
tensely. She didn't want her son to guess at the fear
that enveloped her.

From childhood, she'd always recovered her sense
of equilibrium in Blanche and Beatrice's study. The
book-filled room she entered now was far larger and
more impressive, but its restful atmosphere was sim-
ilar to her cozy retreat at the Lillybridge Seminary.
She walked over to a tall open window and surveyed
the immense lawn which led down to the same bubbling stream that curved through Chippinghelm.

Sandhurst Hall was a rambling country home,
originally built in the standard three stories with
wooden trim and a central pediment, but which had
been added onto through the years in a rather
higgledy-piggledy fashion. Its handmade bricks had
mellowed to a silvery pink, a joy to behold in the
summer sunshine. Indoors, the manor had a comfort-

able, old-fashioned feeling, with everything scoured and polished, but delicately faded. Few of the rooms had been repainted in the last twenty years, creating an aura of peaceful harmony in pale ivory, pink, and blue, gently sprinkled with gold. It was a home in which to raise a large brood of rambunctious children, a home to grow old in with one's cherished mate. This handsome estate and several others, equally fine, now belonged to Kit. Here, he would raise those high-spirited youngsters. And, hopefully, grow old with a loving spouse. The solid, enduring strength of Sandhurst Hall had enticed her back to England. Today, she deeply regretted her decision to come.

Philippa bent her head and covered her face with her hands, allowing the pent-up emotions she'd held in abeyance all day long to sweep over her. God above, she'd nearly come undone in the church when she'd looked up and read the cold ferocity in Warbeck's eyes. Her heart thumped against her ribs at the memory. She'd been foolish, foolish to return! If she'd only accepted Domenico's suit, she and Kit would still be in Venice, safe from Warbeck's wrath.

Lifting her head from her trembling fingers, Philippa stared out the library window with unseeing eyes. She wrapped her arms about her waist in misery as she relived that terrible moment in St. Aldhelm's. Lord, it had taken only a glance for Warbeck to recognize his son. Just one swift glance. She bowed her head and willed her erratic heartbeat to slow. Everything was going to be all right, she told herself. Let him make all the accusations he wanted. There was nothing he could do. Nothing! If he attempted to claim Kit as his own, he'd soon learn to his dismay that the law was firmly on her side. Sandy had seen to that.

A harsh, unforgiving voice cut through her tormented reflections. "So I find you alone at last, madam."

Philippa whirled to discover Warbeck standing in the open doorway. They no longer had an audience, and he made no attempt to conceal his true feelings. Rage emanated from his tense, sinewy form. Encased in a black frock coat, his wide shoulders nearly filled the doorway. His tight gray breeches were molded to the well-defined muscles of his thighs, and the strong calves of his long legs were covered by high, cuffed boots. She'd always found his physical strength intimidating, even when they'd been courting. Now he resembled a man-eating panther that had just been loosed from its cage. Magnificent, powerful, and deadly.

Cautiously, she edged around the large reference table until its substantial bulk stood between her and the man she'd once known so intimately and yet had never really known at all. She'd been foolhardy to believe that she could avoid this inevitable moment. Belle had written that Warbeck rarely ventured into Kent, preferring his other estates to the ponderous, old castle. Philippa had planned to hide Kit from his sight for months, even years, by remaining secluded at Sandhurst Hall. But today Warbeck had done the unthinkable. He'd attended Sandy's funeral.

"What do you want?" she asked, her words coming out in a pathetic croak.

"What do I want?" he grated. "*What do I want?*" He charged across the room to stand directly in front of the wide oak table. "I want my son, madam." He knocked a stack of books off the polished surface in one swoop. Philippa jerked reflexively as the heavy tomes struck the hardwood floor with a bang. Slamming his walking stick down on the table, he braced his palms on its cleared top, leaned toward her, and spoke in a tone as low and chilling as an executioner's instructions on the scaffold. "*I want my son.*"

"I don't know what you're talking about," she countered, as a wave of foreboding washed over her. Her legs trembled so violently, she had to lean against the table's edge to keep from sinking to the floor. "If you're referring to my child, his father was buried today."

"Don't lie to me, Philippa," he warned. His gray eyes were frozen pools of malice. "Admit it. Admit the truth now and save yourself the humiliation of a public trial. The boy is mine."

"The boy is not yours." She struggled to keep the hysteria from her rising voice. "He was born two days after Sandy and I were married. Regardless of what you might claim, in the eyes of the law, Kit is the new marquess of Sandhurst."

"Kit is my son! Dare you look me in the face and deny it?"

Philippa raised her chin in a quick, defensive movement, but she couldn't control the trembling of her lips. Those honeyed lips that he'd once kissed so hungrily. Court dragged his gaze from her mouth to read the evasion in her frightened eyes. Beneath his relentless scrutiny, she gradually lowered her thick-lashed lids and looked away. He could sense how close she was to collapsing in tears, when her answer came in a thready, uneven voice. "Kit is not your son."

"You're a liar."

At his insolent retort, her head came up with a defiant jerk. In the sunlight streaming through the window behind her, the riot of curls that framed her oval face created a helmet of shimmering gold. She stood combative and majestic, like some mythical goddess of war. For one frantic instant, he wondered if this were merely a dream, like all the others. Had he conjured up a son, a son who looked exactly like him, out of the dark recesses of his own tortured soul?

Philippa clasped her hands in front of her, her breasts rising and falling with each rapid breath. "Believe what you choose," she said hoarsely. "I have the documents right here in the library. If you'll promise to remain calm, I'll show them to you."

"To hell with your documents," he scoffed. He flung his hand out in contemptuous dismissal. "Do you think I care what's written on a piece of paper?" She flinched at his movement, as though he'd attempted to strike her. Her unconscious reaction deepened his rage, and he spoke through clenched teeth. "All I have to do is look at the boy to know he's mine."

"What you think and what you can prove to a magistrate are two different things, Warbeck. This is something you can't buy, not with all your newfound wealth. I have the law behind me."

"Then to hell with the law," he roared. He smashed his fist on the tabletop. "I'll have my son, Philippa, no matter what the cost!"

"Mama!" a child's high-pitched voice cried out. Kit tore across the room and around the table to clutch the skirt of Philippa's black silk gown. "Go away!" he commanded with boyish bravado. He glared at Court. "Leave my mama alone!"

The fear in Kit's eyes sobered Court instantly. His anger dissolved, replaced by a keen regret that he'd frightened the child. "I'm sorry I yelled at your mother," he apologized in a gentle tone, as he straightened. He picked up his cane and stepped back from the large table. "I'm your neighbor, Kit. I want to be your friend."

The innocent voice trembled with suspicion. "Were you a friend of my father's?"

Court hesitated for a moment, then nodded. "I was his closest chum when we were both little boys like you."

Kit searched Court's face, seeking the truth in the eyes of a man he'd never seen before that day. "Then I'll be your friend," he conceded with a warning scowl, "if you promise you won't hurt my mother."

"Of course, he won't hurt your mother," Lady Harriet proclaimed as she hurried into the room and placed her square frame between the warring parties.

"Kit," she boomed in her no-nonsense fashion, "this man is my godson, the duke of Warbeck. Come shake hands with the duke and say hello." With an attitude of complete sangfroid, she motioned for the child to step away from his mother's skirts.

Kit's lips puckered thoughtfully. He looked up at his auburn-haired grandmother for a long, hesitant moment and then back to Court. Then he released his tight hold on Philippa's dress and went to stand beside Lady Harriet.

Court gripped his cane and moved to the end of the table, his heart thundering like an artillery barrage. He ignored the pain that lanced through his bad leg as he crouched awkwardly on one knee. Looking into the boy's silvery eyes, he offered his hand.

"Hello," Kit said solemnly, as he placed his small palm in Court's much larger one. "I'm very pleased to meet you, *signóre*."

Court stared down at the little hand engulfed in his and fought back the tears that stung his eyes. As he met the stubborn gaze, so like his own, his chest swelled with pride at the young boy's pluck. This was a son any father would be proud of. And Kit was his. He knew it beyond any doubt, beyond any legal document that claimed to prove otherwise. With an iron will, Court suppressed a nearly overpowering desire to wrap his arms around the stiff shoulders and enfold the child against his aching heart.

"Hello, Kit," he said huskily. "I'm very pleased to meet you, too."

Philippa watched the man and boy with wrenching remorse. She recalled the overwhelming love she'd felt the moment she'd first laid eyes on her tiny baby boy. Could it be that a father would experience the same shattering emotion when he first beheld his son? In the past five years, she'd lain awake countless nights agonizing over her guilty secret. But not until she'd seen the two dark heads so close together and heard the pain in Warbeck's voice had she fully realized the horror of what she'd done.

By denying her former husband any knowledge of his son, she'd perpetrated a monstrous deception. Yet, even now, she refused to tell the truth. For in the eyes of the law, if Kit *was* his son, Warbeck could walk out of the room with the boy and never allow her to see him again. Legitimate issue was the man's personal property. According to English jurisprudence, a father was the legal and moral guardian of his children. Not a soul would question the duke of Warbeck's decision that his former wife was too unfit a mother even to visit her child.

Swallowing back a sob, Philippa stared numbly across the room to find Lady Augusta standing just inside the door. The proud, seemingly aloof dowager was watching her grandson and his child with an expression of unutterable tenderness. At Philippa's muffled sound of grief, the white-haired woman looked up and met her anguished gaze. The sure knowledge of Kit's paternity was unmistakable in the duchess's astute gray eyes. But surprisingly, there was no animosity. No accusation. Only mild reproof, as though Philippa were some spoiled little girl who'd thrown a monumental temper tantrum in order to get her own way. The heat of a flush suffused Philippa's face at the unspoken censure, so well deserved and so understated.

"I think it's time for you to take me home, Court," Lady Augusta said quietly. "It's been a long and exhausting day for the ladies."

Court looked up in surprise, unaware till that moment that his grandmother had entered the room. Reluctantly, he released Kit's hand and rose, fiery darts shooting through his cramped thigh. He gripped his cane, leaned his weight on its solid strength, and smiled at his son. Ignoring an inner pang of disappointment, he nodded in agreement.

The last thing he wanted to do was overset the precarious friendship they'd just established. "Yes, I suppose we should say good-bye for now, Kit. But I'll come back tomorrow morning to see you."

"We won't be here," Philippa said sharply. "Lady Harriet and I are taking Kit on an excursion."

"May I ask where you're going?"

"That's none—"

"We're taking Kit to explore the village," Lady Harriet offered. She flashed a droll smile at her grandchild, indicating that she, for one, was looking forward to the outing. "We plan to visit the toy shop and have lunch at the inn. Why don't both of you join us?"

Lady Augusta shook her head with a weary sigh. "Not tomorrow. These old bones need a little rest." But she smiled at Kit as she held up two childish drawings so the others could see. "Thank you for the pictures of the gondolas, young man. I'm going to have one framed and put above my bed. If you don't mind, I'd like to give the other one to the duke. I think he'd like to have it. Would that be all right with you?"

Kit looked up at Court with an expression of unbounded generosity. "You can have it, if you want, *nòbile*. Have you ever been in a gondola?"

"No, I'm afraid not," Court admitted, his lips twitching in beguiled amusement.

"I have," Kit boasted, "lots of times." He propped his hands on his hips and widened his stance, as though countering the roll and buck of a deck. "I'm going to be a boatman when I grow up."

Court smiled at the boy's artless enthusiasm. "I don't have a gondola, but I do have a schooner. Would you like to learn to sail on one?"

Not allowing Kit to answer, Philippa stepped up behind her son and splayed one hand protectively across his chest. She drew him against her knees as she met Court's gaze with a worried frown. "Kit is far too young to learn to sail."

"But, Mama," Kit protested, wriggling out from under her hold.

"Surely, he can come . . ." Court began.

Before either male could say another word, Lady Harriet snatched the boy's hand and headed for the door, pulling him gently along. "Don't argue with your mother, Kit. There'll be plenty of time for sailing boats. Right now, let's take a walk down to the stream before we're called to dinner."

The two paused in front of the open doorway. Kit awarded Court a wide, ingenuous smile. "*Ciao!*" he called with a happy wave. "See you tomorrow, *signóre.*"

That evening, the dowager marchioness of Sandhurst peeked into Philippa's bedchamber, after first tapping lightly on the door. "Are you still awake, dear?" she asked. "I know it's rather late, but I thought you might not have gone to bed yet."

Attired in an emerald silk wrapper, Philippa sat on the bench in front of her dressing table, brushing her hair. "Yes, I'm wide-awake. Please come in and sit down for a while." She met her mother-in-law's anxious gaze in the mirror and attempted a cheery smile.

Lady Harriet entered the spacious room and closed the door quietly behind her. She wore a lavishly embroidered night robe in the old-fashioned Chinoiserie style. Its bright tangerine satin clashed jarringly with her graying auburn hair, which had already been secured for the night in one long braid down her back. "I was worried that you were still upset," the dowager said.

Philippa put the hairbrush down and unconsciously repositioned the delicate crystal candlestick on the tabletop, moving the candle's flame farther away from the draperies on her canopied bed for the third time that evening. "The duke of Warbeck behaved exactly as I would have expected him to," she replied. "What I don't understand is why you invited him to come with us tomorrow."

Lady Harriet plopped gracelessly down on a soft upholstered chair. "Courtenay is one of our nearest neighbors, Philippa. It would be impossible for you to avoid him for the rest of your life. Why don't you try to sue for peace instead of brangling with him like a fractious schoolboy?"

"Peace?" Philippa gasped. She rose and turned to face her mother-in-law. "Do you actually believe that Warbeck would make peace with me?"

Lady Harriet glanced down at a box of chocolates on a nearby table, lifted the lid, and perused them idly. Then she looked up and met her daughter-in-law's disconcerted gaze. "He seems quite taken with your son. That alone should give him reason enough to want to settle the differences between you."

Philippa searched the dowager's intelligent green eyes, unable to believe the woman could be so thick-headed. Was it possible that she didn't see the strik-ing resemblance between the duke and her grandson because her heart wouldn't let her? "I don't think you understand Warbeck very well," Philippa said cautiously, "if you believe he would show anything but animosity toward me. He's the most ruthless, un-feeling man on the face of this earth."

Snorting in disagreement, Lady Harriet closed the candy box with a snap. "Nonsense. Courtenay is far more sensitive than you give him credit for being."

"Sensitive!" Philippa croaked in astonishment. She strove to keep her voice low, knowing Kit was asleep in the next room. "Have you forgotten that Warbeck refused to give me a chance to explain a thing, after he came upon Sandy and me in the Four Coaches Inn? You know very well that I wrote three letters in as many days, begging my husband to see me. Plead-ing with him to meet me so we could try to resolve the misunderstanding between us. All three letters were returned unopened. And when I went to Warbeck House that last afternoon before I left England, hoping against hope to persuade him to listen to reason, I wasn't allowed to cross the threshold." Philippa pressed her hands to her cheeks, feeling once again the anguish and humiliation she'd suffered as the heavy door of Warbeck House had been shut in her face. "I was turned away from my own home! Do you call that being *sensitive?*"

"I call that being very foolish, indeed," the dowager admitted, a grimace twisting her wide mouth. "But Courtenay was always quick to lose his temper. As a young man, he brawled with anyone who looked at him sideways or dared to utter innuendos about his shameless mother. After his father's death, he was ready to fight the whole world. And who could blame him?"

The two women gazed at each other in silence, neither wanting to put into words the terrible tragedy that had destroyed Court's youth. For after years of ignoring the blatant affairs of his unfaithful spouse, Court's father had shot his wife and her lover in bed. Two weeks later, the embittered, emotionally distant man had been found in the Castle's woods, mortally wounded. The official cause of death was listed as a hunting accident, but whispers of suicide had spread like an insidious plague throughout the county of Kent.

Philippa scowled stubbornly, unwilling to concede that Court's cynicism and lack of faith in mankind were all too understandable. "Court did more than brawl. I was told before we were married that he'd mortally wounded a man in an affair of honor. When he swore to kill Sandy, I knew it was no idle threat."

"Bosh," Lady Harriet disclaimed. "My godson was barely twenty when he fought that duel. The man he shot was fifteen years his senior and had loudly and quite foully besmirched his mother's memory.

Courtenay would never have killed my son. He loved him."

"He loved me once, too." Philippa made no attempt to soften her bitter words. "That didn't keep him from vilifying my name during the divorce proceedings. He falsely accused me of adultery, dragged my reputation through the mud, and left me without a shred of dignity or a shilling to live on. I shall never forgive him for that." She sank down on the bed, clutching the mattress. "I often wondered how Kit and I would have survived without Sandy."

"Mmm," the dowager marchioness mused thoughtfully. "And I often wondered what would have happened if Arthur had not decided to run off with you. For one thing, you might have been forced to stay and resolve your differences with your idiot husband."

Philippa lifted her chin at the chiding tone. "I was determined to go. I'd have left England that evening whether your son came along or not."

"I know, dear," Lady Harriet said with a sigh. "That's why Arthur went with you. I also knew, when I kissed my son good-bye for the last time, that I'd never see him again."

Astounded, Philippa met her mother-in-law's serene gaze. "You knew he was ill?"

Lady Harriet nodded. "I knew." She rose from the chair and moved to sit beside Philippa. Taking her daughter-in-law's hand, she said softly, "I was fully aware that Arthur was dying. He thought I didn't know, but a mother knows. That's why I let him go without a word of rebuke. Caring for you gave him the desire to go on living. I knew that with such an enormous responsibility on his shoulders, he would struggle to survive for as long as possible. You and Kit were his reason for getting up each morning, for putting one foot in front of the other. He wrote only of the happy times in his letters—of Kit's birth, of celebrating your nineteenth birthday, of sitting on the balcony with his family every evening and watching the sun set on the Grand Canal. He never once wrote of the pain he suffered. But, my dearest daughter, I could read between the lines." The dowager squeezed Philippa's fingers as she lovingly met her dumbfounded gaze. "Oh, yes, I knew."

Philippa put her arms around Lady Harriet's large frame and hugged her tight. Tears sprang to her eyes and rolled down her cheeks unheeded. "My dear, dear mother," she said, her heart aching at the loss they'd both endured. "We thought we'd kept it such a secret."

Chapter 7

"**A**h, Courtenay," Lady Harriet said, "I see you've decided to join us after all. I thought perhaps you'd changed your mind. Or did you have trouble finding us? We spent the entire morning chasing about and are enjoying a little respite in the shade." She motioned for him to come and sit down at the table the innkeeper had carried outdoors for them.

Philippa swiveled in the Windsor armchair to scowl at him, unhappily aware that her mounting hopes had just been dashed. Despite all her prayers, Warbeck had shown up before they'd eaten their midday meal and could start back to the Hall.

The tumult of emotions she'd suffered last night had only grown worse in the daylight. His threatening presence now filled her with terror. Kit was all she had. She couldn't lose her only child to a man who'd ignored his marriage vows and cast her aside, leaving her defenseless and alone in a world where she'd never felt safe, never felt she belonged. How could she be certain he wouldn't treat his son the same way? She stared at Warbeck in utter dismay, unable to hide her true feelings. She'd dreaded his appearance all morning.

The duke stood under one of the inn's curved archways, watching them with an enigmatic smile. His hands were folded across his cane. As Philippa's unhappy gaze swept over him, his silvery eyes taunted her, as though he were fully aware of her displeasure at the sight of him. He was dressed for a drive in the country. The brown corduroy riding coat and buff breeches tucked into his high leather boots emphasized the strength of his muscular torso and enhanced his rugged appearance.

Warbeck crossed the flagstones to where the trio sat looking out on Chippinghelm Green and the stream beyond that splashed and gurgled as it flowed beneath the bridge. Removing his gloves, he took Lady Harriet's hand, which she'd graciously extended, and kissed it in brief salutation. Since Philippa kept her own hands folded safely in her lap, he presented her with a casual bow before dropping into the spindle-backed chair opposite her, with the dowager marchioness at his right and Kit to his left.

"Have you visited the toy shop already, then?" he asked, smiling warmly at the boy.

"Yes, *nòbile*," Kit piped up without a trace of yesterday's shyness. It hadn't taken long for her son to make a new friend, blast it all, Philippa thought. "I wanted some wooden soldiers," the boy confided, "but Mama said I'd have to wait."

"First, we're going to explore some trunks in the attic," his grandmother explained. "I'm not certain where Arthur's toys are stored, but we'll find them. There'll be some wooden soldiers in his collection. No sense in purchasing something we already have, is there?"

"No," Kit admitted with a worried look, "but I hope they have red uniforms just like the ones we saw in Mr. Twicken's store. I sure don't want any Frogs."

The adults chuckled at the dire concern on his face. "Well, you certainly shan't have Frenchmen under your command, General Kit," Philippa teased. She playfully rumpled his ebony hair. "But you'll need an army to fight against in your battles."

"I will?"

"Most definitely," Warbeck told him. The duke's eyes twinkled as he bent closer to the boy. They had placed two large cushions on the seat of Kit's chair to bring him closer to table height. "Half the fun of playing with soldiers is planning your battle strategies. You can't let your enemies sneak around your unguarded flanks, you know."

Kit glanced at the black cane with its gold handle and stared up at him doubtfully. "Were you ever a solider, sir?" The perplexed look he sent Warbeck made it all too clear he found it hard to believe that a gentleman who walked with a decided limp had ever been a dashing military man.

"Yes," Warbeck replied, a grin lighting his sharp features. He didn't seem the least bit bothered by Kit's bald skepticism. "I served with the Light Brigade on the Spanish Peninsula. We reinforced Wellington's regiments at Talavera and prevented a hasty retreat from turning into a flight of sheer panic."

"Is that where you hurt your leg?"

The duke shook his head, his cheerfulness fading slightly. "No, Kit, I was injured at Bussaco. If you like, I can offer my suggestions when you start to plan your battles."

"That would be wonderful, *signóre!*" Kit exclaimed. He looked up at Court with growing adoration. "Will you come as soon as we find my father's soldiers?"

"I'd be happy to."

Philippa opened her mouth to object, then resolutely closed it. Now was not the time to tell Kit that he wouldn't be seeing the duke again. She intended to refuse Warbeck entry to Sandhurst Hall, over Lady Harriet's objections, if need be. The less he saw of his son, the better for everyone involved. After all, the man was engaged to be married. His new bride would soon produce an heir for his dukedom. There was no need for Kit to develop an affection for a man who would eventually focus all his interest on his new wife and family.

Philippa wouldn't allow her son to suffer the pain of abandonment. As an orphaned girl, she knew all about that kind of sorrow. She couldn't even remember her own parents. She was determined that Kit would never suffer the aching loneliness that haunted her even now.

Her unhappy thoughts were interrupted by the innkeeper, who brought a tray of drinks to the table. There was a tankard of ale for the duke and tall glasses of lemonade for the others. "It do be an honor to serve ye again, Y'r Grace," the burly man said as he set the refreshment in front of them. "I'll bring ye me finest capon in less than a trice."

"Thank you, Tarbel. And some strawberries and cream for our dessert, if you have them."

Their host's round face shone with pride. "Indeed, I do, Y'r Grace, indeed I do. Sweet an' ripe from me wife's own garden."

They dined al fresco in the pleasant courtyard situated at the rear of the timber-framed building. The Black Swan was a coaching inn dating back to the sixteenth century. The branches of a giant yew tree, as old and venerable as the inn itself, shaded their peaceful haven, casting dappled shadows across the red-and-white tablecloth and over the roast chicken and dumplings on their plates.

During the luncheon, Philippa said very little, the reality of sharing a meal with Warbeck once again making it difficult to do more than listen with half an ear while her thoughts wandered into forbidden fields. Beneath lowered lids, she watched his hands as he used his knife and fork. How many lonely nights had she yearned for the feel of his strong fingers stroking her bare skin? He had used those hands so expertly on their honeymoon, introducing her to erotic pleasures she'd never dreamed of. Pleasures that had haunted her during the empty years of her exile.

Blast it all! Why did his mere presence have to

bring back all the old yearnings? Each time she saw him, the turmoil inside her grew stronger. She *couldn't* still love him after all the pain he'd caused her. For nothing could change the fact that he hadn't trusted her. Would never trust her. And, therefore, she could never trust him.

Fortunately, her unusual silence wasn't noticed by her three companions, who chattered merrily like old friends. Kit plied Warbeck with questions about everything, from what it was like being a soldier and sleeping in a tent to how old the duke had been when he'd had his first pony to ride. Warbeck answered them all with warmth and honesty. Philippa was amazed at his changed demeanor. He seemed a different person from the furious man who'd accosted her at Belle's party and in the Sandhurst library the previous afternoon. With the child, he was patient, good-humored, and understanding.

She was forcibly reminded of their wedding trip, when Warbeck had showered her with tender affection. Sitting across from her now was the engaging gentleman she'd fallen so deeply in love with. She gave herself a mental shake, refusing to allow her thoughts to stray back to those golden days that were gone forever, but thankful that at least Warbeck's bitter hatred was directed solely at her. Apparently, he didn't believe that the sins of the parent were visited upon the child.

By the time they finished their meal, Kit had become restless. He slid off the cushions stacked on his chair, ready for another adventure. "Where are we going next, Mama?" he asked, just as Philippa popped a strawberry covered with thick cream into her mouth. She set the spoon down and waved her hand back and forth, motioning for him to wait until she'd swallowed her food.

Impatient, Kit placed his hand on her forearm and tugged. "Can we go back to the toy store and look at the soldiers one more time?"

"Your mother's still eating," Warbeck said firmly. "Wait politely until the grown-ups are ready to go."

Startled, Kit turned to challenge this unexpected source of discipline. "I only . . ." His words died at the intractable authority in Court's steady gaze.

"Come with me, Kit," Lady Harriet suggested, shooting Warbeck an approving smile. She scooped up several pieces of dark brown bread from a small wicker basket and handed them to Kit. "Here take these. We'll go down and feed the ducks while your mother finishes her sweet. After all those questions you bombarded him with, His Grace can relax a bit while he keeps Mama company."

At her suggestion, Kit took the bread and bounded off toward the stream bank, his hale and hearty grandmother striding close behind. Philippa started to rise, met Warbeck's sardonic gaze, and sat back down. To follow them now would appear nothing less than a craven retreat.

Court moved to Kit's vacated chair, where he would have a better view of the pair now surrounded by a flock of hungry ducks. The two adversaries sat in awkward silence, listening to the raucous *quack, quack, quack* of the greedy fowls. From the corner of his eye, he watched Philippa lift another spoonful of strawberries to her mouth. When she licked a spot of cream from her upper lip with her soft pink tongue, a surge of desire, hot and searing, spread through his groin.

The mottled sunshine played over her lovely face, drawing his gaze to the finely textured skin and the delicate arch of her high cheekbone. He lifted his hand to brush back an unruly tendril that lay against her flawless complexion, then caught himself in time and grasped his mug of ale, instead.

Aware of his intense scrutiny, she glanced up from beneath her long lashes. "Thank you for answering all of Kit's questions so patiently," she said in an obvious attempt at normal conversation. "That was very good of you."

He didn't answer, just sat taking in the exquisite beauty that had haunted his dreams for the past five and a half years. She was wearing a straw gypsy, its round, flat brim perched at a rakish angle on her yellow curls. The somber black of the previous day had been set aside once again, for Sandhurst had been dead for four years, and his widow's required time of mourning was long since over. Today, her blue muslin gown was gaily flowered. The wide satin ribbons that accentuated its fashionably high waist streamed down to pool in her lap.

His eyes followed the curve of her full breasts, suspecting that beneath the softly draped fabric her waist was as slender as it had been when she was an eighteen-year-old girl. He could feel himself hardening as unwanted images of his hands and mouth moving over her silken body battered his senses.

Damn it, hadn't she realized that he'd adored her? If she'd asked for the moon, he'd have tried to pluck it from the night sky and lay it at her feet. What magical words of love had Sandhurst whispered in her ear?

Court cursed silently to himself, all too aware that he'd never been skilled at flowery speeches. Until he'd met Philippa, he'd had no need for them. The women in his life had been satisfied with lusty, hot-blooded tumbles, where the less said, the better. The thought of a wide-eyed Philippa lying in Sandhurst's arms, as he lured her deeper and deeper into his honeyed trap with all the sugary platitudes and sweet endearments that her randy, lustful bridegroom had never uttered, still filled Court with rage. No woman had ever brought him such joy. Or such agonizing pain.

"How long were you on the Peninsula?" Philippa asked, as she looked down at the spoon she twirled idly in the heavy cream. Her cheeks were flushed as though she'd read his lecherous thoughts.

With an effort, Court brought himself back to the present and the harsh reality of her deceitful ways. During those miserable years, when he'd forgiven her and taken her back over and over again in his dreams, she'd kept his own child a secret from him. He ruthlessly squelched every feeling except anger. "I wasn't in Portugal long," he answered, trying to maintain a semblance of calm, though the muscles in his shoulders and back knotted with the effort. "Not much more than a year. After Bussaco, we retreated to Lisbon, and I was shipped home to convalesce."

"Were you caught by flying shrapnel?" she questioned softly.

"No."

She waited, expecting an explanation that didn't come. "A musket ball, then?"

"No." He shifted uncomfortably in his chair as the recollection of that gruesome battle assailed him. His chest ached with the force of his conflicting emotions. Bloody hell, why did she pretend to care now? It was too late to feel any honest concern. Her questions only brought back all the haunting misery that had followed him during those black, awful years.

Giving up her attempt to converse with such a surly companion, she laid the spoon beside the bowl of berries and gazed out across the grass to where their son was chasing a brown speckled duck round and round Lady Harriet's plum-colored skirts. They could hear Kit's chortles of delight each time he reached out and brushed his fingertips across the duck's tail feathers. Laughing at his antics, Philippa turned her head and met Court's eyes. The sound of her rich laughter, deep and unaffected, sent talons of lust raking through his loins.

"Kit won't give up," she said with a brilliant smile, clearly unaware of the heat building inside him. "Not until he's either caught the foolish thing or it gathers the sense to race to the water."

"He's a fine boy." At the hoarsely uttered words, Court watched the amusement on her features change to wary circumspection.

"Yes, he is," she agreed in a near whisper. She placed her forefinger against her lips as though purposely holding back the thought she'd been about to share. Her violet eyes were filled with a poignant sadness, making her seem defenseless and vulnerable.

Court felt himself becoming ensnared once again in the unbridled sexual desire that only she had ever aroused in him. He fought to keep from reaching out and hauling her supple form up against his hard male body. His hands curled into fists as he battled the need within him to touch her, to feel the softness of her sweet femininity one more time. Damn her! She should never have come back to England. All the raw emotions he'd thought buried forever came bubbling back to the surface. Anger, regret, recrimination, hurt, and erotic need combined within him, like some evil sorcerer's poisoned brew, threatening to erupt in a scalding combustion.

Philippa could feel the tension growing between them, as the lighthearted atmosphere of a moment before dissipated completely. "Warbeck," she said haltingly, "I don't think it's wise for you to see Kit again. It would be better for him, for all of us, if you'd not come to the Hall."

The mocking self-assurance on his stern features sent her heart to her throat. "You can't keep me from seeing my son," he stated with absolute conviction. "No one can keep me from him."

"Kit is not your son," she cried, finding it hard, all at once, to catch her breath. "He's Sandy's legal heir. You have no right to push your way into his life. In the future, you will find yourself barred from entry to Sandhurst Hall. Please don't attempt to visit us again."

Warbeck grasped the handle of his cane and lurched to his feet. His deep voice was cool and frighteningly unemotional. "Is this my godmother's wish as well?"

"Lady Harriet has nothing to say in the matter," Philippa protested. She tried to stand up, but he leaned over her, his menacing stance imprisoning her as effectively as iron shackles. "Kit is now the master of Sandhurst Hall," she said, "and as his widowed mother, I have the right to determine who sees my child."

He bent forward and planted his hand on the curved maple armchair, speaking quietly so his words wouldn't carry to the happy twosome capering on the lawn nearby. "You're not going to keep me away from Kit, Philippa. In fact, in the near future, you're not going to have anything to say about my son's life. If I have to spend every shilling I own to regain my child, I'll do it." Before she could make any threats, he picked up his hat and gloves and left.

Two days later, Court was working in his study with Neil Tolander when his elderly butler carried in a calling card that Court had been waiting for impatiently. He scanned the card and nodded his willingness to see the visitor.

As Peel left to bring the man in, Court tossed the card down on the ponderous library table that served as his desk and glanced over at his secretary. "Neil, if you'll excuse us, I'd like to speak to my caller privately."

Tolander looked up in surprise. Since he'd come to work for the duke, he'd been privy to the most confidential information, often in matters that concerned hundreds of thousands of pounds. Court's trust in him was implicit.

"Certainly, Your Grace," his secretary replied. He

jumped to his feet, gathered the stack of papers from
the glowing mahogany desktop, and tucked them
under his arm with a brief nod. "I'll be in my office,
if you need me, sir." As Tolander left the study, Peel
ushered in Mr. Emory Fry.

"Your Grace," the man said in a straightforward
manner as they shook hands. "I came as soon as I received your message." He was in his late twenties,
slender, not above average height, and dressed in a
tweed suit, despite the summer weather. He carried a
matching cap in his hand, and his prematurely balding head was surrounded by a fringe of light brown
hair, cut short and neat. His hazel eyes were large,
round, and slightly protruding.

"Come in and sit down," Court said, indicating the
seat Tolander had recently vacated. "And thank you
for coming so quickly." He sank down in his desk
chair, opened a silver cigar case, and offered it to the
man, who shook his head.

"Don't smoke," Fry explained. "Wife can't abide
the smell." He sat back in the chair and studied
Court with a candid air. "What can I do for you, Your
Grace?"

"My solicitor, Efrain Bowling, recommended you
as the best private investigator in London. In all of
England, he claims. Is that true?"

Fry's response was neither puffed-up nor humble.
"I do my best, sir. I learned my trade under my uncle's guidance, him being a Bow Street runner. But I
prefer to work on my own. More freedom, you understand."

"Quite," Court responded. "Have you any idea
why I asked you here?"

"Not in the least, Your Grace."

Fry had the lean, capable appearance Court had
expected. There was a hint of the wolf beneath the
very proper, middle-class exterior. He looked like a
man who'd seen some violence. Court was certain

that Fry could take care of himself in a fight, but did he have the skills necessary for more subtle intrigue?

Court rose from his chair and walked over to the window. He gazed out through the diamond-paned glass onto Castle Warbeck's rose garden. On this warm June morning, Lady Augusta was busily issuing directives to one of the gardeners, who was following behind her with a huge basket of pink blooms. "What I'm going to tell you is in complete confidence, Mr. Fry," Court said, still facing the glass. "Whether you accept the assignment or not, I'd like your assurance now that nothing said in this room will ever be repeated without my permission." He turned to the man. "Do you agree?"

Fry met his inquiring gaze with a long, serious look. "I do, sir."

"And you are willing to travel in the pursuit of your investigations?"

"I've traveled across most of Europe, at one time or another," Fry said, folding his arms across his chest. "As far east as Warsaw, as far south as Vienna. Where is it you wish me to go, Your Grace?"

"Venice. I want you to investigate the circumstances surrounding the birth of a male child. You're to talk to the midwife who delivered him, the city official who registered his birth, and the wet nurse who suckled him. Bring back everything you can find about the infant. Even the minutest detail could prove to be of relevance."

Fry shifted in his chair, leaned forward, and placed one hand on his knee, his expression thoughtful. "Whose child is it?"

"Mine."

Fry merely lifted his thin eyebrows in polite inquiry and waited for Court to continue.

"I also want you to speak to anyone who knew my former wife, Lady Philippa Bentinck and her deceased husband, the marquess of Sandhurst. The pair fled to Italy five years and ten months ago. I believe that at the time of their departure, the lady was carrying my child."

"You didn't know of her pregnancy at the time?"

"Had I the least suspicion that my wife was with child, I would have followed her to the ends of the earth." Court couldn't keep the bitterness from his voice. "Instead, I obtained a dissolution of the marriage."

"When was the child born?"

"She claims he was born two days after she and Sandhurst were married."

Slowly, Fry shook his head, the compassion in his eyes undeniable. "If that's true, the child is legally the son of her second husband, whether or not he is the result of your seed."

"But if it's not true? If she's lying?"

Fry's domed forehead crinkled in speculation. "That depends on whether the Bill of Divorcement was passed by Parliament before or after the actual date of the baby's birth." The young man paused, as though hesitant to broach the next subject, then continued in his plainspoken way. "The boy could be illegitimate. Neither man's legal issue. There'd be no way to prove which man sired him. If such is the case, it would be better, for the child's sake, to let sleeping dogs lie—if you'll pardon my offering some advice, Your Grace."

Meeting Fry's forthright gaze, Court sank down on the deep stone windowsill behind him. He stretched out his bad leg and absently massaged his thigh. "If you discover that the boy is illegitimate, we will forget this discussion ever took place. He will remain in the eyes of the world the deceased man's son."

Fry nodded in agreement. "And the boy's name, Your Grace?"

"Christopher Bentinck, fifth marquess of Sandhurst."

* * *

Lady Augusta stood amidst the blooms of her favorite flowers and watched a vigorous young man in a rumpled tweed suit hurry down the wide steps that led from the main rear entrance to the curving, graveled driveway and clamber into his hired post chaise. If he wasn't an officer of the law, she'd eat the rose she held in her hand. "Carry on," she called to the gardener over her shoulder as she lifted the hem of her chocolate-colored morning gown and headed into the Castle.

She found Court alone in the austere, high-ceilinged room he called his study. He was standing in front of the fireplace, one hand braced on the mantel as he stared down at the cold grate. "Who was your caller?" she asked from the doorway, trying to sound only mildly interested. "We should have offered him some refreshments before he started on his journey home."

Her grandson turned at the sound of her voice and smiled distractedly as she placed a bouquet of pink roses on his desk. He frowned, however, when she sat down on the leather sofa nearby, giving every evidence of staying for a lengthy chat. "He came on a matter of business," Court answered. "There was no need to trouble yourself."

Augusta snorted in disbelief. "That man is a Bow Street runner or I'm not a dowager duchess," she said without equivocation. "This has something to do with Kit, doesn't it?"

Court wasn't pleased at her sagacity. "Grandmother, this doesn't concern you."

"Don't tell me that," she said with an air of amused skepticism. "Anything that concerns my great-grandson concerns me."

The duke crossed the brown-and-gold Turkish carpet to stare out the window, obviously weighing the possibility that she might accept his refusal to discuss the matter further. Finally, he turned and faced her, his jaw tense with strain. "Mr. Fry is not a policeman.

He's a private investigator. The best there is, I'm told."

"What are you trying to do, Court," she demanded, "prove that Kit is illegitimate? For what purpose? You'll soon be married. You can have as many children as you wish with Clare Brownlow."

"I don't *want* children with Clare Brownlow."

She made no attempt to keep the sarcasm from her voice. "You shouldn't have asked the woman to marry you if you didn't want her to have your children."

Realizing what he'd just said, Court glared at her in exasperation. "I didn't mean that the way it sounded."

"Of course you did," she countered. She rose and walked over to stand beside him. "I hoped that once you became engaged to Clare, you'd soften a little. But your bitterness is worse than ever."

His chiseled mouth became a hard, stubborn line. "I'm sorry if I failed to live up to your expectations. I believed that earning a dukedom and acquiring a fortune would please even the most critical of relatives."

"Pardon me," she said tartly, "if I prefer the rakehell youth, bent on gambling away what was left of his family's fortune, to the cold, ruthless man whose only interest for the last three years has been to amass more money than any other gentleman in England. Since you came back from the Peninsula, you've had no thought for anything but your financial investments. You've turned into an unfeeling martinet."

"Thank you for your vote of confidence, Grandmother. Now if that's all you wanted to say, I'm afraid I'm very busy."

But Augusta wasn't finished. "The only thing that can save you from yourself, Court, is to fall deeply in love again. And not with that ice princess you call your fiancée. You need a woman who can light the fire in your blood, to fill your life with moonlight and romance."

"Romantic love is a myth," Court replied with a sneer. He braced his buttocks on the edge of the desk and met her gaze with a frosty stare. "Love is a will-o'-the-wisp fancy that took my mother down the path of self-destruction. And in the process, she destroyed her husband and orphaned two sons."

"And you're not about to forgive or forget, are you?"

"This has nothing to do with my mother."

Ignoring his derisive smirk, she moved to stand directly in front of him. "It has everything to do with her. You're afraid to trust, afraid that any woman you truly care about will treat you in the same way. That she'll abandon you in the end for her fancy lovers."

Except for the vein that throbbed in his temple, his face was a mask of indifference. "Don't be absurd," he said with a harsh laugh.

"Laugh if you wish, my dear grandson, but I can tell you this. Your cynicism will never bring you happiness. I knew what your intentions were when you asked Clare to marry you. Your proposal was a cold, calculated decision made for the sole purpose of fathering an heir. When you announced your betrothal to Miss Brownlow, I wasn't particularly hopeful that it would result in a happy marriage. But you are, nevertheless, engaged. Need I remind you that the wedding is set for November, the notice has appeared in the papers, the bridesmaids have all been chosen, and you, as a gentleman, cannot withdraw from the betrothal? So for God's sake, why don't you allow Kit and his poor mother to lead their lives without persecution, while you get on with yours?"

With that parting salvo, Augusta flounced out of the room, shutting the door behind her. Her scowl was soon replaced by a wide, self-satisfied smile. She nearly rubbed her hands together in glee. Things were going just as she'd hoped.

Chapter 8

The weather had turned unusually cool for the second week of July, with showers during the past three days that had soaked the lawns and flower gardens. But in spite of the overcast sky that afternoon, several of the tall window casements stood open, allowing the slight breeze to circulate through the crowded library of Sandhurst Hall. Philippa scanned the diverse assembly, grateful that the temperature had remained mild. She gave her mother-in-law, who stood beside her, a halfhearted smile, knowing that Lady Harriet was well aware of her chaotic frame of mind.

"It's time we take our seats," Lady Harriet said, slipping her arm through her daughter-in-law's and patting her wrist gently.

"Yes, if we must do this, let's begin, so we may have it over with all the sooner," Philippa replied.

The moment she'd seen the duke of Warbeck enter the library, a heavy weight had pressed against Philippa's chest. Blast it, she'd *known* that he'd been invited to come. Phineas Larpent, the Sandhurst solicitor, had given her a list of every person mentioned in the will. She took a deep breath and told herself there was no need to panic. Sandy would never have written anything that could harm her or her child. But why, then, had the solicitor summoned Warbeck?

Together Philippa and Lady Harriet walked up the narrow aisle that had been left between the rows of chairs. Philippa smiled and nodded to the people who turned toward her with looks of compassion. She was acquainted with everyone present, though some of them she'd only met earlier that morning. The large retinue of servants, including the butler, the housekeeper, the footmen and lackeys, the cook, the upstairs and downstairs maids, the gardeners, the coachman and stable hands, were all seated together in the back.

In the middle of the room waited the five stewards from the outlying estates, their expensively tailored attire setting them apart from the household staff behind them. The Sandhursts' chief steward, Stanley Tomkinson, had offered to go over the accounts with Philippa when she'd first arrived, but she'd put him off, well aware that nothing in her past had prepared her for such a complicated task. She'd informed Tomkinson that she had no intention of making any changes at the present time. At least not until after the complete will had been read.

During the dark days in Venice, when Sandy knew his death was imminent, he'd sat propped against the pillows in his large bed and laboriously composed his last testament. He'd been in excruciating pain, but the writing seemed to give him some measure of comfort, for when it was completed, he smiled at Philippa and the babe in her arms and told her not to worry about the future.

The sealed will had been carried to England by special courier, where it was locked in the safe of the marquess of Sandhurst's solicitor, awaiting the end of the war and his widow and son's safe return. Sandy had stipulated interim measures, giving Philippa and Kit an allowance during their exile in Venice and his stewards the authority to disperse moneys from his estates for needed purposes. But the full will was not to be read until his body had been returned to England.

Grateful for Lady Harriet's steadying presence,

Philippa slipped into a seat in the first row directly across from Warbeck, leaving the chair closest to the aisle for her mother-in-law. At the large oak table in front of them, Mr. Larpent sat down and immediately picked up the document, several pages thick, that had been placed before him. He bent his head to scan the top sheet of vellum, and his thick, bushy brows hid his heavy-lidded eyes. His jowls hung down in wattles, and his lantern jaw made his lower lip thrust forward in a perpetual pout.

Before he could begin, Lady Augusta, who'd been upstairs visiting with Kit, sank down on Philippa's other side. "Courage, child," she said softly. She ran the edge of her closed fan along Philippa's forearm in a discreet gesture of warning. "No matter what the will discloses, don't let the servants think there is aught amiss. They prattle like children, and nothing delights them more than gossiping about their betters."

"Don't worry, Grandmother," Philippa said with a teasing smile, purposely misunderstanding her words. "I won't swoon if I'm left without a shilling. Is Kit keeping himself out of trouble?"

The duchess's wrinkled face lit up with pride. "Lud, at five years old, that scamp has all the charm of a town beau. You'll have to erect a barricade around the Hall when he reaches fifteen to keep the girls away." She chuckled softly. "By twenty, he'll have half the women in England, married or single, chasing at his heels."

"He's a delight," Philippa admitted proudly. "But he's far too young to be present at what will likely prove to be a very tedious and lengthy proceeding." And if the opposite were true, if her worst fears were realized and Sandy had confessed his sins in the testament he'd left behind, she wanted Kit safe in his bedroom under the eyes of his vigilant nursemaid. Who could know, in the end, what acute regrets a dying man might suffer?

When the widow and the two dowagers were settled comfortably, Philippa nodded, and the solicitor began reading in a gruff, ponderous monotone. She found it nearly impossible to concentrate as the many small bequests for the staff were read. Personal gifts were left to all of Sandy's trusted retainers, their value graduated in worth, not on the importance of the servant's job, but on the years each had served his family. Realizing the opening terms of the will were neither threatening nor surprising, her mind drifted to the source of her present agitation. She turned her head slightly, glancing at those sitting across from her.

His arms folded over his broad chest, Warbeck listened to the reading with an expression of cool detachment. Then he leaned forward slightly, his scowl of irritation making it plain that he was as perplexed as to why he'd been requested to attend she was. But he'd come, nonetheless.

Tobias and Belle, seated beside Warbeck in the front row, were holding hands as though to reassure each other that nothing terrible was going to happen. But behind their spectacles, two pairs of dark brown eyes watched Phineas Larpent with concern. The spouses' obvious need for mutual support during the reading of Sandy's will sent a stab of apprehension through Philippa.

Directly behind Viscount Rockingham, Philippa's uncle, Erasmus Crowther, sat mopping his brow with a kerchief despite the cool weather. A big bull of a man with a head of thick brown hair and a ruddy complexion, he was dressed plainly in the dark frock coat and breeches of a lesser country squire. Her uncle had arrived with the rainstorms, three days before.

"I'm sorry for missing Sandhurst's memorial rites," he'd offered in his usual gruff manner. "The axle of my coach broke, which shouldn't surprise anyone, since I must travel in such an antiquated wreck. I was forced to put up for nearly a week in a wretched inn along the road, which cost me dearly, as well."

"I'm sorry too, Uncle," she said with a cheering smile. "But you've arrived safely for all your inconvenience. And I will gladly reimburse you for any expenses you had to meet on the road." She wondered absently what her uncle did with the salary he received for acting as caretaker of the ruined manor.

"What I need is a decent carriage," he growled.

"Then you shall have one."

She tried to be patient as he complained bitterly and unceasingly of the trials of the journey, yet unexplained feelings of dislike and distrust surfaced from deep inside her. Which really wasn't fair, she told herself. She had no right to blame him for the past.

Erasmus was in his early fifties now and had known extreme poverty after the destruction of the manor house by fire eighteen years ago, for he'd been dependent on his brother-in-law's largess, having no livelihood of his own. When Philippa's parents died, her uncle, like herself, had been left destitute. He had survived on the charity of his neighbors in Hamble Green. It was only natural for him to worry about the future, despite his niece's assurances that he'd be provided for.

Philippa knew full well why Erasmus was here. He'd come to Kent to learn what was going to happen to Moore Manor now that she'd returned. And, more importantly, to discover if the late marquess of Sandhurst had provided for a continuance of the ample living allotment that Erasmus had received during their long absence from England.

As the last of the gifts to the servants were read, Philippa turned her attention once more to the solicitor. The next endowment proved that Erasmus had nothing to fear. His benefactor in life had remembered him in death. A bountiful allowance was to be provided along with funds to rebuild the manor.

The following paragraph dealt with Sandy's bestowal on the dowager marchioness, which, to no one's surprise, was exceedingly generous. Lady Harriet looked at Philippa with a teary smile when the solicitor read Sandy's profession of love for his mother.

The room began to grow warm and humid as Phineas Larpent's voice droned on. "I leave to my beloved wife, Philippa Moore Bentinck, a third of my fortune so that she may continue to live in the style befitting her rank as the marchioness of Sandhurst. The estate, formerly known as Moore Manor of Surrey, and the landholdings surrounding it, which once belonged to her parents and which she brought to our marriage as her bride's portion, are hereby bequeathed to her so that her family's heritage in that district shall not be lost to the passing of time. She shall also be entitled to live in the dower house at Sandhurst upon the death of my dear mother, Lady Harriet, so that she may remain close to her son in her later years."

Oh, Sandy, Philippa thought with inner gratitude, you provided for my future just as you said. God bless you, dearest, noblest of hearts. I shall never face the threat of being homeless again.

Deep inside, she felt an easing of the old terror that had haunted her since the day she'd found Erasmus Crowther's letter and learned that she could have been sent to a factory at the age of ten. The blood-chilling possibility of suffering such a fate would never go away completely. Nothing could ever erase that deeply rooted fear of abandonment. It had sunk into the marrow of her bones.

Mr. Larpent paused. He looked at the faces, one by one, of those who sat listening in the first row. Everyone straightened in their chairs in tense anticipation, for they knew the next paragraph would mention Sandhurst's only child. The room grew still. Phineas cleared his throat with a loud, horsy harumph and continued.

"The remainder of my fortune, my title, and all my estates, I leave to my son and legal heir, Christopher, whom we call Kit. Since his tender years will preclude his supervising the management of these moneys and estates during his minority, I have deemed it necessary to designate a guardian until he reaches the age of twenty-one. I am not making the following request without great thought and enormous prayer. I ask, nay beseech, that my two friends, Tobias Howard, Viscount Rockingham, and Courtenay Shelburne, duke of Warbeck, act as joint guardians of my beloved son."

Philippa sprang from her chair. Reeling in shock, she was unable to utter a word. She looked wildly from Larpent's pumpkin-shaped face to the papers he held in his fleshy hands, certain that someone would shout out that there'd been a terrible mistake. The idiot must be reading someone else's will. This trumpery couldn't be Sandy's wishes!

"Sit down, dear," Lady Harriet whispered. She clasped Philippa's elbow and tugged her back into her seat. "Mr. Larpent is not finished reading."

Philippa looked into her mother-in-law's sea green eyes and realized that Lady Harriet wasn't the least bit startled. Had Sandy written his mother of his disastrous decision? Or did the dowager marchioness suspect what she'd never put into words, never once alluded to—that Kit was not her grandson.

Lady Augusta ceased plying her fan and calmly pulled a vial of hartshorn from her reticule. She offered it to Phillipa, who waved it away. "I'll be all right," she told the duchess. "I'm not going to faint." But the throbbing beat of her heart felt like the roll of the drums before an execution.

The entire roomful of people waited in suspense. Ignoring the dumbfounded spectators behind her, Philippa clasped her hands tightly in her lap, lowered her head to offer a quick prayer for her deliverance, and then looked up to signal the solicitor to continue.

"I hereby request," read Larpent, "that the duke of Warbeck be given full control of my son's trust, knowing that my hotheaded friend is a genius when it comes to financial affairs. Word of his brilliant investments has traveled all the way to Venice, and I was pleased to learn that he made such wise use of the moneys awarded him in civil court. As an absentee landlord, I have not been able to oversee the stewardship of my holdings as I ought. I ask that Warbeck do whatever he deems necessary to set all the estates in order, so that by the time Kit comes of age, he will inherit a strong and steady income from his properties. Further, I request that all other matters regarding my son's education, life-style, etc., be jointly decided upon by the two guardians, in whom I place my complete trust for the well-being of my child, for two truer friends no man ever had. The only stipulation I place on their guardianship is that my son never be forcibly removed from his mother's loving care."

"No!" Philippa cried, jumping to her feet once again. "There's been a mistake. Sandy wouldn't do this!" She turned, her eyes automatically seeking Warbeck's, who, like the rest of the room's occupants, now stood in front of his chair, a look of astonishment on his arrogant features. He was no longer scowling. As he met her gaze, an unholy light blazed in his silvery eyes. The mobile line of his mouth quirked upward in jubilation.

"Hush, dear," Lady Harriet soothed. "This isn't the time to discuss it." She looked beseechingly at Lady Gabrielle, who slipped past the duke and came immediately to Philippa's side.

Belle put her plump arms about Philippa's shoulders and hugged her comfortingly. *"Nom de Dieu,"* she commiserated softly in her friend's ear. "This is incredible. But we must hope it is for the best. Toby will protect your interests, regardless of what Court tries to do."

"Protect me?" Philippa's voice rose hysterically as she looked over Belle's shoulder at the tall, threatening duke. "Why should I have to be protected from my own son's guardian? My God! This is insane!"

The room was abuzz with conjecture. She could hear people whispering madly among themselves. If just the presence of Warbeck at Sandhurst Hall on the day of the interment had been cause for wild speculation, the appointment of His Grace as guardian of his divorced wife's child would rock the ton. Especially when that child was the very image of the duke, himself.

"Let's go up to your bedchamber," Belle suggested as she glanced around at the servants, who continued to stare bug-eyed. "You can lie down until you're feeling more the thing."

"G-good idea," agreed Tobias, who'd come to stand beside his wife. "Why don't you l-let me escort you upstairs, Pippa?"

"No, have the library cleared at once, please," she begged. She fought back the sobs that threatened to clog her throat, making it nearly impossible to talk. "I . . . I want to. . . to speak to Warbeck with my family and friends present. We have to discuss, right here and now, what he plans to do. I must know right now."

While Lady Harriet went to the back of the room to direct the staff to return to their duties, Lady Augusta and Belle stayed close by Philippa's side. They tried to get her to sit down again, but she refused. It was all she could do to keep from pacing back and forth in a maddened frenzy or wailing out loud like some crazed lunatic. Phineas Larpent came over and bowed low, obviously expecting her to offer her effusive gratitude for his services. Sick with despair, she was barely able to meet his gaze as she extended her hand in a perfunctory dismissal. He left the room with a dissatisfied frown, followed by Stanley Tomkinson and the five stewards of the outlying estates, whose pale faces and worried glances indicated their own concern about the abrupt change in the winds of fortune.

Warbeck, with Erasmus Crowther following right behind, came to stand near Tobias. In a few minutes, the room was empty, except for the small group clustered around Philippa. When she could bring herself to look again into Warbeck's eyes, it was exactly as she'd expected. He was gloating. His elation filled her with an icy dread. There was no doubt in her mind that he would use this mighty, two-edged sword that Sandy had delivered into his hands with a vengeance. Her former husband now stood in nearly complete control of her son and her son's trust. And if Warbeck controlled her son, to a great extent, he controlled her as well.

"Do you plan to accept this guardianship?" she demanded hoarsely. "After the infamous accusations you made against Sandy in a public trial?"

His spirits soaring with the fantastic turn of events, Court favored her with a delighted grin. "Without question, I'll accept this guardianship. Whatever else I may have accused him of being, I never implied that Sandhurst was stupid. He knew I could double, even triple, Kit's fortune by the time the boy reaches his majority. Something Sandy, with his lack of practical common sense, would never have been able to do."

Lady Harriet straightened to her full height, her eyes snapping with ire. "Here, now, Courtenay," she warned gruffly, "we'll have nothing scurrilous said about my son."

Court tipped his head in polite acquiescence to his godmother, but his answer was directed to Philippa, who stared at him with the huge, frightened eyes of a wounded animal waiting for the hunter's final thrust. "At this moment, I wouldn't say anything critical about Sandhurst at all. Not after his touching vote of confidence in me. And I intend to meet the responsibilities of my role as guardian and executor of the trust to the fullest extent. I will return to the Hall in the morning to meet with the overseers of all the estates Kit has inherited. Then I'll spend the afternoon getting better acquainted with my charge." He turned to Tobias. "Would you like to join me tomorrow in beginning the process of going over the financial accounts?"

The viscount shook his head. "N-not tomorrow, Court. I'll leave the f-finances completely in y-your hands. It sounds like that's the way Sandy w-wanted it." He looked at Philippa with sympathetic eyes. "B-but I will be coming here frequently to see Kit."

"As a matter of fact," Court said, immediately pressing his advantage, "perhaps it would be better if Kit came to live with me at the Castle. Then I could supervise his rearing and education properly."

"No!" Philippa cried. "You shan't take Kit from me!" Shaken to the tips of her satin shoes, she was stirringly beautiful, Court thought. Her deep lavender-blue gown matched her eyes, brimming now with tears. A tiny cluster of violets nestled charmingly in her curls, highlighting the burnished gold of her hair. At the sight of her trembling loveliness, Court felt a burst of heady exhilaration, part the intoxicating thrill of power and part a surge of vibrant carnal energy. After nearly six years of impotent fury, he had her under his thumb. It felt bloody damn wonderful.

Everyone started talking at once, loudly voicing their own opinions, until Lady Harriet put up her hand in a dramatic signal for silence and addressed her godson with unruffled conviction. "Let's not get carried away by our emotions, Courtenay. The matter has been plainly set forth in my son's will. Arthur stipulated that the boy could not be forcibly taken from his mother."

"No one's going to take Kit from Philippa," Lady Augusta affirmed. She snapped open her black lace fan and waved it in regal self-assurance, sending Court a look of reproach. "We all know a young child belongs with his mother."

"Do we?" Court goaded. "I think Sandhurst was trying to say just the opposite. He knew that it's a man's role to provide the proper guidance and discipline needed in rearing a male child. Especially one who's inherited a title, wealth, and the heavy responsibilities that go with it. The boy's mother can't possibly prepare him for running his estates. Even she must admit that."

"I admit nothing!"

"You never have," he said quietly, "but that doesn't change the truth." Her shocked gaze flew to meet his, and the hurt that registered on her pale face told him his barb had struck home.

"W-wait a minute, Court," Tobias protested, ignoring the interplay. "Th-the will doesn't give you the r-right to make that d-decision on your own. W-we're supposed to agree on everything except the investment of m-moneys in the trust f-fund, which Sandy placed s-solely in your h-hands."

Court turned to his friend. "But don't you agree that Kit would be better off living under a man's guidance?" He fought to hide his relief when he read the indecision in Tobias's gaze. As a future father himself, Toby would naturally favor the male point of view. Besides, the two men had been close friends since childhood.

Philippa clung to Belle, scarcely able to fight back her tears. "Kit stays with me," she insisted in a breathless, strangled voice. "My son stays with me."

"*Mon Dieu,*" the viscountess cried passionately, "of course the child should stay with his mother. Who would be cruel enough to take Kit away from her?" With one arm about Philippa's waist, Belle ran a shaky hand through her own dark curls. She looked at Court and then her husband with horrified eyes.

"Although I sympathize with my niece," Erasmus Crowther said in his gravelly voice, "the law always places the rearing of children in the hands of the father, or the guardian, if that be the case, who is, of course, always male. Only a man can make the intelligent, logical decisions required to transform the little beasties into civilized, responsible citizens."

The four females turned as one to stare in displeasure at Philippa's uncle. Beneath their frigid censure, his pockmarked cheeks grew even ruddier. But the burly man held his ground, returning their glares with stubborn conviction.

"It appears the decision rests with Toby," said Court. He tapped his cane idly against the toe of his boot and waited.

Everyone's gaze swung to Tobias Howard, who stood at his friend's side with a sickened look on his thin features. He fidgeted with his wrinkled cravat, stretching his long neck upward in an awkward, uncomfortable movement. At his nervous hesitation, Philippa pressed the tips of her fingers against her soft, pink lips, as if to stifle a cry of despair. Her face was deathly white. In the long seconds they all awaited the viscount's answer, her world surely must have turned upside down.

"I-I agree with Philippa," Tobias said at last. "It w-would be b-better for the b-boy if he remains in S-sandhurst Hall with his m-mother and gr-grandmother."

"Unless Philippa would like to come and live at the Castle as well," Lady Augusta suggested with a kindly smile. "Since I am always in residence, it would be perfectly proper."

"Never!" Philippa gasped, clearly horrified that Court's grandmother would even suggest such a thing. "The idea is ... is unthinkable."

"Th-then the child st-stays at S-sandhurst Hall."

"Very well," Court conceded, hiding his dissatisfaction behind an air of well-tempered compromise. "We'll leave Kit here for the time being. But everyone surely must agree that I have the right to come to the Hall anytime I please to check on the welfare of my charge."

Philippa raised her chin defiantly. "I don't agree to that at all."

"Neither do I," Lady Gabrielle said. She looked at her husband with narrowed eyes, daring him to disagree. Court had never seen the sweet, soft-spoken gentlewoman so overwrought.

"As Kit's legal g-guardians," Tobias said firmly, "b-both Court and I have the r-right to see the boy at any time. That's what g-guardians do."

Court looked around the circle of people. On this particular issue, only Belle's distraught brown eyes showed any sympathy for Philippa. Lady Augusta waved her fan back and forth, smiling benignly as though everything had been arranged to her satisfaction. Even Lady Harriet, who should have been irate at the presumptuousness of the two men, stood strangely silent.

"Then it looks as though we're all in agreement," said Court.

"Very well," Philippa replied in a hollow voice. Her shoulders slumped in defeat. "I will not instruct the servants to bar you from the Hall." Then she thrust out her lower lip and met his gaze with the pugnacity of a bantam prizefighter. "But I insist upon being present whenever you visit Kit."

He couldn't keep a victorious grin from spreading across his face. "I wouldn't want it any other way."

The next morning, Court started out for Sandhurst Hall later than he'd planned. His own business correspondence had kept him in his study with Neil Tolander until midmorning. Consequently, he'd only slowed his pair of galloping chestnuts as he entered the village of Chippinghelm. He was approaching St. Aldhelm's vicarage when he saw Philippa emerging with the Reverend Mr. Trotter. The two stood for a moment beneath a stone archway, then talking earnestly, they walked side by side down the pansy-bordered path toward the road, where Lady Harriet's brightly painted gig stood waiting, an attendant standing at the horse's head.

Court brought his team to a halt behind the carriage just as the vicar and his guest reached it. He lifted his hat politely. "Good morning, Lady Sandhurst ... Reverend Trotter. You're up and about early." This last statement was directed at Philippa, who stared up at him with solemn eyes.

"You know what they say, Your Grace," Zacariah Trotter quipped in a clergyman's benevolent manner. "The early bird gets the worm."

Court returned his cheerful greeting with an abstracted smile. Philippa was wearing a dress of striped green muslin. The breeze blew the diaphanous material against her long legs, revealing the slender body that still tormented Court's dreams. A lime green bonnet with a bow tied under her chin anchored her thick curls, but several tendrils had escaped to trail after the ribbon streamers that danced gently about her slim shoulders. During the night, the stormy weather had been blown away, and, in the bright morning sunlight, she looked as pure and lovely as a bouquet of spring flowers, all pink and green and gold. He knew without conscious thought that she would smell as fresh and fragrant as the blossoms she evoked. That knowledge stirred a response deep inside him.

"Hello, Your Grace," Philippa said with a coolly polite inclination of her head. "I take it you're on your way to the Hall."

"Yes, I'd hoped to get there earlier, but I had several pressing concerns to attend to first."

"Then I'll see you again shortly," she replied. "Mr.

Tomkinson will be waiting for you in the library. I've instructed him to have all the accounts ready for your scrutiny." Remarkably, the fear that had clouded her eyes the previous day was absent. She seemed calm, even serene. Perhaps her talk with the vicar had eased her guilty conscience.

The liveried driver helped Philippa into the gig. Then he sprang up beside her, gathered the reins in his hand, and waited for her signal to depart.

The Reverend Mr. Trotter moved to stand beside the open carriage. When Philippa offered him her gloved hand, he reached up and took it in both of his. "Thank you for coming to see me, Lady Sandhurst. I'll arrange that matter we talked about as soon as possible. Please don't hesitate to visit myself and Mrs. Trotter at any time. You're always welcome at the vicarage."

With a fond reply for the vicar and a brief nod to Court, she motioned to her coachman, and the gig pulled away.

Pensively, Court watched the back of the retreating vehicle. So Philippa still hadn't learned to drive, not even a light, two-wheeled carriage with a single horse. It was something he'd promised to teach her. As a girl raised in a boarding school, she'd rarely even ridden in a carriage, until the day he'd come courting.

He remembered her thrill the first time he'd taken her driving in Hyde Park behind two prancing dappled grays. She'd been so excited she'd bounced up and down on the seat like a child at a party. He'd had to tell her to stop wiggling and gawking like a fourteen-year-old miss, or everyone in London would accuse him of robbing the cradle. Her musical laughter had pealed out, causing several male riders nearby to turn and stare at her with worshipful eyes. Every one of his acquaintances had fallen in love with Philippa at first glance.

After the gig had drawn out of sight, the Reverend

Mr. Trotter went to stand beside Court's vehicle. "Would you like to come into the house, Your Grace? I'm sure my wife would be delighted to serve you a cup of tea and a plate of her delicious scones. She baked them this morning."

"No, thank you," Court replied. "As you heard, I'm on my way to the Hall." He quirked his eyebrow in mild inquiry. "I was surprised that you invited Lady Sandhurst to visit your home. I find it hard to imagine that Mrs. Trotter or you would welcome a call from such a notorious woman. Unless, of course, she came to confess her sins."

The clergyman returned Court's gaze thoughtfully. "Had the lady come to make her confession, the matter would, naturally, be confidential. As it happens, Lady Sandhurst came to the vicarage this morning to bring several lovely bouquets for our service on Sunday. And to arrange a baptism for her son. Because of their long sojourn in Venice, the little marquess has never been baptized in the rites of the Church of England."

"I must admit," Court said brusquely, "the thought that Lady Sandhurst came for her son's religious welfare hadn't occurred to me. Someone with her spotted past usually doesn't spend much time in church." Court could have bitten his tongue off at the vicar's admonishing frown. Hell, he sounded like a rejected lover, embittered and smarting. Damn it, he'd better get a firm rein on himself, or people would start to think that he was still in love with the woman.

"Don't be too quick to pass judgment," Trotter cautioned. "No man knows what's in another person's heart." He stepped away from the carriage. "Now, as I believe you're in a hurry, I'll let you go. But I'd like to look down from the pulpit some morning and see Your Grace in attendance at Mass."

"I'm afraid you're doomed to be disappointed, Reverend," Court replied, giving him an apologetic smile to soften his refusal. "God and I parted company quite some time ago. I grew weary of His perverted sense of humor."

"Then let me offer you a little unsolicited advice, Your Grace, which also happens to be the topic of my sermon this coming Sunday. *Judge not, that you may not be judged.*"

With that abbreviated lecture, the vicar saluted in farewell, and Court urged his chestnuts into a quick trot. He paid little heed to the vicar's admonishment. Rather, his thoughts raced ahead to the newfound son who awaited him at Sandhurst Hall. Court had been awake most of the previous night, trying to decide the wisest course of action where Kit was concerned. He knew he wanted only the best for the child. And he was willing to set aside his own desires in order to protect Kit from any unnecessary emotional pain.

Court longed to embrace the boy and tell him that he was his real father. But until he could prove his paternity to the satisfaction of an impartial magistrate, Court knew that such a declaration would only cause the child needless doubt and confusion. If Philippa denied the truth, Kit would naturally believe his mother over the word of a man he'd met only a few days before.

In the end, Court had decided to bide his time. He was determined not to show the anger he felt toward Philippa in Kit's presence. For striking out at her with harsh words or disapproving looks would cause Kit far more suffering than it would cause his wayward, headstrong mother. Court was determined to act as if he were Lady Sandhurst's caring friend and neighbor, no matter what the provocation. No matter if it killed him.

Chapter 9

∞

Later that morning, Warbeck remained secluded in the library with Stanley Tomkinson for over three hours. The sound of their voices raised in sharp disagreement could be heard through the closed door. When midday arrived, a lackey carried in a meal for the two men, who waited in icy silence for the food to be set out on the reference table. It had been a long time since an authoritative male voice had issued orders at Sandhurst Hall. The staff seemed to be going about on tiptoe, aware that what was transpiring in the library very likely meant the end of the old, complaisant regime.

During that time, Philippa waited with Kit in his bedroom. At first, she sat at a small corner table with him, helping him practice the alphabet. He could already write his first name and form most of the letters correctly. She'd been planning on hiring a tutor for him at the end of the summer, but she knew that the decision of who should teach her son to read and write now lay in the hands of the duke of Warbeck. It rankled that she had no say in the matter.

Philippa had slept only a few hours the previous night. Warbeck's threat to move Kit to the Castle terrified her. She'd lain awake, tossing and turning, while she tried to decide what to do should he attempt to force the issue. Her only hope lay in convincing Tobias Howard that the young marquess of Sandhurst should live in his own home.

171

The thought of losing her son filled her with an unspeakable, paralyzing dread. If she lost Kit . . . oh, God above, if she lost Kit there'd be no reason to go on living. Unnamed, barely recognized fears from her childhood surfaced to haunt her like old, familiar phantoms. Would she be left alone in this world—totally alone—once again? She was ready to go down on her knees in front of Warbeck and beg him to let her keep her son. But she knew the duke too well to think an impassioned plea for understanding would sway him. She'd tried that six years ago, and he'd rebuffed every one of her attempts to even speak with him.

With a determined shake of her head, Philippa pushed her demoralizing thoughts aside and concentrated on enjoying Kit's efforts to learn his letters. Eventually, he became bored with the lesson.

"Let's go out to the stable and see the horses," he begged. "I'm tired of staying in my room." He hurried over to the tall window and looked out at the beautiful summer afternoon. "It's not raining today. Why can't we go outside, Mama?"

She strove to hide her nervousness with a cheerful smile. "I've already told you, darling. Your guardian wants to see you this afternoon as soon as he's through going over some business matters with Mr. Tomkinson. His Grace asked that you be here waiting for him." She clenched her hands in her lap, praying silently that Warbeck wasn't planning to tell the child that he was his father.

Kit braced his elbows on the sill and leaned his head through the open window. He was dressed in sturdy nankeen trousers and a plain white shirt. White socks and flat black shoes completed his costume, for Philippa believed that children should wear clothes which allowed them a maximum freedom of movement.

"How much longer will the grand *signóre* be?" he asked impatiently.

"I don't know, dearest. You'll just have to wait until he comes."

There was no mistaking the disgruntlement in Kit's voice or the restlessness behind the long, drawn-out sigh. "That's what I've been doing all morning. Waiting."

The sound of footsteps coming down the hall forestalled Philippa's reply. His boredom forgotten, Kit eagerly turned to welcome their visitor. When her son's face lit up with a wide, cherubic smile, she knew, without turning around, who stood in the open doorway.

"I'm sorry I kept you waiting, Kit," Warbeck said, his deep baritone filling the quiet room. "If it's any consolation, I quit before Mr. Tomkinson and I were through with our work because I knew you were up here, waiting and wondering why you couldn't go outdoors to play." He moved into the room and bowed politely to Philippa. "Lady Sandhurst," he added, "thank you for being so patient."

Warbeck was dressed informally in a dark brown jacket, breeches, and high leather boots. He held his cane in one hand and an enormous package under his arm.

"Mama says you're my guardian," Kit announced ingenuously. "I never had a guardian before. What's in the box?"

"Kit," his mother admonished softly, "it isn't polite to ask prying questions." She met Warbeck's glance, worried at what he might say. He'd corrected Kit's manners at the Black Swan without hesitation. She half expected him to do so now. Philippa had no way to gauge what would be considered the ordinary discipline meted out by a guardian, for she couldn't remember her father and her own guardian hadn't come near her. The only man she'd really observed in a fatherly role was Lady Gabrielle's papa, and he was indulgent to a fault.

Warbeck's warm chuckle told her he wasn't offended by Kit's free and easy behavior. He handed the large box wrapped in pale blue paper to the boy. "It's a present for you, Kit," he said. "Go on, open it."

Kit grinned in unabashed delight as he balanced the package on both arms and held it out in front of him. "Is that what guardians do?" he asked happily. "Give people presents?"

"Among other things," Warbeck replied.

Philippa's heart leaped at the tenderness in his words. Perhaps her fears were unfounded. Suddenly breathless, she lifted her eyebrows in a silent appeal, begging him wordlessly not to say anything to upset Kit. Surely he would speak to her first before blurting out any shocking announcements to an unsuspecting five-year-old. But when Warbeck glanced at her again, his silvery gaze was inscrutable.

Kit carried the gift over to where his mother sat. Placing it on her lap, he looked up at the duke, his gray eyes alight with impatience. "Can I open it now, *signóre?*"

"Certainly," Warbeck said. Leaning on his cane, he followed the boy to the chaise longue.

"Go on, then," Philippa encouraged.

Kit slipped a small white envelope from under the blue satin ribbon and handed it to her. "Read it to me, Mama."

Her fingers trembling slightly, Philippa opened the envelope and pulled out a card printed in Warbeck's bold, thick lettering. *"For the finest young man in England,"* she read in a shaky voice. *"Welcome home."*

Lowering her head, she bit her lip and blinked back tears of thanksgiving that suddenly blurred her vision. She could only surmise the depth of emotion behind those few, carefully phrased words, but she was certain that they didn't come close to conveying the message Warbeck longed to write.

"Thank you, *nòbile,*" Kit said, blissfully unaware of the tension that swirled around him. "I'm glad to be in England. But it doesn't feel like home yet. I miss the gondolas on the canals." He tore off the paper and lifted the lid. "Soldiers!" he cried gleefully. "Just like I wanted!" He lifted out a finely carved dragoon and held it up for closer inspection.

Philippa stared down in surprise. The large box contained two entire armies, dressed in uniforms of amazingly accurate detail, including fringed epaulettes, gold braiding, and fur trim. There were hussars, dragoons, cuirassiers, grenadiers, carabineers, and lancers. Magnificent cavalry horses pranced and curvetted, the shiny brass rivets on their saddles and harnesses newly polished. It was a young boy's dream come true.

"They're *magnifico, signóre!*" Kit exclaimed in awe. "They're wonderful!"

"I thought you'd like them." Warbeck beamed with satisfaction at the child's wholehearted enthusiasm. He braced himself on his cane and dropped down on one knee next to the boy. "They're British and French soldiers representing all the arms of service. I had a feeling that Lady Harriet wouldn't find the ones that belonged to . . . ah . . . to your father. I remembered that both of ours had once been stored away in a chest in my old nursery. We often played together when we were your age, so he kept his army with mine."

"What do you say, Kit?" Philippa prompted in a smothered voice, scarcely able to believe what Warbeck had done. Good God, had he forgotten that he was betrothed? The offspring from his future marriage should inherit his childhood treasures.

Sensing Philippa's uneasiness, Court met her gaze. The stricken expression on her face revealed her alarm. Deep shadows beneath her eyes attested to the fact that he wasn't the only one who'd paced the bedroom floor for the larger part of the night. Seeing how pale and wan she looked, compassion assailed him.

Yet even in her exhausted state, she was enchanting. Her bright yellow dress nearly matched the color of her hair, which was piled loosely on top of her head in a bounty of artless curls. The gown's short puffed sleeves left her graceful arms bare, the creamy skin smooth and incredibly alluring. Memories of those sweet arms wrapped around his naked body surfaced, bringing their customary torment.

When he'd finally fallen asleep last night, he'd dreamed of her. A wonderfully erotic dream. But the wanderings of his unconscious mind didn't excuse his present lustful imaginings. Bloody hell, did he have no control over his thoughts even when he was awake? Nothing seemed to make sense anymore. How could he desire a woman he despised? Dammit, when he looked into those enormous violet-blue eyes, he wasn't completely convinced that he did despise her.

"*Gràzie, signóre! Gràzie!*" Kit threw his arms about Court's neck, bringing him quickly back to the present. "They're exactly what I wanted."

Court clasped the child in his arms, hugging him so tight he could feel the energy radiating from the small body. For a brief moment, he brushed his cheek against Kit's thick black hair before setting him free. "You're welcome," he said.

"Will you help me set them up, *nòbile?*"

"Yes, but not now, young man. Right now, we're going to begin your lessons."

The change in Kit's demeanor was unmistakable. "I already practiced my letters with Mama this morning," he said, his face mirroring his disappointment. "And wrote my name four times."

"That's good," Court commended as he used his cane to lever himself to his feet. "I want you to study with your mother whenever she says. But writing the alphabet is not what I had in mind for this afternoon. Today, you'll begin to learn the fine art of fishing."

"Fishing!" Kit bounced up and down in excitement. "Are you going to take me fishing? When, *signóre*? When?"

"Right now. As soon as you're ready."

"Can Mama go too?"

Philippa held her breath. Surely, Warbeck wouldn't try to take Kit on an excursion without her? Or did the fact that he was Kit's legal guardian allow him to do just that? And while the duke was alone with her son, what would he say to him?

Kit, I'm your father?

Warbeck met her gaze, a rueful half smile twisting his mouth. "If your mother wants to join us, she's welcome to come along."

Quickly, Philippa sprang to her feet. "I'd love to go with you. Fishing is one of my favorite pastimes. I'll tell Mrs. Babcock to have a basket of food packed while I change my clothes."

"There's no need to summon the housekeeper," Warbeck said. "I've already arranged that. But if you want to put on a more serviceable dress, you'll have to hurry. And bring a warm shawl for yourself and a jacket for Kit. We'll be late getting back to the Hall, and the evenings are cool. We'll leave in fifteen minutes."

Not wasting a second, Philippa called over her shoulder as she hurried to the adjoining bedchamber, "I'll be ready in five."

Kit held up a large, wriggling earthworm between his thumb and forefinger. "Here, Mama," he offered with a magnanimous smile, "you can have this big, fat one."

"Oh, that's all right, darling," Philippa said brightly, while her insides churned at the thought of touching the crawly thing. "You go ahead and use it. I'll just sit here and watch for a little while longer."

Warbeck looked up from the hook he was baiting for Kit and sent her a taunting grin. He'd removed his coat and cravat and left them on the seat of his open carriage, then rolled his sleeves up, displaying powerful forearms. Dressed in doeskin breeches that were molded to his corded thighs, tall boots, and a plain linen shirt that stood open at the collar, revealing a patch of crisp black hair at the base of his neck, he was the image of the rugged sportsman.

"You can't expect your mother to bait her own hook, Kit," the duke said with an air of male superiority. "Women are too squeamish to touch worms."

"I'm not squeamish," Philippa denied. She folded her arms and tried to look bored with the idea of impaling a living creature on a sharp steel hook. "I'm simply waiting for both of you to begin before trying my luck." What she didn't want to admit was that the idea of actually holding a worm, let alone any hapless fish that might be so unfortunate as to try to swallow it, made her queasy. But she was determined not to make a silly goose of herself by letting her son or her former husband in on her humiliating secret. She'd never been fishing in her life. It was only one more example of how restricted her existence had been. Until she'd met Warbeck, Philippa's life had been circumscribed by a few square blocks in Chelsea.

Sheltered from the warm July sun, she sat on a red-and-black plaid blanket which had been spread on the grass beneath a giant willow tree. The fishing gear lay piled on the ground nearby, and beyond the gear flowed the rushing stream. She'd exclaimed in delight when they'd first arrived. A profusion of alders grew along the bank, casting their shade over the sparkling water. Drifts of comfrey, with their bell-shaped lavender blooms, followed the shoreline. Forget-me-nots grew in the cool of the undercut bank, their sky blue flowers a bright contrast against the dark green vegetation. Philippa sighed with pleasure. The task of learning to fish might be somewhat daunting, but the setting was idyllic.

Kit paused in seeking the fattest worms in the

bucket. "What's squeamish?" he asked Warbeck, his young face bright with curiosity.

"Squeamish is what makes females scream like bedlamites when they see a mouse. Have you ever seen a woman do that?"

Kit's gray eyes grew round with speculation. "I never saw a bed'mite, sir, but in Venice, I saw Cook jump up on a chair once, when a rat ran through her kitchen. Her face turned red and her eyes bugged out. I had to get help 'cause I couldn't catch it myself. It was too fast!"

"You need a good terrier to catch a rat," Court explained. He moved to a fallen oak tree that lay along the edge of the bank. "Do you have a dog of your own?"

Kit trotted after him, carrying the wooden tackle box. He placed the box on the log's rough bark with reverent hands, clearly awed that he had such a marvelous treasure in his possession. Earlier, Court had filled it with several old hooks, an extra line, and assorted flies and lures.

"I don't have a dog of my own," Kit admitted, "but my grandma has five hounds. She lets me pet them whenever I want."

"Every boy needs a dog of his own," Court said absently as he checked the float and sinker.

"Yes, *signóre*," agreed Kit with unreserved enthusiasm.

Court watched his son clamber up on the fallen log to sit beside the scarred, old tackle box and felt an unaccustomed sense of peace seep into his soul. The place was filled with memories, both bitter and sweet. His two companions were unaware that they stood on Warbeck land. The Castle was only a few miles away, hidden from view behind the thick stands of trees that surrounded it. This gurgling, swift-moving stream fed into the river that curved past Warbeck Castle. Court had fished its waters since he was Kit's age.

The spot he'd chosen had once been his favorite childhood haunt. Court and his older brother had spent countless summer afternoons in this shady nook. Chris had shown him how to bait a hook, how to acquire an eye for the haunts of trout in rapid water, how to cast a fly upstream and let it float down, and how to keep a fighter on the line. When his brother died at the age of twelve from a virulent fever, Court had come to this exact spot to mourn. He'd sat and cried for hours until his tutor finally discovered him and took him back to the Castle, where his father roughly adjured him to stop bawling and behave like a man. His mother, of course, was in London for the start of the Little Season, but she returned to Castle Warbeck for the funeral. As beautiful as ever, even in black, she'd been accompanied by her current lover, a mincing, lisping fop. Court had been nine years old.

Once Kit was safely perched on the fallen trunk, Court cast the line out and handed him the rod. His son's little body quivered with excitement as he took the cane pole. Court had chosen to use live bait that afternoon, rather than artificial flies, so that Kit would have a better chance of catching some fish. Angling for trout could be frustrating, even for an adult. If Kit could catch several panfish that afternoon, he would have the grand pleasure of providing supper for his family. Then as he grew older, his father would teach him the techniques required for outsmarting the unpredictable trout.

"Watch that float bobbing about on the water," Court told him. "If you see it disappear, call me."

"Yes, *signóre*," Kit said, staring at the stream's surface with a look approaching ecstasy.

Next, Court baited a hook for Philippa, who sat waiting on the blanket with a wary expression. It hadn't been part of his plan to bring her along, but the heartfelt plea in Kit's eyes when he'd asked if his mother could come had decided the issue. So there she was, all tense and tight, and looking as ill at ease as a vicar's wife at a cockfight. She'd changed from the gauzy yellow gown she'd worn earlier to a worn brown-and-beige striped dress. A faint grass stain was visible across the front of the skirt just below knee level. A gypsy straw bonnet with a wide yellow ribbon lay on the blanket beside her.

"Come on," he said, motioning for her to join them on the bank. "This pole is for you."

"Truly, I'm in no hurry," she countered with a nervous flutter of her fingers. "You two go ahead while I watch."

"Please fish with us, Mama," Kit called. "It won't be nearly as much fun if you don't."

Reluctantly, Philippa rose and went to stand beside Court. A deep frown etched a crease between her delicately arched brows as she stared down at the baited hook. With a grimace of distaste, she cupped her hand beside her mouth and whispered to Court, "Doesn't that hurt the poor creature?"

"It won't feel a thing once it hits the cold water," Court assured her solemnly, trying to keep his amusement hidden. "Would you like me to cast the line for you?"

"No, I'll do it," she said. She pursed her lips in concentration and took the rod, holding it high in one fist like the handle of a parasol. Then she walked up to the stream's edge till the tips of her kid half boots were hanging over the lip of the undercut bank and dropped the hook straight down into two inches of water. Court shook his head in disbelief.

"If you keep the line there," he said with a chuckle, "the fish will start nibbling on your toes before they take the bait on your hook. Here, I'll get you started." He pried the bamboo pole from her grasp and, with a flick of his wrist, sent the line sailing out over the stream. "Relax and don't make so much work out of it," he encouraged. "This is supposed to be fun."

Philippa cocked her head and looked up at him. When she saw his grin, her violet eyes sparkled with devilment. "The young ladies at Lillybridge were never given lessons in anything so practical as acquiring one's dinner with a hook and line," she declared primly. "But we can order from a menu in flawless French, so there's no danger we'll ever die of starvation."

"Nothing you've tasted in the finest restaurant will compare to the fish we'll catch today," he informed her.

"Mmm, that is if we catch any."

"*Signóre!*" Kit called out. "I think something's biting my worm!"

Tightening his hold on his cane, Court hurried over to the boy and discovered he was right. The float had submerged, and the tapered end of the pole was bobbing up and down. "Here, let me help you," he said. He showed Kit how to jerk the line up, snagging the fish. "Now bring it in like this," he instructed, demonstrating how to turn the reel's handle. Kit hooted with glee at the sight of the nice fat perch on the end of his line. After the fish was safely landed, Court started to show him how to attach his own bait.

"Oh, oh, oh! Court!" Philippa cried in a high-pitched squeak. "Something's pulling on my hook! What should I do?"

He sped back to her. From the way the sturdy pole was bending in a deep arc, it had to be a big one. "Jerk up on the line," he instructed. She took far too long to follow his directions, so he dropped his cane on the grass, encircled her with his arms from behind, and covered her hands with his. "Like this," he explained as he set the large fish on the hook. The fragrant scent of hyacinths drifted up from her golden hair. He felt the stirrings of desire deep within him. Aware that he was holding Philippa far tighter than necessary, Court released her and stepped back. He fought to keep his voice even, not wanting her to realize how quickly the sensation of having her in his embrace had aroused him. "Now bring in the line slow and steady. Don't let that big fellow get away."

She was far too intent on her goal of landing the fish even to notice that he'd touched her. "I won't if I can help it," she said breathlessly, laughter bubbling up with her excitement.

All at once, her line went slack.

"Oh, no!" she wailed in disappointment. "I've lost it!"

"Maybe not," Court said. "The wily devil might just be trying to trick you." He put his arms around her once again, and the feel of her slim form pressed against his tense body sent a surge of lust spiraling through him. "Pull up," he instructed, determined to ignore the heat in his groin as he guided the pole in her hands. "Now change your position to follow him. That's it. He'll make several runs, then attempt to fall back on the leader and break it." The line tautened, and they could feel the sharp, strong tugs of the enraged fish.

"Don't let it get away, Mama!" shouted Kit. He came charging across the grass, his own pole forgotten where he'd dropped it. "Catch it! Catch it!"

"Don't worry," she assured him, "I'm not going to lose this Goliath." Her buoyant laughter rang out, floating up to the branches above them. "Egads, it's gigantic!" There was another strong pull on the line, and in her exhilaration, she nearly slipped and fell. "Oh, Court," she said in a worried tone, "I'm not so sure I can land it all by myself."

"Just keep reeling the line in," Court instructed. He bent to pick up his cane and a net. "I'll scoop it up when it gets here."

The brown trout came out of the water fighting mad, thrashing wildly about in the churning foam. Court stepped into the streambed, the water swirling about the calves of his high leather boots, and neatly caught it in his net.

"Hurrah!" Kit shouted, executing an impromptu jig. "Hurrah! It's a monster fish! Mama caught a monster!"

"I did it!" Philippa gasped in elation. Her face was flushed with the victory. "Oh, my! Look at the size of it!"

Court lifted her catch out of the netting and held it up. "It's a ten pounder, at least," he said with sincere admiration.

For the rest of the afternoon, Court helped the two novices bait their hooks, reel in the fish, and add them to their stringers. He'd never seen such successful angling. There was no time for him to cast out his own line, for no sooner had he finished helping one, then the other would need his assistance. Mother and son capered about in jubilation each time they landed a fish. They were a pair of uninhibited madcaps, and he found himself chuckling at their zany behavior. Philippa's spontaneity and effervescence had captivated him from the moment he'd met her. It was no surprise that her son possessed the same endearing qualities. He tried to caution them, without success, that they were going to scare the fish away. After a while, it didn't matter. They caught so many, they had to start throwing them back in, anyway.

The two fishermen finally quit so they could all eat the meal packed in an enormous picnic basket. Soon the delicious aroma of meat pies and raspberry tarts mingled with the pungent scents of trampled grass, damp earth, and freshly caught fish. The Sandhurst cook had included a bottle of port for the grown-ups and a jug of lemonade for Kit. Afterward, replete and content, Court stretched out full length on the plaid wool and pillowed his head in his hands. Kit immediately followed suit, mirroring Court's every movement.

Keeping her gaze away from Warbeck's virile body

lying flat on his back beside her, Philippa gathered the remainder of the food and stored it in the wicker hamper. The sight of him, relaxed and no longer scowling at her, brought a nervous flutter to her stomach. They were so close, she could have reached out and touched him. She'd been agonizingly aware of his strong arms around her as he'd helped her land that first fish. The longing to rest her head against his broad chest, if only for a moment, had nearly overpowered her.

Seeing Kit unconsciously imitating the handsome, dark-haired duke, whom he resembled so closely, brought a sense of sharp foreboding to her. She hadn't envisioned such a strong and immediate attachment could form between them. Yet she wouldn't have missed this lesson in angling for all the world. It had been a marvelous afternoon, rare and fine. One that she and her son would remember for years to come.

"Fishing's fun, sir," Kit confided cheerfully.

"It is that," Warbeck agreed.

Kit rolled to his side and propped himself up on one elbow, regarding his new friend thoughtfully. "I like having you for my guardian," he said at last.

Warbeck turned his head, still cradled in his stacked hands, and returned the boy's scrutiny. "I like being your guardian, Kit."

Minutes passed as the two just looked at each other, and then, out of the blue, the little boy stated in a clear, trusting voice, "You have eyes just like mine, *signóre.*"

Warbeck went completely still. "Do I?" he said cautiously.

From the corner of her eye, Philippa could see her son gazing serenely on his father's stunned face. She sat frozen, her hands outspread over the picnic hamper as though invoking a mealtime blessing.

"Yes, sir," the youthful voice piped without guile. "I never met anyone with eyes like mine. Everyone in Venice had brown eyes, except for Mama. And hers are purple. Do you like having gray eyes?"

Warbeck cleared his throat. "I, ah, never thought much about it, Kit. My father and brother had the same color as mine. So does my grandmother, Lady Augusta." His words were gentle. "Why do you ask? Don't you like having gray eyes?"

Kit sat up and shrugged in abashment. "I didn't use to. I didn't like being different." He smiled shyly at Warbeck. "But now, I don't mind at all."

"Why, Kit," Philippa said softly, her heart aching for her son's sense of isolation. "I never knew you felt that way. Sweetheart, I think you have the most beautiful eyes in the world."

Warbeck's gaze flew to hers, and she realized, too late, what she'd just given away in her attempt to comfort her son. For a moment, the incredulity on the man's face was too much to bear. Then a mask of indifference settled on his hawkish features.

Oblivious to the duke's chagrin, Kit crawled over the man's muscled torso and moved to stand behind his mother. He bent down and wrapped his arms about her neck. "*You* have the prettiest eyes in the world, Mama."

She reached behind her and tickled his ribs. "You'd *better* say that," she teased, "or I'll never tell you another bedtime story again."

Kit doubled up with laughter. "Help me, *signóre!*" he yelled. "She's going to tickle me to death!"

Warbeck sat up and, in one smooth motion, lifted Kit to safety high over his head. "Your only chance is to counterattack," he advised.

"Yes! " Kit agreed. "Let's tickle Mama."

Philippa sprang up. "Oh, no," she cried. "You'll never catch me!" She tore across the grassy clearing and into a stand of trees. With Kit riding on Warbeck's shoulders, and the man leaning heavily on his cane, they followed in hot pursuit. Philippa hid behind an enormous oak tree and listened to them crashing through the undergrowth. Barely able to keep from giggling out loud, she clamped her fingers tightly over her mouth and waited for them to draw nearer. At the last moment, she leaped from her hiding place. "Clever varlets!" she said. "But not clever enough." She dodged their outstretched hands and raced back to the blanket, where she fell to the ground.

"Tickle her, sir!" Kit commanded.

"You're too late," she said on a gurgle of laughter. She lifted her hand in warning. "This blanket is my magic castle. No one can touch me here, or he'll be turned into a warty toad."

"Aw, she always does that," the boy confided to Warbeck. "It's 'cause she's a girl and doesn't play fair."

Warbeck lifted Kit down and placed him beside Philippa, then joined them on the blanket. Still laughing, she gathered her son in her arms and kissed him soundly on his rosy cheek. "It's because I'm a witch," she said with a shrill cackle, "and I eat little boys for breakfast." She turned Kit to face Court and whispered in her son's ear, "You can't tickle me, but what about him?"

Kit leaped upon Warbeck, who conveniently fell over on the wool plaid. "Help me, Mama!" the boy hollered. "Help me tickle him till he surrenders!"

Without thinking, Philippa joined in the mayhem. Before she knew it, Warbeck had a muscular arm about each of them, pinning their arms to their sides and crushing them close to his solid rib cage.

Certain of victory, Court squeezed them against his ribs, till they were the ones who had to cry out in surrender.

"I give up!" Kit yelped between gulps of air. "I give up, *signóre!*"

"I yield, too," Philippa said breathlessly, her eyes alight with merriment. Her nose was only inches from his chin, her full, pink lips just an instant away. Court fought the demented urge to bend his head and cover her mouth with his own. If it hadn't been for Kit's presence, he might have given in to the temptation. She froze and stared at him in startled bewilderment, as though only just aware that she was locked against his body.

With a pang of agonizing regret, Court realized that *this* was what it would have been like if Philippa hadn't run off with Sandhurst. They would have played with their son during the day and lain in each other's arms at night, while their child slept peacefully in the nursery nearby. The bitter ache for what might have been consumed him. He released both mother and child and sat up.

"We'd better start back to the Hall," he said gruffly, withdrawing behind a wall of indifference, lest he reveal to her just how deeply she'd hurt him. "The sun's already starting to set. It will be dark before we get there."

Later, as Court drove his blooded chestnuts along the familiar country road, he glanced down at the two passengers on the seat beside him. Kit had quickly fallen sound asleep, his head pillowed on his mother's lap. For the last twenty minutes, Philippa had fought the drowsiness that threatened to overtake her, but lost the battle in the end. Now, she slept, too, her head resting on Court's shoulder, his arm around her.

Above them in the velvety night sky, a million stars twinkled brightly. Court gazed up at the constellations, picking out Ursa Major and Minor with ease. As he pondered the enormity of the universe, he tried to come to grips with the conflicting emotions that had racked him all afternoon. Certain that logic and practicality would win out, as they always did with him, he made a mental list of his conclusions.

First, he wanted Philippa. Aye, he wanted her, and it would do him no good to deny it. Bloody hell, what was so unusual about a man lusting after the mother of his son?

Second, Sandhurst was gone. No matter how much Philippa had loved him, the man was dead and buried. Court was certain that eventually he could make her forget that smooth-tongued lothario. Nor was it so unusual for a cuckolded husband to forgive his unfaithful wife. Christ, that happened all the time, as well. Why should he wait until she'd formed an attachment to some braying jackass who'd try to push his way into Kit's life as a stepfather?

Third, the three of them belonged together. There was only Court's pride keeping them apart, and he was willing to swallow an inordinate amount of it, in order to regain the family that had been stolen from him. Of course, this time he'd have to keep a strict rein on Philippa. Her naturally high spirits would need to be closely tethered. But he could do it, now that he knew she could so easily be led astray. He was older, more mature, and far more worldly than he'd been nearly a half dozen years ago. And he wanted his family so deeply, so totally, that he was ready to move heaven and earth to get them back.

The fact that he was promised to be married in the fall to a woman of unimpeachable character bothered him only a little. Naturally, Lady Clare Brownlow would have to be the one to break off the engagement. He, as a gentleman, was bound by his word. But when she realized that her fiancé wished to be free, she would surely accommodate him. Clare had no reason to be recalcitrant. There had been no passion between them. They'd exchanged only a chaste betrothal kiss in front of her parents. No one as honorable and upright as Clare would consider forcing an unwilling man to marry her.

As the lights of Sandhurst Hall came into view,

Court called to the house with a cheery hello. He smiled to himself, experiencing a feeling of real hope for the first time in six long years. Tomorrow, he'd begin to set things right.

Chapter 10

"I never saw a lovelier sight."

Philippa looked up with a start from where she crouched beside the row of mossy garden pots. "You're admiring my flowers, kind sir?" she asked gaily.

"Among other things." Warbeck stood in the open doorway of the greenhouse, one shoulder propped against the jamb, his cane held loosely in his hand. With the dazzling morning sunshine behind him, she could distinguish only the outline of his frame, but there was no mistaking those broad shoulders and lean hips or the rich, deep timbre of his voice. He'd caught her by surprise. For most of the morning, the duke had been secluded in the library with Mr. Tomkinson, the head steward.

Holding a large blue-and-white china pitcher half-filled with water, Philippa rose and smiled shyly. When they had arrived at Sandhurst Hall the previous night, she'd awakened to find she had been resting her head on his shoulder while she slept. The feel of his arm placed protectively around her had seemed so natural, she thought she was dreaming about her long-ago honeymoon. Momentarily bewildered, she'd stared up into thick-lashed silvery eyes that seemed to be gazing at her with incredible tenderness. It had probably been the moonlight playing tricks on her sleep-drugged mind. She wished she

191

could see his eyes clearly now, to be certain she'd been deluded.

"Kit's playing in the stables," she explained, convinced that was who he'd come looking for. "You'll probably find him pestering one of the grooms to let him help. I tried to get him interested in assisting me in the conservatory, but to an active five-year-old boy flowers aren't nearly as fascinating as a stable full of horses."

"I know," he replied. "I spoke to Kit before I came here. He was standing on an overturned bucket and brushing the coat of a very gentle mare under the supervision of his pretty nursemaid and an admiring young stable boy named Max." The duke remained in the doorway, the look in his eyes still obscured by the sun's radiant glare. "The nursemaid was doing the supervising," he clarified, "and Max was admiring the maid."

She laughed at the wry observation. "Miss O'Dwyer's charms are admirable, indeed. But I'm surprised Kit isn't trailing behind you like a shadow."

Warbeck made no reply. He walked into the cool recesses of the glasshouse to where she stood next to a cluttered gardening table. Her straw bonnet and dusty canvas gloves lay on one corner, next to a pile of orange clay pots, shears, trowels, and a stack of wicker baskets. Taking the handle of the heavy pitcher she held, he set it beside its twin on the rough wooden tabletop. Only moments before, she'd completed an arrangement of freshly cut blue delphiniums and bachelor's buttons, sweet peas in pastel shades of pink and lavender, Queen Anne's lace, and deep red rambling roses.

"The arrangement is lovely," he repeated. "I didn't know you had such a flair for horticulture." His slow, tantalizing smile seemed almost a caress in the muted light. Good Gad, her brain was playing tricks on her.

She could see his eyes now. They held a glimmer of deviltry, reminding her of the first time she'd met him. He'd teased her unmercifully about her sudden, unexpected, and unannounced appearance on the London scene, till she'd broken into peals of laughter. It had been fun to torment him in return by refusing to tell him more than her name. He'd even tried to steal a kiss, for which he'd received a stinging rebuke. The rebuff hadn't seemed to daunt him, however. Warbeck had been intense and unswerving in his pursuit of her from the moment they'd met.

Philippa smiled at the memory of that initial encounter. "I don't know anything about horticulture," she admitted. She pointed to the flowers that sat in a dented tin bucket of water on the table, waiting to be placed in the second pitcher. "I'm merely making use of Lady Harriet's uncanny talent for growing exquisite blooms. Displaying them to advantage is the easy part."

"Go ahead. Don't let me interrupt you," Warbeck said. "I'll just stand here and watch. I gave you a lesson in trout fishing yesterday afternoon. You can teach me something about making bouquets this morning."

Philippa picked up a short branch cut from a green apple tree and wedged it into the large china pitcher. "I know you didn't come to the nursery for a lesson in flower arrangement," she said. "Was there something in particular you wanted?"

"Not especially," Court lied. Each time he was with her, it became harder to remember that she'd betrayed him. As the months had turned into years, he'd tried to forget his lost bride with a score of other women. It had never worked before. Why should he think it would be any different now? The truth was he couldn't stop wanting her. He wasn't sure anymore that he even cared to try.

The moist air in the hothouse was filled with the scent of summer blossoms. In the light coming through the glass panes above them, Philippa's lustrous hair shone like a bright yellow flag. The tall, dark green fronds growing in slatted containers on the shelves around them cast intricate shadows over her ivory complexion and pale muslin dress.

"Did you enjoy your fishing expedition yesterday?" he asked quietly. Something in his voice must have alerted her. She paused and looked up, her brilliant eyes large and wary.

"Very much," she said on a slow exhalation of breath. "Kit and I had a wonderful time. We hope you did, too."

Court took a step closer, his pulse accelerating wildly at the mere thought of taking her into his arms. His words were thick and husky. "I can't think of when I've had a more pleasant afternoon. We'll have to go fishing again sometime."

She looked at him suspiciously. "I'm sure you've already been invited to stay for our luncheon," she said with a nervous smile. "Since our cook will be preparing the trout you helped land, Kit insists that you join us."

"He mentioned as much when I saw him in the stables a few minutes ago," Court said with a low chuckle. "I told him I'd be happy to stay and feast on his catch, if that was all right with his lovely mother."

She met his steady gaze, clearly surprised at the warmth in his voice. "Of course," she said, her cheeks blooming like the rambling roses she held in her hand. "You're most welcome to stay."

He waited in silence as she returned to her work. When she'd completed the arrangement, she leaned back slightly and cocked her head to study the light, airy effect she'd created. Like its counterpart beside it, the enormous bouquet was asymmetrical, yet pleasingly balanced, its varied blossoms loose and natural.

"There," she said at last, "now I have one for the

library and one for Lady Harriet's sitting room." She reached across the table and picked up a small jasperware vase filled with hyacinths, which had been partially hidden behind the pile of wicker baskets. "And of course, these personal favorites are for my bedchamber," she confided, her lips curving in a winsome smile. She lifted the stalks of spiked blooms to her nose, inhaled, and sighed deeply.

Court took a step nearer. "Philippa," he began, then halted. He stared down at the hyacinths that for centuries had been a symbol of rebirth and renewal. He couldn't tell her that every spring for the last six years, he'd smelled their sweet perfume and longed for her. Instead, he silently laid his cane on the table beside the china pitcher, grasped her by the waist with both hands, and drew her gently to him. She didn't resist. She slid the tips of her fingers up the sleeves of his jacket to rest on his upper arms and leaned toward him, ever so slightly. It was the first hint she'd given that she, too, felt a stirring of their old desire.

Then, as though suddenly realizing what she'd just done, she tried to draw back. "The lesson in floral displays is over," she stated breathlessly, her gaze tangled in his. She ran the tip of her delectable pink tongue over her upper lip, and he groaned deep in his chest. "You can help me carry the flowers into the house, if you'd like," she added in a frantic afterthought.

"I'd like that," he agreed hoarsely. "But there's something I'm going to do first. Something I've wanted to do ever since I helped you land that first trout."

Her violet-blue eyes were enormous. "What's that?"

"This."

He covered her mouth with his, cupping the back of her head to steady her. With the other arm, he pulled her slender form against him, till he could feel her slim thighs and flat stomach through the gauzy lavender gown. A rage of hunger swept through him, insistent and insatiable. He was starving for the feel of her soft lips, the satin touch of her bare skin, the sweet taste of her mouth. He swept his tongue across her closed lips in an urgent demand, and she opened them willingly, allowing him access to the irresistible honey inside. Their tongues tangled in a joyous reunion.

Greedily, his hands roamed down the delicate curve of her spine and over her firm buttocks, bringing her ever tighter, ever closer to his blatant need. The moment she felt his throbbing erection, she tried to pull away, to deny that she wanted this as much as he did, but he wouldn't let her. He shifted his mouth, pressing, coaxing, stroking with his tongue, till he felt her arms tighten around his neck as she returned his embrace.

Gasping for air, she broke the sensuous kiss and tilted her head back, her beautiful eyes squeezed tight. "What are we doing?" she moaned. "This is madness."

He didn't answer, knowing she was probably right. But if this was madness, he didn't want to be sane. He dropped light kisses on her jaw and neck and nuzzled at the hollow of her throat as he worked his way downward to the satin mounds that swelled enticingly above the low, square neckline of her dress. Christ, he remembered every silken inch of her as if it were only yesterday since they'd last made love. Her round, perfect breasts with their uptilted pink tips, the little navel that jutted out, instead of in, the tiny mole just above the cluster of springy, golden brown curls had been forever burned into his brain in the raging fire of their passion. He shuddered as the image of her cool, tapering fingers curving sweetly around his hot, naked flesh nearly sent him to his knees.

"Oh, Court," Philippa whispered, her heart pound-

ing madly. His warm, moist tongue dipped into the
crevice of her breasts, and she clung to him, reveling
in the vibrant hardness of his virile male physique.
She bracketed his face with her hands, and he lifted
his head to cover her mouth with his, once again. It
was a wildly passionate kiss that seemed to go on
and on.

Their breathing grew heavy and ragged as he
rocked her back and forth against his powerful
thighs. She could feel the bulge of his arousal pressing against the juncture of her legs. Deep within her,
carnal desire spread like a thick, enervating mist,
making her limbs heavy and languid. She had the
sensation of lying atop him, the way she'd done so
often in their soft feather bed. Even in their sleep,
they had clung to each other, arms and legs en-
twined. She had sometimes wakened to find him
deep inside her, bringing her to a shattering climax
just as she reached full consciousness.

Now she returned his voluptuous kisses, ignoring
the frenzied voice inside that told her what she was
doing was worse than foolhardy. It was insane! God
above, she knew he would bring only heartbreak. But
her flesh and bones had yearned for his arms, for his
lips, for his passionate embrace, too long to be denied. She knew what it felt like to have his strong
male hands move over her naked skin, the deep, pul-
sating pleasure he could create with his skillful, practiced fingers. He had kept her spellbound all these
years, as though he really were a warlock who had
the power to ensnare a woman's soul forever.

Court cupped her breast in his hand, his thumb
rubbing back and forth over the taut nipple through
the thin fabric of her dress. Her body responded unconsciously, arching back against the strong arm that
held her imprisoned in a band of steel. A plaintive
sob deep in her throat revealed what she'd longed to
keep secret. She wanted him. After all the pain and

sorrow and heartache he'd caused her, she still wanted him.

"I want you, Philippa," he said thickly, as he slipped his fingers inside her bodice to caress her bare breasts.

The intimate touch sent a thrill of desire caroming through her. Shocked by the intensity of her need, she shook her head in denial. "We can't ... We mustn't."

"We can," Court insisted. But despite his words, he summoned his iron will and slowly released her. They could be interrupted at any moment by their son, if Kit took it into his head to come looking for them. Placing his hands on either side of Philippa's slender hips, Court braced his palms on the rough wooden board behind her, trapping her between his much larger body and the heavy table. His breathing was labored and broken, his voice harsh and raspy with sexual desire. "This isn't the way I'd planned my proposal, but it's what I'd come to say."

Dazed, she looked up at him with heavy-lidded, luminous eyes. Her parted lips were reddened and swollen with his kisses, her milky complexion delicately flushed with passion. "What ... what did you come to say?"

"I came to propose marriage a second time."

"A second time?" she asked in a muddled voice. As the realization of what he'd implied struck home, the shock and bewilderment on her finely chiseled features told him how unexpected his words really were. "You're mad!" she cried, attempting to shove his arms away.

He grasped her shoulders and held her in place. "Calm down and listen for a minute," he said soothingly. "There are several very good reasons why we should get married again. First of all, for Kit's sake. Surely, you must know that in the short time I've known him, I've come to love him. And I can see how deeply attached he is to you. I don't want to upset Kit or cause him to suffer in any way, but I fully intend to play a role in his life."

"You already play a role in his life," she pointed out, her voice rising on every syllable. "You're his guardian!"

"I'm his father," Court stated in a tone that wouldn't be denied. "If we were married, it would be so much simpler and better for everyone."

Furious, Philippa met his presumptuous gaze with a scowl of disbelief. "What are your other good reasons?" she snapped.

He ran his hands up and down her arms in an appeasing, conciliatory gesture. "If you marry me, you'll no longer have to worry that I'll take Kit away from you," he assured her. She gasped in outrage at the scarcely veiled coercion. Recognizing his misstep, he hurriedly continued. "Not only that, but we can give Kit the little brother or sister he deserves. He's five years old. He needs a family around him."

She flushed with embarrassment at Court's philosophical pronouncement and all it bespoke. The idea of becoming pregnant again with his seed brought a flood of tempestuous emotions. Speechless, she lowered her head and stared at the toes of his shiny leather boots.

"You can't tell me you don't want another child," Court said, immediately pressing his advantage. She trembled in his hands at the softly spoken words. Elated, he smiled at the top of her golden curls, knowing he'd just discovered the one real chink in her armor. "I've seen you with our son, Philippa. You're a wonderful mother. Haven't you ever thought about having a little girl to primp and pamper? Or another little boy like Kit to love?"

She raised her head, her eyes filled with doubt and confusion. Clearly, she'd thought quite often about having another child. Her voice shook with the strain of her tortured feelings. "How could we ever live together after all that's between us?"

His spirits soared. The first rampart had been breached. She hadn't refused him outright. "Let's set all that aside," he urged huskily. He dropped feathery kisses on her forehead, her fluttering eyelids, and the tip of her dainty nose. When she lifted her lips for his kiss, he wrapped his arms around her and covered her mouth with his own. She returned his kiss and his embrace, pressing eagerly against his rapacious body. "I want to forget about the past," he murmured in her small pink ear. "I'm ready to forgive and start anew."

Philippa stiffened in his arms and pulled back. His smug assumption that he was the injured party slashed her burgeoning hopes to ribbons. The staggering ache in her chest left her momentarily breathless. *"You're ready to forgive me?"* Her words were strident and shrill. "I know what you're after, Warbeck. You're willing to take back a flawed, stained woman in order to gain a child you believe is your son. But I don't intend to play the role of the deceitful wife, who's generously pardoned by her magnanimous husband. Once you had your hands on Kit, you'd lock me in seclusion in the country for the rest of my life."

"That's not true," he said. But his strong jaw tightened at her incisive accusation.

"Oh, no? Then what did you intend to do? Watch me day and night to make certain I remained faithful?" She knew she'd struck the target dead center from the wrathful glower on his hawkish features.

"Naturally, I'll provide you with the direction and authority necessary to keep you from straying again," he said tersely. "This time I won't be remiss in administering the husbandly guidance I failed to give you when you were an impulsive chit of eighteen."

Incensed at his self-righteous attitude when the whole wretched divorce was his own doing, Philippa lashed out bitterly. "Aren't you forgetting something rather important, Your Grace? You're already betrothed. Or did you intend to break your word to Lady Brownlow the way you broke your sworn oath to me?"

"What the hell are you talking about?" he thundered. "I was never unfaithful to you, and you damn well know it!"

Philippa lifted her eyebrows and stared at him in feigned surprise. "Oh, then the talk of all your steamy, sordid affairs have just been rumors?"

"I've been a free man for the last five years," he grated through clenched teeth. He gripped the dragon head cane with whitened knuckles as he glared at her.

"Ah, but I do remember your promising before God and a clergyman to cleave only to me until death. You say you're willing to forgive my past indiscretions, but I'm afraid I can't find it in my heart to be so noble. *I don't forgive you.*"

She tried to slip past him, heading for the door. Before she'd taken two steps, he caught hold of her wrist and brought her to an abrupt halt. "We're not through with this discussion," he roared, all pretense at rational consideration abandoned.

"Don't be so upset about my unexpected refusal," Philippa said scornfully. She jerked on her hand, attempting without success to break his hold. "Your marriage to Clare Brownlow will bring you a large dowry to add to your already fat coffers, unlike the burned-out ruin I brought with me. But now that you've so kindly pointed out the benefits of another union, I can see what splendid rewards of marital bliss I've been missing. I *should* provide Kit with a father to guide him, with brothers and sisters to play with, and myself with a spouse to protect me from unwarranted assaults like this. But I intend to marry a man who loves me enough to trust me."

"You little witch," he snarled, drawing her closer. He bent her arm behind her, exerting just enough pressure to keep her pinned against his larger frame.

"Don't ever forget that I'm Kit's legal guardian," he warned. "It's up to me and Rockingham to decide if any man would make a good stepfather for the boy."

She quivered with indignation. "You don't have the right to say if I can marry again! The permission for me to remarry was stipulated in the Bill of Divorcement."

"Aye, that's true," he admitted with a derisive grin. "But I do have the authority to say if Kit can live in the same house with the bloody sot, whoever the blasted hell you're thinking of." He released her, and she stumbled backwards, caught her balance, and whirled to go.

"One more thing, Lady Sandhurst," he called. She paused in the open doorway, not deigning to look back at him. "I'm taking Kit on a short trip to the seacoast to look at some property I intend to purchase with some of his funds. I want the boy to see the place first, just to be sure he likes it. You're welcome to come along, if you wish."

An icy dread washed over Philippa. She turned slowly to meet his taunting gaze. The man was diabolically clever. He'd take Kit with him under the ruse of instructing the young heir in his responsibilities. If she refused to go along with them, it would be her decision, not his. No doubt, Warbeck would be more than happy to leave her behind at Sandhurst Hall. "You're demented!" she spat out. "I can't go racketing across the countryside with you!"

He stood with his hands folded complacently on the handle of his cane, his sinewy legs widened in a stance of undiluted male superiority. "If you're worried about what people will think, you needn't be," he mocked. "The dowager duchess has agreed to accompany the three of us as a chaperone. I certainly wouldn't want to damage your sterling reputation."

"Whyever not? You've never hesitated to trample on it before."

His aristocratic features hardened. When he spoke,

his voice was chillingly soft and low. "I said I was willing to forget the past, Philippa, but by God . . ." He clenched his fist and took a menacing step forward. "Don't push me too far, or I'll turn you over my knee, here and now, and give you the thrashing you should have received that day in the inn."

She blinked and took two small steps back. The icy fury in his silvery eyes attested to his absolute conviction that she deserved any punishment he chose to mete out. This wasn't the time to bait the enraged bull by professing her innocence or pointing out his patent insanity. "You can't take Kit anywhere without Toby's agreement," she declared calmly. "The two of you are joint guardians, in case you've forgotten." But despite her brave front, Philippa fought the eerie sensation of being trapped in a sorcerer's clutches.

"I already have Rockingham's agreement on the matter," came Warbeck's sardonic reply. "I stopped at Rockingham Abbey this morning before coming here. Kit and I are leaving with Lady Augusta next Wednesday. We'll be gone for a week. I've given orders for his nursemaid to pack his things. If you want to come with us, you have three full days to prepare."

Philippa's heart sank. She was well and truly caught in his snare. He'd known all along that she wouldn't let him take her little boy on a journey without her. Yet the thought of spending time in Warbeck's company after what had just occurred between them filled her with misgiving. She drew a ragged breath and forced herself to speak through dry lips. "I'll be ready."

"Fine," he replied coldly. "Please give my regrets to Kit. I won't be able to stay for your luncheon. I have some business affairs of my own to take care of before we depart. By the way, I plan to dismiss the head steward and most of the other overseers. When we return from our trip, I'll begin searching for their replacements."

Shocked, Philippa took a step closer. "But Sandy trusted those men completely. Most of them have been employed on the Sandhurst estates for years. They all have families. How will they live?"

"How incompetent men make a living is not my concern. Protecting the Sandhurst fortune is. And Stanley Tomkinson's incompetence, if not outright dishonesty, has cost the Sandhurst estates dearly. If he remains in charge of the accounts for many more years, there won't be anything left but an empty title."

"So rather than give the matter closer scrutiny to determine whether there's been a breach of trust or merely a case of poor judgment, you decided to toss the old gentleman and his colleagues into the street. I don't know why I'm surprised. Your reputation for ruthless financial dealings has earned you quite a colorful sobriquet."

His granite jaw clenched, but he made no response to her jeering words. Moments passed as they stared silently into each other's eyes. Then she asked with an insolent toss of her head, "Is that all, Your Grace?"

"This discussion is now at an end, Lady Sandhurst." His frigid gaze raked her. "You have my permission to leave."

Philippa turned on her heel and dashed for the house.

Chapter 11

They traveled in the duke of Warbeck's elegant country carriage across rolling hills toward the sea. It was the middle of July. The early summer rains had left the landscape lush and verdant. Looking out the open window of the coach, Philippa could see why Kent was known as the Garden of England, for they passed through gentle valleys where orchards of cherry, plum, apple, and pear trees grew in abundance. Meadows of tall ryegrass dotted with wild purple orchids, daisies, and white clover stretched between remnants of the vast medieval forest of oaks that had once covered the entire area. Philippa watched the panorama unfold and tried to ignore the fact that Warbeck sat, relaxed and seemingly content, on the seat across from her.

Her thoughts went back to their departure early that morning. Lady Harriet hadn't seemed a bit dismayed to learn that Warbeck was taking her grandson to the coast for a holiday, and that Philippa had decided to accompany them. When the dowager marchioness learned that Lady Augusta was performing the office of chaperone, she'd announced in her usual forthright manner that the sea air and salt water would be a great physic for all of them. Lady Harriet had hugged and kissed each member of the party good-bye, leaving Philippa to wonder how her mother-in-law could be so blindly complaisant.

"Look at my cavalryman, Mama," Kit said from

his place beside her. He held a mounted soldier beneath her nose, heedlessly interrupting his mother's abstracted thoughts.

"He's magnificent," she agreed with a bright, hopefully carefree smile. Philippa was determined to make their visit to the seashore a pleasurable holiday. If she refused to allow her feelings about Kit's overbearing guardian from spoiling it, the trip would be a treasured memory for her son. And should Warbeck purchase the villa with Sandhurst funds, Kit might very likely return there summer after summer for the rest of his life.

She would act the way she wanted to feel, blast it, and not let her deep-seated fears take control of her life. But the fact that they were retracing the exact route she'd taken with her bridegroom after their wedding filled her with an increasing uneasiness.

"That's a captain in the Tenth Light Dragoons," Warbeck explained to the boy. "The regiment's title was changed to the Prince of Wales' Own Royal Hussars after they served with great distinction at Benevente. He's carrying a rifled musket, which is far more accurate than a smoothbore. It's one of the reasons for our eventual success in the Peninsular War."

"Let's have a look at your dashing officer," Lady Augusta said to Kit, who offered it gladly. Leaning forward, she took the mounted horseman in her aged fingers and studied it with interest through her tortoiseshell lorgnette. "La, he is a handsome fellow," the duchess agreed with admiration.

"His Grace gave him to me," Kit told her proudly. He pointed to the large box on the seat beside him. "The soldiers belonged to the grand *signóre* and my father when they were little boys like me."

For a brief instant, Lady Augusta met Warbeck's gaze with an unreadable expression, then she smiled lovingly at the youngster. "I know, child. Arthur Bentinck and Tobias Howard were my grandson's closest friends. They played with their wooden soldiers by the hour when they were your age. We had to threaten to take their armies away and lock them up in a chest just to get those three rascals to come and eat their meals."

Kit nodded knowingly. "That's what my mama does," he confided. He looked over at the duke with a sudden, impish grin. "Did you always eat your vegetables, *signóre?*"

Warbeck chuckled. "Always. My grandmother was a veritable dragon when it came to carrots and peas."

"Ugh!" Kit said. "I hate carrots and peas." His little nose wrinkled in distaste, and the grown-ups smiled at his unqualified disgust.

"Well, you might not like the vegetables we'll have at supper every evening, but you'll like the sea," Philippa assured him.

"Will we be able to sail on your boat, sir?" he asked with wide, expectant eyes.

"Yes," replied Warbeck. "I plan to take you and your mama out on my schooner the very first day we're there."

"Hurrah!" Kit shouted, his face lighting up with excitement. He looked expectantly at Lady Augusta. "Will you come sailing with us, Nana?"

The dowager waved her black lace fan languidly and gave an exaggerated sigh. "Lud, child, I'm much too old to go bobbing up and down like a cork adrift on the water. But I will go down to the seashore with you, if my grandson can promise to set up an awning for shade."

"Will you, sir?"

"I will," the duke promised. "And the four of us shall have a picnic right on the sand. How does that sound?"

"Wonderful!" Kit exclaimed. "Gosh, this is going to be a jolly good trip." He scooted up on his knees on the padded leather seat and threw his arms about his mother in an ebullient hug. "Aren't you glad the grand *signóre* invited us along?"

Philippa returned the hug as she brushed a quick kiss on her son's temple. She met Warbeck's perceptive eyes, telling him silently that what she was going to say was for Kit's sake, not his. "Yes, dear heart, I'm very glad."

Kit scrambled down from the seat and moved to stand in front of the duke, his small shoes wedged between the toes of the large, gleaming Hessians. Bracing his hands on his guardian's knees, he smiled up ecstatically. "What's your boat's name, *signóre?*"

"The *Golden Witch*," Warbeck said, his gaze still riveted on Philippa. Then he looked down at the child and smiled with tenderness. "She's a fine ship, trim and weatherly."

Philippa's heart lurched. From the piercing look he'd given her, she realized Warbeck had christened the yacht with her in mind. And it hadn't been meant as a compliment to her fair coloring. Feeling the heat of a flush creep up her neck, Philippa stared blankly out the window, but not before catching a glimpse of the knowing smile that skipped across the duchess's thin lips. In that brief glance, she realized that the autocratic old woman had her own reasons for agreeing to act as their duenna. But what those reasons were, Philippa couldn't imagine.

She wondered when the duke had acquired the schooner, certain it was sometime after he'd received the enormous settlement for damages from Sandy. For while she and Warbeck were married—though her husband never spoke of fiscal matters—she'd guessed that his finances were somewhat straitened. Philippa had known that a need for available funds was the reason he'd left for a week on business affairs less than two months after their wedding day. She'd often thought that if her husband hadn't gone on that trip, the tragic events that later unfolded would never have happened. She wondered, sometimes, if he'd pondered the same thing.

* * *

They shared a midday meal at the Crown, where they were to lodge for the night. The ancient inn had once offered shelter to the countless pilgrims who thronged to Canterbury.

After luncheon the four of them set out to explore the cathedral community that was the seat of Christianity in England, just as Philippa and Warbeck had done on their wedding trip. As they strolled along the old city wall, with its crenellated stone towers, the breeze from the river whipped the ladies' skirts about their ankles and played havoc with their headgear. Lady Augusta's turban fit snugly on her snowy hair, but one of her ostrich plumes floated away, despite Kit's enthusiastic attempt to save it. The high brim of Philippa's poke bonnet caught the wind like an open sail. Only the wide ribbon tied firmly under her chin kept her hat from following the turban's feather.

Philippa glanced at Warbeck several times when she thought he wasn't looking. He was wearing a tailcoat of deep blue superfine, cut straight across in front at the waist, and his white trousers were sculpted to display his long, well-formed legs. His dark complexion and thick, straight hair, tousled by the wind, gave him the air of a well-dressed pirate. Several young ladies sent him admiring looks, which he failed to notice. Instead he was looking directly at her with a smoldering, deliberative gaze that set her heart pounding. She couldn't blame the silly damsels for gawking, blast them. To give the devil his due, Warbeck was prodigiously handsome in a hard, chiseled, intimidating sort of way.

Next, they visited the massive twin-turreted Westgate that had once guarded the citizens from foreign invaders, and from which radiated ponderous defense works dating back to the twelfth century. After pausing to look in awe at the antiquated military fortifications, they explored the site of the castle, where the ruins of the great Norman keep still proclaimed to the curious visitor its once formidable size and strength.

Filled with energy, Kit frequently bounded ahead of them, exclaiming in fascination at what he saw, then running back to tell them of the magnificent sights.

"Slow down, child, slow down," Lady Augusta complained with a weary smile as she leaned on her grandson's strong arm. "It makes me dizzy just watching you gallop about."

"Are you getting tired, Grandmother?" Philippa asked in concern. "We can stop and go back to the Crown any time you wish." She was walking on the opposite side of Warbeck, but unlike the dowager, Philippa had politely refused his arm when he'd offered it earlier. She sensed that he needed the support of his gold-headed cane on the uneven stones.

Lady Augusta waved her hand in denial. "No, no, I'm not a bit tired. We can't stop now at any rate. We haven't seen the cathedral yet." The three adults watched indulgently as Kit tore off again.

"That's next on our itinerary," Warbeck said. "After that, we'll take you back to our lodgings, and you can rest for a while before supper."

"Fine," his grandmother agreed. "After riding all morning and walking all afternoon, these old bones will need a little cosseting. But I don't want to keep Philippa and Kit from seeing all the sights. Every red-blooded Englishman should make a pilgrimage to Canterbury once in his lifetime."

"Don't be concerned about our missing the cathedral," said Philippa. "If you're growing tired, we'll gladly stop. I've already seen it once. And Kit is really too young to appreciate medieval architecture."

"Ah, that's right. I had almost forgotten. You and Court stopped here immediately after your wedding, didn't you?" The elderly lady's eyes glinted with mischief, belying her dulcet tone. "Still, it's been several years since I've visited Canterbury. I want to see the site of Becket's shrine once more before I die."

At the mention of her honeymoon, Philippa's heart dropped to her toes. Although she could feel Warbeck's gaze upon her, she refused to meet his eyes. Earlier that morning, she'd suspected that their route to the coast had been no happenstance. When they arrived at the Crown Inn, she'd known for certain. Warbeck was purposely retracing the steps of their wedding journey.

The moment the four pilgrims entered the quiet cathedral with its majestic fan vaulted ceiling, Philippa recalled in excruciating clarity the day she and Warbeck had entered the sanctity of its hallowed walls, walking hand in hand. Only the night before, they had made love for the very first time, and then again that morning. He'd taken her in his arms and aroused within her an eroticism she'd never imagined existed. The bond that his passionate lovemaking had forged between them had seemed a living presence, as though their souls had merged to form a new, flawless spirit—one of complete and unconditional love. Captivated bride and doting groom, they had wandered together, gazing upward in wonder at the superbly carved stone ceiling, yet far more engrossed in each other than in the soaring feats of Gothic architecture.

Now it was her son's hand she held, as they walked down the long nave. She was achingly conscious of the fact that Warbeck was only a step behind her, Lady Augusta on his arm. They moved toward the broad flight of steps leading to the choir, which was separated from the nave by a screen, then paused for a moment to look back at the brilliantly colored west window. The choir's graceful arcades of round and pointed arches were adorned with dark marble, its luster a startling contrast against the cathedral's light stone.

"Oh, look, Mama," Kit said excitedly. He pointed

to a tomb on top of which lay a remarkable bronze effigy. "They hung the knight's helmet and shield above his statue."

"That's Edward the Black Prince," Warbeck told him.

"Why did they call him black?" Kit tiptoed up to the bier as though afraid he might wake the sleeping warrior. The stern knight lay with his hands folded across a breastplate emblazoned with the lions of England and the fleurs-de-lis of France.

"Partly because of the dark hue of his armor," the duke explained. "And partly because he was ruthless in battle. But he's not the only member of royalty laid to rest in the cathedral. In the chapel nearby are the remains of one of our many kings named Henry."

With a grateful sigh, Lady Augusta sank down into a nearby choir chair. "But the real reason for the pilgrimages in the early days," she said, "was to see the shrine of St. Thomas."

"Where is it?" Kit asked.

"The shrine was torn down by another king named Henry," she answered. His interest caught, Kit came to stand beside her. The dowager put her arm around him and drew him onto the seat next to her. "The eighth Henry, to be exact. Now all that remains are those beautiful testimonials." She pointed above them, and they all looked up at the stained glass pictures illustrating some of the miracles the saint had performed.

Leaving the others to admire the windows, Philippa walked slowly to the northwest transept and halted to gaze up at the soaring roof of the Bell Harry Tower, magnificently decorated in gold, red, and blue. She heard quiet footsteps behind her and felt Warbeck draw near. When she refused to acknowledge his presence, he slipped his hand beneath her elbow and turned her to face him. He bent his head and gently pulled her closer.

"Philippa," he began, his words low and filled

with contrition. "I'm sorry for the things I said in the greenhouse the other day. I swear that on this trip, I'll guard my tongue and my damnable temper. It won't happen again. I also want you to know that I postponed discharging Tomkinson and the other overseers for at least two months. I'll see how well they perform under my close supervision before making a final decision."

She reached out and clasped his hand, suddenly contrite herself. Her unplanned apology tumbled out in a rush. "I'm sorry, too, for my harsh words. You were right about the past being best forgotten. We don't have to go through life hating each other for things that happened so long ago. We can be friends if we choose to." She paused and smiled at him hopefully. "Let's set our anger aside and enjoy this holiday with Kit. We have our mutual love for him as a foundation for our friendship."

"I'm willing to start with that," Court agreed, knowing he had no intention of being satisfied with mere friendship.

At the moment, however, he was content just to feast on the sight of her. She wore a brilliant green spencer, decorated with mock epaulettes and fastened with frogs, over a light, white dress trimmed with ruffles that seemed to float around her ankles. The emerald velvet of her short jacket contrasted vividly with her violet-blue eyes and golden hair. Her adorable bonnet was adorned with tiny flowers of pink and yellow and shades of lavender. Tearing his gaze from her with a conscious effort, he glanced around him and then up to the roof of the bell tower high overhead. "It seems like only yesterday since we stood on this spot together, doesn't it?" he asked softly.

With her gloved hand still clasped in his, she lowered her head, refusing to meet his eyes. "Yes," she said in a hushed tone. "I was just thinking the same thing."

Court studied her pale features, remembering how she'd exclaimed in excited whispers about the marvels of the Christ-Church Cathedral. At the time, she'd never before been farther from London than Chippinghelm, where they'd been married. She'd been an innocent, green girl, who found everything around her absolutely fascinating. Although he'd been to Canterbury several times prior to his wedding trip, that day, with her at his side, he had seen it all in a new and wondrous light, as though he were beholding for the first time the slender columns, the narrow buttresses, the magnificent vaulted ceilings, and the graceful pointed arches. He'd fallen asleep in her arms on his wedding night and woken up to find the world was suddenly good and right and filled with happiness.

"You were so captivated by its beauty," he said with an ache in his throat, "that I saw the cathedral through your eyes and was entranced as well. For a cynical London gentleman, that was quite a change in perspective."

She lifted her head and met his gaze. A glowing smile appeared on her fine-boned features, brightening her somber eyes with a hint of deviltry. "I don't remember your being cynical," she whispered. "Just in a hurry to finish the sightseeing and get back to the inn."

"I needed my rest," he rejoined, his mouth curving up in a grin of relief, because she was back to her pixie self again. "My duties as a new bridegroom were exhausting."

A soft gurgle of laughter bubbled up in her throat. "I'd never been to Canterbury before," she parried, "so you can't blame me for being a little overzealous. And I certainly didn't realize at the time that entertaining me was such a fatiguing chore."

"I'd been kept awake most of the night, then forced to ramble all over town the next day," Court said thickly, his gaze fastened on her lovely lips. "It was no wonder I had to go back to the inn for a nap."

Her cheeks bloomed, telling him she remembered that particular nap very well. Neither one of them had gotten much sleep in the first few weeks of their marriage. She looked up at the tower soaring majestically above them and blinked rapidly, as though fighting back tears. "It was a perfect honeymoon," she said in a strangled voice. "Did I remember to thank you for it at the time?"

Court's heart did an ecstatic cartwheel. "You thanked me on several occasions," he answered hoarsely, "at which time I assured you that the pleasure was all mine." He reached out and touched a golden curl. The feel of the silken strands between his thumb and forefinger stirred memories of their passionate lovemaking that had been burned into his very soul.

How often had he wondered if he'd done something to hurt or upset her during those few brief weeks of marriage? He'd lain awake night after night searching his memory for every word that had been said between them. Always, he'd berated himself for not telling her in more romantic terms the overpowering feelings of love he'd held locked in his heart. But he hadn't wanted to frighten her with the passionate intensity of his emotions. She was so pure and naive that at eighteen, she'd come to their marriage bed thinking all they would do was sleep together.

For the first two weeks of their courtship, Court had been frustrated at every turn by the constant presence of Blanche and Beatrice Lillybridge and the all-too-frequent addition of a dozen preadolescent girls. True to his promise, he'd taken them to Piccadilly, where the pint-sized females engaged in a shopping frenzy of mind-boggling magnitude. He'd also accompanied the entire group to Astley's Amphitheater, the Tower of London, and Madame

Tussaud's wax museum—a particular favorite of the young ladies. His friends at White's began calling him Pasha Warbeck. They grinned like hyenas and asked him where he was keeping his harem that evening.

Court's first inkling of just how all-encompassing Philippa's naïveté was came at the time they were formally betrothed, and they were allowed at last to go on excursions with Belle and Tobias as their chaperones. When the four of them were returning from Covent Garden one evening, Court slipped his arm around Philippa in the darkened carriage and pulled her close. She immediately cuddled up against him like an affectionate kitten and sighed contentedly. Court's breath caught in his throat at the feel of her sweet body pressed close to his.

"Excuse me," she said as she covered a yawn. "I'm so tired I can hardly keep my eyes open. I'm not used to keeping such late hours."

"Put your head on my shoulder and go to sleep," he suggested. "I'll wake you when we reach Chelsea."

Philippa straightened with a jerk and moved determinedly away from him. From beneath the lush fringe of her lashes, she glanced covertly at Belle and Tobias, as though Court had suggested she disrobe in front of them. "I shan't fall asleep," she said in a tone of deep humiliation.

Court smiled at her needless embarrassment. "I'm glad I'm not boring you, sweetheart."

The next evening at Vauxhall Gardens, he took advantage of the milling crowd that strained to see the magnificent fireworks display. "Come with me," he urged softly in Philippa's ear. Not giving her a chance to argue, he pulled her down a deserted pathway.

Philippa looked back at the Rockinghams, who were watching the colorful pyrotechnics in fascination. "We'd better tell them where we're going. Otherwise, they'll think we're lost."

"Toby will know where to find us," he assured her. He guided Philippa into a dark, wooded area well hidden from view. Leaning against the trunk of a tree, he drew her into his arms and kissed her. Not the brief, chaste kiss he'd bestowed in front of the two eagle-eyed spinsters the evening they became engaged, but a long, scorching kiss, fueled by all the frustrated yearning pent up inside him since the day they'd first met. Philippa wrapped her arms about Court's neck and pressed her slender form against his with undeniable eagerness. Without a second's hesitation, she kissed him in return, her lips pursed tight.

When Court traced the seam of her soft lips with his tongue, her lids flew open. The surprised shock in her violet eyes told him it was an experience she'd never envisioned. But she didn't pull away. Lowering her thick lashes in scholarlike concentration, she imitated his actions. Her tongue peeped out from between her lips and touched his tongue with an ingenuous curiosity. The gentle, feminine grace of her tentative exploration rocked Court to the very core of his soul. Sexual need that had simmered for two long weeks as he'd purposely kept his hands away from her luscious body exploded inside him like a volcano. Churning, steaming, red-hot lava poured through his veins.

"Ah, Pippa," he murmured huskily. "My sweet, sweet pixie." Supporting her head with his hand, he pulled her tighter against him. He thrust his tongue inside her mouth, withdrawing and reentering in a bold imitation of the sex act itself. She clung to him, her breathing growing deeper and more uneven. To Court's delight, she followed his example and swept the waiting cavern of his mouth with her tongue. The lava boiling and seething inside him rushed in a flood to his engorged manhood.

His heart clubbing wildly against his ribs, Court
slid his hand up to her breast, ready to halt if she
drew back in censure. He was moving too damn fast,
and he knew it. But Christ, being with her, yet not
being able to touch her, had left him half-mad with
desire. He couldn't continue to fight the rage of carnal need that slammed through his groin every time
she was near.

Philippa's sigh of pleasure as he rubbed his thumb
across the soft peak of her breast assured him that
she didn't want him to stop. She was as natural and
uninhibited as the fairy sprite she resembled. "You
make me feel so wonderful," she whispered with
guileless honesty.

"The feeling is mutual," he assured her. Cupping
her buttocks, he lifted her to him, molding their
bodies together, bringing the juncture of her thighs
against his thickened staff. A deep groan of pleasure
rumbled through his chest at the heavenly, heavenly
feel of her. How in God's name would he ever be
able to wait for their wedding night?

To his amazement, she chuckled softly. "Court,"
she murmured against his lips, "you have something
hard in your clothing that's bumping against me."

The meaning of her words slowly sank into his
lust-fogged brain. "It's me," he told her hoarsely.

"What?" The confusion in her voice was mixed
with pure, girlish happiness.

"The something hard bumping against you is me."

She pulled back and gazed at him in bemusement.

"You don't understand, do you?" he asked in resignation, knowing he couldn't take advantage of her
artless innocence.

"Understand what?"

Court took her hands and brought them down
from around his neck. With a heroic effort, he regained control of the driving need that pounded
through every pore of his lecherous body. He held
her away from him and searched her trusting fea-

tures, while he waited for his thundering heartbeat to return to normal. His voice was hoarse from the strain of regathering his moral convictions in the face of overwhelming temptation. "Philippa, have you ever seen a naked male body?"

"Court!" she cried in mortification. "What a thing to ask me!"

He smiled tenderly at her shocked expression. "I meant an infant boy's or a painting or a statue."

"Well, hardly," she muttered in an aggrieved tone. "Miss Blanche and Miss Beatrice would never have allowed such a thing."

Court realized she spoke the truth. The two unmarried ladies would have made certain that any renderings of Greek or Roman statues in the books used at the seminary would have a concealing fig leaf strategically placed. And it was obvious that Belle hadn't taken it upon herself to dispel her friend's ignorance after returning from her own wedding trip. Hell, for all Philippa knew about men's private parts, she might as well have been immured in a cloistered convent. The unwelcome thought that she might find him repulsive when she saw him bare-ass naked on their wedding night sent a jolt of uneasiness through him.

He cleared his throat, determined to put that worrisome thought aside for the moment. "Pippa, you know when people marry they usually have children."

"Oh, yes!" she exclaimed with a smile. "I want to have lots of children. Don't you?"

"Yes, I do." He paused, searching for the right words. "Did Blanche or Beatrice ever explain to you exactly how babies are made?"

She laughed at his foolish question. "Of course. They'd never leave anything so important to chance." Her smile faded, and she gazed at him with a suddenly serious mien. "And I know for a fact that even an unmarried woman can have a baby. Once a pretty kitchen maid at Lillybridge became pregnant and had to be dismissed. Cook and all the other servants were crying and carrying on as though it was Doomsday. When I asked my mothers how such a thing could have happened, Miss Beatrice explained that the foolish girl had slept with the greengrocer's son. Miss Blanche said a woman must *never, ever* sleep with a man, until she sleeps with her husband on her wedding night. Otherwise, she could have a baby to raise and no gentleman to support her." Philippa gestured gracefully, as though to indicate that that explained it all.

With a blaze of comprehension, Court realized why, when he'd suggested she put her head on his shoulder and sleep on the way home in the carriage the previous night, she'd jerked away from him as if he'd maligned her character. As long as she stayed wide-awake, no amount of fondling and kissing could be considered dangerous. Apparently, the young ladies at Lillybridge had studied everything but conjugal relations, that particular topic being left to each girl's mother to explore as she saw fit. And Philippa's two spinster mothers had seen fit to ignore it.

Court cupped Philippa's chin in his hand and gazed into her eyes, reading there the untrammeled purity of her soul. He debated telling her the truth. But they were to be married in two short weeks. Rather than risk frightening her with an awkward explanation, he would wait until their wedding night and show her, with all the tenderness he possessed, what it meant for a man and a woman to make love.

In the days left before their wedding, Court made use of every opportunity to get Philippa alone. He taught her the pleasure and joy of kissing and caressing as he aroused within her the need for his touch. She responded to his tutoring with an unguarded spontaneity, eagerly advancing her knowledge of lovemaking without a hint of guilt or shame. It was

Court who always dragged their lessons to a halt before he lost control completely.

During those glorious, torturous fourteen days, he watched every gentleman who came near her with hawklike intensity. He intended to make damn sure no other man took advantage of her incredible innocence. Scowling ferociously, he made it clear that, if any male over fifteen dared to lay a finger on her, he'd break the bastard's arm. . . .

Court felt a sharp tug on the tail of his coat and returned to the present and Canterbury Cathedral. He looked down to find Kit staring up at him.

"*Signóre*," his son announced, blissfully unaware of the intimate memories he'd just interrupted, "Nana says it's time to go back to the inn and take a nap."

Court met Philippa's bemused gaze. "It seems history has a way of repeating itself," he said with a grin. Suddenly, he felt lighthearted enough to soar to the top of the bell tower. He took his son's small hand and nodded for Philippa to take the other. "Come on, you two pilgrims, let's all get some rest, so we'll be ready to enjoy the evening. For supper, I've ordered an extra helping of sweets. And absolutely no vegetables will be allowed on the table."

"What a considerate host!" Philippa twitted with a playful smile.

"What a great idea!" Kit agreed, grinning almost as broadly as his father.

The *Golden Witch* sailed from the sleepy fishing port of Ghyllside with a crew of five and three passengers, the youngest of whom roamed the deck with one end of a sturdy rope tied around his waist and the other fastened to the foremast, for safety's sake.

"She's a beautiful ship," Philippa told Warbeck with sincere admiration as the two-masted schooner slipped away from the dock. They were standing at the railing, watching her long-nosed prow cut through the waves with the grace and elegance of a swan.

"Aye, she's bonny," he agreed. "The *Witch* was made right here in Ghyllside by a master builder, who designed her to my specifications. She's been clocked at ten knots."

"Is that fast?"

Before Warbeck could answer, the sails filled and hardened against the wind. The schooner seemed to leap forward as though she were airborne, gliding faster and faster over the waves, till Philippa felt a thrill of exhilaration.

The duke smiled at her look of delight, and her heart skipped a beat at the tender amusement in his eyes. He was dressed in duck trousers and a white cotton shirt, its ruffles at collar and cuff blowing gently in the breeze. He wore no hat, and his hair shone blue-black in the summer sun. Despite his injured leg, he stood on the deck with the confidence of an experienced seaman.

"When did you learn to sail, sir?" Kit asked as he wedged his way in between them. Fearlessly, the youngster braced his hands on the railing, took a step up on the edge of the bulwark, and peered down at the white crests slapping against the side. "Were you as little as me?"

"No, Kit, I didn't learn to sail until I was nine," Warbeck said, rechecking the knot on the boy's lifeline. "My brother and I came to Gull's Nest with Lady Augusta to spend the summer. We made friends with an old fisherman from Ghyllside, who taught us how to sail a small sloop. We weren't allowed to go out of the bay, however."

Kit looked up at his guardian with ingenuous gray eyes. Dressed exactly like Warbeck in white linen trousers and a white ruffled shirt, his resemblance to the man was extraordinary. "Did you always obey the rules?"

Warbeck gave Philippa a broad wink before answering. "Most of the time."

The trio turned to look back at the picturesque town. Its weatherboard houses and half-timbered shops climbed up the steep hills that rose above the wide sandy shore. The site of the docks, lined with rows of colorful fishing boats, dated back to the time of the Romans and had once threatened to rival the Cinque Ports. But for some reason, resort seekers had bypassed Ghyllside for Folkestone and Ramsgate—not to mention Prinny's fashionable Brighton—leaving the ancient port a remarkable reminder of the past with its medieval gateway and narrow, cobbled streets.

Kit touched Warbeck's sleeve, bringing his attention back to their interrupted conversation. "Did you stay at Gull's Nest often, *signóre?*"

"Only once as a youngster. We were always sent to the seaside for the entire summer with a staff of servants and our tutors. Usually our parents rented a house for us in Broadstairs farther up the coast. That year, however, an acquaintance of my father's offered us the use of Gull's Nest. The three months Chris and I spent there with our grandmother were the happiest ones of my childhood."

Kit gaped at Court in genuine surprise. "Where were your mama and papa, sir? Didn't they want to come with you?"

Philippa kept her eyes fastened on the cresting whitecaps and tried not to show her burning interest in Warbeck's reply. During their brief courtship and marriage, he'd avoided speaking of his formative years. He'd answered her direct questions with jocular, offhand remarks, then redirected the lighthearted talk to her own unusual childhood at Lillybridge.

Early on, Belle had told her of the tragic and scandalous deaths of his parents. Instinctively, Philippa knew that her husband's clever repartee hid a deeply buried pain. So she'd honored his unstated wishes and didn't attempt to pry. Had he once spoken of his true feelings toward his parents, however, she would have confessed with relief the secret of her own shameful heritage. For as wicked and contemptible as his mother and father might have been, they were no more disgraceful than her own. She waited now for his answer, expecting Warbeck to put up the same impregnable wall with Kit that he'd shown to the rest of the world.

The duke scowled out at the sea but didn't brush Kit's question aside with a waggish jest the way he had Philippa's nearly six years before. His words sounded pensive and faraway. "My mother was spending the summer attending one country house party after another, I suppose." He shrugged as though it were of no consequence and continued in a lighter tone. "My father always remained at the Castle, no matter what the season. He hated London and didn't like the seaside much better."

"Where's your brother now, sir? Does he ever come to Gull's Nest?"

The artless interrogation was playing havoc with Court's emotions. Ruthlessly, he shoved aside the image of Chris in his great four-poster bed, calling out in delirium for his absent mother. Court wasn't going to let the anger and despair he'd felt, as his brother lay dying that long-ago morning, spoil this glorious day with his son. He looked down at the trusting, upturned face and spoke gently. "My brother's dead, Kit. That summer we spent with our grandmother at Gull's Nest was the last summer we had together. He died in the autumn of a fever."

"He's in heaven with my father, then," Kit stated matter-of-factly.

"No doubt," Court replied, unwilling to tell the boy that heaven was the last place the late marquess of Sandhurst would be found. He knew Kit could have no recollection of the man, since he'd died when the boy was only a year old. That thought brought a surge of intense satisfaction. Sandhurst lay rotting in his grave. And *he* was here, by God, alive, and with Philippa and Kit at his side. No ghosts from the past were going to ruin this glorious day.

"I wish I had a brother," Kit said with a confidential air. The startled grown-ups waited for his next remark. "I asked Mama if we could get one when we came to England, but she said she didn't think so. She said we'd have to get a daddy first, and daddies are even harder to come by than little brothers. But I'm going to get a pony for my next birthday."

"When is—"

"Oh . . . oh, look at the naval ship," Philippa blurted out. She turned her head so the brim of her bonnet hid her face, but not before Court caught a peek at her mortified expression.

"Where?" Kit cried, instantly diverted.

His mother pointed to a sleek cruiser, close-hauled on a starboard tack, her course set for the Strait of Dover. "There," she said breathlessly.

"That's the H.M.S. *Ferrett*," Court told them. "She's probably heading into the channel to lie in wait for some smugglers this evening."

"I'd like to be the captain of a boat like that," Kit announced with childish bravado. "I'd catch the smugglers and send them to prison."

Philippa turned to look at her son with an entrancing smile, her coloring vivid. Court wasn't certain the heightened glow was caused by the brisk sea air or Kit's unexpected disclosure that he wanted a daddy and a little baby brother. "I thought you wanted to be a boatman on a gondola," she teased, touching the tip of Kit's nose with her forefinger.

"Couldn't I be both?" he demanded with a frown.

Court's deep chuckles were joined by Philippa's bell-like laughter. "What do you think, Your Grace?" she asked, her violet eyes dancing with pixieish delight. "Can he be both?"

"I think Kit can be anything he wants to be," Court

answered, making no attempt to keep the pride from his voice.

His heart swelling with joy, he pointed out the sights along the shore to his two chattering companions, who rivaled only each other in their insatiable curiosity.

The schooner, expertly crewed by a captain, two mates, a cook, and a steward, sailed northward along the coast beneath a blue sky dotted with cumulus clouds. The *Golden Witch* was a magnificent yacht, with high bulwarks and broad teakwood decks. There were touches of elegance everywhere. Teak grabrails, beautifully made hatches, and brass-trimmed portholes showed the care with which she'd been crafted. Belowdecks was a spacious galley, an aft cabin, and a main salon with a wood-burning stove. The *Witch* could take her passengers anywhere in the world in comfort and bring them back safely to England.

Sometimes, as he'd watched the schooner being built, Court had dreamed of sailing her to Venice. Sailing her right up that damn Grand Canal to dock in front of a certain palazzo. He hadn't given the dream up entirely until he'd become engaged to Clare. He smiled, now, with a flash of insight. Maybe that was *why* he'd become engaged. So he'd be forced to give up the dream. Hell, after all his tortured soul-searching, here he was, right back in the golden-haired witch's pocket. And he hadn't felt so happy in years.

The thought of Lady Clare Brownlow intruded on his cheerful musings. He would have to go back to London when this holiday was over and explain the complicated situation to his fiancée. When she learned that he had a son—who he never knew existed until two weeks ago—and that he hoped to reconcile with his former wife so the three of them could be a family, the genteel young woman would naturally release him from their betrothal contract.

Lady Clare was known for her exemplary Christian charity and her unselfish interest in the plight of the poor. He'd settle the unfortunate business with a substantial monetary gift in her name to whatever orphanage or asylum she chose. None of this was Clare's fault, and he could afford to be generous.

As they skirted a wooded headland, Court pointed toward a small inlet bordered on both sides by high cliffs. "There's the entrance to Gull's Nest Bay," he told them.

"Can we go into the bay and sail past our house, sir?"

Court rumpled the boy's thick hair affectionately. He'd been told that children asked a lot of questions. He was learning that with his irrepressible son, it was one eager query after another. "No, Kit, the passage is too narrow for anything larger than a small ketch. The outcroppings of rocks along this strip of coast make it dangerous for ships to approach any nearer than we are right now. But you'll be able to see Gull's Nest in just a few minutes."

As the *Witch* steered past the mouth of the inlet, all sails set and running free before the wind, they spied the villa. It sat high on a bluff that overlooked the sandy beach at the back of the bay. The summer home stood three stories tall, its first floor built of a rich gray stone local to the area. A white wooden veranda ran the entire length of the building, its flat roof forming a railed balcony for the second floor. Gabled windows on the top story looked out over the cliffs that protected the bay, to a magnificent vista of unending sea and sky.

To Philippa, the great house appeared totally isolated, even though Ghyllside was a mere five miles away. The only other approach was from the land side along a narrow, curving road. How well she remembered all the opportunities the villa's unique privacy afforded.

She and Court had spent their honeymoon there.

The bedchamber that she'd been given that morning upon their arrival was the one they'd shared together. The large oak bed she would sleep in tonight, she'd once slept in with him. The very thought of lying down on its feathery mattress made her ache with longing. Blast the man, if his intention was to turn her emotions upside down, he was succeeding far better than he knew.

"Do you think Nana can see us?" Kit asked hopefully.

"If she's looking through the telescope she can," Court replied. "Go ahead and wave. She just might be watching for us to sail by."

Exuberantly, Kit raised both hands high over his head. He continued to wave until they'd left the narrow waterway behind.

"And now," Court said, untying the rope from about Kit's waist, "I'm going to take you both belowdecks and show you the hold."

Kit bounded across the teakwood planks to the companionway, then turned abruptly, his eyes alight with excitement. "Can we sleep on board the *Witch* tonight, *signóre?*"

"Not this time. We'll have to get Mama back to her own bed this evening. On another cruise, though, all three of us can bunk down below. There's nothing so peaceful as sleeping at sea on a moonlit night." He looked back at Philippa with an indolent, sensuous gaze that left no doubt as to the exact sleeping arrangements he had in mind.

At his shocking proposal, Philippa folded her arms and glared in outrage. Unable to speak, she tapped the toe of her white sandal on the deck and narrowed her eyes meaningfully.

Warbeck met her speaking gaze with a lazy, wicked grin. "Don't worry, Lady Sandhurst, there's lots of space belowdecks," he explained, as though completely misunderstanding the silent rebuke. "The berths are comfortable and the passenger cabins are roomy. Come on, you two landlubbers. After I show you both around, we'll have that luncheon the ship's cook has spent all morning preparing."

Pinning a complacent smile on her face for Kit's sake, Philippa walked toward the waiting menfolk. She intended to glide regally past the duke and afford him scant attention the rest of the day by way of punishment for his outrageous suggestion.

Suddenly, the schooner lurched sideways, pitching Philippa off balance. She crashed against Warbeck, and his cane fell to the hard deck with a noisy clatter. Her first thought was to protect his injured leg. Throwing her arms around his waist, she sought to regain her equilibrium on the swaying deck, while at the same time preventing him from falling.

Too late, she realized that he was keeping her firmly upright with one powerful arm. In a quick, reflexive movement, he'd dropped his cane and grabbed the rail above the hatch. He held her now, smashed up against him, her toes barely touching the deck. She could feel the strength of his muscular frame as he supported her effortlessly. The faint scent of sandalwood on warm male skin battered her senses. He bent his head till their lips were scant inches apart.

Philippa's breath caught high in her chest. She tipped her head back and stared into silvery eyes agleam with warm amusement. "I appreciate your concern for my lameness, Lady Sandhurst," he drawled, "but I thought it would be more romantic if I saved you."

"I thought . . . I was afraid . . . I tried to . . ." she spluttered.

"There was no need for alarm," he assured her. "Had I ended up sprawled out flat on the deck, it would have been nothing new. I've already fallen head over heels for the second time. What further indignity could happen to me now?"

For a moment, she thought he was going to kiss

her. The look of hunger in his compelling eyes sent a jolt of desire straight through her treacherous body. "Kit's here," she reminded him in a husky whisper.

"I know," he whispered back, his cool breath fanning across her face.

Simultaneously, they looked down to find Kit watching them in fascination, his face aglow with wonder and joy. Philippa prayed that Warbeck was unable to read the message so clear in her son's bright eyes. Blast the man to hell and gone, she knew exactly what Kit was thinking: The grand *signóre* would make a wonderful daddy.

Chapter 12

"**E**xactly how much of the town do you own?"
Philippa asked Warbeck, then immediately
swung her gaze back to the harnessed horse in front
of her. They were on their way to Ghyllside, and the
duke had just informed her that he was going to
check on several of his properties there while she and
Kit did some shopping.

"A considerable part of it," he answered. "You and
I have a few mutual friends who've also invested a
substantial share of their fortunes in the port."

Philippa nodded, her thoughts more on her task
than on financial investments. "Am I doing this
right?" she asked, nervously moving the reins from
one gloved hand to the other.

"You're doing fine," Warbeck said with a reassuring smile. "But always keep the ribbons in your left
hand. That way your right is free when you need to
shorten or lengthen a rein. Even for a man tooling a
coach and four, the goal is to have the least visible
motion of hands or reins. But the steady position of
your left hand doesn't mean you should keep a dead
pull on the horse's mouth," he cautioned.

"I understand," she said, as she readjusted the
reins accordingly.

They were riding in a light, two-wheeled gig
pulled by a pretty, piebald mare. When they'd
emerged from the villa to leave on the day's outing,
Warbeck had assisted Kit up to the farther edge of

the carriage seat, guided Philippa up, and climbed in
himself. Then he'd surprised her by announcing with
a lazy grin that she was going to have her first lesson
in driving a coach that morning. Without waiting for
her reaction, he'd placed the ribbons in her hands
and shown her the correct way to lace them through
her fingers. Determined to master every driving skill
he tried to teach her, Philippa had followed his instructions precisely.

"Even with a light-mouthed horse like your little
mare," he reminded her now, "you should hold the
reins tight enough so that you can feel her mouth at
all times. Otherwise, she won't be able to feel immediately the slightest movement of your hand. It's
called driving up to the bit."

Court watched his intent companion with a sense
of complete gratification. Philippa's face had lit up
when he'd handed her the reins, giving him all the
reward he needed. She wore a bright yellow gown
and a pert straw hat that sat on her upswept curls at
a rakish angle, reminding him forcefully of the way
she'd looked the first time they'd ridden into
Ghyllside on their wedding trip.

The previous evening, the four of them had eaten
supper on the veranda and then played jackstraws
until there wasn't enough light to see by. Lady Augusta had retired with a genteel yawn, leaving the
other three sitting on the steps of the wooden porch,
watching a great orange sun go down on the bay.
Leaning heavily on his cane, Court carried a sleepy
Kit up to his bedroom, while Philippa traipsed behind. The two males listened, enraptured, as she
spun a tale of sorcery and high adventure until the
boy was sound asleep. Court realized that she'd
made the story up as she went along, weaving in fascinating facts about geography and history as she
talked.

He'd felt a contentment he'd never known as he
watched her bend and kiss their son's forehead and

smooth the covers over his slim shoulders. She was
everything—and more—he'd glimpsed in the vivacious young schoolteacher with whom he'd first
fallen in love. For now he saw what a gentle, loving
mother she was. Aye, she'd been a faithless wife, just
as his own mother had been. But with the deceased
Lady Warbeck, tawdry indiscretions had been a way
of life. Philippa would never leave her child for
months on end to follow the fashionable rounds of
balls and country house parties. Her love for Kit was
too deep, too abiding.

And therein lay the answer. For if Court had complete custody of her son, he would hold sway over
Philippa, too. And where one child would bind her
to him, three or four would keep her at Castle
Warbeck forever, too busy with her growing offspring to even look at another man.

Her passionate fling with Sandhurst had been an
aberration, an impulsive misdeed contrary to the innate goodness of her nature. She'd been captivated
by the bastard's polished charm and had paid the
dire consequences. Now they'd both been given a
chance to start anew. Court smiled inwardly. He had
everything he wanted just within his reach.

Philippa was barely able to contain her excitement
at being allowed to drive. She knew, however, that
other people somehow managed to keep up a conversation while they did so. "Is Toby one of the other
investors?" she asked.

"Yes. And both of his brothers-in-law. André and
Étienne Mercier have invested nearly everything they
could scrape together. Among the four of us, we own
most of the inns in Ghyllside and a great many of the
shops. Toby intends to purchase a summer home
close by. And the villa that I'm going to inspect for
Kit is just south of the old city walls. That estate
stretches from the hillside down to the ocean shore. It
will be an extremely valuable piece of property
someday."

She frowned in disappointment. "I thought you were going to acquire Gull's Nest with Kit's funds."

"Gull's Nest is not for sale."

Until that moment, Philippa hadn't realized how much she'd counted on her son acquiring the secluded villa on Gull's Nest Bay. The idea of going there every summer to stay with Kit had captivated her. "How can you be so certain it's not for sale?"

His response was low and absolute. "Because I own it."

Unconsciously, she jerked on the reins, and the black-and-white mare threw her head up and down in annoyance. "Blast it," she said under her breath. "I didn't mean to do that."

"You'll soon get the hang of it," Warbeck encouraged. "The first thing to learn is to drive with a light hand. Never strike your horse with the whip unnecessarily or job her in the mouth with the bit. Well-trained cattle will do their best for you without being coerced."

She nodded in understanding, then grinned down at the reins in her hands. A tremor of exhilaration ran through her. "I can't believe I'm actually driving."

"Gosh, you're doing great, Mama," Kit told her with a bounce of encouragement. "When do I get to learn, sir?"

Warbeck chuckled. "You'll be considerably younger than your mother is now, I can promise you that. But first, you need to learn how to ride."

"Why? Mama can't ride."

"That's the next thing I'm going to teach her."

Astonished, Philippa made no attempt to hide her joy. "You are?" she asked, her voice squeaking like an adolescent's.

"I told you once that I'd teach you how to ride and how to drive a carriage," he reminded her softly. "I always keep my promises."

Startled by the intensity in his gaze, Philippa

stared straight ahead, hoping her son had failed to catch his guardian's answer.

But Kit hadn't missed a word. "When did you tell her that, sir?"

The duke reached behind Philippa and playfully rumpled the child's thick hair. "When she was younger."

"As young as me?"

Warbeck grinned. "Not that young, though sometimes she behaved like a five year old."

Philippa stuck out her tongue at him. "When are you going to teach me how to loop the reins?" she demanded cheekily.

He gave a crack of laughter. "When you're ready to drive a four-in-hand, I'll show you how to loop the reins and point the leaders. Meanwhile, we'll concentrate on skills for a beginner."

"Oh, gosh," Kit said with another happy bounce on the seat. "I can hardly wait to learn how to drive."

"Your turn will come soon enough." There was an underlying wistfulness in Warbeck's voice, and Philippa felt a stab of deep remorse.

More and more each day, she realized how much she'd denied Warbeck when she'd fled without telling him of their unborn child. She'd cheated him out of five years with his son. Precious years of childhood that could never be recaptured.

At the time, she'd been certain that he would reject her baby, just as he'd rejected her. What else could she have thought? She'd been abandoned by the last living member of her family when she was only six years old. Horrified by Warbeck's threats to divorce her and kill her supposed lover, Philippa had believed that he would prove no more reliable to the babe in her womb than her uncle had been to her. 'Twas her destiny to be alone in the world, but she intended to make certain her baby was not taken from her, only to be later forsaken.

Yet by keeping her child, she'd stolen him from his

father. In Canterbury Cathedral, Warbeck had spoken of forgiving and forgetting. But suspecting what she'd done, could he ever truly forgive her? And God above knew, he would never, ever forget.

"Why have you and the others bought so much property in Ghyllside?" Philippa questioned, hoping to divert her guilt-ridden conscience.

Warbeck rubbed his injured thigh absently as he watched the road before them. "We're going to develop the town into a seaside resort. The ocean air has always been known for its tonic effect. In recent years, people have taken a new interest in sea bathing as well. At Brighton and other popular coastal towns, bathing machines are rolled out into the water so that ladies of all ages can bob up and down in the salty waves with some degree of privacy. They believe it will help cure every complaint from rheumatism to biliousness."

Philippa looked at him warily. On their honeymoon the two of them had splashed about in the sea together. It'd been shocking of her to go into the water with him, even though the seclusion of a small cove on Gull's Nest Bay had afforded them complete privacy. At first, she'd refused to even consider the idea, but he'd been so charmingly insistent that she'd finally given in. As he'd pointed out with a devastating grin, they were husband and wife and had every right to know each other in the Biblical sense of the word.

All she'd worn was a white cotton shift that clung to her body like a second skin once it was wet. He'd dived into the waves stark naked. The memory of his sinewy form slashing through the blue water stirred warmth deep inside her, and Philippa's thoughts turned back to their wedding night, when she had seen his unclad body for the first time.

She wondered now how she could have been so naive at eighteen about the facts of life. But given that she'd been raised in a boarding school for females by two bookish, middle-aged spinsters, she supposed it was understandable. During the last two weeks of their engagement, Court had showered her with physical demonstrations of his affection. His long, lingering kisses and caresses had set her body tingling with an excitement she'd never known before.

When she confessed to her fiancé that she felt an unfamiliar ache deep inside her whenever he touched her, he smiled knowingly. The light in his silvery eyes glowed with warm amusement as he explained that what she was feeling was perfectly normal for a bride-to-be. He didn't mind at all that she wanted to rub up against him like a kitten begging to be petted. In fact, he encouraged it.

On their first evening together as husband and wife, she was looking forward with sweet anticipation to being held in his arms while they slept, something he'd promised to do when they were married. After arriving in Canterbury late in the day, they shared a light supper in their room at the inn. Following the meal, Court used an adjoining dressing chamber to change out of his street clothes, while Philippa stood behind a screen and slipped into her nightdress. The long, voluminous gown was made of white lawn so fine it was nearly transparent. It was a gift from Belle, who'd dimpled merrily at Philippa's squeal of surprise when she'd lifted it out of the box. But her laughing friend had made Philippa promise she'd wear the gown on her wedding night, in spite of the future bride's protests that she'd likely catch an inflammation of the lungs attired in such a wisp of a garment.

Philippa took the ivory combs from her hair, shook out her long tresses, and glanced at herself in the mirror. Feeling awkward and self-conscious, she waited beside the glowing hearth for her bridegroom to return. She told herself not to be a silly goose. After all, they were married now and would be seeing each other in their nightclothes for the rest of their lives. As Court stepped back into the room, she peeped up at him from under her lashes and smiled shyly.

Her husband stopped just inside the doorway and stared as though seeing her for the first time. His gaze swept down her sheer nightdress to her bare toes and back up to linger on her mouth for a few brief seconds. Then he met her eyes and smiled encouragingly. "You're a diamond of the first water, Lady Warbeck," he teased in his usual way. But a spark seemed to ignite in his thick-lashed gray eyes.

"You look quite marvelous yourself," she said truthfully. His dark blue dressing robe ended just below his knees, revealing powerful calves covered with wiry black hair. Like her, Court was barefoot. Yet for some unaccountable reason he seemed taller, his shoulders broader, his strength more intimidating than a few moments before. She stepped backward as he moved to the small table in the center of the room.

Court poured a glass of wine, then sprawled comfortably on the sofa in front of the fire. "Come and join me," he encouraged. She accepted his invitation with delight. But when she started to sit down beside him, he guided her onto his lap instead. "The wine is for you," he told her as he placed the crystal goblet in her hand. He wrapped his arms around her and pulled her close.

"This will be my third glass this evening," she reminded him. "I'm liable to get tipsy."

Brushing a kiss against her temple, he cuddled her to him. "Go ahead and drink the wine, little pixie. It will help you relax."

She sipped the ruby liquid and sighed contentedly. "If I drop off to sleep in your lap, you'll have to forgive me. It's been a long, busy day."

"It has, hasn't it," he agreed. He nuzzled the hollow at the base of her neck, and a thrill of excitement reverberated through her. "Did you enjoy our wedding?" he murmured.

"It was wonderful," she said dreamily. "It was the most beautiful wedding I've ever attended." She closed her eyes, reveling in the feel of his warm lips nibbling her bare skin.

"How many have you attended?" he asked curiously.

"Two. Mine and Belle's. But our wedding was definitely the most beautiful."

"It could be that you're prejudiced," Court said with a chuckle. He lifted his head to meet her gaze, and the glow of love that burned in the depths of his gray eyes made her breath catch in her throat.

With a trembling hand, Philippa caressed his stubbled cheek. He'd told her during their courtship that he loved to have her touch him, so she didn't hesitate to trace the arch of one black brow and the line of his cheekbone with her fingertip. "I'm certain ours was the most beautiful," she said with a gurgle of laughter. "What other bride ever had twelve schoolgirl bridesmaids precede her down the aisle? Or two spinster headmistresses give her away at the altar?" She smiled with happiness at the memory. "And now we're married," she added softly.

"Yes," he agreed, his voice low and raspy. He took the glass of wine and set it on the stand beside the sofa. "And now we're married."

Philippa wriggled closer, relishing the hardness of his muscular frame and the strength of his arms about her. Court groaned deep in his chest at her movements, and she sat up in concern. "Aren't you feeling well?" She glanced at the table that had been laden with food earlier in the evening. "Perhaps it was the Yorkshire pudding."

"I feel wonderful," he assured her. He slid his hand up her rib cage and boldly cupped her breast.

The heat of his touch seeped through the thin material of her nightdress, and Philippa drew in a quick draft of air. She released a long, drawn-out sigh of pleasure as his fingers played with her nipple, and the now familiar ache spread through her body. For the past two weeks, he'd been caressing her in just this way, and she'd come to yearn for the sweet sensations that coursed through her at his touch.

Drawing her nearer, Court kissed her, his tongue entering her mouth and stroking her enticingly. His lips molded against hers, readjusting for a deeper, longer kiss, as he supported her head with his hand. When he pulled away, she looked up at him in disappointment.

"Pippa," he said gently, "there's something we need to discuss before we go to bed tonight."

"I don't care which side I sleep on," she replied, her languid gaze fastened on his generous mouth. All she really wanted was for him to kiss her again.

He rubbed his hand up and down her arm in a slow, soothing motion. When he spoke, his tone was suddenly serious. "Sweetheart, men are very different from women."

"Oh, I know that!" she replied with a laugh. To prove her point, she placed her hand beside his much larger one. The tapering oval tips of her slender fingers contrasted markedly with his wide, blunt nails and darkly tanned skin.

"Not just in the way you're thinking," he answered with a tender smile. "Men are not merely bigger and stronger and hairier. Males are basically, fundamentally different from females in their physical anatomy."

She lifted her brows and looked at him with open curiosity.

"It has to do with the way babies are made," he said almost gruffly.

Philippa sat up straight, giving him her undivided attention. She'd always wondered exactly how that occurred. Now she was about to learn. "You mean while I'm sleeping?"

"What's important is what happens *before* we fall asleep," he explained. "Tonight, while you're still wide-awake, I'm going to place my seed deep inside you, darling. So deep that our baby can grow protected and nurtured by your luscious, beautiful body." He paused, and when she only stared at him in mute fascination, he continued. "In order to get my seed inside you, I have what's called a male member. I'm going to insert it here." His hand moved to cover the space between her legs, and she stiffened in surprise. She tried to bring her thighs together, but he kept his hand there and began to slowly caress her.

From somewhere in the back of her mind, Philippa recalled a fellow student once trying to describe the differences between girls and boys. The description had seemed so outlandish, Philippa had refused to believe it. "You're sure that's how babies are made?" she asked incredulously.

"I'm sure."

"Well, then, let's do it," she said, attempting a plucky smile. "I'm not certain exactly how this is going to work, but I'm willing to try."

Court pulled her against him, burying his face in her unbound hair. For a moment, she suspected he was laughing at her, but when he lifted his head, his eyes shone with tender affection. "Yes," he agreed, "let's try."

He rose and carried her to the bed. Setting her on her feet, he untied the ribbons at her throat and the gossamer nightdress drifted to the floor. Then he swept her up in his arms and laid her on the feather mattress.

Philippa pulled the sheet up to her chin, then turned her head on the pillow, watching him expectantly. Court untied his belt and slipped the blue robe off his shoulders. With a gasp, she scooted up against the carved headboard, dragging the sheet with her to cover her bare breasts, as she stared at him in wide-eyed wonder. He hadn't a stitch of clothes on.

He was right. Males were fundamentally different. Her astonished gaze swept over his naked body. His powerful shoulders and upper arms bulged with sinew, a mat of dark hair covered his chest, and his taut abdomen was ridged with muscles. But that wasn't the most important difference. At the juncture of his massive thighs, the male member he'd told her about stood straight out from a mass of wiry black curls.

Philippa dragged her disbelieving eyes up to meet his and gulped convulsively. How could such a large, jutting appendage have been concealed beneath his pantaloons? Inch by inch, she sidled to the far side of the bed, ready to leap up, if necessary. Her mesmerized gaze flew back to his groin. Something was definitely wrong. They should never have married each other, for they were grossly mismatched. Court ought to have chosen a much larger woman, and she'd have been wiser to remain single. There was no possibility whatsoever that he could insert his enormous male member into her body.

"This is not going to be possible," she warned in a shaky voice.

Ignoring her nervous pronouncement, Court sat down on the bed beside her. With his back propped against the headboard, he gathered her to him before she had a chance to scramble away. "It will," he assured her calmly. He buried his fingers in her hair and rubbed the nape of her neck in a soothing, circular motion.

Philippa folded her arms tightly across her chest, careful to keep the sheet over her breasts. "You've done this before?" she asked skeptically. At his silence, she glanced at him from the corner of her eye. "Of course you have," she added in a disgruntled tone. The heat of a blush spread over her cheeks. Lord, she felt like such a fool!

Court ran his fingers down the slope of her shoulder and over her arm in a comforting gesture, seemingly unperturbed by her rigid posture or the way she jumped at his touch. Beneath the white sheet, she felt his hairy thigh brush against hers and quickly pressed her legs together. He bent his head and traced the shell of her ear with his soft, moist tongue. "We're not going to hurry," he whispered.

"We're not?" she asked, and he smiled at the relief in her words.

"No," he reassured her, "we're going to take all the time we need. We're going to touch each other and become familiar with each other's bodies. You do like to touch me, don't you?" he cajoled.

"Yes," she admitted. She could hardly deny it. Lured on by his whispered encouragements, she'd been touching him for the last two weeks. His clothed upper body, that was. Not . . . not down there!

In an unhurried, leisurely manner, Court slid her down on the mattress beside him. Under the concealing sheet, he slipped his arm around her waist and turned her toward him. "Go ahead, little pixie, touch me," he urged huskily. "Touch me wherever you want. I'm your husband. My body belongs to you."

At his words, a thrill rocketed through Philippa. Tentatively, she placed her hand on his bare chest. His pectoral muscles bunched beneath her fingertips, and he released a harsh, pent-up breath. She froze in doubt as she met his gaze. "Go on," he rasped.

And at the urgency of his words, something inside Philippa burst like a flood. She stroked her hands over his magnificent body, learning the feel of every ridged muscle and hard bone, tracing the bumps of his rib cage and the firm line of his lean flanks. He caught her hand and carried it down to his male member, and she gasped at the feel of smooth, satiny skin and hard manhood.

When she had touched him everywhere, he rolled her beneath him and explored her body with his mouth and tongue. He covered her smaller frame with his larger one, rubbing his bare skin against hers. Startled at the intimacy of his caresses, Philippa's breath came in quick, short pants. She was on fire, burning with a need that had been smoldering inside her for two long weeks. She lifted herself against him, seeking some unknown goal which only he seemed to understand.

"Oh, Court," she moaned in confusion, caught in a maelstrom of sensations, her eyes shut tight. "What's happening to me?" She raked her nails across his back and buried her fingers in the thick hair at the nape of his neck.

Kneeling between her legs, Court spread her quivering thighs and slowly, carefully eased his stiff member into her tight, resisting womanhood. "Pippa," he called hoarsely, and she lifted her lids to gaze into his eyes. "This is the only time it will hurt," he promised with aching tenderness. "Darling, I love you." With a powerful thrust of his hips, he buried himself deep inside her. Philippa cried out in surprise at the searing pain. Tears sprang to her eyes.

"Ah, sweetheart, sweetheart," he whispered as he kissed her eyelids, her chin, her nose. "Don't cry, little love, don't cry," he soothed. "Oh, God, I want you so much." He kissed her with his open mouth, his tongue delving and retreating, coaxing her to forgive him for the hurt he'd just inflicted, as her body gradually became accustomed to the shock of his invasion.

Little by little, the pain turned to pleasure. A feeling of fullness spread through her groin and with it a mounting sense of excitement. When Court began to move inside her, gradually building a slow, steady, unhurried rhythm, Philippa gasped with delight at each stroke. "Oh, Court," she moaned, "I never knew . . ."

"Come with me, sweetheart," he urged. "Let me take you to paradise."

Philippa wrapped her arms around her husband, pulling him closer, straining to bring him deeper inside her. God above, it felt so wonderful! Court rocked and pounded and drove into her as her muscles clutched and spasmed around him. An explosion of pure pleasure spread through Philippa at the same moment his straining body stiffened and jerked spasmodically. With a soft, ululating cry, Philippa floated to paradise, the sound of Court's harsh groan of release echoing in her ear. . . .

Gradually, Philippa realized that she'd been daydreaming. She glanced at Warbeck, wondering if he had been thinking of their wedding night, too. The smoldering glow in his eyes told her he remembered it all quite clearly.

Frantically, she tried to recall what they'd been talking about before her thoughts had drifted into the past. Sea bathing and the tonic effects of ocean air and salt water. "People have come a long way from merely drinking the waters at the Pump Room in Bath for their apoplectic disorders," she commented.

With Kit beside them, there was nothing Warbeck could say about her long silence. "In the years to come," he stated prosaically, as though their wedding trip was the furthest thing from his mind, "more and more people will be spending their summer holidays at the ocean shore. We're going to make Ghyllside an important and fashionable retreat."

"I hadn't realized you were so deeply involved in the town," she said, struggling to keep her wayward thoughts on financial concerns.

Court rested his arm on the seat back behind her, leaned closer, and spoke in her ear, his words low and husky. "What I'm deeply involved with is right here beside me." He raised his voice and continued, "You can go a little faster, Lady Sandhurst. When you have a fine, well-bred mare who's naturally fast, you'll weary and annoy her by always holding her back."

She loosened the reins slightly, and the piebald broke into a trot. Court smiled at her obvious delight in driving a swift, high-stepping horse.

"I was surprised to see how few outsiders were visiting Ghyllside when we were there yesterday," she said. "The town is so quaint and lovely, it's as though time has passed it by. I would have thought many more people would be coming to see it."

Court lifted a golden tendril that curled at the nape of her neck and idly rubbed it between his thumb and forefinger. She sat so near he could smell the perfume of spring flowers that rose from the silken strands. How long would it take him to coax her into his bed? He was determined to seduce her before they returned to Chippinghelm, even if he had to delay their departure indefinitely. And how many times would he need to bed her before he succeeded in getting her pregnant? Philippa must have been with child by the time they returned home from their honeymoon. Yet she and Sandhurst had never had a baby, even though they'd lived together for well over a year. Court knew the odds were against his getting Philippa with child before they left the villa this time, but that sure as hell wouldn't stop him from trying.

"Ghyllside has been overlooked in the past," he answered as though his thoughts were entirely on the discourse at hand, "because there's a lack of good transportation into the town. A public coach comes from Ramsgate every day, but the main road into the port is winding and narrow, making it difficult and uncomfortable to reach the town by any means other than sail. It's far easier for people to go to more accessible seaside resorts."

"But won't that continue to be a problem?"

"Not in the future. We're going to bring the visitors in by coaches driven over rails."

Philippa stared at him, her eyes incredulous. "You

mean the steam engines you were talking about at Belle's dinner party? The ones that ride along iron tracks?"

"Exactly. I'm going to build a road of iron rails from London to the sea."

She burst out laughing. "What a preposterous notion! Do you think people will willingly ride behind one of your incredible steam-driven machines? Lady Augusta was right. The passengers would be afraid of being blown to kingdom come."

"Oh? I seem to recall that you once said you were willing to ride on it," he countered with an ironic smile.

Philippa snapped her mouth shut, remembering his pithy comment on her impulsive nature. She had no wish to bring up that controversial topic again, especially with her son seated right beside her.

"I'll ride on it, sir," Kit piped up.

"You'll do more than ride on it, young man," Warbeck told him. "You're going to be one of my major investors."

Philippa scowled. "Don't you think it's a little risky to put Kit's funds into such a newfangled contraption? Wouldn't it be wiser to wait for a few years until it proves itself feasible?"

"Trevithick has already proved the feasibility of the steam locomotive," he answered smoothly, unperturbed by her skepticism. "An engineer named George Stephenson is working right now on a new type of rail at the Killingsworth Colliery in Newcastle. He plans to conduct experiments on reducing the rolling resistance on a graded roadbed. One of the major obstacles in the past has been the lack of capital required to build a roadway in accordance with Stephenson's theories. I'm willing to invest heavily in the graded roadbed because I believe that someday steam-powered railways will serve the entire population. By the time Kit is a grown man, they'll provide a whole new method of transportation for the masses."

"I still think it sounds risky," she said stubbornly.

"You have to take financial risks," Warbeck informed her with an arched brow, "or you never make a substantial profit. And if we don't move forward on this idea now, there are plenty of potential investors who'll see the practical advantage of these new inventions in the near future. We can't wait for the rest of the nation's financiers to wake up. We stand to make millions on this investment."

"Pooh," she replied in disbelief. "No one could make that much money on any investment." Philippa felt a stirring of unease. What would happen if Warbeck's grand idea came to naught? The whole thing could prove unworkable. Good Lord, a steam engine could literally blow up in their faces. The thought of a substantial part of Kit's trust being invested in such a fantastic scheme alarmed her.

They were approaching Ghyllside from the north, which meant descending a hill that led down to the seaport. Philippa focused her attention on her driving.

"Don't hurry your horse off the top of the rise," Warbeck advised, "or you're liable to find you're going too fast. A pulling horse is inclined to start off suddenly when he's relieved of the weight of the carriage and then get out of control on the descent. It's better to start off slowly at the crest of the hill, so you're able to maintain a firm check on your animal, if need be."

"Shouldn't we put on the brake?" she asked nervously. The decline suddenly looked steeper and possibly even dangerous.

"No, you've got the carriage and your little mare well in hand. Whenever you clap on the drag, the horse is forced to pull the full load of the vehicle. Try to make her work as easy as possible. Only put the brake on if the descent is steep." He pointed ahead.

"We want to turn up that first street. Give her a gentle hint which direction we're going to take by slightly feeling the rein."

Worried that she might turn too sharply going around the corner and bump the gig against a lamppost or the edge of the cobblestone pavement, Philippa fought the urge to draw back suddenly on the reins and signal the piebald to halt. But blast it, she refused to give up at the first challenging moment. Following Warbeck's continued instructions, she safely rounded the corner, feeling absolutely splendid at her accomplishment.

She'd always wanted to drive a carriage. When they were first married, Warbeck had promised to teach her, but somehow the opportunity never arose.

Warbeck was a renowned whip. She'd seen him drive every kind of team and vehicle with consummate skill. To think that he would be there to help Kit learn how to drive filled her with maternal satisfaction—until she remembered that Warbeck was betrothed. Would the duke's new bride allow him to spend time with his ward after they were married? The uncompromising line of his jaw told her one thing. If he wanted to spend his time teaching Kit how to drive, the future duchess of Warbeck would have very little to say about it.

Philippa was extremely aware of the compelling man who sat beside her. Dressed in a tan hunting jacket and trousers, he rode with one strong arm resting on the padded leather seat back. His long legs were stretched out in front of him, his booted feet braced casually on the footboard. His muscled thigh was less than an inch from the skirt of her lemon-colored promenade gown. He'd used the opportunity of instructing her to draw steadily closer, till she was achingly conscious of his every move. More than once he'd brushed against her, seemingly by accident. Several times, she'd felt his fingertips lightly stroking the curls at the nape of her neck. Her entire body reacted with a dreamy longing to that familiar, seductive touch.

Had he planned her driving lesson with that reason in mind, knowing that by placing the reins in her hands, his own would be free to explore? Intuitively, she realized that only Kit's immediate presence protected her from a further, much more aggressive assault on her senses. Thank God, her son was seated right beside her.

Under Warbeck's direction, she drove carefully down St. Dunstan's Lane, which led to the center of Ghyllside, and pulled into the courtyard of the Eight Bells.

"Is this your inn, sir?" Kit asked. He craned his head to look up at the half-timbered building with its rows of diamond-paned windows sparkling in the sunshine.

"It is," his guardian replied, climbing down from the carriage. "What do you think?"

"It looks awfully old."

Warbeck smiled and lifted the boy to the cobbled pavement. He extended his hand to Philippa and guided her down from the gig. "The interior of the inn has been completely renovated," he explained, "but it was once the meeting place of a band of notorious smugglers. They hid their contraband in the cellar. The men used to haul their stolen goods straight up over the seawall during the night."

"Gosh, smugglers!" Kit's eyes glowed with anticipation. He peered up at the inn as though hoping to see a swashbuckling pirate at one of the windows. "Do they come here any more, *signóre?*"

"No, Kit. Fortunately, the port is much too civilized for that now." Warbeck looked at Philippa, and the warm amusement in his silvery gaze stirred an answering tenderness deep within her.

A budding awareness of what a wonderful father he would be both terrified and enthralled her. How could she have believed that he would have spurned his own child? He loved Kit. Her vision misted with tears, and she turned away quickly, as if to study the inn's carved oak door. "Shall we investigate the scene of their crimes?" she asked in a cheery voice. She bit her lip and quickly wiped the tears from her lashes before they were noticed.

"Let's explore Ghyllside first," Warbeck suggested. "We can come back to the Eight Bells for our luncheon. After which, I'll take you and Kit down to see the secret hiding chambers where the smugglers stowed their booty."

She turned back to find them standing hand in hand, waiting for her. The tall, imperious, autocratic duke and the sturdy, bright-eyed little boy. Blue-black hair, patrician features, intelligent gray eyes stared back at her. A person would have to be blind not to know they were father and son. A person would have to be deranged to think she could keep one from the other. Like a jagged bolt of lightning cracking open the heart of an oak, the surety of her coming loss split her heart asunder.

She was going to lose Kit. Eventually, inexorably, Warbeck would take him from her. And once the duke realized the full extent of her duplicity, he would turn his back on her forever. Philippa forced a gay, carefree smile to her trembling lips. What was done, was done, and could never be undone. Whatever small measure of time there was left, she was going to spend it happily with her son, treasuring every precious moment.

The trio explored the seaside town together. They visited the shops which lined the narrow lanes and the ancient town hall with its four-hundred-year-old clock. They watched in amazement as two voluptuous brass mermaids struck the quarter hour with their tails.

From the height of the old seawall, they looked down at the quay, where a cluster of large buildings provided shelter for the fishing boats being constructed by the craftsmen whose Huguenot ancestors had come to Ghyllside from France four generations ago.

As Kit scampered ahead of them, Warbeck pointed to the hills west of the town. "Along the cliff we'll build a broad promenade with a commanding view of the Channel," he told her. "One day there will be lawns and flower beds for nearly two miles, connected to the shore road by footpaths and more gardens below. Eventually, we'll construct a promenade pier and a concert pavilion."

Philippa turned in a circle, amazed at the sheer beauty in every direction. "I'm beginning to comprehend what you and the others envision. But in a way, it will be a shame for Ghyllside to lose its isolation."

He caught her hand and drew her closer. "My villa will always be the only home on Gull's Nest Bay," he said thickly. "I own all the land that surrounds it." His eyes glowed with a fierce carnal message. One of primal need and taut, male sexual hunger. "Believe me, Philippa, I wouldn't give up the privacy it affords for all the money in the world."

Entrapped by the blatant sensuality in his gaze, she stood absolutely still, reading the pagan eroticism he willed her to share. Her pulse beat frantically. In that instant, she knew, beyond a doubt, that he was keeping himself on a tight leash, biding his time until Kit was asleep or otherwise occupied. But sooner or later, Warbeck would attempt to seduce her. Her heart hammering, she released a pent-up breath and tore her gaze away. She prayed he hadn't read the answering hunger in her eyes.

The port had a busy marketplace close to the wharf. Early each day, fishermen brought in their morning's catch of whiting and flounder fresh from the Channel. Farmers from the surrounding countryside carted in their produce and livestock. Warbeck, Philippa, and Kit wandered through St. Dunstan's market, enjoying the marvelous sights and smells. They stopped to buy hot oat buns topped with honey and drink tall glasses of cool apple cider.

Philippa was aware that everyone who saw them assumed that they were a family. She found it much pleasanter to pretend it was true, if only for the day, than to dwell on the harsh reality.

"Oh, look, Mama!" Kit called, his mouth full of food. "There are three little puppies over there. Can I pet them?"

She looked at Warbeck. "We're in no hurry, are we, Your Grace?"

He smiled at her with easygoing complaisance, as though he were completely unaware of the turmoil inside her. "Of course, you can pet them," he told Kit. "Let's all go over and take a closer look."

The Welsh terriers were adorable, with long, thick, wiry coats and sturdy, compact bodies. They put their small, catlike paws up on the edge of the wooden crate and peeked at the newcomers, barking a frantic welcome. A rotund farmer's wife turned from her booth heaped high with radishes, cucumbers, and potatoes. "Would the little master like to hold one?" she asked with a friendly, gap-toothed smile.

Kit needed no further invitation. He lifted a black and tan terrier up in his arms, and the puppy lavished kisses on his smooth cheek. "*Buon giórno, fanciullo,*" Kit said happily. The puppy seemed to understand Italian, for his little upright tail sped back and forth in a frenzied response, while his compatriots yipped and pleaded for their share of attention.

Philippa picked one up and looked into its dark eyes. The tan-and-gray puppy squirmed and barked excitedly. "Hello, little girl," she cooed. "You're sure a pretty thing."

"Ye may buy 'em if ye wish, Y'r Lordship," the farmwife said, wiping her hands on her green-and-white striped apron. She was as round and ruddy as one of her shiny radishes. "Me husband breeds 'em for rattin', but they're equally good chasin' after the fox."

"Could we, *signóre?*" Kit asked, his heart in his eyes. "Could we get them?"

"Oh, Kit," Philippa interjected sympathetically, "we'd have to take them back to Sandhurst Hall in our coach. His Grace and Lady Augusta wouldn't want to ride all the way back to Chippinghelm with three little puppies crawling over their laps." She looked at Court, trying to keep the entreaty from her eyes.

Ignoring the painful twinge in his thigh, Court dropped slowly and carefully down on one knee and scratched the third terrier behind its small, folded, V-shaped ears. He ran his hand over the wide skull and clean-cut muzzle and felt the strong neck and sinewy legs. The tan puppy was square and robust, giving every indication that he and his siblings would make game, courageous, affectionate playmates. Weighing the prospect of a two-day journey in the company of a yapping, chewing, restless little puppy against the disappointment he'd encounter in both Philippa's and Kit's expressive eyes, he came to a quick conclusion. "One," he said in a voice that brooked no further questioning. "We can get one."

"Hurrah!" Kit squeezed the puppy to his chest and performed an ecstatic jig.

"Which will you choose?" Philippa asked Kit with an encouraging smile. The look of gratitude in her violet eyes almost made Court forget that the puppy probably hadn't even been trained not to wet indoors. It was going to be a long ride home.

One by one, Kit picked up the terriers and held them close. He patted their backs, scratched under their chins, and nuzzled their velvet noses. But the first little fellow had already captured his heart. "I'll take this one."

"What will you name him?" his mother asked.

"Fanciullo."

"Ah, Little Boy," Court said. "A good name. He looks like he'll be a strong hunter. I had a terrier like this when I was young. He'll make a fine companion."

Court paid the beaming woman, and they turned to go, the puppy wriggling excitedly in Kit's arms. As they walked away, Philippa caught Court's sleeve and leaned closer. "Thank you," she whispered, squeezing his arm gratefully.

He met her gaze, basking in the admiration he found there. This was going to be easier than he'd thought. Every time he did something for his son, he improved his own standing in Philippa's eyes. Wait until she saw what was going to sail into Gull's Nest Bay tomorrow morning. He'd have her in bed with him by nightfall.

The muscles in his groin tightened at the thought. He ached to cover her slender body with his, to bury his throbbing flesh inside her sweet warmth and plant his seed deep within her. God, if he could just get her pregnant as easily as he'd done the first time. His blood surged through his veins at the thought. If he could outmaneuver the gods of fate, he could have it all.

"Every boy needs his own dog," he said softly, so Kit wouldn't overhear. "But I was hoping we could wait till we returned to Chippinghelm before we got him one."

"I know this wasn't the most convenient time," she apologized, "but I think it was love at first sight."

"Well, I can certainly understand that," he answered with a provocative grin. "I've suffered the same experience myself." To his satisfaction, she blushed charmingly. "Now what would you like to do next?"

Philippa pointed to a ladies' apparel shop across the street. "I want to go into the *Salon de la Mode*, if you gentlemen won't be too bored. There's an item displayed in the window that I'd like to look at more closely."

"Kit can accompany you," Warbeck answered, "while I walk down to the docks for a few minutes. Take all the time you'd like in the shop, and I'll meet you there."

"I'd rather go with you, sir," Kit said, jerking his chin up to keep the puppy from smacking him on the lips while he talked.

"Next time, you shall," Warbeck promised. "But right now, I want you to keep your mother company while I take care of a business matter."

Though disappointment was plain in the child's clear, gray eyes, he accepted his guardian's instructions without a quibble. "Thank you for the puppy, *signóre*," he said with a grateful smile.

Warbeck returned the smile. "You're welcome, Kit. Now you take good care of Mama. I'll meet you both in the ladies' shop."

Chapter 13

Court walked around the small sloop, eyeing it from every angle.

"What do you think, Your Grace? Will she do?"

He nodded in appreciation. "She'll do."

The two men stood inside the tall wooden building that housed the shipyard of Bonnet and Sons. The single-masted craft they studied was sleek and graceful. She was the simplest form of rig, having only one headsail and one mainsail. It would be several years before Kit could handle her all by himself, but eventually he'd be able to cruise around Gull's Nest Bay with expertise. And one day, he'd have a brother or sister to sail with him. Maybe both. Maybe more.

"The jib can be changed to a larger or smaller size, giving greater or lesser sail area as you require, Your Grace," Paul Bonnet said proudly. He removed his workman's cap and ran a blue-veined hand through his thinning hair. "I designed her especially for single-handed sailing. She's small, but she's swift and weatherly."

Court met the old man's honest gaze with complete trust. Bonnet had built The *Golden Witch* to Court's exact specifications, producing a craft that was strong, watertight, buoyant, and stable. He knew the same qualities were present in the sloop. He'd be damned if he'd let his son go out on the water in any vessel that wasn't entirely seaworthy. "Can you sail her into Gull's Nest Bay tomorrow morning?" he asked.

The master shipbuilder touched his cap to his forehead. "I'll be happy to, your lordship. We'll bring her around the point just after sunrise."

"Good." Court's mouth turned up at the thought of Kit's reaction when he saw the sloop. "It's going to be a surprise."

"Ah, for your young son, no doubt."

Court stared at the man in mild astonishment, wondering how he could have known about Kit. In all his dealings with Paul Bonnet, he'd never discussed anything about his family—or lack of one.

"I saw you at the marketplace earlier this morning with your lovely lady and child, Your Grace," Bonnet explained. "I assumed you were purchasing the sloop for him." He beamed with pleasure at his own astute conjecture.

Nonplussed, Court paused for a moment and then smiled in resignation. Hell, he couldn't keep Kit's paternity a secret, no matter what the investigation he'd launched eventually proved. All people had to do was see them together to know he'd sired the boy. "The sloop is a gift for my son," he admitted.

"Children, themselves, are a wondrous gift," Paul Bonnet said, his chest swelling with pride. He was nearly toothless, and his sunken smile highlighted the folds of his craggy, weathered face. "My wife and I have eight all together. Four girls and four boys. Our sons are shipwrights, everyone of them, and our grandsons will follow in their footsteps. The love of the sea and sailing craft is in our blood."

"I hope to have more children, myself," said Court. He tried not to grin like an idiot, but the thought of Philippa swollen with his child sent his spirits soaring. "Eight sounds like a pretty large number, however. I think I'll be satisfied with an even half dozen."

Bonnet rubbed the side of his nose with his callused forefinger and cackled gleefully. "Oh, six are quite enough, Your Grace. Quite enough, indeed."

The two men moved toward the sloop to admire it closer. The beautiful little craft was a work of art, its regal lines flowing gracefully.

"The only thing left to be completed waits on your pleasure, Your Grace." The master craftsman tilted his head and looked at Court in jovial expectation. "Have you decided what you're going to name her?"

"Yes," he said. "We'll christen her *Sea Gull II*."

Bonnet raised his shaggy eyebrows inquiringly. "I recall seeing a sloop by that name around these waters some years ago. Was the craft yours, Your Grace?"

"Mine and my brother's." For a moment, Court felt once again the familiar disquiet that always came at the thought of Chris and their last summer sailing on Gull's Nest Bay. Then he looked at the brand-new sloop and the faded ache of disillusionment turned to hope. Like the pristine sailing craft before him, Kit was a symbol of life renewed, stronger, better, wiser. In his son, Court would see the resurrection of all his boyhood dreams. He understood, with heartened insight, his grandmother's immediate and unprecedented attachment to her only great-grandchild. Kit was the thread that linked the past to the future.

Court placed his hand on the elderly man's shoulder and squeezed it gratefully. "Thank you, Bonnet. You've done a magnificent job."

The shipbuilder looked startled, more moved by the nobleman's touch than his words of praise. "Your young son will be safe on board the *Sea Gull*, Your Grace," he said in a throaty voice. "You have my word on it."

They shook hands, man to man, father to father, neither of them having to ask why the other suddenly had tears glistening in his eyes.

* * *

Court made his way up from the docks and turned down a narrow alley that led to St. Dunstan's Lane. As he neared the corner, he heard a puppy barking wildly. He rounded a building to see two junior naval officers crowding close to Philippa. His gut tightened in rage when he realized that one of the men had dared to put his hand on her arm.

He'd kill them.

He started up the street, cursing fluently. Never had he regretted his injured leg so much.

The one holding Philippa had massive shoulders and a queue of dark brown hair hanging down below his tricorn hat. The other was blond and thin. They were both in their early twenties, intent on enjoying their brief time ashore and eager to sow their wild oats before their ship headed back out to sea.

Philippa batted at their hands ineffectually. Step by faltering step, she backed down the street, trying to draw them away from her son. Several packages lay on the cobblestones in front of the clothing store, where she must have dropped them when the men first approached. "Go back into the shop, Kit," she urged in a frightened voice. "Do as I say. Now!"

"Let go of my mama," Kit cried, ignoring his mother's instructions. He tugged on the long tail of the skinny man's dark blue coat. "Leave my mama alone!" The game little terrier raced around their feet, yapping ferociously.

With a frustrated oath, the junior officer turned and shoved Kit aside. The boy flew backward and landed on his rump with a yowl of outrage. He scrambled to his feet, hollering a fluent and pithy obscenity in Italian.

Philippa screamed in terror for her son. "He's just a little boy!" she cried. "How dare you! How dare you!" Furious beyond reason, she started pounding her fists on the larger man's face and chest—anywhere she could land a blow.

The dark-haired assailant jerked his head back out

of range, laughing uproariously. "Stap me, if you ain't a scrapper," he chortled. "Hey, George, boy, I don't think the little petticoat likes me."

The two midshipmen were so engrossed in their quarry, they didn't hear Court coming. The moment he was within striking distance, he smashed George Boy on the head with the gold head of his cane. The impact caught the lanky blond directly behind his ear. The bastard dropped like a stone.

Shocked into silence, the brawny naval officer foolishly retained his grip on Philippa's arm. He turned to face her would-be rescuer with a sneering grin, the long, deadly barrel of his sidearm pointing straight at Court's chest.

Philippa met Court's gaze, her face pale and drawn with fright. Her eyes darted to where Kit stood watching, frantic that he might try to intervene.

"It's all right, mate," the midshipman sniggered. His glazed, bloodshot eyes glittered dangerously. "We're just havin' a little sport. We ain't gonna hurt her none. Not a fancy-dressed lady like her. We were only tryin' to introduce ourselves proper like. She treated us like we were scum, no better'n bilge water." The pockmarked man had been drinking heavily, which explained why he'd had the temerity to accost a decent woman and her child on the street. But he wasn't weaving or slurring his words. He was just drunk enough to be dangerous.

"Get your hand off my wife, mate," Court drawled, his eyes on the pistol, "and we can forget this ever happened."

The end of the barrel wavered unsteadily. "Your wife?"

"If your captain should get wind of the fact that two of his junior officers tried to force their attention on a member of the peerage, he'll flog your worthless hides."

The man squinted at Court with glassy eyes and

suddenly realized the seriousness of his mistake. He swung a stunned gaze to the wealthy and titled lady he held in his grasp.

In that instant, Court struck the seaman's wrist with his cane and the gun fell, crashing to the cobblestones. Using the cane for leverage, Court put all his strength behind his blow, smashing his antagonist squarely in the face with his fist. Court grunted with satisfaction as he felt several teeth and the cartilage of his opponent's nose give way. The midshipman's head snapped back under the onslaught, his cockaded tricorn falling to the ground. He staggered, but managed to regain his balance and crouch in a street fighter's stance. With surprising speed, he drove his ham-sized fist into Court's stomach.

Court reeled under the force of the vicious blow and felt his weak leg buckle under him. As he fell, he slipped the cane between his adversary's ankles and rammed it hard against the man's shin. They collapsed to the pavement together. Court ignored the searing pain that lanced through his thigh and smiled in morbid gratification. Flat on the ground, they were equals. He flung himself on top of his burly opponent before the man had a chance to recover his senses and pinned him to the rough stones with his weight. Holding the cane in both hands, Court shoved it against his foe's throat.

The midshipman clawed desperately at the cane, as the polished hickory wood pressed relentlessly against his windpipe. Blood flowed from his mangled mouth and broken nose. His face turned red, then purple. His eyes bugged out grotesquely.

"You can release the bloody cove now, your lordship," an unfamiliar male voice suggested calmly. "We'll take care of him for you."

Court caught sight of a constable's uniform from the corner of his eye. Dredging up every ounce of willpower inside him, he forced himself to remove the cane from his adversary's throat. He braced his weight on the sturdy hickory wood and clambered awkwardly to his feet, cursing softly at the throbbing pain in his thigh. Behind him, the seaman choked and gagged on his own blood as he clutched his neck with both hands and tried to drag in enough air to remain conscious.

Court's gaze swung to Philippa, who was crouched beside Kit. Her arms were wrapped around her son and she was staring at Court as though he were a stranger.

Dragging his numb leg, he moved to stand beside her. "Are you all right?" he asked sharply, still feeling the rage pounding through every pore. "If those bastards hurt either of you ..."

She shook her head, then jerked her chin up and down in a trembling affirmative. "No ... I'm ... I'm fine. So's Kit. We're fine." She pressed the tips of her fingers against her lips as though she were about to burst into tears. "I thought ... I was afraid you were going to ..."

A second officer of the law came over to join them. He lifted his hat politely to Philippa, then addressed Court. "I warned those two rotters last night to be on the coach leaving Ghyllside today. They should have listened to my advice. We'll keep them in the town jail until they sober up. Would you like me to place them under arrest, your lordship?"

Court turned to watch the other policeman jerk the dark-haired midshipman up by his navy blue coat collar. The man weaved about precariously, holding his hands to his swollen face. "No. Just make sure their captain learns what happened here today. He'll see that they're duly punished. And see that the word is put out, Constable," he rasped. "If any man in Ghyllside lays so much as a finger on my wife or my son, I'll kill him."

Philippa drew an audible breath as she rose to her feet. "Your Grace," she said in a low, shocked voice,

"I don't think those men would really have harmed me on a public street."

Court whipped around to face her. The fear he'd felt for both of them was still a tight knot in his gut. "You let me be the judge of how seriously they could have harmed you," he said curtly. "I told you to wait for me inside the shop. Next time, follow my instructions." He scowled down at Kit, who was clutching her skirt with one hand and holding the tan-and-black puppy with the other. "And you, young man, when your mother tells you to do something, you do it. Understand? You should have gone into the shop immediately and called out for help. Trying to stop a grown-up was a foolish thing to do. You could have been badly hurt."

"*Sí, nòbile,*" Kit said meekly. But despite the tongue-lashing, he looked up at Court with open adoration.

Court turned to the peace officer who waited politely nearby. "Have the shop send someone to the Eight Bells with my wife's packages."

The man touched his hat in reply.

Gradually, Court's pulse returned to normal, his heart stopped pumping blood at a frenetic pace, and the feeling of rage subsided to a tense, smoldering anger now that he was certain they were both unharmed. He took a deep, calming breath and offered Kit his hand. The child took it without hesitation. "You two were extremely courageous," Court said tenderly. "As a matter of fact, I'm very proud of you both. Now let's go back to the inn."

Kit grinned in relief at his guardian's words of forgiveness. "You beat the stuffing out of them both, sir," he said worshipfully. "I never saw anything so wonderful."

Court shook his head in mock dismay. "What a bloodthirsty little Tartar you are. Tell me something, Kit. How on earth did you learn to swear like that?"

"I heard the boatmen yelling it at each other from

their gondolas. I used to practice in secret." Kit essayed a little hop of joy. "But I'll have to learn to curse in English, now that I'm in England. I've picked up some good words from you already, *signóre.*"

Court tried his best not to laugh. It proved impossible. He gave up, tipped his head back, and whooped out loud.

Philippa was not nearly so forbearing of the stern scolding she'd just received. Nodding a curt goodday to the policemen, she took the puppy from Kit and grabbed his hand. Then she marched stiffly alongside the two of them without saying another word. Fanciullo, however, was as quick to forgive as Kit. He barked wildly and smacked her chin with his pink tongue. This time, Court had the wisdom not to crack a smile.

They returned to the Eight Bells for their midday meal. At Kit's request, they sat in the public dining room so he could watch the comings and goings of all the guests. Philippa tried to concentrate on the poached sole and sparkling wine, but found herself looking at Warbeck. His savage behavior had brought back vivid images of the day he'd discovered her with Sandy at the inn in Kensington. Until the afternoon he'd charged into the Four Coaches, she had never seen him enraged, had never even had a glimpse of his terrible temper or his reputed skill with his fists. She'd been frightened to death that he was going to murder Sandy on the spot.

Now he sat chatting with Kit as though nothing untoward had happened. He had no injury to show for his brawl except a small cut across his knuckles. His tan hunting jacket wasn't even torn. She'd sustained the loss of a blue satin bow from the puffed sleeve of her gown and a tiny rent along the seam at her shoulder. When he'd noticed the slight damage, it had looked as if he were going after the two midshipmen to thrash them all over again. She'd assured him that it was an old gown, due to be replaced and ridiculously out of style. He'd calmed down again, but she felt as though she were sitting next to a powder magazine that could explode at any moment.

Warbeck had repeatedly tried to bring her into the conversation, but she couldn't reconcile the charming gentleman who had taught her how to drive that morning with the infuriated male who'd nearly killed someone in a street fight only minutes before. She felt the same shocked confusion she'd felt when he'd turned his wrath on her and Sandy, calling his childhood friend terrible names and threatening her with a divorce.

When she'd first met the earl of Warbeck, she'd been swept off her feet by a tall, handsome, titled gentleman who wooed her with dazzling gallantry. During their month-long courtship and two brief months of marriage, she'd only started to get to know him. He'd been extremely possessive, jealous of any man who foolishly tried to flirt with her. And they'd had several arguments over his arrogant assumption that he would make all the important decisions. His attitude of unquestioned authority had rankled Philippa's strong sense of independence. After all, she'd been supporting herself as a schoolmistress and had been in charge of her own life for over a year when they met. But most of the time the newlyweds had been very loving and enormously happy. Until the day he found her hugging Sandy and went berserk ...

Her thoughts were distracted by the arrival of the public coach from Deal. Passengers swarmed into the dining room, in a hurry to order their food. They'd be given exactly twenty-five minutes to eat their meal and get back on the coach, or risk the danger of being left behind. The big, thickset coachman, wearing a many-caped benjamin with huge mother-of-pearl buttons and a bunch of daisies stuck in his lapel, wandered about the room offering his up-turned hat. Various people threw coins into the low-crowned, broad-brimmed headpiece with a murmur of thanks.

"What's that man doing?" Kit asked.

"He's collecting tips," Warbeck explained. "It's called kicking the passengers. In addition, those who are taken up for only short distances don't have to pay the full fee. The coachman gets to keep any fare not exceeding three shillings."

"What if they don't want to tip him?"

"Oh, a passenger can get by without it, if he's clever enough to slip away before the coachman notices him. It's called tipping the double. Lady passengers are especially notorious for it."

"I'd like to ride on a coach," Kit said cheerfully. "I think someday I'd like to be a coachman."

"Would you now?" Court asked with a fond smile. "Maybe that can be arranged."

Philippa watched in surprise as the duke rose and went over to the ruddy-faced coachman. While the two men spoke, the burly driver became more and more animated. Then Warbeck reached into his inside coat pocket and pulled out a money pouch. He dropped a stack of guineas into the coachman's outspread palm. To Philippa's growing astonishment, the bulky man presented Warbeck with his whip in return.

The duke returned, his eyes glinting with mischief. "Well, Kit, let's go take a try at driving a coach."

"Wow!" Kit jumped up from his chair so fast it tumbled over with a crash. The terrier barked his excited agreement.

"Whatever do you mean?" Philippa demanded. "Surely you're not going to attempt to drive a stage-coach?"

Warbeck lifted his straight black brows at the absurdity of her question. "How else can Kit learn what it's like? He has to decide if coaching is the right profession for him." He turned and started to walk away, then called back over his shoulder. "You're welcome to come along, if you wish."

Philippa gasped. He was using that same ploy again. She could either go with them or wait by herself till they returned. They started out the door, and she followed at their heels, right behind the gamboling little puppy. "How far do you intend to drive?" she asked in exasperation as they walked across the inn yard. "All the way to Ramsgate?"

Warbeck shrugged imperturbably. "Not that far, surely. Kit can get a feel of what it's like riding up on the box in five or six miles."

"Then what will you do? Walk back?"

"No, the coachman is going to follow along behind us in our gig. Luckily, there are no elderly passengers, so no one inside the coach will suffer an apoplectic fit if they get jostled about a tad. You can either ride with Hortimer Budd in our carriage or up on the box with us."

"This is insane," she protested, though the idea started to seem inviting.

Kit scrambled up to the coach's high front seat and waited expectantly while all the passengers who were going on to Ramsgate climbed into or on top of the Folkestone *Flyer*. There were eight in all. Four inside and four on the roof, not counting the guard, who'd ride in the rumble on the hind-boot, and the various packages, parcels, and trunks that were piled on top of the coach or in the boot.

"Come on, Mama," Kit pleaded. "Ride up here with us. It'll be fun."

She turned to Warbeck with a questioning scowl. "Do you know how to drive a stagecoach?"

"Certainly," he replied with a wicked grin. "How do you think I traveled back and forth to Eton?"

"I didn't say *ride* in one. I said *drive* one."

"That's what I did. I always sat up on the box of the Bristol *Defiance* with the coachman. The celebrated Tommy Brown started letting me take the reins when I was barely thirteen. I assure you, I was taught to drive by one of the best."

"Haven't you ever been afraid of anything?" she asked with a grudging smile.

He paused, his thick-lashed gray eyes suddenly thoughtful. "Yes," he said quietly. "I was afraid I'd never see you again."

She stared at him, her chest compressing painfully. He had voiced the very fear that had haunted her for over five years. "I was terrified of the same thing," she whispered.

"Come on, Mama, let's go!" Kit cried.

The guard, dressed in a scarlet coat smart enough to wear to a fox hunt, came up and lifted his hat politely. "Name's Amos Tufton, y'r lordship. With all due respect, sir, we'd better get on the road, if we're goin' to stay on schedule. Mr. Budd prides hisself on being punctual."

"Are you coming with us?" Warbeck asked her.

Philippa looked up at her son, high on the bench, and then back to the duke. His beckoning eyes issued an invitation for her to join them, not just for the ride, but for the rest of their lives. With a resigned shake of her head to indicate that she really ought to know better, she took his elbow and let him lead her to the coach. "Drive carefully, will you please?" she asked in a belated afterthought.

He touched the whip to his forehead in a salute. "You're talking to a member of the Four-in-Hand Club," he answered glibly. "I'll spring the team and have you three miles down the road before you're aware we've left the inn."

"That's what I'm afraid of," she murmured. But a ripple of anticipation went through her. With his assistance, she climbed up to the high seat and moved Kit to the center, where he'd be safer between them. Kit had set Fanciullo down in the front boot at his feet, and the puppy was happily chewing on the hem of the boy's duck trousers.

Philippa had never been on a public coach before. She hadn't realized she'd be so far from the ground. The fresh team waited impatiently, two grooms standing at the leaders' heads. This was one more first she was about to experience with Warbeck. She wondered if it would be as exhilarating as all the others.

After checking every buckle and ring on the harness and inspecting the coupling reins and curb chains, Court handed his cane up to Philippa and pulled on his gloves. He took the ribbons from their place above the tug-buckle and held them and the whip in his right hand. The difficulty of climbing aboard with his stiff leg sent a shaft of pain through his thigh, but he made it up to the driver's seat without suffering the ignominy of having to ask for anyone's help. He'd pay for the day's escapades later, when the ache in his old wound would keep him awake for hours, but it was a small price to render for the enjoyment of tooling a coach and four with Philippa and Kit beside him.

He turned to the passengers on the roof. A red-faced farmer holding a carton of peeping chicks, two spirited university students on their summer holiday, and a plump, painted doxy they'd obviously invited to come along, stared at him with varying degrees of interest. Court lifted his whip in a polite salutation and sat down. Then he passed the reins to his left hand, making sure they were in order and adjusted to the correct length.

The inn yard was crowded with ostlers, porters, stable boys, chambermaids, waiters, post-boys, boot-blacks, and grooms who'd heard that a London swell was going to wagon it out of Ghyllside. Everyone wanted to see the grand sight. Someone had decorated the bridles with hollyhocks, giving the adventure a festive air.

Court looked down at the restive horses—four dark browns, all sixteen hands—checking to be sure that no rein, or either of the inside lead-traces, were twisted, and that the coupling reins were crossed. The coachman had already warned him about the team. Two were jibbers, one was a bolter, and the fourth was an inveterate kicker. But the mark of a true dragman was to be able to drive any sort of team through any kind of country.

He glanced at the wiry guard, who immediately released the drag and scrambled to his place on the rumble at the back of the coach. "Sit fast!" Amos Tufton called out in warning.

Court nodded once to the grooms who held the leaders' heads. At the moment the horses were released, he tightened the reins to feel their mouths, giving them the office to start. Then he yielded his hand, and the team sprang forward.

The bystanders cheered as the clatter of hooves and the crunch of iron wheels on the cobblestones echoed around the courtyard. Traces tightened and creaked, pole chains clanked and banged, and swingle bars came up with a groaning lurch. The terrier braced his front paws on the top edge of the footboard and barked enthusiastically. Two thousand pounds of coach bounced and swayed as it passed under the stone archway of the Eight Bells Inn.

The guard carried a keyed bugle rather than the usual yard of tin. To Kit's elation, Tufton played "Rule Britannia" as the stagecoach rolled down St. Dunstan's Lane gathering speed, while passersby stopped to stare and shout encouragement.

Court glanced across the top of his son's bare head to look at Philippa. She held one hand pressed flat against her chest, the other to the brim of her bonnet. An expression of astonished delight shone on her beautiful face. She turned her head to meet his gaze, her eyes brilliant with excitement. "It's thrilling," she managed to gulp. She looked down at Kit, and the two of them burst out laughing. Laughing for joy at the sheer fun of it.

Court had the skittish, mettlesome team well in hand as they left the paving stones of Ghyllside and turned into the open road that led to Ramsgate. He slackened the reins, and the horses moved into a quick-stepping trot up a steep hill.

"I thought you said to take the crest of a rise slowly," Philippa called over the rattle and clang of the harness and poles.

"There's no need to worry," he assured her. "The team's a bit restive. They need to stretch their legs a little."

The *Flyer* topped the crown of the hill and fairly soared over it.

"Hurrah!" Kit cheered. "Make them go faster!"

"We don't need to go any faster," Philippa protested with a squeal. "We're flying now." But the look of jubilation on her face told Court she was having a wonderful time.

"They're not doing too bad for running blind," Court confessed.

"Blind!" she cried.

"Just the two wheelers," he explained with a grin. "Mr. Budd warned me about them before we left the inn."

They rolled down the long hill and into a valley. With a flick of the whip, Court touched the shoulder of the off leader, who was hanging to the side of the road. Then giving a slight turn of his wrist, he neatly caught the thong.

Kit watched in wide-eyed admiration. "Will you teach me how to do that, sir?"

"When you're a little older," he promised. "I practiced using the whip on a wooden chair by the hour, till I had the stroke and return of the thong down to perfection by the time I was ten."

At Philippa's look of astonishment, Court shrugged

good-naturedly. "Not everyone's a scholar," he told her with a grin.

When they had safely passed a slow moving farm wagon, he let the team gallop full out on a flat stretch of road. The breeze whipped their hair into their eyes and tugged on Philippa's straw bonnet. She finally gave up and held it in her lap. The marvelous sensation of speeding over the ground behind four fast-moving horses was intoxicating.

When they came to the tree-lined road that led to the villa, Court pulled back on the reins and brought the coach to a slow, gliding halt, then put on the brake, and descended. Amos Tufton quickly scrambled from his perch and raced around to the front of the *Flyer*, where he held the reins of the near wheeler, while Court helped Philippa and Kit down from the high seat.

"Can we do it again?" Kit entreated. He held Fanciullo in his arms, and the puppy barked and wriggled as though asking the same question.

Philippa smiled engagingly. "Yes, can we?"

"We've had enough excitement for one day," said Court. He gripped the handle of his cane and moved to the off leader's head. "But I promise to take you both for a ride in my private drag when we get back to London. I have a team of four matched chestnuts who refuse to let anyone pass them."

At that moment, Hortimer Budd drew up in the gig, and Philippa and Kit switched places with him. The coachman had kindly brought her packages, which had arrived at the Eight Bells before he left. They watched the stagecoach drive away, and then Court climbed into the two-wheeled carriage and turned the piebald mare down the shady, winding lane that led to Gull's Nest.

"Well, did you enjoy that?" he asked.

"Yes, sir," Kit stated emphatically. "I'm going to be a coachman when I grow up."

Court looked at Philippa. "How about you? Did you enjoy the ride?"

"Oh, my, yes!" she exclaimed. "That's the most thrilling thing I've ever done in my life!"

He leaned close and spoke softly in the pink shell of her ear. "Goddamn, you really know how to hurt a man."

Philippa's head snapped around. The startled look on her face told him she knew exactly what he referred to. Her cheeks turned crimson as she smashed her bonnet on top of her disheveled curls and tied the ribbons under her chin. "Well, it . . . it was exciting," she stammered lamely.

Court raised his voice so Kit could hear his reply. "I'll have to see if I can't think of something even more stimulating for tomorrow."

"What, sir?" his son asked.

"Oh, I don't know," Court drawled lazily. "I guess I'll have to sleep on it and tell you in the morning."

Chapter 14

Philippa awoke in the night to find moonlight streaming in through the French doors of her bedchamber. After their eventful day, she'd fallen sound asleep the moment she'd climbed into the large oak bed. She listened for a moment, wondering if Kit might have called out restlessly in his sleep from the adjoining room. Only the usual night sounds of the rambling summer home disturbed the silence, and she realized that it was the adventures of the day that had brought her to consciousness.

The enigma of the man who slept in the chamber next to hers continued to baffle her. Seeing him with Kit these last few days, she had begun to glimpse the innate goodness of Warbeck's inner character. It was as though, through his love for his child, she'd seen into his very soul. She had begun to perceive the father he could be, not just to Kit, but to any children he would sire in the future.

That he cared for Kit was without question. But it was more than merely male pride that he had produced a son in his own image. He truly loved the boy. Warbeck's deep feelings for Kit, combined with his determination to teach his son everything from fishing to coaching, had forced her to look at the temperamental man who had divorced her in a whole new light. Yet those characteristics of familial loyalty and unqualified love had been present in the

275

charming gentleman who'd originally wooed and
won her.

Not that she'd chosen the earl of Warbeck because
she believed he'd make a good father. Theirs had
been a very passionate, very physical relationship.
She'd been overwhelmed by his masculine presence,
his unabashed virility, and his unquestioned air of
authority. Even now, she knew very little about members of the stronger sex. At eighteen, she'd known
absolutely nothing.

Since returning to England, she had learned of
Warbeck's years of dissipation and debauchery after
their divorce and of his reputedly ruthless acquisition
of wealth. Now she understood her own part in it.
Cheated out of his bride, he had struck back at the
world with savage intensity. Was it any wonder that
the boy who'd been virtually ignored and eventually
forsaken by his parents had grown into a man who
believed that his wife would betray him, too? If she'd
stood her ground when he'd accused her of infidelity
and threatened to divorce her, there might have been
a chance that she could have convinced him of her
innocence. But running off with Sandy had furnished
the proof that Warbeck needed to obtain a Bill of Divorcement. In trying to protect her unborn child from
the abandonment she had suffered, she'd cheated her
son out of knowing his real father and herself out of
the happy family she once dreamed of. As for attempting to find another husband who could be a
stepfather for Kit, she'd known it was a lie when
she'd told Warbeck that she was considering it. For
no man would love Kit the way his own father loved
him. And she would never love any man but
Warbeck.

Sleepless, Philippa shoved the bedcovers aside and
rose. Picking up her dressing robe, she pulled it on
and opened the double doors that led to the balcony.
The July night was still and balmy. A giant moon
hung over the bay, turning the cresting waves phos-

phorescent in its silvery light. She walked to the railing and stared out into the evening's magical beauty. Memories of another summer night, when she and her handsome bridegroom had left their bedchamber and stolen down to the cove, filled her with an incredible longing. If she could only turn back time, how differently she would act. Instead of running like a scared rabbit, she would fight tooth and nail to prevent the estrangement that had separated her from her husband. She would have risked everything to keep them a family—even the chance that Warbeck might have killed Sandy. Even the chance that he might have taken her baby away from her.

From the shadows of the balcony, Court watched Philippa in silence, feasting on every delicate curve and graceful line. She stood looking out at Gull's Nest Bay, pensive and lovely. The moonlight bathed her in its soft glow, turning her long hair, loosened from its usual pins, into a cascade of pale curls. She wore a dressing gown of fine white lawn, the outline of her slim legs barely discernible in the muted light.

Unable to sleep for the pain in his old wound, he'd been sitting with his leg propped up on a soft ottoman, listening to the gentle crash of the waves hitting the sandy shore below him. Barefoot, he was dressed in a loose-fitting cotton shirt, open at the collar, and duck trousers. On the small table nearby sat the bottle of brandy he'd carried outside with him and the now empty glass. He'd been waiting for its effects to dull the ache in his thigh.

"It's a beautiful night, isn't it?" he asked quietly.

Startled, she whirled to face him. "Yes," she whispered. "I'm sorry to intrude. I didn't mean to disturb your solitude." The peignoir rustled about her ankles as she took a small, hesitant step toward her room.

"Don't go," he said thickly. "I can't sleep. Stay here and keep me company for a while."

"Your leg is bothering you?"

"A little." He shrugged. "I'm used to it."

Her glance flickered across the brandy snifter and half-filled bottle and then back to him, sympathy in her eyes. "Is there anything I can do?"

Yes, he thought, you can come to bed with me and hold me in your sweet arms and tell me you'll never leave me again.

"No," he said.

She turned and, resting her hands on the railing, gazed up at the full moon, the silence between them heavy with sensual tension. Court studied her finely chiseled profile, the high forehead, the aquiline nose, the full, generous mouth, the stubborn chin. "Were you having trouble sleeping?" he asked. "I can recommend the brandy, though we'll have to share the glass." He reached over to pour the liquor.

She shook her head and turned once more to face him, her expression serious. "I wanted to thank you for rescuing Kit and me from those naval officers today. I don't think I told you how brave you were to fight two men with your ... your injured leg."

He smiled. "I had a feeling you were angry at me for treating them so harshly."

"I ... I guess I was a little confused. When you threatened to kill anyone who touched Kit or me, I was frightened."

"Of me?" He couldn't keep the censure from his voice. "Surely you know that I would never raise my hand against you, no matter what the provocation."

"Yes," she whispered. "I know that."

Her answer brought a gut-twisting wrench of pain. "Then why did you tell everyone that I'd beaten you during our marriage?" The terse words were out before he could stop them. He grasped the arm of the chair, damning himself to perdition. Hell, he already knew the reason. She'd accused her bridegroom of brutality in order to justify her involvement with her lover.

Philippa took a step toward him, clearly stunned

by his accusation. "I never told anyone such a despicable lie!" she said hoarsely.

"Then someone else did. The newspapers were merciless in their depiction of me as a callous brute of a husband."

Her hand flew to her throat. "It must have been my bruised eye!" she said with sudden comprehension. "When you wrestled with Sandy, you accidentally struck me with your elbow. You probably weren't even aware of it." As she drew nearer, she clutched the edges of her dressing gown together, clearly agitated. "But I don't understand how anyone could have learned of it. We warned the servants at Sandhurst House to say nothing."

"Apparently at least one of them blabbered like a fishwife. That kind of gossip was too juicy to keep to themselves."

"No, I feel certain they didn't," she disclaimed. "Their pledges of silence were given with honest sincerity." She moved closer, the soft folds of the embroidered lawn stirring about her slender form. "But one of your servants may have said something."

"Mine?" Court refused to consider it. "How could they have even known?"

"I . . . I came to your town house to try to talk with you," she said in a hushed tone. "I was refused admittance, but your butler saw the bruise on my cheekbone and the swollen eye. He must have jumped to the wrong conclusion."

At her words, Court felt, once again, the exquisite torment of knowing that she'd stood on his doorstep and he'd refused to see her. At the time, he'd been filled with mindless rage because she'd betrayed him. In the years that followed, he'd have given anything to have that chance again. To go back in time and be allowed the opportunity to talk with her before she'd eloped with Sandhurst. Maybe something he might have said would have deterred her from her reckless course. But even in his ranting state, vowing to kill her lover and threatening to divorce her, he never dreamed she'd do anything so unbelievably scandalous as to run away. With an effort, he kept his reply calm and reasonable. "Even if Nash had seen your bruised face, he would never have repeated a thing to a living soul. I'd stake my life on his loyalty."

With a start, Philippa put her hand to her forehead and closed her eyes. The contrition in her voice was unmistakable when she spoke. "Your neighbors saw me. The countess of Flintshire and her daughter were standing on their front stoop when I turned to leave. They must have seen my face and told everyone that you'd beaten me."

Court was silent, relief flooding him. All these years he'd been certain she was to blame for the scathing portrayal of him in the public prints as an abusive fiend, a vile warlock who tortured innocent maidens.

She reached out her hand imploringly. "Court, I swear I never told anyone that you struck me. You must know I would never have uttered such a malicious falsehood."

He grasped her slender fingers and drew her down into his lap. Her eyes shone brilliant in the moonlight, and he read the anxiety on her worried features. "I believe you," he said huskily. He brought her close, savoring the wonderful sensation of holding her in his arms again. She smelled of spring flowers and fresh rain. He could feel the soft curves of her bare body beneath the gossamer lawn, and the muscles of his groin tautened reflexively. His heart thundered wildly as the blood rushed to his swollen sex. He groaned deep in his chest.

"Your leg . . ." she protested. "I'm hurting it."

"To hell with my leg." He captured her face in his hand and bent his head. Their lips met in a kiss filled with a feverish yearning that had never ceased. He stroked her tongue with his, telling her wordlessly how much he wanted her, how determined he was to have her.

Philippa slipped her arm around his neck and returned his kiss. She drew in a ragged breath as his hand cupped her breast, the heat of his touch burning through the thin material of her nightclothes. He tugged on the lavender ribbon that fastened her robe and slipped his hand inside. His thumb flicked across her nipple, and she arched in vibrant response.

"Ah, Philippa," he murmured, his voice hoarse with desire. "It's been so damn long." He bent his head and suckled her through the sheer linen.

The drugging pleasure he brought her was exquisite and irresistible. Yes, it had been a long, long time. Yet the memory of his fiercely erotic lovemaking was as clear and fresh as if it had been only yesterday. She wanted him to touch her. To build within her that all-consuming fire that had raged between them each time they'd come together.

She laced her fingers through his thick hair, her thumbs tracing the streaks of silver at his temples. He raised his head to meet her gaze. His gray eyes were filled with a savage intensity, as he caressed her breasts and watched the emotions that flitted across her face. He kissed her again, a blatantly seductive kiss of sensual need and carnal intent. A thrill of excitement caromed through her. She met his tongue with hers, telling him of her longing. Then she eagerly explored his warm mouth, her heart beating an ever-faster rhythm. He tasted of brandy and heady male ardor.

Philippa felt his large hand slide under the hem of her nightgown and caress her bare calf. The touch of his fingers on her inner thigh awoke a memory of passion so powerful her whole body shuddered. "Court," she protested breathlessly against his lips, "we shouldn't be doing this. It's wrong."

Warbeck gave a groan of primitive male need. "Ah, little pixie, nothing could be more right."

She drew back to look into his eyes. "We have to be absolutely certain," she said. "This time there's more than just ourselves and our wishes to consider."

Court slid his hand up her silken thigh and cupped her mound with his fingers. "I'm certain," he said hoarsely. "And I'll do whatever it takes to convince you." He caressed her velvet folds and felt her body respond with heat and moisture. "Tell me you don't want me, Philippa," he insisted, as he gently explored her delicate flesh. "Tell me you don't want me, and I'll let you go back to your room without another word."

Her eyelids slid shut. Her breathing grew shallow and jagged with need. Slowly, languidly, she shook her head back and forth, as if to deny the pleasure he was bestowing. But he saw the passionate response he sought in her softened features and knew her denial was a lie.

He kissed her, all the while stroking and building the need within her, till he felt her stiffen and arch upward in a shattering climax. He took her long, drawn-out cry of surrender into his mouth, as he continued to fondle her, enhancing her orgasm till she was writhing with pleasure in his arms. This was how he remembered her. Holding nothing from him. Giving herself over to him with total trust.

When she'd relaxed completely, he drew back and gazed at her. Her eyes were closed, her mouth soft with spent passion. He tenderly kissed her forehead, her lowered lids, her sweet lips. "Philippa," he said in a hoarse whisper, "come to bed with me. I'm aching with need for you."

In a haze of sexual languor, Philippa's lids drifted open. She looked up at Warbeck and recognized the stark hunger in his eyes. More than anything, she wanted to let him lead her to his bed and lie down with him, naked and trembling in his arms. But he'd turned against her before, without allowing her any explanation of the wrongdoing he'd accused her of. She couldn't bear that rejection a second time. She didn't think she could live through that much pain again. She reached up and touched his lips with one finger. "If only I could trust you . . ." she began in a plaintive whisper, the words torn from deep within her.

He stiffened. The smoldering heat of passion in his eyes turned to cold, banked anger. "Trust me?" he grated. "Haven't you got that backward? It's I who can't trust you."

She tried to sit up, but he held her against his arm, his strong hand splayed across her belly. She could feel his leashed power, feel the bulge of his hardened manhood pressed against her buttocks. She met his gaze and saw the raw, primal need flare up once again. "Then how could you speak to me of marriage?" she asked angrily. "How could you possibly pledge your life to someone you don't trust?"

He smiled sardonically. "Over half the men in England are married to women they don't trust. But the clever husbands make it impossible for their wives to be unfaithful."

"How?" she scoffed in disbelief.

"Oh, there are many ways. For one thing, a dead paramour makes an excellent example to any cur who might otherwise attempt a future liaison. For another, an obviously pregnant wife is rarely the target of carnal flirtations."

"And if you married me, which one of those strategies would you follow?" she challenged.

"Both."

Philippa fought to keep the shock from her voice. "At least you're honest." She squirmed in his grasp, trying to regain her feet. He held her fast. "The answer is no," she said.

"To which question? Will you marry me? Or will you go to bed with me?"

"To both. Now please, let me up."

Court recognized the determination in her eyes. He'd given the wrong answer, that was clear. But could she honestly expect him to trust her after she'd run off with his closest friend? He wanted her. And not just to regain his son. Even if Kit were Sandhurst's child, he'd still want her. But did he trust her? Hell, no.

He released her slowly. "How much longer will you continue to deny that you want me?"

She scrambled to her feet. "I don't deny that I want you, Warbeck. But I won't consider marriage without love. And loving someone means trusting them. Totally and completely."

Scowling, Court rose to stand beside her. "You're asking too much, Philippa. Perhaps, after years of fidelity, I could begin to trust you."

"Years?" she scoffed. "How many? Ten? Twenty? Fifty? Besides, you're missing the point. It is I who don't trust you." Without giving him a chance to reply, she turned and hurried into her bedroom.

He was tempted to follow her. There was nothing he wanted more than to pin her to the mattress with his greater strength and pound his turgid flesh into her, over and over, till his ravenous lust was slaked. She wouldn't call out, fearing that Kit or Lady Augusta might awaken and come to see what was happening. She wouldn't want their son to see his father ravish his mother.

But he couldn't take advantage of her for that very reason.

"Look, Mama," Kit called, "I've built another tower." He stood barefoot in the warm sand, wearing only a pair of short nankeen breeches. His black hair was tousled by the sea breeze off the bay. Fanciullo jumped about at his heels, yipping ecstatically.

"Yes, it's marvelous," Philippa said with an encouraging smile. She moved to her feet and stood back to admire their handiwork. "This has to be the most wonderful castle anyone ever built."

"It looks just like Castle Warbeck," Lady Augusta offered from her chaise longue beneath the yellow-and-white-striped awning.

Philippa cocked her head and studied the edifice. "Yes, it does, doesn't it?"

"It should," Warbeck said with a satisfied grin. "I planned it that way." He was on his knees beside Kit, giving the final touch to the tower they'd just added to the enormous sand castle. Like his son, he was attired in only skintight breeches that came just to his knees. His swarthy complexion had turned golden brown, attesting to other days spent in the sun. He looked more like a pirate than an English nobleman.

Philippa knew that if it weren't for the presence of his grandmother, Warbeck would have gone into the water without a stitch on. All day long, she'd tried without success to keep her gaze off his broad chest and strong back, but the sight of his muscles, sheened with water and rippling as he moved, was simply too captivating. A mat of black, curly hair covered his firm pectorals and tapered to a narrow line at the waistband of his black breeches. His biceps bulged enticingly with every movement of his powerful arms. She longed to smooth her fingers over his bare skin, feeling the play of sinew and bone. She knew from past experience that the corded muscles of his back would spasm and clench beneath her lingering caress.

"Can we play in the water again, sir?"

Warbeck jabbed his shovel into the sand, braced himself on its long handle, and moved to his feet. "Grab Mama's hand and let's go."

"You two go without me this time," said Philippa. "I'll stay here and keep Nana company." She moved to the other chaise longue beneath the colorful awning, and, together, the ladies watched the two males splash through the gentle waves and plunge into the cool blue water, the little terrier paddling behind them. Warbeck held his son as they went under. They soared out of the water with a mighty splash. The duke was a powerful swimmer, and in the buoyant salt water he was unimpeded by his injured leg. Kit howled with joy each time they crested a wave. Philippa leaned her head back and sighed contentedly. "It's been a wonderful day."

"I would like to see it last forever," Lady Augusta agreed.

They watched in companionable silence as Kit and his father splashed and played. Philippa turned her gaze to the beautiful sloop tied to the dock nearby, recalling Kit's incredible joy at waking that morning to see the *Sea Gull II* sailing into the bay. She shook her head at the memory. Only the unpredictable Warbeck would give a five-year-old boy a sailboat of his own. The three of them had spent the entire morning sailing all over Gull's Nest Bay. Then the dowager duchess had joined them on the beach for a picnic lunch, which the villa's staff had carried down the white wooden staircase that led from the top of the cliff to the sand.

"When we return home, I'd like you and Kit to visit me," Lady Augusta said. "Would you come and spend a few days at the Castle?"

Philippa looked down at her lap. How could she admit to the autocratic duchess that the thought of entering the castle that once had been her home frightened her? She was terrified that, seeing the familiar rooms where she was once so happy, she would lose control of her emotions. "I'm certain that Lady Harriet has made plans for our entertainment when we return," she hedged. "I couldn't promise anything until I spoke with her."

"Afraid to beard the lion in his den?" The dowager's gray eyes twinkled with amusement. "Remember, Castle Warbeck is my home, too. I assure you, you are most welcome. And I have a feeling that

there is nothing my grandson would like better than
to see you and Kit ensconced in his castle perma-
nently."

Philippa met the elderly woman's perceptive eyes
and read there the knowledge of Warbeck's attempts
to seduce his former wife. Lady Augusta knew her
grandson too well to believe otherwise. "And would
you like to see us live in the Castle?"

"That is my devout wish."

"What would people think?" Philippa protested.
"The gossipmongers would relish the chance to vilify
us once again."

The duchess closed the book she'd been reading
and ran her gnarled fingers along its spine. "I've
lived a long time, my dear. I'll give you some advice
I've learned through the years. Don't ever make your
decisions based on what other people might say. You
have one responsibility and one only. Be true to yourself."

"Sometimes it's hard to know how to do that. I
thought I knew once and found out that I'd made a
tragic mistake."

"You must ask yourself, Philippa, what is best for
you. And for your son. Nothing would please me
more than to see you and Court remarry. But, in the
eyes of the law, that would make you and Kit his
personal property, with no legal rights of your own.
Only you know if you have the courage to place
yourself in his power once again. I pray each night
that you will find it within you to do so."

"And if he turns against me a second time?"

Lady Augusta chuckled softly. "Of one thing I am
absolutely confident, my dear. If Court wins you
back, there is no power on earth that could ever
wrest you from him again."

Philippa was silent. The conviction in the dowager's voice reassured her. It was a reassurance she
desperately needed. To marry Court a second time

would be to step off the edge of the world and trust that he would catch her.

"Now, you go on and enjoy the water with those two jackanapeses," Lady Augusta urged. "Don't let that lovely bathing dress go to waste."

Philippa laughed as she looked down at her seaside gown. She had purchased it at the *Salon de la Mode* the previous day. Made of royal blue serge, it had long sleeves and three layers of ruffles at the hem. Another deep ruffle was strategically placed across her bosom. It was further adorned with white braid and nautical brass buttons. The dress was fashioned especially for ladies who liked to dip in the ocean from bathing machines. But in the secluded privacy of Gull's Nest Bay, there was no need for a machine to get her modestly into and out of the water.

Warbeck had teased her when he first saw her costume, saying she would sink like a stone with the weight of all those ruffles. And she had to admit that she had been more comfortable in the light cotton shift she'd worn when they were alone. Even so, the bathing dress was the first Philippa had ever owned, and she felt rather audacious.

"I never thought I'd wear anything so daring," she admitted as she fluffed up the ruffles on her chest self-consciously.

"Be daring, Philippa," the duchess exhorted. "Seize the day, child, so that when you're an old woman like me, you won't look back with regret at the things you wanted to do and never did because you were too timid." She waved her tortoiseshell lorgnette toward the shore. "Go on, now. I'll take a little nap while the three of you play in the water."

Philippa gently squeezed Lady Augusta's fingers. "All right, if you insist."

She ran across the sand, and Fanciullo raced to meet her.

Warbeck looked up to see her splashing through

the waves. "Look who's coming to swim with us," he said to Kit with a wicked grin. "Your mama, in her fancy new bathing dress. We'd better help her, or she'll sink to the bottom and we'll never find her again."

With a spontaneous trill of laughter, Philippa grasped their outstretched hands and took a deep breath. All three of them submerged together.

Philippa stood at the railing, staring up at the full moon. This time, when she'd left the stillness of her bedroom, Warbeck hadn't been waiting on the balcony. Perhaps the exertions of the day had overshadowed the pain in his leg, and he'd fallen asleep immediately, just like Kit. She wondered what Court would say if she entered his chamber and he awoke to find her standing beside him. Would he raise his arms to invite her into his bed? Her heart skipped a beat at the thought.

Lady Augusta's advice echoed in Philippa's mind. Would she one day be an old lady filled with regrets? She leaned her elbows on the wooden rail and raised her eyes to the clear night sky. For the past hour, she'd been asking herself what was best for her and Kit. Only her fears had kept her from admitting the truth. For who knew better than she what it was like to dream of a father you'd never known? Gazing up at the star-filled heavens, she acknowledged the truth with bruising candor.

Her son needed his father.

And so did she.

Restless, she descended the stairs that led to the sloping lawn at the back of the house. The thick grass felt wet and cool on her bare feet. Moving to the edge of the cliff, she stared down at the bay, bathed in moonlight. Whitecapped waves crested and rolled onto the sandy shore. She drew a large gulp of the fresh sea air and exhaled it slowly, sweeping her gaze across the magnificent vista of ocean and velvet black sky.

It was then that she saw him coming out of the water. He was naked and more beautiful than any man had a right to be, despite the wicked scar that crossed his right thigh. He looked up and froze in his tracks when he saw her. She must have resembled a ghost with her long hair wisping about her and the flowing white nightdress billowing in the breeze. He made no motion to summon her down, but simply gazed up at her.

For long moments, they stood enthralled, caught in the magic and mystery of the night. Then she slowly moved to the wooden stairway that led to the beach and descended the steps, her gaze never wavering from him.

Court watched Philippa walk across the sand and wondered if he'd just stepped into a dream. She wore only a thin nightgown that blew about her bare ankles in the gentle wind. As she drew nearer, he stood unmoving with his hands at his sides, making no attempt to hide his potent male erection. He watched her in silence, hoping against hope that this wasn't a figment of his tortured imagination. That tonight she would lie willingly in his arms. At the last moment, when he realized her intention, he opened his arms wide in invitation, and she flew to him. He braced himself, his heels digging into the sand, as she flung herself against his wet chest.

"Oh, Court," she whispered, "I need to tell you—"

"Shh," he crooned, "don't say a thing. There will be lots of time to talk later."

He kissed her, his hands roving across her straight back and firm bottom. She shivered in his arms, her fingertips tracing the muscles of his shoulders and neck. Then he broke the kiss, snatched up his cane and dressing robe from the beach, and took her hand. Leading her out of view of the house, he guided her around a curve of the shore to a secluded cove.

Dropping his cane, he spread his burgundy dressing gown across the sand and turned to her.

Philippa stood watching him with enormous eyes, her pale hair falling in loose tendrils around her slim shoulders. Bracketing her beautiful face with his hands, he kissed her, his tongue tasting her sweet, honeyed mouth. He moved his questing fingers across her slender form, touching every delicate curve as he feasted upon her like a man dying of starvation.

His pulse beating madly, Court tugged her night-gown upward, bringing it over her head, then drew back to look at her. Her bare skin shone like polished ivory in the moonlight. Her full breasts were up-tilted, their round crests pink and lush. Her long-legged body was sleek and supple and meant to drive a man wild with desire. Court felt his sex grow heavy and hard as his gaze drifted downward, across her flat stomach to the cloud of golden brown curls at the juncture of her pale thighs.

He dropped slowly to his knees and brought her to him, his hands encasing her narrow hips. He smoothed first one rough cheek and then the other across the silken skin beneath her breasts. Kissing her with an open mouth, he ran his tongue across her soft flesh, inhaling the intoxicating floral scent of her. Then with a low, savage groan of need, he raised his head and suckled the firm, velvet nipples, until she was gasping for air, her chest rising and falling in an ever-increasing rhythm.

"Oh, Court," she moaned above him, as she stroked her fingers through his wet hair.

He dropped to the outspread silk robe and pulled her down beside him. Lifting her hands above her head, he covered the entire length of her body with his much larger frame, moving across her trembling form like a blind man learning the touch and feel of her.

With a shivering sigh, Philippa looked up into

Court's heavy-lidded eyes. His silvery irises were pools of liquid thunder. He was still damp from the ocean water, but the heat of his body warmed her in its slow fire. Holding her wrists in one hand, he bent his head and kissed her, a wild, voluptuous kiss filled with undeniable male desire. His breath flowed hot and fierce over her bare skin.

A tremor of vibrant sensations rocketed through her as he traced a scorching path of seduction down her neck, delving his tongue into the hollow of her collarbone and kissing the frantic pulse in her throat. With his open mouth, he explored every inch of her, nudging her breasts and making them shimmer with sweet vibrations. He kissed the sensitive underside of her arms, her shoulders, her ribs, her jutting hipbones.

Releasing her hands, he circled the raised bump of her navel with his tongue, as his fingers smoothed across her thighs in a lingering, sensual promise of ecstasy. He spread her legs and lifted her knees over his broad shoulders, then scooped his hands beneath her buttocks and pulled her closer.

She gasped as she felt his warm breath caress the most secret part of her. "Court," she moaned, "oh, Court." She flung her arms out wide on the sand, thrilled by the knowledge of what he intended to do to her.

Her breath coming faster and faster, she arched reflexively as his mouth covered her. He laved her with his tongue, licking and sucking and tasting her, till she was half-crazed with passion. He held her fast in his strong hands, immobile against his mouth, giving her such exquisite pleasure that she thought her frantic heart would beat out of her chest. She climaxed with a deep, prolonged moan, barely conscious that he was spreading her legs wider for his entry. He called her name as he plunged his thick, turgid sex into her, the penetration eased by her convulsing tissues, slick and moist from her orgasm.

Court felt her delicate muscles flutter around him as he buried his heavy shaft deep within her. A primal shudder raked though him. He pulled back, nearly withdrawing, and drove into her sweet warmth again. With his hands braced on either side of her head, he watched the desire build within her once more, as he stroked a steady, unceasing rhythm.

"Pippa," he said hoarsely, "look at me."

Her eyes flew open, an expression of drugged enchantment glowing in their violet-blue depths.

"I'm going to give you every pleasure imaginable, sweet pixie," he told her. "I'm going to make love to you in every way possible, night after night, till just my presence arouses you." He bent his head and kissed her, letting her taste herself on his lips. She moaned and arched beneath him, her hips matching his rhythm, her breathing broken and harsh. "Tell me you want me," he demanded.

"Oh, Court, I want you," she cried. She clutched his upper arms, her nails gently scoring the taut, bulging muscles. "I need you so much."

He reached between them and gently caressed the swollen bud of her femininity, smiling victoriously as she cried out in a pleasure so keen, so vivid, that it was nearly pain. He thrust his hard, swollen rod into her, over and over, till he exploded inside her, burying his seed deep in her womb. His shout of release was a cry of male conquest and total possession.

Philippa gasped for breath, her heart racing madly. She nestled her face in the hollow of his shoulder, nearly sobbing with spent emotions. Court rolled to his side, bringing her with him. Still buried deep inside her, he turned onto his back and eased her on top of him.

She lay across his massive torso, spent and lethargic, her fingertips buried in the thick, curly hair on his chest. His hands moved over her buttocks and lower back in a gentle, lingering caress. Bracing her palms on his chest, she pushed upward as she brought her knees beside his lean flanks. She needed to look at him. Needed to see herself straddled across him, his manhood still wedged tight inside her. He filled her completely. The feeling was indescribably wonderful. Splintering sensations of pleasure radiated through her as she gazed into his hooded eyes.

A contented smile played across his chiseled lips. "You're more beautiful than ever," he said huskily, as he cupped her breasts in his hands, his thumbs sliding across their erect peaks.

"No," she said, shaking her head. "It's you who are beautiful, incredibly beautiful." She slid her fingertips across his large flat nipples and smiled as his pectoral muscles tensed reflexively. She bent and traced the sensitive twin circles with her tongue. He made a mesmerizing male sound deep in his throat when she began to suckle him. A heady feeling of sweet female power washed over her as she felt his shaft harden and thrust upward inside her.

"Kiss me," he said hoarsely. She lifted her head and covered his lips with her mouth, probing him sensually with her tongue. He buried his fingers in her tousled curls and captured her head in his hands. "Now ride me, sweetheart," he urged. "Ride me like I'm a stallion, swollen and hot with lust for you."

Philippa sat back up, her engorged breasts swinging gently. He tugged on her nipples with his fingers as she moved rhythmically on his hard staff. Her delicate tissues convulsed around him, drawing him deeper. This time they reached fulfillment together, welcoming their release with shuddering cries of ecstasy.

When they finally regained their strength, they cavorted about in the water, naked and glorying in each other's beauty. Back on shore once again, Philippa knelt and tenderly kissed the long, vicious scar that ran across his thigh. Court teased her, telling her there was a far better place to lavish her kisses, and she promptly followed his advice. They made love twice more before the sun began to rise over Gull's Nest Bay. Then laughing like schoolchildren on a holiday, they hurried back to the villa before the servants awakened and began the new day.

Chapter 15

St. Mark's Square
Venice

They were waiting for Emory Fry when he came out of the Doge's Palace. Two swarthy henchmen with massive shoulders and arms the size of an average man's thighs.

"*Mi scusi, signóre,*" the larger one said with the ingratiating smile one would give a lost child. "We would like you to come with us, please. There is someone who wishes to talk with you." He spoke with a nearly unintelligible accent, as though he'd memorized the words in English but had no real understanding of the language.

Emory looked from one to the other and debated his chances of escape. As though reading his thoughts, the second man opened his coat just far enough for him to see the carved-bone handle of a knife. He returned their smiles. "Gentlemen, lead the way."

They each took an elbow and guided him past the Campanile and across the Piazza San Marco. Emory glanced at the dark-haired man on his right, who outweighed him by at least eighty pounds. He had a bulbous nose, which had been broken more than once. The fellow on the left appeared even less civilized. A jagged scar crossed his hollow cheek, reaching almost to the corner of his thin mouth. Dark

brown hair, tied in a queue with a leather thong,
hung down to his shoulders. Though not as big as
his comrade, he was lean and wiry.

"Can you tell me where we're going?" Emory
asked, as they turned down a dark passageway between two buildings. The narrow alleys of Venice,
crisscrossed with countless canals and bridges,
formed a maze that only the local populace traversed
with ease.

Neither man bothered to answer. They hustled him
into a gondola waiting beside a high arched bridge.
The boatman nodded curtly as the three of them sat
down and then shoved off, leaving no doubt that
he'd been expecting them.

The long, slender vessel glided out into the Grand
Canal. Emory watched the famous landmarks go by,
as they slid past the magnificent homes and domed
churches. They passed the Palazzo Grimani, with its
massive Renaissance facade, and the Ca'd'Oro, a
Gothic palace once covered entirely with gold-leaf
decoration. More than two hundred palaces lined the
Grand Canal, glittering like jewels in the sun. Pinna-
cles and towers in hues of pale pink and faded ocher
were touched here and there with gold and azure
and made twice as beautiful by their shimmering reflections. Emory hadn't yet become accustomed to
the sheer glory of Venice.

The gondolier turned his sleek black craft, and
they glided between two red-and-white striped poles
to come to a halt in front of the ornate portico of a
Byzantine palace adorned with domes, rounded
arches, minarets, and mosaic tiles. Emory looked up
to see a lacy facade of delicate pink marble and white
stone. The intricately carved arches of the loggia on
the first floor ran the entire length of the building.
Whoever wanted to see him lived in the sumptuous
luxury of a Turkish potentate.

Without a word, the two brawny men guided him
across the elegant portico and into the ground floor.

They hurried up a grand staircase and led him down a tiled corridor to a pair of tall doors. With a discreet knock, they entered, silently ushering him into the room in front of them.

A tall, handsome man turned from his view of a peaceful inner courtyard and smiled graciously. He spoke in English, with only the slightest trace of an accent. "Mr. Fry, how kind of you to visit me."

Emory approached the gentleman and bowed his head politely. "And whom do I have the honor of visiting?"

"I am Domenico Flabianico, duke of Padua, Vicenza, and Verona." The nobleman gestured to a sofa. "Please sit down." At his nod, the two hulking lackeys left the room, closing the doors quietly behind them.

The mere mention of the duke's name sent Emory's heart smashing against his breastbone. Domenico Flabianico was one of the richest and most influential men in Venice. In all Italy, for that matter. Time and again, in the course of his investigation, Emory had heard mention of the Italian noble, who'd been in exile since Bonaparte's armies invaded the mainland. It was rumored that he had been the protector of the beautiful English marchesa. One informer had even claimed that the powerful duke had offered his hand in marriage after the lady's husband died.

The duke of Verona sat down in a gilded chair across from Emory. He steepled his long fingers and pressed them thoughtfully to his lips as he gazed at the Englishman with coal black eyes. Somewhere in his mid-forties, he had a full head of black hair, a slender build, and the graceful white hands of a gentleman. "It seems that you have been asking questions about a certain English lady," he said softly. "Questions about the birth of her child. Questions that, I believe, might best remain unanswered."

Emory swallowed convulsively. How much did the

nobleman know? he wondered. "*Nòbile*," he answered nervously, "I am merely trying to ascertain information requested by my employer. I mean no harm to the lady or to her child."

Flabianico rose and went to a marble side table. He poured two glasses of sherry and handed one to Emory. Returning to the chair, he lounged back comfortably and signaled for his guest to drink.

The specter of poison rose in Emory's mind. He lifted the glass in a salute, raised it to his lips without drinking, and set it down on a low table beside the sofa.

"I understand that you have spoken with Isabella Conegliano at great length," the duke said. His cultured voice rumbled like the dangerously deceptive purr of a panther.

Christ, there was no point in denying that he'd talked to her. If Emory had been followed by those two thugs, the duke would have received a complete report including the time and place and length of his visit. "Yes," Emory said, clearing his throat in apprehension. "The midwife who delivered the child was gracious enough to grant me an interview."

"And she told you the exact date of the infant's arrival into this world?"

Emory nodded. "There was no doubt in her mind. The baby was born on the feast day of her favorite saint." He wondered if the duke knew he had the old woman's signed statement, written in Italian, in his coat pocket.

The duke of Verona sipped his sherry and contemplated Emory Fry as though he were a piece of sculpture displayed at an auction. "Do you know how easy it would be for me to have you disappear completely?" he asked in a conversational tone. "Venice has been under Austrian rule since Napoleon traded the city like a piece of merchandise in the Treaty of Campoformido. The bodies of foreigners are often found floating in our canals. No one has the time or the inclination to track down their country of origin, let alone their murderers."

"Killing me won't solve your problem," Emory pointed out boldly. "My employer would merely send another investigator, who would eventually locate Signora Conegliano."

"And who is your employer?"

Emory hesitated. Telling the truth wouldn't do the wealthy peer in England any harm, and it might mean the difference between life and death for him. "The duke of Warbeck."

The black eyes lit up with understanding. "I see. However, sending another hireling to Venice wouldn't do the English duke much good. Sadly, the *vecchia* died in her sleep last night."

Emory leaned back against the sofa, staring at the nobleman in horror.

"I didn't have her killed, if that's what you're thinking," Flabianico said. "The old crone knew she was near death. That's why she wanted to make her last confession. There's nothing like the fear of the everlasting fires of Hell to force the truth out of us."

The duke stood and moved to an elegant black-lacquered table. Picking up a blue velvet pouch, he untied its braided gold cords and spilled the contents carelessly across the tabletop. Emeralds, rubies, sapphires, and diamonds bounced and rolled across its smooth surface.

Emory rose and walked over to gaze in awe at the mound of jewels, sparkling with every color of the rainbow. "Jesus," he murmured fervently. He ran a finger under his stock and waited for the wily Venetian's offer.

"Enough for a king's ransom, wouldn't you say, Mr. Fry?"

Emory nodded. The worth of even a fraction of the precious gems would allow him and his family to live in luxury for the rest of their lives.

"How much is your employer paying you?"

"Not as much as that," he admitted gruffly. "But I make it a habit not to betray the person who's hired me. It's bad for my professional reputation."

The duke of Verona smiled charmingly. The deep crinkles around his dark eyes conveyed an engaging sense of humor. Emory began to see what had attracted the marchioness of Sandhurst to the sophisticated patrician, aside from his piles and piles of money.

"I'm not asking you to betray the duke of Warbeck," the nobleman said. "I'm not even going to demand that you hand over that document you carry in your pocket. Nor will I impede your exit from this city."

Emory released a pent-up breath. "That's good to hear."

"What I do want, Mr. Fry, is to hire you, myself. Now, sit down and enjoy the sherry. I swear to you on my dear mother's grave that it isn't poisoned."

He waited as Emory returned to the sofa and picked up the fluted crystal goblet. Then he sat down in the chair opposite. "When you return to England and discharge your duty to the duke of Warbeck, I would like you to begin an investigation for me."

Emory lifted his eyebrows in surprise. "In England?"

"Yes. First of all, I want you to find out everything you can about a fire that destroyed a country home in Surrey by the name of Moore Manor. Second, I want you to discover the date of onset of the late marquess of Sandhurst's illness. His beautiful wife nursed him with the tender faithfulness of a guardian angel. Yet from the moment they set foot in Venice, I am convinced that they lived as brother and sister. I am also convinced that the marquess knew he was dying before he left England. Locate the doctor who treated him. Find out everything you can."

"And report back to you?"

Domenico Flabianico rose and gestured gracefully.

"Not to me, Mr. Fry. I want you to present this information to the duke of Warbeck."

Emory jumped to his feet. "Warbeck?"

The nobleman smiled. "Precisely." Walking to the door, he grasped the handle and then turned to look back at the stunned Englishman. "Oh, and one more thing, Mr. Fry. Please give my deepest respects to the marchioness of Sandhurst and tell her . . . tell her my humble offer still stands." He tipped his dark head toward the ebony table. "The baubles are yours."

Court sat at a writing table in the villa's east drawing room, reading over the papers that completed the purchase of a summer home for Kit. Everything seemed in order. He planned to carry the deed back to the Castle for Neil Tolander to place in the boy's trust.

Two days before, Court had taken Kit and his mother to see the property. They had explored the empty Georgian mansion together, Philippa exclaiming over the large, airy rooms that faced the sea. She was thrilled for her son. Her happiness shone in her magnificent eyes. It was obvious that her love for Kit was the bedrock of her life.

"Now you'll always have a place to come when you want to visit the seashore," she'd told the child, laughing gaily. "And you'll never have to worry about being here alone, for I'll always be with you."

Court had sensed the underlying sadness in her words. What she'd left unsaid was that she'd never had a home of her own, nor a mother or father, for that matter. If not for the kindness of the two eccentric spinsters who'd taken her into their boarding school, she would have been left completely alone in the world at a very tender age. Had Philippa been placed in a factory, as her uncle had suggested, her chances of survival would have been minimal. The drudgery and ceaseless toil inflicted on the small laborers would have snuffed out the spirit of the happy little girl like a candle flame in a gale.

Seeing Philippa with Kit, knowing how frightened she was of losing him, Court had begun to perceive the inner terror of being abandoned that lay beneath her outward facade of bubbling gaiety.

He reached for his cane, rose, and walked to the window where he could look out on the wide veranda that ran along the ocean side of the house. Lady Augusta and Philippa were watching Kit play with his new puppy. The boy's excited shouts rang out as the frisky terrier raced round and round at his feet. Court studied the laughing young woman who sat in a chaise longue on the other side of the glass.

She was beautiful, beyond a doubt. Her fresh loveliness was what had first attracted him. But he'd quickly become entranced with her bright disposition and intelligent mind. Only now, nearly six years later, did he truly understand the hidden anguish beneath that gay masquerade. Had he not been so filled with blind, unreasoning jealousy, he would have realized at the time that Philippa might have run away because she was convinced that she was doomed to be abandoned all over again. Like a self-centered idiot, he'd been so engrossed in his own bitter misery and wounded pride that he'd failed to consider any other reason for her to flee the country than simple lust.

Court smiled as he watched her through the window. They had made love each night since the evening in the cove three days ago. She had come to his room and shared his bed until almost dawn, when she'd quietly stolen away. In the hushed stillness of the night, they had silently agreed to set aside all recriminations, as they once again relived the magic they had felt on their honeymoon. Each time he took her in his arms, it was a bonding of two lonely, heartsick souls, who responded to each other's healing touch in a near-wordless communion.

They'd soon be returning to Chippinghelm and the seaside idyll would be over. It was time to announce their plans to remarry, though she hadn't, as yet, actually agreed. He wanted to do so immediately, on the chance that she might be carrying his child.

Court knew he was putting his pride on the line. He'd been the butt of vicious gossip during the divorce and mercilessly pilloried as the cuckolded husband in the gossip columns. If he should place his faith in Philippa and be betrayed a second time, he would be a complete laughingstock, an obscene joke for the rest of his life. That was why it was so important that she admit her wrongdoing. After all, no matter what the circumstances, she *had* run away with another man. For his own peace of mind, he needed to hear her ask for forgiveness and to promise that it would never happen again.

Court's pensive thoughts were interrupted by the villa's housekeeper. "Mr. Crowther is here to see you, your lordship," she announced.

At Court's nod, the big, strapping man was ushered into the drawing room. "Erasmus," Court said, moving from the window, "this is a surprise."

Crowther, dressed in a dusty coat and worn breeches, strode across the room and shook Court's hand. The ingratiating smile on his ruddy face didn't quite reach his eyes. "I hope you'll pardon me, Warbeck, for intruding on your holiday like this. But I have the plans for the rebuilding of Moore Manor for you to examine. I arrived at Castle Warbeck, only to find that you'd come here. Rather than return to Surrey, I decided to continue on to Ghyllside." He handed Court a set of documents rolled into a tight cylinder.

"I can look at these in the morning," Court told him. "You'll be staying the night?"

Hunching his broad shoulders, Crowther rubbed his stubbled chin and grimaced apologetically. "If you don't mind, Your Grace, I'd hoped you could go over the designs immediately. I want to return to the manor as soon as possible. I'm anxious to begin the reconstruction. I've taken a room at the Eight Bells for the night and plan to leave at the crack of dawn."

"Very well." Court unrolled the sheets of parchment and glanced over the drawings. "Would you like something to drink?" he asked, his eyes on the plans. "The liquor is on the side table."

"No, thank you. While you're looking them over, I'll go out and say hello to my niece."

Court nodded absently. There were no close feelings between Philippa and her uncle. Since she was six years old, Erasmus Crowther had made no attempt to see her until the day Court had gone to Surrey to ask him for her hand in marriage. She was only eighteen and legally still Crowther's ward at the time, and his written permission was necessary. Although Philippa had never uttered a word of criticism, Court suspected that she believed the only reason her uncle had wanted to renew their severed ties was because of her bridegroom's title and wealth. Whenever she was around Erasmus, Philippa grew edgy and ill at ease, in spite of her scrupulous courtesy to the man. Considering the fact that he'd failed her utterly, Court could hardly blame her. He didn't much care for the irascible fellow, himself.

Crowther returned in twenty minutes. "I think I'll just have that drink now," he said. "May I fix one for you, Your Grace?"

"Not for me." Court leaned back in his chair and stretched his legs out in front of him, rubbing his thigh. "The layout of the house seems excellent. I take it the architect has made every attempt to rebuild the manor just as it appeared before the fire?"

"He has. And a fine job he's done, too, sir. We worked on the plans together, since I'm the only person alive who remembers the house as it was. I tried to recall every cornice and arch down to the tiniest detail." After pouring a glass of Madeira, he sat down on an overstuffed chair nearby.

"It looks like you've succeeded. Congratulations. You can tell the builders they can begin as soon as you return."

Philippa's uncle sipped the wine. "I'm glad to see my niece is taking an interest in her child," he confided. "I have to admit that when I heard she'd returned from Venice, I was more than a little worried."

"Why is that?"

"Why, because she's the exact image of her mother," Crowther said with a confidential air. "I don't like to speak ill of the dead, Warbeck, but when I saw Hyacinthe Moore's daughter grow up to look enough like her to be her twin, I was appalled. They say blood will out. When Philippa eloped with that fancy lord, I knew she'd inherited more than just her mother's pretty looks."

"Are you saying that her mother ran away with another man?" Court grabbed his cane and stood, the legs of his chair scraping harshly across the planked oak floor.

"Plague take it, she didn't need to run off. She dangled her lovers right under her poor husband's nose. Nigh drove him crazy, she did." Crowther ran his thick fingers through his shock of brown hair and stared down at the amber-colored wine swirling in his goblet. "That was the cause of the fire, you know. They were arguing about her indiscriminate love affairs."

"No, I didn't know." Court moved to the side table and poured a splash of bourbon into a glass. He swallowed it in one gulp, letting the fiery alcohol burn its way down his throat. "How exactly did the fire start?"

"Hyacinthe threw a burning candelabrum at her husband in a fit of anger. The drapes in their bedroom caught fire. They were both trapped." Crowther placed his empty glass on the table. He took the plans and carefully rolled them up. "But the greatest shame's on me, sir," he added glumly, his gravelly voice low and gruff. "Even knowing the kind of woman she was, I fell into her sugar-coated trap, myself. When Hyacinthe fluttered her long lashes and gazed up at me with those big violet eyes, I forgot I was married to her sister, Anne. Forgot everything, but her soft white flesh and her long yellow curls." He looked at Court, his eyes filled with remorse. "My poor, innocent wife died in the fire caused by that depraved vixen. I tried to tell myself that I wasn't to blame. That I'd been only one of many who'd bedded her like some horny old goat. But all my excuses never eased the guilt that's tortured me all these years."

"I'm sorry," said Court, trying to hide his disgust at the sordid tale. Hell, the man was Philippa's only living relative.

Crowther waved his large hand in deprecation. " 'Twas many years ago." He stood and walked to the window to look out at his golden-haired niece. "Philippa's got her mother's personality, all right. The quick smile, the bubbly laugh, the joy of life. They attract a man like a moth to a flame. But when she ran off to Venice, I knew she'd inherited her mother's fatal flaw." He turned and solemnly met Court's gaze. "Hyacinthe had no conscience."

"If you're intimating that Philippa has none either, you're wide of the mark," Court said tersely. He clutched the crystal glass in his hand so tightly that his knuckles turned white.

Crowther's ruddy complexion deepened. His broad face was scarred from a bout of smallpox, giving him a rough, plebeian appearance. "I hope you're right, Your Grace. However, when I tried to talk her out of going to meet Sandhurst at the inn that day, Philippa laughed at my fears and called me a foolish old man."

"You were in London at the time?" Court asked in surprise.

"Didn't she tell you? I was visiting Warbeck House. If you remember, we'd spoken about restoring Moore Manor when you were first married. I came to talk to you about it. When I learned you weren't expected back till the end of the week, I returned to Surrey without ever seeing you. Next thing I heard, Philippa was on her way to Italy and you were seeking a divorce." Crowther tucked the plans under his arm. "Well, I must be going. I want to be back in Ghyllside before the sun sets. And thank you again, Your Grace."

Court nodded abstractedly and watched the burly man leave. Only minutes later, Philippa hurried into the drawing room. She wore a light summer gown that matched the rosy hue of her cheeks. Court felt his body respond to her nearness and ruthlessly suppressed the urge to take her in his arms. "You missed saying good-bye to your uncle," he said.

"I know," she answered with a pixieish smile. Her eyes twinkled mischievously. She came up and put her slender arms around his neck and kissed him full on the mouth, then wrinkled her nose enchantingly. "I did it on purpose. I understand he brought you the plans for rebuilding the manor. How do they look?"

"Since we have only Erasmus's memory to go by, we have to hope we'll be successful in an exact reconstruction. At any rate, the building itself will be sound and attractive." Court grasped her arm and held her away from him. He searched her glowing features intently. "Philippa, your uncle said he tried to talk you out of going to meet Sandhurst that day. Is that true?"

Shocked, Philippa met Court's accusing glare. She could feel the tension in the strong fingers wrapped around her upper arm. "Yes," she told him truthfully, as she fought back a wave of panic. "I happened to mention that I was joining Sandy for a luncheon at the Four Coaches in Kensington. My uncle acted as though I was behaving outrageously. I explained to him that the outing was completely harmless. Sandy had asked me to meet him there because he wanted to tell me something."

"Just what did he want to discuss?"

"It was a private matter."

Court's mouth twisted in a sardonic grin. "I'll bet it was private."

Her breath constricting in her throat, Philippa stared into his cold eyes and said nothing. She had given her solemn pledge to Sandy that what he told her that day would never be repeated.

Court released her. Leaning on his cane, he moved restlessly across the room, then turned and pinned her with his frosty stare. "Erasmus also told me how the fire started."

Philippa's heart plummeted. She closed her eyes, willing herself to stand there calmly, while her whole world shifted beneath her feet. She drew a painful breath and forced herself to meet his aloof, ironic gaze. Somehow, she managed to keep her voice utterly calm. "You mean he said that my mother was an immoral jade whose ungovernable temper cost the life of her family as well as herself?"

"Then you knew?"

"Yes."

"How?"

"I told you during our courtship that when I was fifteen, I found a letter sent by my uncle to the Lillybridge sisters saying that he was penniless and couldn't afford to send my tuition any longer. It was written when I was ten. In that same letter, he also told them about my parents and their part in the fire that destroyed our home."

Warbeck studied her with displeasure. "Why didn't you ever tell me?"

"How could I have confessed such a horrible

thing?" She raised a trembling hand to push away an errant curl. "How could I have told the charming, titled gentleman who came to court me that my mother was a despicable slut and my father a cowardly fool?"

"So you kept it a secret," he said derisively. His jaw clenched as he looked down his aristocratic nose at her.

Philippa blinked away the tears that sprang to her eyes. Somehow, she had to make him understand. "During my childhood, I dreamed of my parents night after night. I created marvelous images of them in my mind. My father was tall and handsome and brave. My mother was beautiful and all that was good. I prayed to them at bedtime, telling them that I knew they loved me." Her voice broke in spite of her resolve to be strong. "When I discovered that they were nothing but the fabrication of a foolish girl's imagination, I couldn't bear to talk about it. I was too ashamed of who they were. And of who I was."

Court walked back to stand beside the writing table. He clenched the back rail of the wooden chair with one hand. "I'll be leaving for London in the morning," he said quietly. "I have business there that must be taken care of. There's no need to cut short your holiday, however. You and Kit can stay for the rest of the week with Lady Augusta and return to Chippinghelm on Saturday. Now I need to tell one of the staff to pack my clothes."

Philippa watched in despair as he left the room, his posture rigid and disdainful. The tears rolled down her cheeks as she told herself that she'd expected it all along. The unpredictable duke of Warbeck was like a loaded gun, ready to go off at any moment. Given the least provocation, he would turn his terrible temper on her. And, inevitably, she would be left alone.

* * *

"His Grace, the duke of Warbeck," the butler announced.

Lady Clare Brownlow looked up from her needlework and forced a polite smile as her fiancé limped across the drawing room rug of her parents' London home. She graciously held out her hand, pleased that he'd found her wearing one of her most attractive morning gowns. Only minutes before, her mother had told her that the pale pink silk set off her blue eyes and flaxen hair to perfection.

Dressed in a severe black coat and gray pantaloons that were molded to his corded thighs, Warbeck bent and perfunctorily kissed her outstretched fingers. "The wanderer returns," she said with a brittle laugh. "Is it of your own volition or did you receive my summons?"

"Both," he said smoothly. He spread his arms wide and smiled with the engaging humor of a naughty schoolboy. "And as you can see, I am here."

"Please sit down," she told him, trying to appear serene as he took a seat on the orange-and-white-striped sofa nearby and braced his cane against its padded arm. Continuing to ply her needle and thread, she spoke in the carefully modulated voice cultivated by wealthy young ladies of the ton. "Rumors have reached London, Court. My mother and father are sorely distressed." She glanced up from her work, waiting for him to begin a profuse apology.

"I'm sorry to hear that Lord and Lady Brownlow are unhappy."

When she realized that was all he was going to say on the matter, she lifted her eyebrows admonishingly. "You remember, Your Grace, that when we first discussed our betrothal, I insisted that you give up your notorious, rakehell ways."

Warbeck had the nerve to chuckle softly. "You have to agree that I kept my part of the bargain, Clare. I haven't been in a major escapade that made the newspapers for over six months. No duels or brawls of fisticuffs, no mad carriage races, no wild gambling bets."

She carefully compared the threads from her basket, making a show of choosing the right shade of blue. She was angry, but she didn't want to push him too far. She'd accepted the duke of Warbeck's proposal, in spite of his unsavory reputation and the fact that he was a cripple, because of his wealth and title. And because he was probably her very last chance. She deftly resumed her stitching. "People are saying that you've adopted a child."

"Not adopted, exactly. The young marquess of Sandhurst has been named my ward."

Astonished, she looked up at him, meeting his calm gray eyes. "You are his legal guardian, then?"

"I am."

"People are repeating all kinds of insanity," she continued brightly. "Some say that you have taken up with your former wife. Naturally, I ignored such ridiculous tittle-tattle. What man in his right mind would want a divorced woman, even if she has been widowed?"

Warbeck crossed his legs, resting one booted ankle on the opposite knee. His silky voice held a tinge of warning. "I didn't come here to listen to you vilify Lady Sandhurst. I want to discuss our engagement."

"It's the rumors about the child that have upset me," she continued as though she hadn't heard him. "People are saying that the boy is your son. That you see the brat every day. That you've given him countless gifts, including a pony, and that you've even taught him to ride." Clare paused and pursed her lips.

"The child is mine," Court stated baldly. "It is my wish to remarry his mother so the three of us can be a family."

Clare sprang up, the hoop and threads scattering at her feet. "But we are engaged!" she cried. With conscious effort, she regained control and smiled at him beseechingly. "Lud, I never expected to keep you in my pocket. After all, our betrothal is one of convenience, and we are both aware of it. If you wish to carry on a discreet liaison with your former wife, that is entirely your affair."

His words were coolly unemotional. "It's our betrothal of convenience that I'm here to discuss."

Dizziness struck her, and she put a hand to her forehead, suddenly afraid she was going to faint. "But I believe that we would suit perfectly," she protested. He arched a black eyebrow sardonically, and she wrung her hands. "Oh, I am well aware of my reputation as an ice queen," she confessed. "But the very qualities of feminine modesty and cool reserve which have earned that title can assure you that I'd never run off with another man, chasing some idiotic notion of romantic love. I would never be so thoughtless as to flout convention and irrevocably destroy my social standing."

The duke rose to his full height. His silken tone dripped with sarcasm. "In other words, you'd carry on any affairs you might have after we were married with discretion."

She tittered nervously. "Fie, sir, you put words in my mouth."

"Clare, I'm asking you, as the kindhearted Christian woman you purport to be, to release me from our betrothal so that I can regain the family I lost. In return, I will donate any sum you name to whichever orphanage or asylum you choose."

"What do I care about orphans and lunatics?" she gasped. She folded her hands in front of her in a pleading gesture. "I will give you a son and heir, I promise."

"I already have a son," Warbeck said quietly.

"You mean your first wife's little brat?" she shrieked. "The child is a bastard! You can't really want the whelp of a whore to inherit your title."

Sickened by her vitriolic outburst, Court was

forced to admit what he'd suspected all along. Lady Clare Brownlow had all the outer trappings of the righteous, but it was merely a show. Her inner spirit was cold, selfish, and unforgiving. She delighted in ministering to the misfortunes of others because it made her appear favored by God. "The boy is my son," he said implacably, "and I'm going to make him my heir."

She lifted her chin and glared at him. Her pretty face was distorted with a scowl that etched two deep ridges between her carefully plucked brows. By the time she was forty, the lines would be a permanent reminder of her mean-spirited disposition. "I won't rear your bastard, Warbeck, if that's what you're thinking," she stated haughtily. "And I refuse to release you from our engagement. If you fail to keep your promise to marry me, I will see that the entire ton knows what a contemptible knave you really are. You won't be able to hold your head up in the meanest gambling hell in London."

"I don't think it's your modesty and reserve that earned you the title of the Snow Queen of Almack's," Court said in a cold, clipped voice. "You're as cynical and pessimistic as I am. But if you force me into this marriage, Clare, you will be a kind, loving mother to my son, whether you like the idea or not."

Clare recognized the white-hot fury on the duke's face. She stepped back, suddenly frightened of what he might do to her. *Good God, his father had murdered his mother in her own bed.* "Please leave," she croaked. As he stalked from the room, she groaned in relief and sank limply down in her chair.

Court charged into his town house in Grosvenor Square, seething with anger. Entering his bedchamber, he threw his cane on the green velvet comforter and braced one hand against the carved bedpost. Bloody hell, he had only himself to blame. Becoming betrothed to Clare Brownlow was one of the stupidest things he'd ever done. He had wanted to prove to the world that he could marry a lady of unimpeachable reputation. He'd coldly and methodically searched through a list he'd drawn up of available females on the marriage mart and chosen a woman whom all society deemed virtuous.

But the heartless stand she'd taken against his son proved her true character. Clare was a self-righteous hypocrite, who'd willingly look the other way if he kept a mistress, provided he acted with discretion. And in time, after an heir had been sired, she'd probably take a lover, as well. But she'd never run off with her paramour, as Philippa had. Just like so many other bored wives of the upper class, Clare would be outwardly circumspect, while her love affairs were well-known secrets. Nor would she ever protest his hard business practices, as long as it made them both wealthier. She'd tried to reform him so that he'd *appear* more respectable in the eyes of the ton. For appearances were all that really counted with the jaded aristocracy.

Court moved to the night table, pulled open the drawer, and rifled through its contents. Slowly, he withdrew the miniature of Philippa Hyacinthe Moore. The painting in the seashell frame had been her wedding present to her besotted bridegroom. He studied the beguiling young woman whose lavender-blue eyes shone with playful innocence.

No, Philippa hadn't been discreet. She'd tumbled headlong into love with Sandhurst and followed her heart down a disastrous path. It wasn't the fact that she'd taken Arthur Bentinck as her lover, but that she *ran away with him*, and was subsequently divorced by her husband, that made her a notorious woman in the eyes of society. Yet Philippa was a far better person than the insensitive, selfish ladies of the ton in the way she treated people—her loved ones, her friends, and even strangers. Her heart was filled with joy, tenderness, and love for all mankind.

Court recognized his own part in the tragedy. He'd used his status and wealth to dazzle the naive young schoolmistress, sweeping her into marriage before she had a chance to meet any other eligible gentlemen. He'd known at the time what he was doing. But his fear of losing her to someone more worthy had been like a fever in his blood. Court had lived with his scarred past too long not to feel uneasy and vulnerable. He hadn't wanted Philippa to hear any of the evil gossip, the snide insinuations that he was as hot-tempered and capricious as his parents, until after they were safely married.

Erasmus Crowther's suggestion that Philippa was as conscienceless as her mother, simply because she looked like the unfortunate woman, was utter rubbish. Hell, Court resembled his father, and that didn't make him a craven dolt who withdrew from his sons and looked the other way while his wife carried on her flagrant affairs.

Court closed his eyes, seeing the mortification on Philippa's lovely face as she confessed the truth about her parents. How well he understood that feeling of shame. Damn, he should have put his arms around her and comforted her, but he'd been too shocked that she'd failed to confide in him. From the moment they'd met, she'd tried to hide the truth from the one person who could have truly commiserated with her anguish. The irony of it brought a harsh bark of laughter. She'd only done exactly what he had done—kept her ugly secrets locked safely in her heart.

Court set the picture down on the stand, walked to a bombé chest, and jerked open the top drawer. He searched through the stack of folded shirts till he found what he was looking for. The folded note was tied with red ribbon. He opened it and studied the ugly, spidery scrawl, reading once again the name of the inn, the date, and the time his wife would meet her lover.

He sank down in a soft chair, recalling everything that had happened during those few short days so long ago. He'd left his bride of two months to go into Yorkshire to meet with a buyer for some property he wanted to sell. Philippa had planned to go with him, but the morning they were to depart, she'd felt ill. He'd left her reluctantly, worried about her health. For the almost six years since then, he'd been certain that she'd feigned the illness as an excuse not to accompany him. He realized now that she was probably suffering from nausea caused by her pregnancy.

The trip to Yorkshire had turned out to be a wild-goose chase. When he got there he was told that the buyer had changed his mind. He returned to Warbeck House two days earlier than expected, to find the anonymous letter waiting for him. How many countless nights in the lonely years that followed had he lain awake wondering what black-hearted villain had sent it?

Just as the note had foretold, he'd found Philippa and Sandhurst in Kensington. Court had charged into the private dining room of the Four Coaches Inn, ruthlessly shoving aside the serving man who tried to stop him. The lovers were standing beside a small table set for two, wrapped in an intimate embrace. Philippa's head rested lovingly on Sandhurst's broad chest. His chin was buried in her thick golden curls. They weren't saying a word, just holding each other close, as if the need for idle chatter wasn't necessary between two people so deeply in love. The poignant silence of that tender moment sent a white-hot shaft of pain straight through Court's heart. This was more than a passing, flirtatious affair. This was a bond of affection that would last a lifetime.

"You bloody bastard!" he roared. "You rotten son of a bitch!"

The startled pair leaped apart, the look of absolute astonishment on their faces almost comical. Clearly, they never expected the betrayed husband to barge into their secret rendezvous.

"Court!" Philippa gasped. "What are you doing here?"

Ignoring the guileful, lying witch, Court grabbed Sandhurst by his knotted white stock and jerked him forward.

"What the hell are you doing?" Sandy cried, his handsome face distorted in surprise. He clutched Court's hand, trying to break his hold.

Court released him with a snarl of contempt. He smashed one fist into Sandhurst's mouth, the other into his unprotected abdomen, and had the satisfaction of seeing the bastard stagger like a puny schoolboy under the vicious blows. But Court wasn't about to let the conniving, two-faced hypocrite slide to the floor. Not until he'd beaten him to a bloody pulp.

"Court, stop it!" Philippa screamed. "Stop it! This is insane!" She tried to grab his arm, but he pushed her away. By then Sandhurst had regained enough of his senses to land a wild punch of his own. The blow glanced harmlessly off Court's chin.

Court grinned with diabolical glee. "That's it, you cowardly snake," he taunted, "come on and fight me. I'm going to break every goddamn bone in your body."

Pulling back his fist, he drove it like a sledgehammer into Sandy's right cheek, rasping the flesh from his cheekbone, then followed up with a strike to the bridge of his nose that sent the traitorous dog sprawling against the table. Crystal goblets, fine china, silverware, and a bouquet of red roses crashed to the floor. A shrill keen rent the air, and Court realized vaguely that Philippa was screaming for help.

He bent over Sandhurst's supine form, intent on his prey. Before he could drag the whoreson up by his ruffled shirtfront, three burly men jumped Court from behind. He tried to shake them off, so blindly enraged that all he could see was Sandhurst's dazed green eyes staring up at him in stupefaction. But Court was outnumbered and outflanked. The beefy innkeeper and two husky servants gradually overpowered him, pulling Court away from the stunned, battered man on the floor.

"Here, sir, that's enough," the red-faced proprietor wheezed. "You can't brawl in this establishment. We'll have to call a constable if you don't cease this bout of fisticuffs at once."

Amidst the splintered glass and broken plates, Philippa dropped to her knees and slid one arm under Sandhurst's shoulders. Cradling his head against her breast, she wiped away the blood on his gashed face with her lacy handkerchief. The look of tender compassion on her lovely features ripped through Court's haze of fury. She looked up at him in dumbfounded shock. "You're mad," she whispered unsteadily. "You're out of your mind."

Court stared at the two lovers through a red fog of hate. "My seconds will call on you this afternoon, Sandhurst," he barked, struggling to regain control. "Swords or pistols, I don't give a damn. It makes no difference to me whether I run a blade through your yellow liver or put a bullet in your black heart." He turned on his heel and strode to the door.

"Court!" Philippa pleaded, her voice cracking pathetically. "You can't do this! You can't kill your best friend. We've done nothing wrong. This is all a dreadful mistake."

With a savage curse, he pivoted and faced her. Philippa's enormous violet eyes glistened with tears. Locks of her silken hair tumbled around her slender shoulders, and one capped sleeve of her muslin dress slipped slowly down to reveal a tantalizing expanse of creamy skin. Even in her disheveled, frightened state, kneeling beside her half-conscious lover, she was unbelievably alluring. For the first time since he'd entered the room, he spoke directly to his treacherous wife.

"Your tears aren't going to save him, Philippa. Nothing can save him now. So keep your lies and your worthless explanations to yourself. And God help you if I ever see your deceitful face again, for I won't be responsible for my actions." He heard her gasp of horror as he stalked from the room.

After trying to drink himself into a state of unconsciousness, Court returned to his town house late that night. He awoke the next morning with a man's silk stock tangled around his bare feet. The initials stitched in one corner were those of Arthur Bentinck, marquess of Sandhurst: his good friend—and his wife's lover. At that moment, something warm inside Court, something that had started to blossom on the day he'd first met Philippa, withered and died.

The next day a parade of petitioners called at Warbeck House, seeking a reprieve for the condemned man and forgiveness for the erring spouse. Lady Harriet and Lady Augusta both sought an audience, which Court spitefully denied. He spoke only to Tobias, who reluctantly agreed to arrange the duel.

That afternoon Philippa herself stood on Court's doorstep, begging to see him. His heart filled with an icy rage, he watched her climb back into the Sandhurst coach from his bedroom window. Then he picked up a chair and threw it through the glass.

The morning of the duel, Court waited impatiently in his bedroom for Toby to arrive. On the chest of drawers sat a gleaming walnut case with a pair of flintlock duelers. Court lifted a pistol out of the box, held it down at his side, and then suddenly raised it toward his own reflection in the mirror on the wardrobe door. Relishing the feel of the finely balanced weapon, he smiled mirthlessly at the man in the glass. Twenty paces would pose no challenge.

The Joyner duelers had belonged to his father. On more than one occasion, the smoothbore flintlock in Court's hand had sent its ball into a practice target nine out of ten times at a range of ninety yards. And on more than one occasion, it had proven lethal to a human target.

At the polite tap on the door, Court returned the gun to its case. "Enter," he called.

Without waiting to be announced, Tobias pushed his way past Dawkes and hurried into the room. He came to a sudden halt and stared into Court's eyes, his own bespectacled ones wide with dismay. "D-dash it all, y-you're ready," he complained.

"Of course, I'm ready. I've been waiting for half an hour." Court snapped the lid of the walnut case shut and picked up his riding crop and gloves. "Let's go."

"W-wait a m-minute," Tobias pleaded.

"Don't try to dissuade me, Toby. You're supposed to be acting as my second. For the past two days, you've spent more time and energy trying to talk me out of this duel than you've spent arranging it."

"F-fiend seize it, I t-told you the truth!" He stepped closer, his forehead furrowed with concern. "Philippa s-swore to me on a B-Bible that she was blameless."

Court smacked the riding crop against his thigh in exasperation. Again and again, Tobias had urged him to reconsider and give Lady Warbeck the chance to explain. He'd beseeched Court not to believe her guilty on the basis of one scurrilous, unsigned letter. What Rockingham didn't know was that there was far more damaging evidence than that bloody note. But Court couldn't bring himself to mention the silk stock he'd found in his bed—not even to his closest friend. He picked up the pistol case and anchored it under his arm. "Let's get on with it."

Nervously, Tobias pushed his wire-rimmed eyeglasses farther up the bridge of his prominent nose and gulped. "W-we can't." At Court's ferocious scowl, he took a small step back, and then held his ground. "It w-won't do you any g-good to g-go to Hampstead Heath this morning. S-sandy won't b-be there."

With calm precision, Court replaced the box on the chest of drawers and laid his gloves and whip beside it, certain this was some fool scheme to postpone the encounter until his friends and family could talk him out of the duel. He folded his arms and glared at Tobias. "All right," he demanded, "what the devil is going on?"

Tobias opened his mouth to speak, but nothing came out. His brown eyes were filled with incredulity.

"Rockingham," Court warned in a low, threatening tone, "you'd better start explaining. Now."

His friend swallowed convulsively and then blurted out the news. "S-sandhurst has b-bolted."

"He's taken to his heels?"

Tobias nodded, a look of commiseration on his haggard features.

Sinking down on the edge of his bed, Court stared at his friend in amazement. "Sweet Jesus, who'd have thought that charming, smooth-tongued Lothario was a coward?"

"I c-couldn't believe it, either," agreed Tobias glumly. "When I l-learned of it an hour ago from his seconds, I w-went to his town house to demand an explanation. He wasn't there, blast his eyes. I spoke to his mother, though. Lady Harriet confirmed it. S-sandy's gone." Shaking his head in bewilderment, he walked over to the settee by the fireplace and dropped onto its soft cushion.

Silence descended on the room. It was an incomprehensible turn of events. For a gentleman to flee from an affair of honor was nearly unheard of. It indicated the depths of cowardice.

At last, Tobias spoke. "W-would you have r-really killed him?" He shifted uncomfortably on the settee, sorry, no doubt, that he'd dared to ask. The tragedy of Court's parents permeated the stillness of the room. Given that the previous earl of Warbeck had killed his wife and her lover, perhaps the question was better left unanswered.

"What would you do if you found Belle in Sandhurst's bed?" Court queried softly.

"I'd kill the s-son of a bitch."

"My thoughts exactly." Court yanked the bell pull. When Dawkes appeared, he ordered his traveling carriage brought round immediately. Then he strode to the chest, picked up his gloves, and tugged them on with quiet determination.

"Where are y-you going?" Tobias exclaimed.

Court lifted one eyebrow sardonically. "Where else, but to Sandhurst House to collect my wife?"

"B-but you swore over and over you were g-going to divorce Philippa!" Tobias leaped to his feet, a look of horror on his flushed face.

"Now that her lover has slunk away like a jackal, leaving her alone to face the tempest they both created, I imagine she'll be relieved to find herself under my protection once again. Whom else does she have to turn to?" Court made no attempt to hide a vindictive, triumphant smile. "I'll take her to Kent to stay with my grandmother. For all I care, Philippa can rusticate in the country for the rest of her life. It'll take that long for the scandal to die down. God knows, she'll never be able to show her pretty face in London again."

Tobias placed his hand on Court's sleeve. His fingers trembled; his shaky voice revealed a tinge of hysteria. "Y-you can't t-take Philippa to the c-country."

"And why can't I?" Court demanded. "She's my wife. In the eyes of the law, the countess of Warbeck is my personal property. I can do anything in the bloody hell I choose with her." He jerked one gloved thumb toward his chest. "Philippa belongs to me."

"B-but you wouldn't want her now," Tobias protested, clutching Court's arm. "N-not after all that's happened in these past three days!"

"Let's just say I've learned from my father's mistakes," Court replied with a sneer. "A man doesn't throw away a perfectly good shirt, just because there's a stain in one corner." He pried his friend's fingers from his sleeve and brushed past him. With his hand on the doorknob, he paused and spoke over his shoulder. "Besides, I think Philippa needs a bit of disciplining. I want to hear that little baggage plead for forgiveness. She'll have the entire trip to Castle Warbeck to try to convince me of her innocence. Then I'll have the pleasure of hearing her heartbroken sobs as I ride away." He opened the door with a violent jerk.

"Warbeck!" Tobias called in warning.

Something in that one word sent an icy premonition spiking through Court's brain. He stopped, turned, and waited for the explanation he didn't want to hear, an ache of suffocation lodging deep in his chest.

Tobias spread his hands in heartsick resignation. "They've r-run off together. The two of them s-sailed from London on last evening's tide. S-sandy's not the only coward among us. 'Fore Gad, I didn't w-want to be the one to t-tell you. My dear friend, I'm s-sorry." Behind his spectacles, Toby's eyes were filled with pity.

Court clutched the doorjamb with one hand, bracing himself against the emotional maelstrom that whirled around him. In the cold, empty place that was once his heart, a volcano of fury and hatred erupted. And a burning resolve to exact retribution. By the Lord above, he would know the sweet taste of revenge.

Growling an obscenity, Court shoved past Tobias to stare in blank frustration at the gleaming walnut pistol case. He snatched it up in both hands, lifted it high over his head and hurled it against the mirror on the wardrobe door. As the wood and glass shattered with a gratifying boom, the magnificent flint-lock duelers crashed, undetonated, to the floor.

Court stared at his distorted reflection in the broken looking glass, the jagged pieces revealing the splintered likeness of a wild-eyed madman. He was looking at the image of his shattered soul. From deep in his throat had come a howl of rage and despair as he damned them both to hell. . . .

The sound of the tall-case clock in the hall striking the hour brought Court back from his painful introspection. He stood, folded the infamous letter, and placed it in his coat pocket. Returning to the open drawer, he ran his hand under the neatly pressed garments till his fingers touched the fine silk of a man's scarf. He lifted out the long white stock with the initials of the marquess of Sandhurst embroidered in one corner. Moving to the edge of his bed, he sat down, holding the neckpiece gingerly across his open palms. He had never revealed the incriminating piece of evidence to anyone, not even while the divorce was being argued in Parliament. Pride had sealed his lips. What man would willingly admit that he'd been cuckolded in his own bed?

Court stuffed the neckpiece into his pocket. He glanced around his luxurious bedchamber as though seeing it for the first time. When next he returned to Warbeck House, he'd have his erring wife with him. They'd lie down together in his high, four-poster bed, and he'd make love to her till every memory of Arthur Bentinck was erased from her mind.

After returning to Sandhurst Hall from Gull's Nest Bay, Philippa wrestled with her conscience for five lonely nights. She hadn't the courage to reach a clear decision, but she knew she had to start by telling someone the truth about Kit's birth—even if it meant that she would lose her little boy.

On the sixth day, she called on the Reverend Mr. Trotter to make the final arrangements for Kit's baptism at St. Aldhelm's. In the privacy of the vicar's study, Philippa explained the circumstances surrounding her flight from England. She was completely truthful about her relationship with the marquess of Sandhurst and the fact that he had not fathered her son.

"I made a terrible mistake in my panic to protect my unborn child," Philippa admitted to the kindly vicar. "And because of it, the two people I love most in this world have suffered grievously. How can I possibly make amends to my son and his father?"

"You must start by being totally willing to right your wrongs," Zacariah Trotter counseled. "And the next step is to christen your son as the duke of Warbeck's legitimate offspring." Although the clergyman's eyes revealed a warmhearted compassion, his words rang with unwavering conviction.

Philippa's lips trembled at the thought of what might happen should she embark on such a dangerous course. Once the proof of Kit's heritage was inscribed for all to see in the baptismal ledger at St. Aldhelm's, Warbeck would have the power to declare Kit his son and legal heir. She took a deep, steadying breath and blinked back the tears that burned her eyes. "I'm not certain I have the courage to risk losing Kit, Reverend Trotter."

"Place your trust in the Almighty," the vicar advised, "and you'll find that you have more inner fortitude than you think. You can't go on living a lie, Lady Sandhurst. The deceit and evasions would destroy you in the end. And whatever the outcome, we both know the boy will come to no harm with his father."

Philippa covered her face with her hands and lowered her head in resignation. "Yes," she replied in defeat. "My fears for my unborn baby were groundless. Warbeck would never have rejected his own son, no matter how much contempt he felt for the mother. He loves Kit as deeply as I do."

Solemnly, Trotter laid his hand on her bowed head in a silent blessing. He was too wise to dismiss her trepidation as a woman's foolish imaginings. Neither of them could predict what the enigmatic duke would do.

Regaining her composure, Philippa straightened and reached for her reticule. She withdrew two folded sheets of parchment and handed them to the clergyman. "I want you to keep these, Reverend. They are the documents I brought back from Venice containing the falsified dates of my marriage to the marquess of Sandhurst and Kit's birth. Do whatever you wish with them. Burn them, rip them to shreds, lock them away forever. I don't care, as long as I never see them again."

Trotter nodded his approval as he took the papers. "You've made the right decision, Lady Sandhurst, although I'm sure you doubt it at this moment."

Attempting a shaky smile, Philippa rose and extended her hand. "I'll see you tomorrow morning at the baptism, Vicar. It will be a small gathering. The only guests who've been invited are Lady Harriet and Lady Augusta. And of course, Lord and Lady Rockingham will be Kit's godparents. They have all pledged their secrecy in this matter until I gather the courage to face the duke of Warbeck and tell him the truth in person."

The Revered Mr. Trotter took Philippa's hand in both of his. "You have the valor of ten men," he told her. "Don't underestimate your strength of will or the duke of Warbeck's capacity for forgiveness."

Philippa gave him a plucky smile, but as she left the room her heart dropped to her feet like a ball of lead. Tomorrow Kit would be baptized according to the rites of the Church of England. She should have been filled with pride and happiness. But her joy was marred by a very deep, very reasonable dread of the future.

Chapter 16

Rockingham Abbey blazed with candlelight. The entry hall and drawing rooms overflowed with flowers. On the second floor, swaths of pink silk and white trellises of summer roses turned the ballroom into a fairy garden. It was early in the evening, and the first guest hadn't as yet arrived, although Lord and Lady Rockingham had invited all the members of the peerage and landed gentry from the surrounding district to their ball.

Philippa waited on the terrace with Belle, enjoying the peace of the August evening before the crush of people arrived. They were wearing diaphanous gowns with fashionably high waists and tiny capped sleeves that left their shoulders nearly bare. A nervous fluttering in Philippa's stomach reminded her that this was going to be her first real excursion into polite society since her return to England. Unlike Belle's small dinner party in London, there would be more than just the loving Mercier family in attendance.

It had taken the combined forces of the Viscountess Rockingham, the dowager duchess of Warbeck, and the dowager marchioness of Sandhurst to induce Philippa to come tonight. They'd insisted that, as the widowed wife of the late marquess, she had every right to participate in the rural society of Kent. Philippa knew better. But she also knew the three ladies were held in such high esteem that her own notoriety wouldn't affect their standing in the social hierarchy. If the worst happened and no one came, she alone would carry the stigma of an outcast. That unhappy possibility sent a cold shiver through her.

It had been over a week since Philippa had last seen the duke of Warbeck. Philippa was aware that he'd been invited to the Rockinghams' gala that evening. But he'd remained in London on whatever business had taken him there. Her heart sank as she recalled his frigid disapproval when she'd admitted the shocking truth about her parents.

She turned to Belle, who was busily rearranging an already-perfect bouquet of peonies on a garden table. The viscountess's translucent pink gown contrasted lushly with her smooth brown ringlets. Without conscious thought, Philippa moved the burning candelabrum on the table farther away from the gauzy material of her friend's dress. "I'm so grateful that you and Toby were willing to be Kit's godparents," Philippa told her. "Your loyalty has transcended the bounds of friendship into the role of guardian angels."

"*Quelle absurdité,*" Lady Gabrielle scolded. She blinked at Philippa, her dark eyes twinkling merrily. Rather than wearing her spectacles, she carried a fashionable pair of scissors glasses. "We were honored to be at Kit's christening. When Toby and I have our first child, you'll be our baby's godmother." Looking down at the fragrant flowers, the viscountess frowned thoughtfully. "Though sometimes I feel as if there's no hope that we'll ever have a child. *Mon Dieu,* we've been married for six years now and still no *bébé.*"

Philippa clasped Belle's hand with sincere compassion. She knew how desperately the couple wanted children. "It will happen when you least expect it," she assured her friend. "When your mind is preoccupied with other things, all of a sudden you'll realize you are *enceinte.*"

"I hope so, *chérie.*" Belle shrugged her shoulders and sighed. "We've consulted a London physician. He told us not to have conjugal relations too frequently, as that exhausts the female and she's not able to conceive. But we love each other so much, we find his advice very difficult to follow. He also said that it was important that we not become too passionate in our marriage relationship." Lady Gabrielle rolled her brown eyes. A mischievous smile hovered about her lips. "We've tried, but we don't seem to be very successful in detaching ourselves from what we're doing."

Philippa burst into laughter. Releasing her companion's hand, she fluttered her lacy white fan as though the topic had suddenly become too torrid. "I can assure you, Lady Rockingham, passionate lovemaking doesn't stop a married couple from begetting a child. If it did, we wouldn't have been celebrating Kit's baptism two days ago." She sobered, remembering her own good fortune in knowing that she herself was not pregnant. The nearly disastrous interlude at Gull's Nest could have resulted in her carrying Warbeck's second child.

Lady Gabrielle gazed into Philippa's eyes and, uncannily, seemed to read her troubled thoughts. Her quiet words were deeply sympathetic. "Toby believes that Court, as Kit's father, should raise his child at Castle Warbeck. He thinks that the best solution to this whole problem would be for you and Court to remarry."

"I couldn't possibly marry Warbeck again!" Philippa cried. She hadn't confided to Belle that the duke had asked her to marry him. How had the couple envisioned what should have been an unthinkable idea? "Has Toby forgotten that my former husband's wild accusations completely destroyed my reputation? And that Warbeck would have murdered Sandy, if the two of us hadn't fled?"

Belle raised her dark brows skeptically. "*Vraiment,*

Toby and I are not convinced that Court would have actually killed his childhood friend."

"Believe me, he would have," Philippa said with conviction. "You weren't there at the Four Coaches Inn, so you didn't see him. I did! Warbeck came charging into the dining room, shouting expletives and raving like a madman."

Lady Gabrielle nodded sadly. She picked up her long white gloves from the table and pulled them on. "Toby tried to talk some sense into Court at the time, but he refused to listen to anyone. He was insanely jealous, Philippa. But he wasn't a madman, even if he behaved like one temporarily."

"Excuse me, your ladyship," the butler said quietly from the open door that led onto the terrace. "The first coach has just started up the driveway." He bowed and retreated to his post at the front entrance.

"Come on," Lady Gabrielle said with a smile that displayed the charming dimples in her cheeks. "Let's forget about the problems of the past and simply enjoy the evening." She slipped her arm through Philippa's and led her through the green salon.

"I only hope I can," Philippa answered honestly. "The butterflies in my stomach are beating their wings in a delirious effort to get out." She glanced down at her apricot silk gown, nervously smoothing her hand over the fragile material. An enormous weight seemed to have settled on her chest, threatening to impede her breathing. "Let's pray I don't become paralyzed with fright and make a complete idiot of myself."

The viscountess patted Philippa's hand soothingly. "You'll be fine, *mon amie*. Everyone knows that you are our honored guest. No one will come tonight unless they are ready to accept you as a member of genteel society."

"That's the problem," Philippa replied with a half-hearted smile. "What if nobody comes?"

Belle's laugh tinkled merrily. "They'll come, you

silly cabbage. Toby and I have many good friends, who will attend our party simply because we asked them to. And Lady Harriet and Lady Augusta have given you their unqualified support. Those two indomitable dragons have spent the entire week paying visits to all the high sticklers around Chippinghelm, letting everyone know they intend to see that you're accepted into our local milieu. With them as your champions, you don't have a thing to worry about."

Philippa and Belle were joined by Lord Rockingham in the flower-bedecked entry hall. His tall, spare frame was splendidly garbed in a deep blue evening coat and trousers. Lady Gabrielle's family was already waiting for the guests in the main drawing room. The count and countess de Rambouillet, along with their sons, daughters-in-law, and new grandchild had descended on the Abbey only the day before. They planned to spend the week visiting their daughter before returning to their own estates.

"We're ready, *mon cher*," Belle said to her husband. "How about you?" Holding her glasses up in front of her eyes, she lovingly inspected the folds of his stock and straightened the points of his high collar.

The lenses of his spectacles glinted in the candlelight as Tobias grinned at them. "This is a l-lot harder than c-conducting chemistry experiments. B-but if I have to d-dance with all the l-ladies, I'd just as soon get it over with."

"I'm expecting you to dance with me," Philippa warned him. "You'll probably be the only gentleman willing to step out on the floor with a notorious woman."

"I d-doubt that," he answered. "F-for one thing, André and Étienne have their wives' permission to gallop around the fl-floor with you most of the night. And Belle's father will m-most certainly ask you for at l-least one waltz."

"Ah, that sets my worries to rest," she told him

with a teasing smile. "With so many handsome gentlemen in attendance, I shall be the envy of all the other damsels."

Tobias blushed. "Egad, P-pippa," he disclaimed, "I ain't handsome, and y-you know it!"

Philippa looked at Belle with wide eyes. "Why, Lady Rockingham! You assured me that your husband would be the finest-looking man at the ball tonight. You weren't quizzing me, were you?"

The viscountess slipped her plump arm through her husband's thin one and rested her dark curls on his shoulder. "Oh, la-la, in my eyes, he'll be the handsomest man here."

"Y-yes," Tobias pointed out, "but that's because you w-won't be wearing your spectacles." The two ladies smiled at his serious expression.

"Don't worry," Belle advised Philippa with an encouraging smile, "there will be a much more disreputable female than you in attendance tonight. Lady Bowring and her husband are coming. Everyone knows she's conducted one illicit liaison after another. Throughout most of the county, her five children are known collectively as the 'Bowring Menagerie,' since it's apparent that no two of them share the same sire."

"I refuse to believe such a Banbury tale," Philippa said with a giggle.

"Oh, it's true," the viscount affirmed. "People have pl-placed wagers on who the v-various fathers might be. The only tr-trouble is, no one has the n-nerve to ask Lady Bowring to p-point the gentlemen out." The three friends burst into gales of laughter.

They were soon busy welcoming a steady stream of guests. The first to come through the Abbey's high-arched doorway was Lady Harriet with Blanche and Beatrice Lillybridge. The two diminutive spinsters had arrived at Sandhurst Hall earlier in the week to spend a few days visiting their adopted daughter and get acquainted with their grandson.

"Pippa," Beatrice said joyfully, "you look exquisite." She kissed Philippa on the cheek and beamed at her proudly.

"Yes, dearest pixie, you couldn't be lovelier," Blanche agreed, slipping her arm around Philippa's waist and giving her a maternal peck on the cheek.

Philippa returned her mothers' hugs wholeheartedly. "Both of you look wonderful," she assured them. They were dressed in identical gray satin gowns trimmed with the fine *Point de Venise* lace she had brought back for them from Venice.

As the exuberant twins turned to tell Belle and Tobias how handsome they looked, Philippa embraced Lady Harriet. The big-boned woman wore a dress of pale green the exact color of her eyes. Her graying auburn hair was nearly hidden beneath a matching turban with one enormous white ostrich feather drooping down in front. "Is Kit behaving himself?" Philippa asked.

"The boy's perfectly fine," her mother-in-law announced in her practical manner. "He ate dinner with us, and then his nursemaid took him up to his room. He was cheerful as could be when we bid him good night." Lady Harriet brushed the feather out of her eye. "Now don't you be fretting about Kit. O'Dwyer will read to him till he falls asleep."

Philippa breathed a sigh of relief.

The next to arrive was Lady Augusta, regal and elegant as ever in rich purple taffeta. As Philippa welcomed the white-haired lady, she felt a pang of disappointment that the dowager's grandson wasn't standing beside her. Since their return from the seashore, Philippa had spent sleepless nights wondering if Warbeck would ever forgive her for concealing the truth about Kit. And pondering what she should do, if he did.

One after another, the families of the surrounding countryside began to arrive at Rockingham Abbey. Philippa met, once again, the landed gentry and

members of the peerage who'd come to Sandhurst
Hall following Sandy's interment at St. Aldhelm's.
Flanked by Tobias and Belle, and with Lady Harriet
and Lady Augusta hovering close by, Philippa was
reintroduced into Kentish society as the widowed
marchioness of Sandhurst. If some of the older
women remained a little distant, at least no one made
any outward show of condemnation.

Philippa smiled with sincere warmth when the
Reverend Mr. Trotter and his wife appeared. "Thank
you for coming," she said. She clasped their hands
gratefully, knowing that with the appearance of the
respected clergyman and his spouse, her acceptance
by his flock would be hastened.

"We wouldn't have missed a ball at the Abbey for
anything," Reverend Trotter reassured her. "And
we're doubly happy that you're here this evening, as
well."

"Thank you for your help with Kit's christening,"
Philippa whispered to Mrs. Trotter. "The church
looked especially pretty that morning."

"It was my pleasure, Lady Sandhurst," Rachel
Trotter replied with a warm smile. Then the couple
moved on to allow the guests behind them to approach.

People continued to squeeze into the crowded ballroom all that evening. It seemed that everyone for
miles around had come to Rockingham Abbey. The
lilting strains of a country dance filled the large
room, enticing even the shyest young gentleman out
onto the floor. In the various salons, card games were
being played by some of the elderly, more inveterate
gamblers.

As the dancing began, Philippa stepped onto the
polished oak boards on the arm of the count de Rambouillet. Lucien Mercier insisted that, as her honorary
father, the privilege of sharing her first dance belonged to him.

After joining in a contredanse with Tobias and waltzing with each of Belle's brothers, Philippa expected to sit down for the rest of the evening. But to Philippa's surprise, Reverend Trotter asked her to join him in a lively Scottish Reel. Afterward, other gentlemen requested the pleasure of her company, including several widowers and even a few brave bachelors undaunted by Philippa's past. Executing the spirited steps of the écossaise and the cotillion, she discussed politics, music, and art with her partners, relieved that none of them had the poor manners to ask about her life in Venice.

She was waltzing a second time with Étienne Mercier when the duke of Warbeck entered the ballroom. Philippa was aware of his presence even before she saw him. Couples around her began craning their necks to watch the duke make his way through the throng to the dowager duchess, who stood chatting with the Lillybridge sisters.

Warbeck was magnificent in formal black evening wear, the severity of his tailored garments enhancing his unabashed masculinity. The streaks of silver in his blue-black hair highlighted the pale eyes beneath their straight ebony brows. He exuded an unconscious aura of power, mystical and omnipotent, and Philippa could easily see why his enemies referred to him as Warlock.

He bowed and kissed the three elderly ladies' hands in turn. Philippa's adopted mothers, initially flustered at his approach, seemed to melt like beeswax in a flame beneath his irresistible smile. Their steel gray heads tipped back as they listened with fascination to his every word. Philippa and Étienne whirled past, and Warbeck looked over and caught her eye. Her heart leaped at the warmth in his searing gaze.

When the waltz ended, she waited anxiously for him to approach, her pulse racing madly. He continued his animated conversation with Blanche and

Beatrice, instead. It belatedly occurred to Philippa that he was making public amends to the twin schoolmistresses. He had once promised to pay the salaries for two teachers at the Lillybridge Seminary for Females and then reneged on that promise at the time of his divorce. From the glowing look in Blanche and Beatrice's jet eyes, they had forgiven him completely.

At Philippa's request, Étienne led her over to the chattering group. Warbeck made his excuses to his grandmother and the Lillybridge sisters and stepped forward to meet them. With a polite greeting to the duke, Mercier rejoined his wife, leaving Philippa in the sole company of her former spouse.

Warbeck bowed formally. "Lady Sandhurst," he said in a low, sensuous voice, "you look exceptionally beautiful tonight." She put her gloved hand in his large one, and he slowly lifted her fingers to his lips.

Philippa ignored the hush that came over the crowded ballroom. She looked into his silvery eyes and smiled tentatively. "I didn't know you'd returned from London."

"I got back just an hour ago," he said. "I'm sorry I'm late." His smoldering gaze drifted over her, taking in her bare shoulders and lingering provocatively on the low décolletage of her gown.

As the familiar melody of a waltz soared around them, she tried to ignore the fact that she was suddenly breathless. "And did your business go well?"

Frowning slightly, he searched her eyes as though looking for an answer to some perplexing puzzle. "Well enough," he said at last. His chiseled features softened, a smile playing at the corners of his sensual mouth. "How's Kit?"

"Oh, he can't stop talking about his trip to the seashore. You'd better get used to being a young boy's idol," she warned. "Kit thinks the sun rises and sets on the grand *signóre*."

He chuckled softly. "I always wanted to be someone's idol." He offered her an enthrallingly apologetic smile. "And how about Kit's mother? Has she forgiven my hasty departure?"

Lowering her lids, Philippa toyed with her fan, opening and closing the fine Venetian lace with quick, jerky movements. Her throat was clogged with emotion. "We need to talk, Court ... but not here."

Warbeck stepped nearer. He bent his head and answered huskily, "I'm at your disposal, Pippa Pixie."

She looked up to meet his eyes. Philippa thought her heart would break at the tenderness she found there. Somehow, she had to find the words to tell him about the baptism before he learned of it from someone else. She had to reveal the true date of Kit's birth—even if it meant she would lose her son forever. "Perhaps we could ..." Her voice broke, and she swiped at her lashes, furtively brushing away the tears.

Seeing her distress, Warbeck quickly intervened. He took her elbow and led her farther away from the dance floor, his large frame protecting her from curious eyes. "We'll talk about this later, sweetheart. Tonight, I want you to enjoy the ball. I'd ask you to dance with me, but I'm no longer very light on my feet." He tipped his head to one side and studied her thoughtfully. "Your twin mothers tell me that you've been discussing the idea of endowing a progressive school for females in Kent."

"That shouldn't be such a surprise," she told him, amused by the mild astonishment in his deep voice and thankful for his tact in quickly changing the subject. "I loved both learning and teaching at the Lillybridge Seminary. I want to see other young girls have the same opportunity. Girls whose families can't afford to send them to London for their education. The school will also provide a living for several female teachers. And I don't know of anyone more knowledgeable about establishing an academy for young women than Blanche and Beatrice."

"I think it's a wonderful idea," he agreed. "In fact, you can put my name on your list of donors. I'll match your funds pound for pound." A gleam of amusement lit up his gray eyes. "Naturally, I'll expect to be on the board of trustees."

It was her turn to be astonished. "That's very generous of you," she said eagerly. "I didn't know you were interested in the education of females."

He grinned at her. "It's something long overdue."

"What?" she teased. "The education of women or your interest in it?"

"Both."

They broke into soft laughter just as the last strains of the waltz died down. Philippa realized with a start that everyone who hadn't been dancing was watching them in mute fascination. She felt the heat of a flush creep up her cheeks and sobered immediately. Blast it! She'd been so engrossed in Court, she hadn't paid any attention to the others in the room or considered how strange it looked for her and her former husband to be on such warm, friendly terms.

A woman's shrill voice cut through the silence. "That disgraceful female shouldn't be allowed in polite society."

People around them gasped in shock. Heads turned to seek the source of the cruel jeer. A cold, unnerving stab of horror sliced through Philippa. In a haze of mortification, she felt Court's strong hand reach out to support her. He stood straight and stiff beside her, fierce displeasure emanating from his powerful body.

Her pretty face contorted with outrage, Lady Bowring rose from her chair and lifted her chin in patent disgust. She was a voluptuous woman, who stood several inches taller than her husband. That heavyset gentleman, at least fifteen years her senior, placed a warning hand on her arm and murmured something in her ear. She shook off his pudgy fingers and glared at Philippa with diabolical intent. "My God," she sneered, "I refuse to stay in the same room with that hussy."

The weight that had sat on Philippa's chest earlier in the evening suddenly threatened to crush the breath out of her.

Sensing that Philippa was about to bolt, Court held her firmly at his side. He met Hester Bowring's imperious stare and knew the real reason for her sudden attack. The forty-year-old woman had tried to seduce him three months ago. She'd been irate when he'd made it clear that he had no interest in being the father of her next child.

Gripping his cane, Court dragged Philippa beside him as he moved to stand directly in front of the Bowrings. Ignoring the vicious-tongued harpy, he glowered at the stunned, cowering husband, who seemed to shrink inside himself under Court's gaze. "Since you're unable to stay a moment longer, Bowring," Court snarled through clenched teeth, "we'll make certain your carriage is brought round at once."

Hester Bowring gathered her India shawl about her plump, white shoulders. She glanced haughtily around the room, her screechy voice carrying to the farthest corner. "I'm sure there are other scandalized women who will need their carriages as well, Your Grace." She waited expectantly for at least one self-righteous female to follow her example. Not a soul said a word. No one wanted to be considered a protégé of the infamous Lady Bowring.

"Let's go," Jasper Bowring muttered to his wife. "You've caused enough trouble for one night." He grabbed her arm in a tight hold and hauled her toward the door. Wordlessly, the crowd opened a path to let them through.

As the couple departed, the cultured voice of the dowager duchess of Warbeck could be heard clearly throughout the hushed ballroom. " 'Fore Gad, that's the first time I've seen Hester Bowring follow her husband's instructions."

"Aye, and good riddance to them both," Lady Harriet declared in her booming contralto. At her matter-of-fact summation, the guests began buzzing among themselves.

The Rockinghams hurried over to Philippa's side. "You're the only m-man I know," Tobias chided Court with a disbelieving shake of his head, "who'd t-take it upon himself to th-throw two fractious g-guests out of another man's h-house." He punched his friend's shoulder playfully. "If you'd given m-me half a chance, bl-blast your eyes, I'd have d-done it myself."

"Are you all right, *chérie*?" Belle asked. The viscountess's face was pale with concern.

"Yes," Philippa whispered.

But Court could feel her trembling with humiliation. "I'm going to take Philippa out onto the balcony for a while," he told Lady Gabrielle in an authoritative tone. "In the meantime, you and Toby can circulate among the guests and ease the awkwardness of the situation. Have André and Étienne help you get people back on the dance floor as quickly as possible." Without waiting for them to answer, he guided Philippa through the open French doors and into the night air.

As soon as they were out of sight of the inquisitive onlookers, Court put his arm protectively around Philippa's shoulders and gently drew her to him. She stood rigid in his embrace, her hands clenched at her sides.

"Take a deep breath," he urged, trying to keep the cold wrath from his voice. "It's over now."

He was furious at the way she'd been publicly pilloried. Furious at the certainty that, if Philippa ever returned to London, she'd be subjected to degradation by other sanctimonious hypocrites like Hester.

The sure knowledge that Lady Bowring had ripped out at Philippa to get revenge for being scorned frustrated Court even more. Hell, he could call a man out for defaming her, but there was nothing he could do to shield Philippa from the cruel gossip of petty females. And the fact that he wasn't able to protect her enraged him still further.

"I don't need your pity," she murmured, her stilted voice muffled by his chest. He could sense the abject shame in her wooden stance.

"I'm only trying to help," he said, his own words gritty with anger.

Her head snapped up, and she glared at him. "I don't need your help, either."

"Why are you so goddamn stubborn?" he demanded, lashing out in his fear for her. "You need all the help anyone can give you, Philippa. Christ, you're like a wayward child who's too obstinate to admit that you've brought a painful, but well-deserved, punishment upon yourself." He gritted his teeth before he said more. Surely she realized that her past had made her a social pariah. She didn't need him to tell her that this evening.

Somewhere in the far recesses of her mind, Philippa knew that she should be grateful for the way Warbeck had come to her defense in the ballroom. But the awful foreboding that had enveloped her all evening had left her nerves raw and jangled. The very justifiable fear of losing Kit—now that she was resolved to tell Court the truth—left her unable to think clearly. And Lady Bowring's verbal attack had been the final blow to Philippa's pretense of serenity.

She felt as if she were splintering into a million pieces. How could Warbeck heap more calumny on her head, when he was the very cause of it to begin with? If he hadn't falsely accused her of adultery, none of this would have happened tonight. She felt as though she'd been led out to be stoned like the sinning woman in the Gospel. And like that hapless woman, only divine intervention could protect her from excruciating scenes like this in the future.

Visibly quaking, she stared at the perfect folds of his white stock and willed herself not to cry. "Yes, I know that I'm being punished for what I did," she said through dry lips. "But I don't need your interference or your lectures. I can manage my life in my own way. Now please, just go and leave me alone."

"Fine," he growled. "I will." He released her and stepped back. His hard eyes raked her. His voice was low and filled with exasperation. "But first, I want to know if Sandhurst was worth it."

Tears blurred Philippa's vision. She wanted to strike back, to hurt him as deeply as he had hurt her. "I may have been reared in a boarding school," she said with bitter sarcasm, "but I do know the consequences of a married woman running off with another man. I knew it at the time. And under the same circumstances, I'd do it again."

She turned her back on Warbeck and walked to the balcony's iron railing. Behind her, she heard the soft thud of his cane as he reentered the ballroom. Philippa stared up at the starry sky, certain from the unbearable ache in her chest, that her heart was broken.

Two weeks after the Rockinghams' ball, Court sat in his study at Castle Warbeck, impatiently waiting for the imminent appearance of his hired investigator. Emory Fry had posted a letter from Dover, giving the date of his arrival in Chippinghelm. Restless, Court rose from behind his mahogany desk and moved to the diamond-paned window. The casements had been thrown open, allowing the fragrance of his grandmother's roses to drift into the room. He scowled impatiently at a large bush covered with magnificent red blooms. In his note, Fry had given no hint of the success or failure of his mission.

Throughout the countryside, gossip about the Warbeck divorce had surfaced again after the barbed taunts of Hester Bowring. A few people dredged up old, yellowed copies of the *Times*, the *Standard*, and the *Morning Post*. The press had not been kind to the earl of Warbeck. His bride had been portrayed as a poor orphan girl, who must have been very frightened, indeed, to have been provoked into running away from her bridegroom of barely two months.

Prattling matrons brought up the fact that there had been no real proof of criminal conversation, or crim. con., as a suit on the grounds of adultery was called. The one piece of hard evidence produced by the angry husband—an anonymous note telling of a lover's tryst—had been scoffed at by the members of Parliament as unsubstantiated hearsay. The divorce had nearly been scuttled in Commons. The House of Lords refused to condemn the missing wife absolutely, passing a Bill of Divorcement which noted only her elopement with another man as the grounds for proof of adultery. There was even the generous inclusion of the right for the wife to remarry.

The staggering financial settlement was again discussed by wagging tongues. Lord Sandhurst had been ordered to pay an astonishing £50,000 in damages to the injured husband, a sum the marquess's solicitor hadn't bothered to quibble with. The irate husband, in lieu of an annuity for his young wife, had returned the burned-out shell of a manor in Surrey that she'd brought to the marriage. It was a shocking piece of business. Everyone in Kent knew that Court had used the money from Sandhurst to finance his investments, which had grown into an enormous fortune. His town house in London was refurbished in splendor. Castle Warbeck had been restored to its former glory. That was when people started referring to Court as Warlock. But never to his face, of course.

Court gripped the head of his hickory wood cane.

He was well aware of the insinuations against him, knew that many people still considered Philippa's desertion his fault. The neighboring gentry all remembered the sweet eighteen-year-old bride he'd brought home to Kent. They were also well aware of the dishonorable circumstances surrounding his parents' deaths. As they'd watched him grow up, they had remarked upon the same defects once displayed by his mother and father. He was short-tempered, brooding, licentious, and cynical.

Court left the window and walked to a side table. He poured a glass of brandy, sat down in a wing chair, and stretched his legs out in front of him. Resting his head on its high back, he stared up at the ceiling, going over in his mind the events of the past two weeks. He smiled grimly to himself. One ray of light had been the appearance in the *Morning Post* of the announcement by Lord and Lady Brownlow that their daughter, Clare, wished to end her betrothal to the duke of Warbeck. The welcome news had been printed the day after he'd returned to Kent.

Another source of pleasure had been his visits with Kit. Court had driven over to Sandhurst Hall nearly every day. He'd bought his son a pony and supervised the lessons in riding given by a competent Sandhurst groom. They'd gone fishing together, taking the frisky little terrier with them. Kit's mother had refused to go along.

Since their embittered words on the balcony that awful night, Philippa hadn't been alone in Court's company once. She'd hidden behind Blanche and Beatrice's skirts, taking them sight-seeing, shopping in Chippinghelm, and looking over half the county for possible sites for the proposed academy, until her indefatigable mothers had returned to London at the end of the first week. After that, she'd tagged along with her mother-in-law everywhere, till it was a wonder that patient lady didn't feel like a dog with a tick burrowed under its fur.

With Lady Harriet seated between them in the Hall's comfortable back drawing room, Court had tried to reason with Philippa. He'd apologized for the fifth time for his sharp words the night of the ball and for his asinine behavior when she'd told him about her parents. Philippa looked at him blankly, as though not even comprehending what he was saying. Hell, it was no wonder he finally lost his temper and swore like the ex–cavalry officer he was. She'd lifted her eyebrows and looked over at the dowager marchioness as though to say, "See, the man's a slavering beast, but we have to tolerate his vile presence because he's my son's legal guardian."

That had been three days ago. He hadn't returned to the Hall since he'd received Fry's message. Court sipped his brandy thoughtfully. Everything depended on what the investigation had revealed. If Court couldn't coax Philippa into marrying him, maybe he would have to coerce her, instead.

At that moment, Peel ushered Emory Fry into the study.

"Mr. Fry," Court said. "I'm very glad to see you." He rose and set his glass on the side table. They shook hands, and Court gestured for the man to sit on the leather sofa across from him.

"Thank you, Your Grace. It's good to be back in England." Fry carried a portfolio under his arm.

Court studied the young man with interest. Gone was the rumpled tweed suit. Instead, Fry wore an expensively tailored coat and trousers, undoubtedly from one of the finest shops in Italy. And he'd put a few pounds on his slender frame. Outwardly, he looked like a prosperous banker, but there was still the hint of the wolf in his shrewd eyes. "Would you like a brandy?" Court asked.

"Don't drink while I'm working, Your Grace," Fry replied. "In my profession, it's best to keep your wits about you at all times."

Court nodded and sank back down in his chair. "Please begin," he encouraged.

"The first document I have for you is a copy of the marriage decree of Arthur Robert Bentinck and Philippa Hyacinthe Shelburne née Moore. The two English Protestants were wed by a Venetian city official in a brief civil service at the personal request of the duke of Verona. The date is listed as the twenty-first of March, 1809, three weeks after your Bill of Divorcement was signed in the House of Lords. The news of the divorce had been brought to the marquess from England by special courier. I can assure you, sir, that the couple was legally and duly married." Fry slipped a sheet of fine parchment out of the folder and handed it to Court. "It's written in Latin, of course," he added.

Court scanned the florid writing of some junior scribe and then looked up to meet Fry's round, protuberant eyes.

"The second copy I have, Your Grace, gives the certified date of birth of a baby boy born in Venice to the marquess and marchioness of Sandhurst two days after they were joined as man and wife. The original document has the signature and seal of Domenico Flabianico, duke of Padua, Vicenza, and Verona. No name is given for the infant, but there's no doubt in my mind, sir, that the child is the very same one you spoke of."

Disappointment slammed through Court. He took the vellum from Fry's hand and stared down at the date. Damn! Damn! Damn! He'd been so hopeful that he could prove Kit was his legal son. He looked up and met the investigator's calm hazel eyes. "Thank you for your efforts, Mr. Fry," he said, trying to hide his chagrin. "You will receive the sum I promised, regardless of the discouraging results you've brought back with you."

Fry lifted his hand in a warning gesture. "One minute, Your Grace." He withdrew a third piece of paper and held it up in front of him. "The last document is the signed confession of Isabella Conegliano, the midwife who delivered the baby boy. The old woman swore to me on her deathbed that the child was actually born on the twenty-fifth of February, the feast day of her favorite saint."

"That's three days before my divorce was passed in Parliament!" Court snatched up his cane and levered himself to his feet. He grinned in exultation. "Kit is my legitimate son, and I can prove it!" He took the paper from Fry's outstretched hand and read it with glee. "Mr. Fry, you've just earned yourself a handsome bonus."

Emory Fry gazed up at him solemnly. "The marchioness of Sandhurst does have two official papers," he warned. "The marriage and birth certificates supposedly prove that the boy is legally her late husband's son. In addition, of course, the deceased peer named the child as his heir in his will. In a court of law, the midwife's written oath might not convince a magistrate, although a deathbed confession is usually taken rather seriously. The trial would probably hinge on which person holds the most influence, the plaintiff or the respondent." Fry held out his hands in a gesture of uncertainty. "Only you know the answer to that, Your Grace."

"I'll win," Court declared. "And when I do, I'll generously reward you for your help."

Fry ran a hand over his balding head. He looked at Court with worried eyes. "You may change your mind, sir, when I tell you that I've been hired by the duke of Verona to continue gathering information on the late marquess of Sandhurst and his widow."

Court scowled. "Whoever the hell he is, this Italian duke seems to have played a suspiciously large part in this whole bloody farce."

"Domenico Flabianico is the wealthiest and most powerful noble in Venice. I was interviewed by the duke personally." Fry gave Court a rueful smile. "I can assure you, it wasn't a pleasant experience. For a while, I feared for my life."

Intrigued, Court sat back down in his chair. "Go on," he said.

Pursing his lips thoughtfully, Fry leaned forward and rested his elbows on the leather case that lay across his knees. "The duke of Verona befriended the two English émigrés upon their arrival in Venice. Some people I spoke with claimed that he was deeply in love with the beautiful marchioness. After meeting him, I believe it still to be true. The nobleman hired me to find out everything I can about the fire that destroyed Moore Manor. And about the illness that took the marquess of Sandhurst's life."

Stunned, Court stared at Fry in disbelief. "What on earth does he want with that information?"

"He wants me to present it to you, Your Grace."

"Why?"

The investigator shook his head. "Perhaps we'll understand when I complete my inquiries."

"Is there anything else I should know?" Court asked gruffly.

"Yes. From what I discovered, Arthur Bentinck was ill from the moment the couple arrived in Venice. Mortally ill. He improved somewhat, for short periods of time, but he was never totally well. According to the Sandhurst servants, his wife nursed him with the utmost devotion until his death. And their housekeeper swore to me that the English lord and lady lived as brother and sister from the first day they moved into their palazzo to the last, even after they were legally married."

"That's preposterous!"

"The duke of Verona believed it." Fry lifted his shoulders in a bid for appeasement, but his unruffled tone indicated that he felt it was true.

Court stood and walked to the window. The illogical revelation didn't fit his jaded view of the world or his intimate knowledge of the weaker sex. And

Sandhurst was sure as hell no saint. Court had known the glib, personable ladies' man since they were boys. Damn it, he had found the bastard's neck-cloth between the sheets of his own bed. Leaning one hand on the edge of the casement, he looked back at Fry. "Something must have been garbled in the translation."

"No." Fry moved lightly to his feet, the empty portfolio once again tucked under his arm. "However, I do have a concession to beg, Your Grace. Before you initiate legal proceedings, will you give me a month to complete my investigation? From what I learned in Venice, I'm convinced the lady was truly innocent of all wrongdoing."

Court gripped the dragon head handle of his cane so hard his fingers ached. "If you can prove that the former countess of Warbeck was innocent of adultery, I'll give you half my fortune."

The man flashed a glowing smile. His hazel eyes gleamed with happiness. "I already have a fortune, Your Grace. The duke of Verona was exceedingly generous."

Emory Fry had no sooner left than Lady Augusta swept into the study. Court grinned at her triumphantly.

"Good news from your Bow Street runner?" she asked, glancing down at the documents scattered across the leather sofa.

"The best news possible," he told her from his spot by the window. He breathed in the heady perfume of roses and could barely keep from shouting with joy. "I have proof that Kit is my legitimate son."

The duchess picked up the papers and sat down, calmly straightening them on her lap. Her face registered mild displeasure. "And just what do you plan to do with this proof?" she asked.

He stared at her in disbelief, unable to comprehend her disapproving attitude. "I'm planning on getting my son back, Grandmother. What the hell do you think I'm going to do?"

"Before you attempt to wrest the boy out of his mother's arms," she said with a sniff of disapproval, "I suggest you pay a call at the vicarage."

"What the blazes are you talking about?"

She smoothed her blue-veined hands across the fragile vellum. "While you were in London getting rid of your fiancée, the rest of us—Lady Harriet, the Rockinghams, and myself—attended a private christening at St. Aldhelm's. I think you might find the child's baptismal record interesting."

"*Kit's?*"

"The name written on the church ledger is Christopher Courtenay *Shelburne*, not Bentinck." She smiled as she rose, handed him the sheaf of documents, and glided toward the door, where she turned and met his astonished gaze. "Philippa asked us to keep the baptism a secret. She wanted to be the one to tell you, in her own way, and in her own time. Considering the fact that she stands to lose her only child by admitting the truth, I think she deserves better than to have her name dragged through the courts once again. Put your legal papers aside, Court. For once, try to think with your heart and not your rock-hard head."

As she left the study, Court dropped down on the wide stone windowsill. He smiled in stunned amazement at the empty room. Bloody hell, this was a day for surprises.

Chapter 17

Three and a half weeks after returning from Gull's Nest Bay, Philippa had exhausted all her excuses for not visiting Lady Augusta at Castle Warbeck. Once Blanche and Beatrice had returned to Chelsea, the dowager refused to listen to any more reasons why Philippa couldn't bring Kit to stay for several days. Lady Harriet abetted the duchess's scheme by telling Kit that when the grand *signóre* returned from his present trip, he would enjoy hearing his ward's opinion of his ancient home.

The minute Philippa learned that the duke had left for London, she put Kit into the green-and-white gig, climbed in herself, and drove to the Castle. Lady Augusta received her with a wide, welcoming smile, while the stunned butler stood in the massive doorway, gawking at the gray-eyed boy in amazement. Philippa suspected it was the only time in his life the unflappable Peel had ever been at a loss for words.

The first day of their visit, Lady Augusta had insisted on showing Philippa her grandson's new collection of antiquities from Egypt and the Byzantine Empire. Warbeck's handsome secretary accompanied them, describing in detail the date of the artifacts and their exact origins. When he met Kit, Neil Tolander was nearly as shocked as the elderly butler, though he did his best to hide his surprise behind a studied demeanor. Philippa caught him glancing sideways at her son whenever he thought no one was looking.

She had to bite her lip to keep from bursting into laughter at the expression of disbelief on the young man's face.

Kit had the run of the duke's stables by the second day. He became intimately acquainted with the coachman and grooms, who fell all over their big, booted feet welcoming the young marquess. Indeed, the entire staff, indoors and out, were clearly captivated by the small boy who so closely resembled His Grace. And their kindness to Philippa, whom they all remembered, brought tears to her eyes on several occasions.

During the course of their stay, Lady Augusta took Philippa all over the Castle, pointing out the extent of Warbeck's recent improvements. Built in the thirteenth century on the site of a Saxon stronghold, the original motte and bailey fortress had been enlarged and refined with each successive earl. The latest wings dated back only to the time of the Stuarts and formed the present comfortable sleeping quarters, while in the great hall, the medieval stone vault rose the whole height of the castle. Massive Norman arches, elaborately carved woodwork, and brilliant tapestries combined to give the home a rich, barbaric splendor. The new furnishings were magnificent, yet the duke had retained the feeling of ageless beauty.

To Philippa's surprise, she found herself ensconced in the same chamber she'd slept in as a bride. Despite the fact that most of the castle had been completely refurbished, the spacious room, with its graceful Queen Anne furniture, was exactly as it had been on the morning Philippa left Castle Warbeck with her bridegroom for their London town house. Even her clothes from six years before remained in the armoire, covered with tissue paper to protect them from dust. Since she'd arrived, Philippa hadn't been able to dispel the uncanny feeling that she'd stepped back in time.

On the third and final evening of their stay,

Philippa stood in her bedchamber, not knowing whether to cry in relief that she would be returning to Sandhurst Hall in the morning or from a heartfelt sorrow that she'd be leaving the Castle and its haunting memories behind. It had been a painfully nostalgic visit. During her brief marriage to Warbeck, she'd spent only two weeks at the Castle, yet she'd quickly come to love it as her home.

Philippa walked over to the dressing table and opened the intricately decorated lid of a japanned box, just as she had for the past two evenings. There on the case's red velvet lining lay the diamond and amethyst necklace and earrings her husband had given her on the day they were married. Her wedding ring, which she had traded for her passage to Venice, had somehow been retrieved and now rested beside them. The gold locket and chain Warbeck had placed around her neck the evening she'd accepted his proposal of marriage was there as well. Someone must have brought the jewelry back to the Castle from Warbeck House after she'd left England. She suspected Lady Augusta.

Philippa's fingers trembled as she lifted the heart-shaped locket, turned it over, and read the words engraved on the back.

Promise me forever

Tears rolled down Philippa's cheeks. She replaced the locket and closed the black-lacquered box, then glanced up to meet her solemn reflection in the mirror. Despondent violet eyes stared back at her. Moving to the tall window with its bright crewelwork hangings, she looked out at the starry night sky, her soul filled with anguish for all that once might have been and now could never be.

She had put off the inevitable for too long. Somehow, she had to find the courage to tell Court the true date of Kit's birth before the duke learned of the

surname inscribed in the baptismal registry from
someone else. Philippa knew that she should be the
one to tell him. Once Court learned that the documents she'd brought home with her from Venice
were false, he would insist upon removing Kit from
her care.

Until the evening of Belle's ball, Philippa had held
on to the slender hope that she and Court could remarry and the three of them would be a family. But
their argument on the balcony of Rockingham Abbey
had made it clear that, though Warbeck claimed he
wanted to marry her, he would never believe she
was innocent of adultery.

Little by little Philippa's melancholy thoughts were
replaced by the increasing awareness that she was no
longer alone in the room. She looked over her shoulder to find the duke of Warbeck standing just inside
the door that led to the adjoining chamber. His chamber.

She stared at him, speechless.

He wore a long dressing robe that nearly reached
his ankles. His feet were bare. She suspected that he
was naked beneath the lustrous black satin. The
thought of all that sinewy male flesh sent a thrill of
desire rocketing through her. Her heart stalled for the
breadth of a second, then started to race.

"Welcome home, Philippa," he said softly.

"You're supposed to be in London," she replied.
"You left four days ago."

His shuttered gaze hid his thoughts. "My journey
to London was an unsubstantiated rumor."

"A rumor your grandmother willingly spread."

"Lady Harriet helped, as well," he admitted as he
came into the room. "I convinced both dowagers that
I had to talk to you without an audience listening to
every word. And without interruptions."

"Just how far away did you travel?" she asked.

There wasn't a hint of apology in his reply. "To
Chippinghelm. I've been lodging at the Black Swan

for the last two nights. I wanted to give you time to feel at ease in the Castle once again. And for Kit to become acquainted with his true home at last."

Philippa took one quick step toward the closed door that led to the hallway. Blast the man! His stratagem had succeeded far better than he knew. In these past few days, both she and Kit had come to feel as though they belonged there. "I was just going to peek in on Kit before I retired," she parried.

"There's no need," Warbeck said. He moved to stand directly in front of her. "I looked in on him before I came here. Our son is sound asleep in the four-poster bed where he belongs. His nursemaid is close by in an adjoining chamber. Both Miss O'Dwyer and his great-grandmother will hear him, if he should waken and call out."

Philippa glanced down at her dressing gown and then looked up to study Warbeck's inscrutable features. "In any case, you really shouldn't be here," she told him with a coaxing smile. "Whatever you wish to discuss can surely wait until morning." She held her breath as she turned and busily rearranged several perfume bottles on the polished tabletop.

Court stepped nearer. "No," he said firmly. "This discussion can't wait until morning." He had come to demand some answers, and he wasn't going to be swayed by the stricken look on her beautiful features or her charming appeal for modesty.

She was attired in a white silk *robe de chambre* with short puffed sleeves and pearl buttons that ran all the way down the front. She hadn't yet pulled the ivory combs from her hair. The golden mass of curls was still piled loosely on top of her head. Wispy tendrils fell in front of her ears and curled at the nape of her neck. She looked like an angel.

Court clenched his hand at his side to keep from reaching out and dragging her to him. "We're going to have that talk you wanted the day long ago when you came to Warbeck House and I stupidly turned

you away. I was a pigheaded ass. I freely admit it.
But I'm listening now. What were you going to say to
me?"

Her apprehensive gaze flew to meet his. "How . . .
how should I remember?" she cried, her distraught
eyes enormous in her pale face. "That was nearly six
years ago!"

"You can remember," Court prodded. "Think!
What had you come to say? Were you going to tell
me that you were carrying my child?" He waited
anxiously for her answer, the pain in his gut like a
raw, open wound. A wound that had festered and
spread, fed by his brooding cynicism and insane jealousy, till it had almost eaten him alive. "Were you
going to beg me to take you back for the sake of our
unborn baby?" he persisted, unable to keep the
throbbing ache from his voice.

"No," she whispered with excruciating honesty. "I
wasn't going to tell you I was pregnant unless you
first believed I was innocent."

"You expected to convince me that there was nothing between you and Sandhurst?" He gripped the
dragon head cane and advanced another step.

"I prayed that I could."

Court pulled the long, rectangular piece of white
silk from the pocket of his robe and held it in his fist
before her. "And could you have explained this?" he
asked hoarsely.

With a frown, Philippa stared at the wadded material in his hand, unable to follow his meaning. "What
is it?"

"Surely you recognize it, sweetheart?" The question was low and frighteningly calm. "Sandhurst
probably had a dozen more just like it."

Philippa took the neckpiece and stared at the embroidered initials in the corner with bewilderment. "I
don't remember seeing one like this."

"But you do agree that it's Sandhurst's monogram?" Warbeck insisted. He loomed over her, his large frame intimidating in the quiet, candlelit room.

She looked at him through narrowed eyes, wondering why he was acting demented. "Of course, it's Sandy's. What difference does it make whose stock it is?"

A bitter, ironic smile twisted Warbeck's mouth. "Do you know where I found this, Philippa? I found the bloody thing in my bed the night after I interrupted your tryst with Sandhurst in Kensington."

Dazed, Philippa looked down at the stock. An icy chill went through her. "How did it get there?"

"That's what I've waited all these years to learn," he bit out savagely. "How the hell did the marquess of Sandhurst's monogrammed neckcloth end up between the sheets of my bed?"

She tried to shove the white silk back at him, as though it burned her fingers, but he refused to take it. "I have no idea!" she exclaimed. "Someone else must have put it there."

"Who?" Warbeck demanded. "Who would have put Sandhurst's stock in my bed?"

She gaped at him in mystification. "Perhaps it was someone playing a cruel joke."

"Then the jester must have laughed himself silly when the divorce bill was passed in Parliament."

Philippa clutched the cloth to her breast. Her strangled words caught in her throat. "Court, I . . . I swear before God that I know nothing about this."

Court looked into her bewildered eyes and sensed she was telling the truth. Intense relief swept through him. Whatever else she might have done, Philippa hadn't betrayed him in his own bed. "I believe you," he said, the words torn from the deepest part of his being. He cursed softly under his breath. There was no one who would have gained by perpetrating such a cruel trick. "Maybe Sandhurst placed it there himself, hoping that I would jump to the wrong conclu-

sion and divorce you," he suggested. But he knew he
was grasping at straws.

"No," Philippa said with absolute conviction.
"Sandy would never have done that. He loved you
till the day he died." Carefully, precisely, she draped
the neckcloth across the back of the chair in front of
the dressing table, then met his gaze. She took a
deep, audible breath and squared her shoulders.
"Court, I know you probably aren't any more ready
to hear this now than you were six years ago, but I
need to say it for my own peace of mind. When you
charged into the Four Coaches Inn and found me in
Sandy's arms, there was nothing between the two of
us but innocent friendship. It was a harmless embrace, nothing more."

Court closed his eyes as he felt the agonizing
doubt cleave through him like an executioner's
blade. Everything he knew about Philippa told him
she was telling the truth. Had it been his own irrational jealousy that had sparked the entire conflagration?

He'd fallen in love with her at first sight. Yet he'd
felt unworthy of her love from the moment they met.
Hell, his own parents had never loved him. Why
should a woman like her?

But he had wanted Philippa so badly. He'd been
determined to win and keep her as a priceless possession, a treasure to guard from every other man
who might try to steal her affections. Yet deep in his
tormented soul, he'd been afraid that one day she
would leave him for someone worthier, someone
finer. Someone like Arthur Bentinck.

The excruciating ache in Court's chest nearly
brought him to his knees as he admitted to himself
what he'd always been afraid to confront. His fierce
determination not to lose his adorable bride could
have been the very catalyst that caused her to flee.
His ungoverned temper had propelled Philippa into
Sandhurst's waiting arms.

Court opened his eyes and met her troubled gaze. "I want to believe you," he said thickly. "But more than anything, Philippa, I want to put it all behind us."

Her violet eyes grew bright with tears. "Oh, my darling," she whispered shakily, "so do I."

Court leaned his cane against the dressing table and took her in his arms. He kissed her with all the love he felt, telling her without words how much he adored her. Telling her that the past was truly over.

He broke the kiss and held her close against his bruised and battered heart. "One thing I promise you, Pippa," he assured her as he brushed his chin across the top of her curls. "I will never question you about this again. I vow, from this day forward, I will trust you completely."

She drew back and lifted her eyes to meet his. Teardrops glistened on her thick lashes. "There is something I have to tell you," she said with a sob, her tear-drenched eyes filled with anguish. "Three weeks ago while you were in London, Kit was christened with his true name, Christopher Courtenay Shelburne. Your son was born before our divorce was passed in Parliament. Kit is your legitimate heir."

"I know, darling," he said soothingly. "While I was in Chippinghelm, I visited St. Aldhelm's and saw the baptismal record." He pulled her close, brushing his lips against her temple and inhaling the sweet scent of her. "Thank you for telling me the truth and for giving me back my son."

"I love you, Court."

The softly whispered words rocked him to his core. He framed her face in his hands. "Ah, God, how I love you, little pixie." He kissed her tenderly, his tongue gently exploring the wet warmth of her mouth. He slid his hands down her arms and cupped her breasts. Beneath his touch, their pliant softness grew full and firm, sending the blood rushing to his groin.

He was suddenly hard and heavy and wild with desire.

The kiss grew deeper and more passionate. Impatient, he yanked at the fastenings of her white silk robe and the tiny buttons popped, spilling across the floor.

"Court!" she yelped in surprise.

"I'll buy you three more just like it," he murmured against her lips, as he shoved the puffed sleeves downward, kissing her all the while. When he'd torn off her gown and she stood in naked splendor before him, he jerked at the belt of his robe. The black satin fell open to reveal his thick male erection. Court sank down on the chair nearby and pulled her astride him. The feel of her soft, womanly folds nestled against his taut flesh brought an almost unbearable pleasure. All the romantic phrases he'd practiced in his head were lost to graphic words of eroticism. He clenched his teeth as he struggled to regain control.

"It's been too long," he said hoarsely, hoping she would understand his raging need. "I can't wait a minute longer."

"Neither can I," she admitted in a shaky whisper.

Cupping her buttocks in his hands, he lifted her up and suckled the pink velvet tips of her breasts. Then he gently guided her onto his swollen sex with a deep groan of satisfaction.

Philippa felt his hard staff ease into her, bringing her an incredible feeling of warmth and fullness. In place of the aching emptiness, tightly coiled sensations throbbed inside her. She buried her fingertips in his thick black hair and returned his feverish kisses. He fondled her as she rocked in slow, rhythmical strokes against him, her breath coming in shallow pants. Every movement brought an exquisite, radiating pleasure. "Oh, Court," she sighed, "I can't get enough of you." She felt his answering smile on her lips.

Through a sensual haze, Philippa listened to his

husky words. "That's good," he murmured. "Because I intend to spend the entire night making love to you."

He caressed her engorged breasts and teased their taut buds with his thumbs, all the while thrusting his manhood deeper and harder inside her, burying himself up to her womb. She gasped as she felt her delicate muscles clench around him. With a long, low sigh, she surrendered to the sweet gratification of her release.

"We're going to be married as soon as possible," he rasped in her ear, while wave after wave of ecstasy washed over her. "And I intend to have lots more children." Then with a muffled shout, he found his own release.

Philippa rested her head against his strong neck as her breathing slowed to a normal pace. In the lethargic afterglow, his words echoed faintly in her mind. "I haven't as yet agreed to marry you," she reminded him in a ragged whisper.

He grinned rapaciously. "You will, after tonight." One by one, he removed the four combs that held her heavy hair and buried his face in the tangled curls. "God, I adore the smell of you," he said with a throaty laugh. Then he lifted her gently off him. "Let's move to the bed, sweetheart, where I can hold you in my arms while we sleep."

They made love again, slowly, lingeringly, caressing each other's bodies with a reverence that came from the knowledge that they had lost nearly six precious years.

Philippa woke in the middle of the night to find Court watching her, just as he'd often done on their wedding trip. "Haven't you slept?" she whispered.

He was braced up on one elbow, his stubbled chin resting on his palm. He traced the line of her upper lip with the tip of one finger. "No," he said, his eyes alight with deviltry. "I was just waiting for you to get a little rest." He splayed his fingers across her belly and slid them slowly downward in an enticing gesture.

"Mmm," she breathed softly. "I've never felt so well rested." She turned to him and ran her hand over his muscular thigh, her fingers halting as they brushed across the long, wicked scar. The words came out in a rush. "Please tell me how it happened, Court. I need to know."

He tensed beneath her touch, then rolled onto his back. Placing his hands under his head, he looked up at the ceiling and spoke in a low, gruff tone. "The evening before the battle of Bussaco, Toby brought orders from Wellington to our encampment. I'd been on the Peninsula for sixteen months, and in all that time I hadn't heard even the tiniest scrap of news about you. I didn't even know if you were alive. Rockingham told me that you and Sandhurst were safe in Venice and had had a child the previous year. A beautiful little son."

At Philippa's soft exclamation of regret, Court's voice grew harsh with self-mockery. "I was filled with rage and despair. I told myself I was angry only because I'd hoped that the two of you had suffered a shipwreck and drowned." He turned his head and looked at her. Philippa had never seen so much pain in a man's eyes. "I cried that night for the first time since my brother died when I was nine years old. I stood beside my horse, looking blindly across the heather to the wooded hills where sixty thousand Frenchmen waited, and felt the tears run down my face because, more than anything, I wanted you to still be my wife. And that little baby boy to be ours."

"Darling, I'm so terribly sorry," Philippa said in a choked voice. Unable to fight back her own tears, she bent and tenderly kissed the puckered laceration, praying the drops that fell on his injured leg would heal his wounded heart. "Can you ever forgive me?"

Court cupped her chin in his palm and gently

lifted her face to his. "It wasn't your fault I acted like a damn idiot the next day. When our supply train was about to be cut off, I led my men on a near-suicidal mission to rescue it. The slash was from a French hussar's saber. I was lucky the bastard didn't slice clean through the bone." He paused, his face twisted in a grimace of remorse. "Ironically, I learned later that by the day of the battle, the marquess of Sandhurst was already dead."

In the silence that followed, Philippa bent and tenderly traced her tongue over the discolored gash. As her long hair brushed across his groin, his swollen manhood leaped upward as though with a life of its own. Court groaned deep in his chest. "Jesus, Pippa, if you keep kissing me there, you're going to turn me into a stark, raving lunatic."

"That's good," she said. "Because you have already driven me to the brink of insanity."

A week later they were all packing for London. Court left several days ahead of the ladies, who insisted they needed more time to fuss over their clothes. He considered taking Kit with him, but he knew there would be a stack of work waiting for him at Warbeck House. The child would be better off spending the last week of summer in the country with his pony and his little terrier.

Before he started for London, Court told Philippa that he would be keeping Stanley Tomkinson on as the chief Sandhurst steward, as well as all the overseers of the other estates, with the exception of one man, who'd proved too lazy. Court admitted that their failures had resulted from a lack of supervision by their absent employer, rather than incompetence or thievery. The appreciative light in Philippa's eyes more than made up for his certainty that he would have to spend a great deal of time overseeing the Sandhurst estates in the future. Still, he had to agree that her gentler approach toward her fellowman had its rewards. He felt buoyed with hope for the future, more optimistic and carefree than he'd been in years.

The first week of September, Philippa arrived in London with Kit and the two dowagers. The Little Season was just beginning. When Court called at Cavendish Square, Philippa insisted that no mention of their plans to remarry be made, until more time had passed. She was worried that the gossips might blame her for the dissolution of his recent betrothal. It did Court no good to point out that his broken engagement with Lady Clare Brownlow had everything to do with her and Kit—and his former fiancée was well aware of it. Philippa was certain, however, that Clare would keep the true reason a secret for pride's sake.

"If we give the poor woman a little more time," Philippa declared with a smile, "perhaps she might even become engaged to someone else." She stood in front of the drawing room's wide bay window, sunlight sparkling on her lustrous hair. She fairly glowed with happiness.

Her day dress, the color of hyacinths, made her eyes appear larger and more brilliant than ever. She was wearing the locket he'd given her as a betrothal gift. He'd placed it around her neck the morning she'd returned to Sandhurst Hall from her visit at the Castle.

"I refuse to wait until Clare snags another idiot," Court warned. He crossed the rug to where she stood and slipped his arm about her waist. "It could be ten more years before someone comes along stupid enough to offer her a proposal."

Philippa's laughter rang out. "That's not saying too much for your own intelligence, my darling." She buried her fingers in the hair at the back of his neck and pursed her lips in a taunting pout. "Besides, I'm not asking you to wait until Clare's married. Just until the gossips have found something more interesting to talk about."

"Which, knowing London as I do, should be in about a week."

Her eyes grew serious. "We must wait at least until after the ball Lady Harriet has planned. I tried to talk her out of inviting the entire ton. She told me she hadn't, only the ones who mattered. I explained to her that those are the very people who'll never come as long as I'm in the same house. I warned her to be prepared for a social disaster."

Court set aside his cane and rubbed his hands comfortingly over her back. "They'll come," he said. "Maybe not everyone your mother-in-law invited, but enough. If you let me announce our plans to remarry, sweetheart, you'll have the added protection of my wealth and influence. A great number of people would attend the gala because they'd be afraid to offend me."

"The Brownlows have many friends and acquaintances, also," she hedged. "If we announce our intention to remarry before the date you were originally supposed to wed Clare, people will feel it's necessary to snub me in order to defend her. I'd like to avoid as much ill feeling as possible. It will be difficult enough for me to face the guests at the ball. That's why I think we should wait awhile."

"One month," he stated unequivocally. "I'll wait exactly one month and no longer." He paused and leered at her suggestively. "Unless you're willing to move into Warbeck House right away. Lady Augusta could play the role of chaperone."

"Your grandmother is the poorest excuse for a duenna I've ever known," Philippa asserted. Her eyes glittered with amusement. "You can't tell me she doesn't at least suspect what happened between us at Gull's Nest and at the Castle. After all, she knows you. Yet she persisted in looking the other way, while her grandson openly pawed her houseguest."

"I never pawed you," Court protested.

"What are you doing right now?" she asked sweetly.

"I'm touching you. Intimately."

A week later, Court smiled to himself as he climbed into his curricle and signaled his team of blooded chestnuts to start. In the last seven days, he'd made use of every opportunity to touch Philippa intimately.

That past Wednesday evening, she had attended a dinner party with her mother-in-law, given by Lord and Lady Holland. It had been Philippa's first appearance among the London ton. She'd been nervous, despite the fact that Lady Holland was a divorced woman, herself. In her younger years, Elizabeth Vassell, then Lady Webster, had left her husband for the arms of Lord Holland.

Their home in Kensington was the site of fashionable Whig society. The Holland House Circle included politicians, writers, artists, and poets. Only the most scrupulous wives, in silent condemnation of Lady Holland's past, refused to attend the affairs, insisting their husbands go alone.

That evening the table had been crowded with self-proclaimed intellectuals, wits, and bards. The domineering and eccentric hostess developed a soft spot for Philippa and introduced her to the Whig lord chancellor, though it was well known that Lady Holland favored the other party. When she learned that Philippa also supported the Tory cause, she drew her into a conversation that tested all of Philippa's wit and knowledge of politics. Impressed, Lady Holland took the young woman under her wing and presented her to Lady Granville and Lady Gray.

Court had arrived later in the evening to find Philippa surrounded by a large group of male admirers. He immediately coaxed her outside into the lovely formal gardens. She'd been flushed with jubilation at her success. Bubbling with high spirits, she laughed in delight as he teased her about her Tory leanings and poked fun at several of the serious young politicians who'd been hanging on her skirts when he arrived. Little by little, he led her deeper into the garden's high, concealing hedges. In the center of the maze, Court dropped down on a stone bench, lifted her onto his lap, pushed her skirts up to her waist, and made passionate love to her. He'd ignored her breathless protests that someone might find them, knowing they'd have to marry immediately should that occur. Nothing would have made him happier.

Court's pleasant reverie was interrupted by the need to check the directions he held in his hand. Glancing down at Emory Fry's cryptic note, he read the name and address. When he was certain he'd found the right street, his thoughts returned to Philippa.

She'd begged Court to wait to tell Kit he was his father until after they were married. Court had reluctantly agreed, realizing it would be easier for the boy to handle one surprise at a time. For although Kit had heard the vicar baptize him as Christopher Courtenay, the five-year-old wasn't yet aware that his surname was Shelburne. Once they were all living as a family, he and Philippa could tell Kit the truth together.

Court intended to conceal his own feelings about Sandhurst from the boy. He didn't want to sully the child's image of the man he held in such high regard.

The thought of holding his son in his arms and telling him that he was his father filled Court with joy. He was determined to be married by November. They could reveal the truth to Kit before Christmas and celebrate the holidays as mother, father, and child. Perhaps by then, there might even be a little brother or sister on the way.

As Court pulled on the reins, signaling his team to halt in front of a redbrick house on Harley Street, he felt his spirits soar. Against all odds, he had reclaimed his wife and son from the black-hearted bastard who'd stolen them. He had truly outwitted fate. Everything Court wanted was right in the palm of his hand.

His red-haired tiger jumped down and raced to the team's heads as Court descended. "Tool them up and down the street a few times," he told Slaney. "I shouldn't be long."

Court walked up the stone stairs that led to the three-story house. A large white sign hung beside the red door. OBADIAH DURNFORD, PHYSICIAN AND HEALER was painted in big block letters. A plump housekeeper answered the clanging bell, and Court was ushered into the spotless home. The smell of camphor, calomel, and mercurial ointment assailed him. Court fought back the oppressive memory of the weeks he'd spent in the gruesome field hospital.

"The doctor's expecting you," the woman said with a cheery smile. She led Court past an empty examining room to a small office in the back.

A portly man sat before a cherry desk and secretary. Its cylinder front was open, revealing haphazard piles of loose papers and stacks of books. On the opposite wall, shelves held medical tomes and various surgical tools.

Durnford and Court shook hands, then the physician gestured his visitor toward a high-backed bench. "Mr. Fry told me you'd be coming," he said, as he pulled his desk chair over and sank down in front of Court with a weary sigh. He held out a box of cigars.

Court shook his head and waited impatiently while the doctor clipped the end of a cigar and lit it.

Durnford leaned back, the smoke wreathing upward around his face. The man, somewhere in his late fifties, was totally bald. In the far corner of the room, an old-fashioned wig rested on the skull of a complete human skeleton that dangled from the ceiling. "I expected you four years ago, Your Grace," he said. "Three at the latest. After a while, I gave up and decided you weren't interested."

Court leaned forward with a scowl. "I didn't know you existed, Dr. Durnford, until two days ago when my investigator sent me your name and address. How is it that you were expecting me?"

"I thought you were interested in your friend, the deceased marquess of Sandhurst." He folded his hands over his paunch and puffed calmly on his cigar.

"You were his physician?"

"I treated Arthur Bentinck for six months prior to his leaving England. He'd been referred to me by his family's physician." He rubbed his double chin pensively. "The relationship between doctor and patient is confidential, Your Grace. However, in this case, I have the young man's instructions—written just before he died in Venice—to answer any questions you might ask, should you ever come to see me."

Court straightened and clenched the gold dragon's head with tense fingers. "Emory Fry seemed to believe that Sandhurst was mortally ill when he fled England. Is that true?"

"Yes. Arthur knew he was dying. I had given him less than eight months. Only his insurmountable will to survive can account for the fact that he lived for over a year in Venice."

"What did he die of?"

Durnford stood and paced restlessly back and forth across his office floor, puffing madly on the cigar. Finally, he stopped and stared at Court. "I followed the news of your divorce in the public papers six years ago with interest, Your Grace. I must say, your accusations against the marquess of Sandhurst astounded me. But, being his physician, my hands were tied. At the time, Arthur chose not to reveal the nature of his illness. There was nothing I could do. But I knew, without a doubt, sir, that he had not seduced your wife. The man was dying of cancer."

Court lurched to his feet. "Sandy? That's impossible! He was only thirty."

"This particular disease strikes young men in their prime. It's rare, but not unknown. I've had two other patients suffer from the same thing, though neither of them lived nearly as long as Arthur. All three men died of cancer of the testis."

"Jesus!"

"That's why there is no doubt in my mind that the marquess of Sandhurst did not carry on an illicit liaison with your lovely young bride. By the time I examined him, the cancer had afflicted the second testicle and was spreading throughout his groin. Arthur Bentinck had been impotent for six months before he sailed from England." Durnford spread his hands in compassion. "You can understand why he wished to keep his illness a secret."

Court sank back down on the bench, reeling from shock. He put his hand to his forehead as he tried to assimilate the unbelievable news.

"I know this must be a terrible surprise, Your Grace," Durnford said quietly as he rose and started for the door. "I have a patient waiting for me right now, but please stay here in my office until you've had time to come to grips with the information I've just shared."

Court stared at the book-lined wall in front of him in blank devastation. Comprehension, painful and tortuous, came at last as Philippa's words echoed in his mind. *Sandy asked me to meet him there because he wanted to tell me something. It was a private matter.* Court knew now why Sandy and Philippa were clinging to each other so tightly when he'd discovered them at the Four Coaches Inn. It hadn't been a lover's embrace, but one of infinite compassion. For Sandy had just told Philippa that he was dying and had begged her to tell no one of his terrible secret. At that very moment, Court had rushed in like a madman, accusing them of adultery.

Later, Sandy had probably tried to reassure Philippa that her fool husband would calm down and realize it was all a preposterous mistake. But Philippa had been eighteen, pregnant, and frightened. She must have refused to listen, certain that her hotheaded bridegroom would kill his best friend and then divorce her. What must have filled her with absolute terror was the possibility that Court would learn of the pregnancy, wait for the birth, and then take the child from her. That was why she'd decided to flee! And Sandy, knowing he was dying and too proud to admit to anyone the nature of his illness, had gone with Philippa to see that she came to no harm. Court had suffered the loss of his wife and child, not because of his friend's treachery, but because of his own jealousy and cynicism.

Court leaned his head on the bench's high back and closed his eyes, making no attempt to deny the overwhelming guilt that assailed him. The duke of Verona had been right in his assumption that the English couple had lived in Venice as brother and sister. What Philippa had claimed all along was true. Both she and Sandy had been blameless. Court had cold-bloodedly planned to kill his beloved childhood friend, who'd been dying by inches at the time.

Like the loathsome ogre he'd been portrayed, Court had wrongly branded his angel wife an adulteress before the entire country. He'd foully besmirched an innocent young woman's reputation in a fit of irrational jealousy. Christ, he was no better than the evil warlock people accused him of being. What he'd done was so vile, so abhorrent, he had no right to ask for forgiveness.

Court moved with unseeing eyes to the door. He left the house and walked up the street in a daze, going over again in his mind the horrible accusations he'd lodged against Sandy and Philippa in Parliament.

What he'd done was unspeakable.

Somehow, Philippa had found it in her heart to forgive him, but he could never forgive himself. He knew that he had to allow her to live free of his despicable person. And he had to give up all claim to her child. He owed them both that much, for God knew, he certainly didn't deserve to keep them.

"Y'r Grace! Y'r Grace!" Slaney called. He brought the chestnuts to a halt beside Court. "Gor'elp us, Y'r Grace! I thought yer didn't even see me."

Without responding to his servant's worried remarks, Court climbed into the curricle and stared straight ahead, making no attempt to take the reins.

His redheaded tiger gaped at him in growing consternation. "Do yer want I should drive yer home, Y'r Grace?"

When Court failed to answer, Slaney gave a piercing whistle to the leaders and raced the team back to Warbeck House.

Chapter 18

Court had regained a measure of control over his reeling emotions by the time he reached his town house. Nash met him at the front door and took his hat and gloves. "Mr. Fry is waiting to see you in your study, Your Grace," the butler said. "There's a woman with him as well."

Court struggled to concentrate on the servant's words. He assumed the investigator had come with his wife to collect his bonus for finding Dr. Durnford. He wondered how much Emory Fry knew about the nature of Sandy's illness and whether he realized that Court had wrongly accused his wife and best friend of adultery. He nodded. "I'll see him now."

Nash opened the study door, and Court entered to find the young man seated on the green settee by the wall. Beside him was a woman in her late forties with an enormous bosom and a small pug nose. The Frys were a mismatched couple. She was at least fifteen years his senior and a good fifty pounds heavier. They both stood as he entered.

Fry stepped forward to shake Court's hand. "Your Grace, I took the liberty of bringing Mrs. Penny Gibbs to see you. We just arrived in London this morning. When I traced her to York, I was so taken with her story that I felt you would want to hear it at once."

Court turned his attention to the woman he'd mistakenly thought was Mrs. Fry. "Hello, Mrs. Gibbs," he said with a faint smile. "Thank you for coming to see me. Won't you sit down?" He tried to conceal his impatience. The last thing he wanted was to listen to a complete stranger tell him a story. His thoughts were still focused on the staggering discovery. He went over and over in his mind the harrowing news of Sandy's hellish disease and his own reprehensible actions toward a dying man.

When the two visitors were reseated, Court crossed the room and leaned his backside against the edge of his desk. "Before we begin, Mr. Fry, I want to thank you for finding Dr. Durnford. You'll be generously recompensed for your trouble."

Emory Fry placed his hands on the knees of his expensively tailored trousers and leaned forward with eagerness. "That won't be necessary, Your Grace. I appreciate your generosity, but I was well paid for that work before I left Venice." He glanced at the woman. "If you'll be so kind, my lord, I'm anxious for you to hear what Mrs. Gibbs has to say."

Court turned his attention to the rotund female. She wore a bright orange carriage gown with a matching turban and plume. It was, without a doubt, the most garish costume he'd ever beheld. But her smile was pleasant, showing a wide gap between her two front teeth. And her deep blue eyes were warm and friendly. He returned her smile absently.

The woman stared curiously at Court in return, raised her thin brows, and tipped her head forward. "Mr. Fry said that yer wantin' to ask me some questions 'bout Hyacinthe Moore, Yer Grace," she prompted.

Court straightened at the mention of Philippa's mother. "You knew Hyacinthe Moore?" he asked in astonishment.

"Oh, aye, for ten years, Yer Grace," she replied. "I was 'er lady's maid from the day she came to the manor as a blushin' bride till the night she died." Mrs. Gibbs looked down at her folded hands and sighed deeply. "I've often wondered what 'appened to me mistress's little girl. I wrote several times to the child's uncle, but never got no answer. Knowin' the man as I did, I wasn't really expectin' one."

Court's gaze flew to meet Emory Fry's intense eyes. "That's correct," the young man added with suppressed excitement. "I discovered that there was a third survivor of the fire that destroyed Moore Manor."

"Please tell us everything you know about the fire, Mrs. Gibbs," Court urged.

"Aye, I'll tell ye what I know, Yer Grace," she said. "Though, i'faith, it 'tisn't wery much. 'Tis only by Gawd's blessin' that I'm alive meself." Her eyes were focused on something faraway. " 'Twas on a loverly June evenin', it was. Mistress Hyacinthe was terrible upset 'cause 'er knave of a brother-in-law persisted in tryin' to seduce 'er. She'd kept the blackguard's gropin' and pinchin' a secret from 'er 'usband to protect 'er sister's feelin's. But things had come to sich a point that Mistress Hyacinthe knew she couldn't 'ide the truth no longer.

"Me lady loved Master Philip dearly. Her world was centered round 'im and 'er little girl. Erasmus Crowther was a bloomin' idiot to think a foine lady like 'er would 'ave even looked at the likes of 'is bleedin' arse." She paused, flushing with sudden embarrassment at the private nature of her disclosures and her free choice of words.

"Go on," Court said quietly.

She shifted uncomfortably on the sofa and continued. "Dear Gawd, 'e was always there, tryin' to touch her when 'e thought no one else was lookin'. That day, 'e wrote 'er a note, tellin 'er to meet 'im in the folly at sunset. He threatened to tell 'is wife, me lady's sister, Anne, that she'd seduced 'im. The mistress took me with 'er to the folly. She wanted to 'ave someone with 'er, for she didn't trust the sneaky devil to keep 'is 'ands to 'imself. She also wanted to

'ave a witness when she told 'im that she was goin'
to tell Master Philip the truth."

Mrs. Gibbs passed her hand over her eyes, then
bracketed her cheek with her palm. "I was there
when Crowther joined Mistress Hyacinthe in the
folly. He didn't even try to speak with 'er. Just stood
starin' at 'er with wild, excited eyes. He wasn't there
no more'n a few seconds when we 'eard shouts from
the 'ouse. We looked up in 'orror. Flames were
shootin' out of every window. In minutes, the entire
manor burst into a ball of fire before our wery eyes.

"Mistress Hyacinthe screamed, 'My baby! My
baby!' Before either Crowther or me could hold 'er
back, she raced into the burnin' buildin'." Mrs. Gibbs
took a deep breath, as she dug into her reticule and
pulled out a handkerchief. When she continued, her
words were creaky with anguish. "It was 'orrible, it
was. The stench and the screams and the roar of the
fire. I'll never forget it. Never. Everyone inside was
burned to death. Charred beyond recognition. The
master, me lady, her sister, all the servants. No one
was spared."

"Except Philippa," Court corrected softly.

"Aye." She raised her face to meet his eyes. "Except for me lady's little lovie." She wiped away the
tears and spoke in a tone of awe. "Fanny Biddle 'ad
been Mistress Hyacinthe's nurse when she was
naught but a babe 'erself. Biddle and Pippa were
trapped in the girl's bedchamber. Biddle took the
child in 'er arms and leaped from a third floor window. She died of a broken neck, but, by a miracle,
Pippa survived. Her fall was broken by 'er nursemaid's body."

Court went to the woman and crouched down on
one knee before her. "Mrs. Gibbs, I must ask you this
question, and you must be very, very truthful. Don't
try to protect the dead. Nothing can help them now.
Are you absolutely certain that Hyacinthe Moore had
repulsed Erasmus Crowther's advances?"

"Oh, yes!" she exclaimed, a look of revulsion on her face. "Me mistress loathed the bloody bugger."

Court gripped his cane and moved to his feet. "Thank you, Mrs. Gibbs. I know that Lady Philippa will want to meet you. You are the only person who can tell her the truth about her mother and father. Will you go with me now to Cavendish Square to see her?"

The large woman jumped quickly to her feet. "Oi, Yer Grace, I'd love to see little Pippa Moore again! After the fire, the poor thing wasn't even able to speak. I tried to comfort 'er, but she didn't seem to know what 'ad 'appened. Even at the burial, I don't think she realized who it 'twas they were puttin' in the ground. She just stared ahead of 'er, not sayin' a bloody word.

"I'd hoped Mr. Crowther would let me stay to care for the little mite, but he told me I was no longer workin' at Moore Manor. That didn't surprise me none. He knew what I thought of 'im, 'e did. But 'e let all the stable 'ands and gardeners go as well, which was wery strange, indeed. So I went to live with me sister in York." Mrs. Gibbs smiled through her tears. "I met me 'usband there, I did. We 'ave an inn not far from the cathedral."

Court was about to ring for a carriage, when Nash tapped politely on the door. At Court's summons, the butler entered. "Lady Augusta is wondering if you're going to join her for tea, Your Grace. The dowager marchioness of Sandhurst is here for a visit."

"Have them come to the study instead," Court instructed. "There's someone I want them to meet."

When the two dowagers entered the room, Court frowned in disappointment. "I was hoping Philippa was with you."

"Oh, haven't you read her note yet, Courtenay?" Lady Harriet queried. "I gave it to Nash when I arrived. Her uncle asked her to come to Surrey to look at the progress of the new manor. Philippa left with Kit this morning."

A premonition of dread snaked through Court's body. "They went to stay at Moore Manor?"

"Apparently Erasmus wrote her a long letter about the rebuilding. He wanted her opinion on the draperies and rugs."

Penny Gibbs looked from one to another in surprise. "After eighteen years, the manor's still bein' rebuilt?" she asked incredulously. "Whyever has it taken so long?"

"Lack of funds," Court explained briefly. "Philippa was left penniless."

"Gawd, what a lie!" the woman cried. "That little ducky was a bloomin' 'eiress!'"

"And Erasmus Crowther was her legal guardian," Lady Augusta added in a strangled tone.

Court met his grandmother's horrified eyes. "I'm on my way to Surrey," he said. He pushed back the sense of impending disaster. With an iron will, he forced himself to remain composed and collected as he rang for his carriage. But the story he'd just heard had made his blood run cold. He turned to the shrewd investigator beside him. Fry's alarmed expression told Court the young man had reached the same dire conclusions.

"Please see that Mrs. Gibbs remains in London, Mr. Fry. Lady Philippa will want to meet her when she and her son return."

Unable to sleep, Philippa lay awake in the tower room of what remained of her childhood home in Surrey. Kit was snuggled up beside her on the straw-filled mattress, his breathing deep and regular. From the foot of the bed, she could hear Fanciullo snoring contentedly. They'd arrived at Moore Manor late that afternoon in response to her uncle's letter begging her to help him choose the furnishings for the mansion now under construction. Although she and

Court had talked about rebuilding the fire-ravaged home when they were first married, this was the first time Philippa had actually visited the manor.

Earlier that evening, Erasmus Crowther had tried his best to entertain her and Kit at the dinner table, but Philippa had become more and more ill at ease in his presence. No matter how often she told herself that her uncle was the only living tie to her lost loved ones, she couldn't bring herself to like the man. He was rough and uncouth and absorbed in his own concerns. But it was more than just his complaining and irascibility that bothered her. Something she could never quite put her finger on stirred a cold foreboding deep inside. Although she'd forgiven him for abandoning her as a child—after all, he'd been destitute and living on the charity of others at the time—she had never overcome her intense distrust of him.

And it wasn't just her uncle that left her feeling so unsettled. The moment she'd set foot in the tall stone tower, an eerie premonition of doom had enveloped her. She regretted coming to the manor and intended to leave the following morning, no matter how much Uncle Erasmus protested that he needed her assistance.

In spite of her troubled thoughts, Philippa dozed at last. She woke in the middle of the night to hear Fanciullo howling. The puppy ran to the bed and whined plaintively, then raced back to the door. Standing up on his back legs, he scratched at the wood with his front paws and yelped with unwavering persistence.

"What is it, Mama?" Kit asked sleepily.

"I don't know," she said. She reached out to light the candle on the night table, careful to keep the flame away from the stack of Kit's drawings nearby. "I think I'll get up and see what's bothering the little fellow."

Philippa crossed the room and opened the bedroom door. As Fanciullo darted out, the faint, acrid smell of smoke touched her nostrils.

Fire!

She slammed the door tight and leaned against it, pressing her forehead to the hard oak board. Clutching the candlestick in one hand, she splayed the other against the wood in sheer, numbing panic. Her mind went blank. Icy terror filled her, oozing through every vein to the tips of her fingers and the bottoms of her toes.

Fire! Fire! Fire!

Where was Mummy and Daddy? She needed them!

From faraway, she heard a child call out. "What is it, Mama? Where did Fanciullo go?"

Philippa whirled and stared in paralyzed confusion at the strange little boy on the bed.

She couldn't talk to him now! She had to hold tight to Nurse's hand! She could hear the flames crackling and feel the heat of the fire coming under the closed door. "I'm so scared," she told Fanny.

"Mama," Kit said with a deep yawn. "I'm going to get my puppy and bring him back in here." He shoved the coverlet off and swung his legs over the side of the bed.

"No, Kit, no!" she cried as she came to her senses. She fought to push back the swirling haze that threatened to engulf her. "Wait, dear! Stay where you are."

Philippa hurried across the room. She set the candle down on the stand and went to peer out the small slit of window at the moonless night. She could see nothing but darkness. There was no sign of life. No hint that anyone had discovered the fire. Her heart pounded in frenzy as the rising hysteria threatened to overwhelm her again.

"You'll be fine, little love. Just hold on tight," Fanny said. "Close your eyes now. And whatever you do, Pippa, keep your arms around my neck and don't let go."

With shaking hands, Philippa reached out to open

the casement, then stopped, her breath coming in great gulping sobs. My God! They couldn't jump! They wouldn't fit through the narrow opening. Not even Kit. And even if they could jump, they'd never survive the fall. They were at the very top of the tower. Four floors up. She covered her face with her quivering hands. She had to think!

It'd do no good to wait in the room and hope that help would come. No one was here but *him* and his half-deaf housekeeper. The only way to safety was down the winding stone stairs.

Racing back to the bed, Philippa knelt down, put her arms around Kit, and hugged him close. She was shaking so violently, he stared up at her with enormous, frightened eyes. "Listen to me very carefully, dearest," she said, struggling to keep her voice steady and even. She knew she had to remain calm for his sake. "There's a fire in the tower. We're going to have to go down the stairs. There's no other way out."

She stood and grabbed the pitcher from the night table, then turned back to where Kit sat on the edge of the mattress. "Don't be startled, dear. I'm going to wet you down." She poured the water over his head, letting it soak the striped material of his nightshirt. Kit jumped when the cool stream splashed over him, but he waited obediently till she was done. Then she dumped the remainder of the liquid on a Paisley shawl that she'd tossed over the back of a chair before retiring. She wrapped the rectangular wool around Kit's head and face, so only his eyes were visible.

"Keep this around you, darling. Keep your face covered and breathe through the wet cloth. Do you understand?"

"Yes, Mama," he answered, the cheerful words muffled beneath the wool. She could tell that he had no idea of the danger they were in.

"I mean it!" she said severely. She held his face in

her shaking hands and looked into his eyes. "Don't you dare pull this away from your face. Do you hear?"

He recognized the panic in her voice and was immediately subdued. "*Sì, mamma.*"

Philippa wet her cotton night robe in the water that was left in the basin and tied it around her face, covering her mouth and nose. She took the candlestick in her trembling hand. It would be pitch-black in the stairwell. They would need its light to find their way down. "Now, hold on to my hand, *carissimo,*" she said. "I won't let you go."

"I'll hold on," he promised solemnly. "I won't let you go either."

With a deep breath to gather her courage, she led Kit to the door. She pulled the cloth down under her chin so he could hear her final instructions. "It may become very smoky out there," she warned, "and the candle might not help us to see. But if we brush one shoulder against the outside wall and always step down, we won't get lost. Do you understand, dear?"

Kit nodded. His eyes were huge and frightened peering out from the makeshift turban.

"Whatever you do," she cautioned, "don't get scared and try to come back up here. Keep going down. That's the way out. And we won't run. We don't want to chance falling and hurting ourselves. We'll just walk as quickly as we can."

The tower was much older than the rest of the former manor. It dated back to an earlier building on the same site that had once been used as a fortification. Made of thick local stone, its narrow, curved staircase had been designed to provide protection from invaders. Only one person at a time could ascend the stairs, sword in hand, making the upper levels much easier for the inhabitants to defend. If she and Kit were lucky, the fire was on one of the top levels, and they would find fresh air below. But if the worst had happened, and the site of the fire was on the ground floor, they would be walking directly into the smoke and flames.

Sheer terror rose up inside her at the thought. Philippa couldn't face what was waiting for them behind that closed door. Her nightgown was soaked from the sweat of her fear. Her mouth was so dry she couldn't swallow. She closed her eyes, trying to fight the mounting despair in her heart. She didn't have the courage to look into the flames or smell the smoke or feel the scorching heat again. She would start to scream and scream and never stop.

"Don't be afraid, Pippa," Mummy said softly. *"Daddy and I are right here beside you."*

Suddenly, a feeling of peace came over Philippa. Drawing the wet cloth up over her mouth and nose, she reached out for the latch and breathed a sigh of relief. The metal was cool beneath her touch. Slowly, slowly, she opened the door, bracing herself against the frighteningly familiar sound and smell of fire. In the light of the candle she held in her hand, wisps of smoke curled up the stairwell, hovering along the ceiling. But there were no flames. Not yet.

Fanciullo appeared from out of the darkness, yipping at them in a spirited greeting. He seemed to be encouraging them to follow him. Gathering all of her strength, Philippa took Kit's hand and drew him out into the hallway. She closed the door behind her on the chance that they'd be forced to retreat back into the bedchamber. With a prayer to God for their deliverance, she took her son's hand and started down the narrow, curving stairs.

Court pushed open the door to the tower and saw the flames leaping high. A great hole had burned through the ceiling, allowing the smoke to go straight up to the second floor. The furniture had been piled against the far wall and was raging like a harvest fire. Once the flames reached the roof, the tower would become a giant chimney.

Erasmus Crowther stood in front of the burning jumble of broken chairs and tables with a torch in his hand. At the fresh draft of air, the flames jumped out at him. He turned with a start and saw Court standing in the open doorway.

Philippa's uncle darted across the room and came to a halt in front of the staircase that led to the upper floors. The burly, big-boned man was nearly dancing with excitement. His eyes glittered strangely in the wavering glow of the blaze.

Fear squeezed Court's heart in a painful vise. He begged God to let them be alive. He would sacrifice anything, *anything*, if only they were still alive. He glanced back at Slaney, who stood right behind him. "Get my pistol and a blanket from the phaeton," he instructed. "Quick!"

Without a word, his little tiger darted out into the night. Court shoved the heavy door closed.

"So, Warlock," Crowther sneered with a contemptuous grin, "you've come to join the bonfire. Pity my niece and her son can't come down to greet you. But they're trapped, you know. It's really quite hopeless."

With a roar of blind fury, Court charged across the stone floor. "Get the hell out of my way, you bastard," he shouted. The hatred he felt for the murderous swine was overpowering. Erasmus Crowther had done far more than cheat an innocent child of her parents and her fortune. He'd stolen a little girl's dreams of the mother and father who'd loved her.

Crowther moved to the second step. He swung the flaming brand in a wide arc before him. "Don't come any closer," he warned, "or I'll have to set you on fire. You'll flare up like a torch, just like Pippa's father did when he tried to save her." He chuckled with fiendish glee. "I couldn't let Master Philip live, you know. Hyacinthe would never have looked at me as long as her prig of a husband was alive. I wanted the pretty thing to be all alone, grieving for her lost loved ones. And I would have been the one to comfort her."

As Crowther talked excitedly, Court inched steadily forward. Crowther jabbed the firebrand at his face with a snarl, and Court was forced to jerk back from the flame, nearly losing his balance.

"You're as big a fool as Philip was!" Crowther jeered. "You never knew who sent that anonymous note, did you? Or who put the marquess of Sandhurst's stock in your bed."

Court wasn't shocked at the taunting revelations. On the ride to the manor, he'd had time to reach the same chilling conclusions. Philippa's uncle was the only person in the world who would have profited from her death.

"I knew someday Pippa would remember," Crowther said with a smug grimace. "As jealous and possessive as you were of your fetching new bride, I thought for sure you'd kill her and Sandhurst when you found out about their love affair." He shrugged philosophically. "When she ran off to Italy, it served my purpose just as well."

"But when Philippa came back to England, you knew you'd have to silence her before she recalled how her parents died. The rebuilding of the manor only made it inevitable that she'd one day remember everything." Court edged forward as he spoke, ready to strike the torch from Crowther's wrist with his cane.

Just then, Fanciullo came tearing down the staircase, barking at the top of his lungs. The game little terrier took hold of Crowther's trouser leg and growled ferociously. With a curse, the brawny man glanced down in surprise.

At that moment, Court lunged toward him, driving the tip of his cane straight into his opponent's breastbone with all his might. Crowther crumpled with a grunt. His head struck the stone wall as he fell to the floor.

Court stepped around the unconscious man, reached down, and snatched up the torch. Lifting it high to light the dark stairwell, he whistled to the excited terrier, who was whining at the closed front door. "Take me to them, Little Boy," he urged. "Show me where they are. Go on, now! Go find Kit!"

The puppy raced up the stairs, barking ecstatically.

"Philippa!" Court yelled as he climbed the stairwell. "Kit! Where are you?" He took the steps as fast as he could. Pain lanced through his thigh, and he gritted his teeth. "Where are you?" he called frantically.

"We're here, *signóre!*" Kit's indistinct voice came from just above him. Thank God, they had made it past the smoke-filled second floor. The courageous terrier's barking grew more and more furious.

Then Court heard Philippa gasping for breath. "Go on, Kit," she croaked. "Go on. Go to your father."

Court was upon them in an instant. She sagged against the wall, scarcely able to breathe through her fits of coughing. She'd covered her nose and mouth with a cloth that was now blackened from the smoke. Kit stood beside her, his face wrapped in a shawl.

"Come on!" Court shouted hoarsely. The smoke seared his lungs each time he drew a breath. "You can't give up now. You're almost down. Just a few more steps and you'll be safe."

Wracked with coughs, Philippa grasped Court's arm and regained her feet. She leaned weakly against him, unable to say a word.

"Crouch down by the floor and follow your puppy," Court told his son. "Don't wait for us, Kit. We'll be right behind you. And keep that turban around your face."

Kit crawled down the stairs behind Fanciullo. Holding the torch in one hand, Court leaned heavily on his cane as he led Philippa down, step by labored step. The heat of the flames increased when they neared the bottom level. The smoke grew denser, till they were unable to see at all. But the terrier's bark led the way. At last, they could feel the draft of fresh air from the open doorway.

Without warning, a firearm exploded just ahead of them in the darkness. The blinding flash lit up the smoke-filled staircase for a brief second. Philippa clutched Court's arm, unable to scream.

"Y'r Grace," Slaney hollered. "Y'r Grace. This way! This way!"

In the glow of the flames, they could see him standing over the body of Erasmus Crowther, the big carriage pistol in his hand, a blanket thrown over his shoulder. "Jesus!" the freckle-faced tiger exclaimed as he hurried to help Kit. "The bloody sod rushed at me like a lunatic. I had to shoot the bloomin' son of a bitch!"

They stumbled out into the night. The shapes of people racing with buckets to the newly rebuilt framework of the manor could be seen in the flickering firelight. When Slaney was certain they were safe and unharmed, he ran to help the others.

Gulping the fresh air, the three of them lay sprawled on the thick grass. Court quickly wrapped Philippa in the carriage blanket and removed the cloth from her face. He held her in his arms as she coughed up the smoke in her lungs in exhausted spasms. Kit tore the shawl off his head, and the frisky puppy crawled over him, licking his face in a joyous reunion.

The moment she stopped choking, Philippa pushed the blanket aside and staggered to her feet. Court levered himself up with his cane and put his arm around her waist to draw her close. She stared at the flames shooting out of the tower windows as though bewitched. In the burnished light from the fire, her skin glowed rosily. She blinked her smoke-stung, reddened eyes, never taking her gaze off the conflagration.

Clearly distraught, Philippa lifted her hands and

held them out as though pleading for someone to come to her. Tears streamed down her soot-stained face.

"The man with the torch," she wailed in a keen of heartrending anguish. "The man with the torch was my uncle! We saw him from the landing, Nurse Fanny and I. He was lighting the tapestries and draperies on fire. My daddy was calling to me, 'Pippa! Pippa!' Then my uncle set him on fire! Oh, my God! Oh, my God! Nurse covered my eyes with her hand. She pulled me back into my room and over to the open window. I could hear Mummy screaming for me. 'My baby! My baby!' she screamed over and over."

Weeping with immeasurable grief, Philippa turned into Court's open arms. "Oh, Court," she cried, "they loved me! Mummy and Daddy loved me! They died trying to save my life!" Great, wrenching sobs wracked her body.

Court held her in his arms and rocked her back and forth. "Shh," he whispered tenderly. "Shh, it's all right now. Everything is going to be all right."

Kit came to his mother and threw his arms around her. "It's all right, Mama," he repeated consolingly. "The grand *signóre* and Fanciullo saved us. You don't have to cry anymore."

Philippa dropped down to her knees and pulled him to her. "Oh, Kit, I know! I don't have to cry anymore."

Court knelt on the grass and wrapped his arms around them. He couldn't speak for the tears that clogged his throat. He just hugged them tightly against him, wanting never to let them go.

All around them, workmen and stable boys stood by and watched the tower burn. They had tried to save the manor's new scaffolding, but it had been hopeless from the start. The entire building was now a raging inferno.

* * *

Three mornings later, Philippa sat in bed with a tray of hot cocoa and toast in front of her, wondering why Court hadn't yet come to call. The night of the fire, he'd bundled her and Kit into the Sandhurst traveling carriage and ridden with them to Cavendish Square. While Kit and his puppy slept, stretched out on the opposite seat, Court held Philippa in his arms. The shock of the fire had released countless memories of her mother and father. In the hushed quiet of the dark coach, she told Court about her early years in an awed, reverent tone. She described her parents in detail, marveling at how clearly she remembered them. The images were bright and strong and filled with happiness. It was as though it were only yesterday that they'd celebrated her sixth birthday together. Just as she'd dreamed when she was a little orphan in the boarding school, her father had been tall and handsome and courageous. And her mother had been beautiful and all that was good.

In the early hours of the morning, Court had carried a sleeping Kit up to his bedchamber in Sandhurst House. Then after Lady Harriet helped Philippa put on a nightgown, Court came into her room and insisted on tucking her into the canopied bed. He'd refused to leave the chamber until she was sound asleep. She knew that he had sat watching her long after she'd drifted into an exhausted slumber.

Philippa hadn't seen him since.

The next day, a polite young man named Emory Fry had brought a woman to visit Philippa at the request of the duke of Warbeck. The moment she saw that round, cheerful face with the gap-toothed smile, Philippa recognized her mother's personal maid, Penny Longley, and burst into tears. Before Mr. Fry left, he further astonished Philippa by explaining that he had searched out Mrs. Gibbs—for that was Penny's name now—under the direction of the duke of Verona. The investigator gravely delivered a message entrusted to him from the Italian nobleman. The caring words touched Philippa deeply. Domenico Flabianico had proven a true and loyal friend.

Penny Gibbs had spent over four hours reminiscing with Philippa, telling her everything she could remember about her parents and her sweet Aunt Anne. It was a joyous and poignant afternoon. They had both been emotionally drained when they'd said good-bye.

Lady Harriet tapped on the bedroom door, interrupting Philippa's stirring reflections. When Philippa called for her to enter, the auburn-haired dowager carried a copy of the *Times* over to the bed and placed it on the flowered coverlet beside her. "London is absolutely agog," she announced in her usual brisk manner. "All of the public prints, including the *Morning Post* and the *Standard*, have the same article. Everyone is duly flabbergasted. You'd better read it, and then hurry and get dressed, my dear. You have a drawing room full of callers, all eager to be the first ones to welcome you back into the bosom of polite society. In the meantime, I've got to offer them tea and crumpets." Before Philippa could say a word, Lady Harriet left the room, closing the door firmly behind her.

With a perplexed scowl, Philippa scanned the front sheet, wondering what her sensible mother-in-law could have found so interesting in the morning news. She caught her breath as she read the bold, black letters directly in the center of the first page.

AN OPEN AND PUBLIC APOLOGY
FROM THE DUKE OF WARBECK
TO PHILIPPA HYACINTHE BENTINCK,
MARCHIONESS OF SANDHURST

Six years ago, I publicly accused my innocent young bride of adultery. I named my equally innocent friend, the Fifth Marquess of Sandhurst, as the party guilty of trespass, assault, and criminal conversation. I deeply and humbly apologize for the actions which I directed against them in the court of common law and in the Parliament. These accusations were spurious, unsubstantiated, and based solely on my own irrational conclusions.

I have been guilty of wrongly defaming her character. In grievous error, I claimed that she had broken her marriage vows and deserted me, when in reality, she had journeyed to Venice to nurse our dying and beloved friend, Arthur Bentinck.

I, Courtenay Shelburne, First Duke of Warbeck, take full responsibility for the shame and guilt heaped upon them during the divorce proceedings. I, hereby, publicly admit my terrible wrongdoing. In an attempt to make some small reparation for the unwarranted suffering and humiliation my actions have caused, I have donated the sum of £180,000 to the Lillybridge Seminary for Females, Chelsea, where the Marchioness of Sandhurst was reared and educated.

Philippa read the article three more times before her tears completely obliterated the print. There for everyone to see were the words she'd yearned to hear for six long, heartbroken years. But Court had restored her dignity in the eyes of the world at the cost of his own reputation. Her heart ached for the proud man who had sacrificed his honor and self-respect in order to vindicate her.

She knew now why he hadn't come to see her since the fire at Moore Manor. Somehow, he had learned the tragic truth about Sandy's illness. While she'd been agonizing over Court's unexplained absence, he had been drowning in guilt and self-reproach.

Didn't he realize that she loved him more than ever? As a naive, eighteen-year-old schoolteacher, she'd been dazzled by the handsome nobleman who'd wooed and won her. But she hadn't really known him. Not all the heartbreaking secrets of his past or the unrelieved grief he'd kept hidden in his tortured soul. They had both suffered painful childhoods, which had left them vulnerable and filled with self-doubt. But in the end, their individual tragedies had only brought them closer, for out of their suffering had come a fuller understanding of the other's sorrow. She loved Court much more deeply now as a man with his own wounds, both physical and emotional, than she had when she'd thought he was a perfect, titled gentleman.

Philippa tossed the paper aside and set the breakfast tray on the bed table nearby. She would see her callers first, then go over the lists of things to be done in preparation for the ball only four days away, just as she'd promised Lady Harriet. As soon as she found a moment to herself, she would decide how to end Court's self-imposed exile.

Later that day, Belle arrived at the Sandhurst town house in a flurry. She was filled with excitement about the article and carried a copy of every one of the many newspapers it had appeared in that morning. When Philippa confided that she hadn't seen the duke of Warbeck since the night of the fire, Belle listened with compassion. Knowing how stubborn and intransigent Court could be, the viscountess promised to ask her husband to speak to his friend. But it was clear from the concern in Belle's dark brown eyes that she was worried as well.

The next afternoon, Philippa called at Warbeck House, determined to see Court. Just as she feared, he wasn't at home. She visited with Lady Augusta, who was eager to hear about the plans for the ball, but never once mentioned her exasperating grandson.

Finally, Philippa lost her patience. "What do you

think about Court's apology in the papers, Grand-mother?" she demanded.

The dowager duchess smiled serenely. "Lud, child, I never read the public prints. They only prove my worst suspicions about the frailties of human nature. But my grandson has announced that he will be stay-ing this fall at another one of his town houses in Lon-don, so that you may feel free to visit me here at Warbeck House any time you wish."

"Why?" Philippa asked in horrified dismay. "Does he intend to avoid me forever?"

Lady Augusta lifted the rose-patterned teapot and poured the hot liquid into Philippa's empty cup. "My grandson spent the last six years gnashing his teeth in thwarted plans for retribution. I believe he even once considered sailing to Venice on the *Golden Witch.*" At Philippa's gasp of surprise, the dowager smiled at her fondly. "Now he apparently intends to spend the next six years of his life doing penance. Even as a child, Court never did anything in half measures. If he's going to wear sackcloth and ashes, he'll do it better and longer than anyone has ever done it before."

Philippa's voice shook pathetically. "What about Kit? Doesn't Court want to see his own son?"

"Court feels that he isn't worthy to be a father. He stated that the best thing for Kit would be to have a fine stepfather he could look up to. A man who'd serve as an example to the boy of a true and honor-able gentleman. A man like Arthur Bentinck."

"Well, I'm not waiting six more years for that blasted idiot to get over his self-pity," Philippa de-clared angrily. "We've lost too much time as it is! Kit needs his father now. And so do I."

The duchess peered at Philippa over the gold rim of her cup. "What exactly do you intend to do, Pippa?"

Philippa pursed her lips as she debated the best course of action. "I think I know exactly what I'm going to do." She stood, picked up her reticule, and bent to kiss Lady Augusta on the forehead. "I'll see you at my ball."

The duchess caught Philippa's hand and held it firmly. "You're not going to tell me, dear? 'Fore Gad, I'm too old to take all this suspense," she complained. "I'll die of curiosity."

Philippa brought the gnarled fingers to her lips. "All I'll tell you now is to be sure to read Friday's papers."

Lady Augusta's gray eyes danced in mischievous delight. "You mean . . . ?"

"That's right," Philippa said as she moved to the door. "What's good for the goose is good for the gander." She threw the duchess a kiss. "See you at the ball, Grandmother."

Two days later, the duke of Warbeck shoved his untouched plate of steak and eggs aside and wearily unfolded the morning newspaper. He had a blinding headache, the result of attempting to drown his sorrows in brandy the evening before. Every night since the fire, he had tried, unsuccessfully, to forget a pair of violet eyes by drinking himself under the table. It hadn't worked so far, but that wasn't to say it wouldn't work eventually. Hell, he had the rest of his life to get over her. The specter of facing month after lonely month without Philippa tore at his insides, till the thought of being hanged, drawn, and quartered sounded like a welcome reprieve.

Court blinked at the print with bleary eyes. He could have sworn he'd just read his own name. He shook his head to clear it. A jolt of sheer agony stabbed through his befuddled brain. Clutching the sheets in stiff fingers, he stared at the article printed in the center of the first page.

MARCHIONESS OF SANDHURST ACCEPTS THE APOLOGY OF THE DUKE OF WARBECK AND HUMBLY ASKS HIS FORGIVENESS

I have read the generous and courageous apology of the Duke of Warbeck and accept it without reservation. I pray that he will forgive me, as well, for keeping the birth of his son a secret from him for over five years.

I implore His Grace to attend the Dowager Marchioness of Sandhurst's ball, which will be given at Cavendish Square tomorrow evening, so that I may know he has accepted my humble apology.

I will be saving the last waltz for the Duke and pray he will not leave a lady standing alone on the dance floor.

Court read the article three times. Then he reached for his cane, struggled to his feet, and left the town house to wander for hours through the streets of London.

The night of Lady Harriet's ball, every person who had received an invitation attempted to squeeze into Sandhurst House. It seemed that the rest of the city stood on the paving stones outside, hoping to get a glimpse of the duke of Warbeck as he arrived. Bets had been placed in the book at White's as to what time Warlock would appear in Cavendish Square. *If* he came at all, the gloomsayers reminded the feverish gamesters.

Inside, the drawing rooms, music room, and library were crammed with guests. It was an adventure akin to navigating the Congo just to essay a waltz, the dance floor was so crowded.

Everyone had come. Even two of the patronesses of Almack's, Lady Cowper and Lady Sefton, arrived, the first with her lover, Lord Palmerston, and the second on her husband's arm. Complete strangers gushed sentimental nonsense as they flattered and fawned over Philippa. No one dared mention the newspaper articles out loud, but even the most notorious gossips tried to imply that they'd been convinced of her innocence all along.

Philippa smiled and chattered, while she strove to hide her mounting anxiety. She still hadn't heard a word from Court. If her gambit hadn't succeeded, and he didn't come tonight, there was little hope that she'd ever convince him that what he'd done was not unpardonable. The thought of living without him was a nightmare that had plagued her for the past four days. She couldn't give in to despair, but she knew she'd placed all her hopes for happiness on one roll of the dice. She prayed to God she hadn't made a mistake.

Trying to remain outwardly serene while surrounded by a jostling, vociferous crowd, Philippa fluttered her Venetian lace fan and looked around the packed ballroom. The count and countess de Rambouillet were executing the steps of the waltz with consummate grace. André and Étienne were also on the dance floor with their wives. Belle and Tobias stood visiting with the two dowagers. Even Blanche and Beatrice were there, their jet eyes sparkling in fascination at their foray into the fashionable world of the ton. Kit was watching from the upstairs gallery with O'Dwyer and Fanciullo. With a smile, Philippa looked up and waved at them.

All her loved ones were there except for the man who held her heart in his hands. Philippa fought a growing sense of hopelessness. Her brilliant success in reentering society would be a hollow victory without him.

She had dressed with special care, choosing a satin gown of lavender-blue, the color Court always said matched her eyes. That afternoon, the diamond and amethyst necklace and earrings he'd given her on their wedding day had arrived along with a bouquet of violets. There'd been no note. Philippa couldn't be certain whether Court or the dowager duchess had sent them. She hadn't questioned Lady Augusta about it. She didn't have the courage to learn the truth.

Her thoughts spinning in her muddled head, Philippa told herself to stay calm and enjoy the party. She smiled at Tobias, who shyly drew her onto the dance floor. "Come on, P-pippa," he said. "This is your n-night to shine. You shouldn't be m-missing a single dance."

They waltzed around the crowded ballroom in companionable silence. The candlelight from the chandelier above them glinted on Toby's spectacles, making it impossible for Philippa to read his thoughts. She longed to ask the viscount if Court was coming tonight, but she couldn't put her dear friend in the terrible position of having to tell her he didn't think so. She smiled gaily as they whirled around the floor, and prayed that she could maintain her sanity until the evening was through.

A sudden hush fell over the ballroom. Gradually, all the dancers stopped in their tracks. The music faded away. Clutching Tobias's elbow for support, Philippa turned to face the door.

Court stood there, straight and tall in his severe black evening clothes. He gripped his cane and began to walk slowly toward her. His silvery eyes never wavered from hers. The regret, the pain, and the burgeoning hope in their haunted depths made her heart leap with joy. She closed her eyes for one brief second and thanked God for the miracle of love. Court had forgiven her. And he had forgiven himself.

In absolute silence, the onlookers opened a path for the duke of Warbeck.

As he came to her on the dance floor, Philippa waited in breathless anticipation. She wanted to reach out to him, but something in his gaze told her to wait. His pale eyes glittered with unshed tears. When he was directly in front of her, Court leaned on his cane and slowly dropped to one knee. Without a word, he caught the hem of her gown in his hand and brought the lavender silk to his lips.

Philippa's vision blurred with tears. She bent and took his hand in hers, and the crystal drops splashed on their joined fingers.

Court tightened his hold on the cane and pushed himself painfully to his feet. The love in her beautiful eyes shone like a beacon, leading him home. "I was wrong," he said hoarsely. "And there is nothing I can do to make up for the infamous way I've treated you. But if you let me, by God, I'll try. Can you ever forgive me, little pixie?"

"Oh, yes, my darling," she said in a shaky voice. "I've already forgiven you." Her sweet, breathless words were a balm to his grieving heart. The warmth of her love surrounded him.

Court handed his cane to Tobias. He slipped his arm around Philippa's waist just as the musicians began playing a waltz. Slowly, haltingly, they danced in a small circle, swaying to the lilting strains.

Then Court stopped and captured Philippa's face in his hands. His heart overflowed with love and happiness. "I promise that if you'll marry me a second time, Pippa Pixie, I will never, ever be jealous again. You can go anywhere, see anyone, do anything you please, and I won't question you."

Philippa smiled through her tears, knowing he could never behave so sensibly where she was concerned. "Yes," she whispered. "Oh, yes, Court, I'll marry you again."

She lifted her lips to his, and they pledged their undying love, while the watching crowd broke into spontaneous applause.

Epilogue

Gull's Nest Bay
2 July, 1830

It was the twins' fifteenth birthday. Philippa found it hard to believe that her little girls would soon be young women. They were like two tightly furled rosebuds, just ready to bloom. Yet it seemed only yesterday they'd been crawling around on the carpet, gurgling and jabbering to their doting father. She'd never forget the look of overwhelming male pride on Court's face the moment he first saw his twin daughters. And the incredible love that shone from his tear-brightened eyes as he watched her nurse them.

Her sentimental thoughts were interrupted when Kit stuck his head into the drawing room and motioned for her to come with him. "You're wanted on the veranda this instant, Mama. The Terrible Twosome refuse to start opening their presents without you."

Philippa looked up from her gift wrapping and smiled. "Come here, dear, and help carry these outside for me."

Kit hurried to take the packages stacked up on the table. "How many more presents do you have hidden away?" he teased.

"This is the last of them, I promise." She playfully pinched his cheek. He'd matched his father's height when he was still in his teens and had added another

inch since then. "When children come in twos," she
told him, "everything is doubled. The shoes, the
stockings, the hats, *and* the presents."

Kit leaned over his pile of gifts and pecked her
on the forehead. "And the fun," he added.

"And the fun," she agreed with a laugh. "Your father always claimed that having a set of twins was
the only way he could make up for lost time."

"Papa never does anything in half measures," Kit
said, the respect and affection in his voice unmistakable.

Philippa gazed at her firstborn son, her heart overflowing with love. Kit was twenty-one and the image
of his father. Black hair, gray eyes, broad shoulders,
and the sharp, hawkish profile that attracted the
young ladies in droves. But it wasn't merely his
physical features that tantalized them. Kit's unconscious self-confidence was combined with an easygoing tolerance for his fellowman that radiated warmth
and vitality. She picked up the remaining packages
and wrinkled her nose at him. "Let's join the party,
carissimo."

The family was gathered on the villa's wide
wooden porch overlooking the bay. On that brilliant
summer afternoon, the turquoise water sparkled beneath a clear azure sky. The sound of the waves
rolling onto the sandy shore below the cliff could be
heard as a faint echo in the distance.

"Oh, Mama, you're bringing more presents!"
Gussie cried in delight as they placed the boxes on
the tabletop. Her dark blue eyes glowed with happiness. Tall and slender, she was perched on a stool in
front of a round garden table, attired in a bright jon-
quil party gown. Her golden brown hair, tied back
with a matching yellow ribbon, shone thick and lustrous.

Gussie's twin, identical except for the rose of her
dress and ribbon, sat at the table beside her. "Oh, my
goodness, we'll never open them all before sunset,"

Cindy said with a giggle. She covered her face with her hands and peeked down at the presents through her fingers. Her sister caught her infectious hilarity, and the two girls broke into peals of laughter.

"You'll have them unwrapped in less than five minutes," their father predicted with a teasing grin. "Then you'll be looking under the table to see if there are any you missed." Court stood behind his youngest son, his hands on the boy's slim shoulders.

Arthur was ten and far more serious than his impetuous, irrepressible sisters. He had the dark brown hair and hazel eyes of Philippa's father. More and more each year, her little boy resembled the handsome man she remembered with so much love.

"*Papa!*" the twins protested. They gave their father a look of mutual reproach. The Ladies Augusta and Hyacinthe were constantly striving to overcome the fact that they had been born into a family of males who never seemed to take them seriously. They'd been twitted and petted and played with by their father and eldest brother—and their younger brother, too, as he'd grown older. Now that they were young ladies, they wanted to be treated like adults, with respect and courtly politeness. Maybe even a little adulation. After all, the male half of the county of Kent was already at their feet, and they hadn't even made their debut.

For the last two winters, they'd attended the Moore Female Seminary in Chippinghelm, which Philippa had established in memory of her parents with Court's unqualified support and Blanche and Beatrice Lillybridge's experienced guidance. But as their father was quick to point out, even the study of Latin and geometry hadn't given the twins an iota of common sense.

Philippa smiled to herself. If their father had his way, the two wouldn't celebrate their coming out until they were twenty-one. Court was nearly as jealous and possessive of his little girls as he was of his wife.

Oh, he strove to hide it. But the sight of all those calf-eyed adolescents swarming over Castle Warbeck like an invading army drove him to muttering dire threats about what he'd do to any male foolish enough to touch their dainty hands. Since two of those handsome young bucks were Belle and Tobias's sons, he couldn't bar them from the door entirely, much as he jolly well wished to.

The Rockinghams had pined for children for six barren years. Then to everyone's delight, Belle had discovered she was pregnant the same month that Philippa and Court were married for the second time in a poignant, soul-stirring ceremony in St. Aldhelm's.

Kit sat down on a garden chair beside Lady Harriet, who was resting on a chaise longue. She fondly patted his arm. "I want to hear about your adventure on the railway, dear, as soon as Gussie and Cindy have opened their presents."

"I'll tell you all about it, Grandma," he promised. "In fact, I plan to persuade you to take a ride on the railroad yourself."

"Bosh!" she protested in her hearty way. "Your great-grandmother was right, Kit. Someday one of those newfangled locomotives is going to slide right off its track and kill everyone on board."

Kit laughed at her fears. "That's not going to happen, I assure you. I'm only sorry that Nana isn't here to come with us," he added with a rueful smile.

Philippa looked across the veranda and met her husband's nostalgic gaze. Lady Augusta had passed away in her sleep at the age of eighty-one, three months after the birth of her youngest great-grandson. She had been tremendously proud of all the children, but there'd been a special bond between her and Kit.

Court's prediction of an unwrapping frenzy proved correct. Once given permission to begin, the energetic twins tore through the ribbons and paper, crying out in excitement at the new gowns, gloves, parasols, and shawls. When the gifts had all been opened and the refreshments served, the four siblings decided to take the *Sea Gull II* out on the bay, and the girls hurried into the house to change their party dresses for more practical clothes.

Closing her eyes, Philippa leaned back on her chaise longue and stretched like a cat in lazy contentment. "Now, Kit," she said, "tell us about the railway." She peeked at her husband from under her lashes and smiled sheepishly. For years, she had remained skeptical about his belief that steam-powered locomotives could pull coaches of people along iron tracks. But time had proved Court to be a brilliant financial investor, and she no longer questioned his predictions about the future.

At his mother's suggestion, Kit propped his booted foot on the opposite knee and cheerfully complied. "In June, I and three classmates from Oxford rode on the first train to run the whole length of the rail line from Liverpool to Manchester. We made the trip in an hour and a half going twenty-seven miles per hour."

"Mercy on my life!" Lady Harriet boomed. "What a world we live in!" She fluttered her fan in astonishment at such an extraordinary feat.

The dowager marchioness was nearing seventy, but she remained as stout-hearted and vigorous as ever. Kit still considered her his grandmother, although he was no longer the marquess of Sandhurst. He'd relinquished the title when he became his father's legal heir and the future duke of Warbeck.

Court had launched an extensive search that uncovered a distant cousin of Arthur Bentinck, who agreed to take the family name in order to inherit the title and estates. Lady Harriet lived in the dower house and visited Court and Philippa frequently. The new marquess had a son who bore an uncanny resemblance to Arthur Bentinck. Through the years,

William and Kit had become close friends, attending Eton and Oxford together.

"Now that you've completed your studies at the university, what do you plan to do, Kit?" Lady Harriet queried.

The young man winked at his father conspiratorially. "I'm going to study for a year with George Stephenson, the fellow who engineered the laying of the Liverpool-Manchester railway. Then I'm going to help my father build a line from London to Ghyllside. The seaside resort he's established is going to become one of the most popular spots on the Kentish coast."

"Just be sure all those swarms of holiday-seekers don't try to invade Gull's Nest Bay," Philippa warned.

"Don't worry," Court interjected. "Our privacy won't be disturbed by sightseers." His amused gaze met hers, telling her he knew exactly why she was so concerned about the continued seclusion of their villa. Through the years, they had brought their children to Gull's Nest to enjoy the warm summer months by the water. And many nights, Court and Philippa had spent the midnight hours lying in each other's arms in their secluded cove. She was certain Arthur had been conceived there.

"I'm going to ride on the railroad with my dad," Arthur told Lady Harriet. "We're going to Liverpool as soon as our holiday is over."

"Well, you two are not leaving me behind," Philippa admonished. "I said a long time ago that I'd be willing to ride on the railway, and I will."

Court's lips twitched. "Your mama always has been willing to live life dangerously," he told Arthur. "You should have seen her riding up on the driver's box of the Folkestone *Flyer*."

Arthur plopped down on the chaise beside Philippa. "Wow!" he exclaimed, looking up at her with newfound awe. "I'd love to ride on the top of a stagecoach."

"Well, ask your father to take you." Her teasing gaze slid to meet her husband's, and she could barely resist the temptation to stick her tongue out at him in retaliation. "He can drive a team of blind horses at a gallop."

"Were they blind, Papa?" Arthur cried.

"Only two of them," Court admitted, "and they were the wheelers."

"You'd better not wait too long to take that ride," Kit warned. "Before we know it, the railroads will completely replace the public coaches."

"Kit!" Philippa reproached. "Don't be filling your little brother's head with such nonsense!"

At her reproving look, her son and his father tipped their heads back and laughed uproariously.

Just then the twins hurried out onto the veranda. "We're ready," Gussie called to her brothers with a bright smile.

"Yes, let's go," Cindy echoed impatiently.

The girls were attired in the latest beachwear fashions. Their dresses of lightweight cotton were banded with ribbon at the natural waistline and adorned with lace at the collars. The hems, high enough to show off their trim ankles and thin summer slippers, were embellished with ruffles. Wide straw bonnets and parasols completed the costumes. Wisely, they'd left their corsets and bouffant petticoats behind. The two young ladies were veteran sailors. They knew the importance of being able to move around freely on a small craft. All four of the children were strong swimmers.

At their sisters' prompting, both brothers dropped down on the wooden steps of the porch and pulled off their shoes and socks, then rolled up their trousers and shirtsleeves.

"I'll race you to the dock," Arthur called. He tore off across the lawn. Forgetting their newly acquired dignity, the sisters picked up their skirts and ran after him, laughing with glee. Three Welsh terriers, who'd been resting in the shade, scrambled to their feet and joined the parade, yelping joyously.

Kit shook his head at the antics of his younger siblings. "We'll be back in time for supper," he promised. "Don't worry, I'll take good care of them." He waved to his parents and headed toward the stairs.

"Well, I'm going to go in and have a little nap," Lady Harriet said with a yawn. "That way I'll be able to keep up with those high-spirited youngsters this evening. I'm sure they have an exhausting program of entertainment already planned for us."

When the dowager had retreated into the house, Court and Philippa stood side by side at the porch railing and looked down at the bay. The children had already hoisted the sails, and the sloop was flying across the water. From his spot in the stern with the three barking dogs, Arthur waved happily to his parents.

Philippa leaned against her husband's broad chest and sighed with heartfelt satisfaction. "Did you ever want to stop time?" she asked. "Just keep everything exactly as it is at one given moment?"

"Right now would be the perfect moment, wouldn't it?" Court agreed as he brushed his lips across her temple.

"Mmm," she said softly. "How could we ever be happier?"

Court turned her in his arms and gently kissed the tip of her nose. His silvery eyes gleamed with affectionate laughter. "We couldn't, Pippa Pixie. But you wouldn't want to cheat our children out of having families of their own someday."

Philippa slipped her arms about his neck and leaned against his tall frame. "No," she admitted readily. She traced his upper lip with her finger, relishing the faint smell of sandalwood on his warm skin.

"Or from knowing the kind of love we've shared through the years," he continued, his words low and enticing. He cupped her bottom and drew her against his muscular body.

"Definitely not," she agreed. She could feel his hardened arousal pressing boldly at the juncture of her thighs. A thrill of excitement went through her. She'd been right on that score. After sixteen years as his duchess, she still couldn't get enough of him.

"I think Lady Harriet had a very good idea," he murmured. He bent his head and ran his tongue along the shell of her ear in erotic persuasion. "Why don't we take a nap so we can keep up with our lively brood this evening?"

"I think you may be right," she said, trying her best to look pensive and thoughtful. Despite her intentions, the corners of her mouth curved up in a playful smile. "And if we're lucky, my darling husband, we might even sleep a little, too."